MW01128420

Last Lorry
to Mbordo

(Misadventures in Nation Building)

A Novel
By
John C. Kennedy

© Copyright 2003 John C. Kennedy. All rights reserved.

No part of this publication may be reproduced, stored in a retrieval system, or transmitted, in any form or by any means, electronic, mechanical, photocopying, recording, or otherwise, without the written prior permission of the author.

This novel is the product of the author's imagination. The characters, situations, incidents, institutions, and the West African nation that is the setting for the story are fictional.

Printed in Victoria, Canada

National Library of Canada Cataloguing in Publication Data

Kennedy, John C. (John Calvin), 1943-
   Last lorry to Mbordo : misadventures in na-
tion building / John C. Kennedy.
ISBN 1-4120-0048-3
   I. Title.
PS3611.E55L37 2003   813'.6   C2003-901373-1

This book was published *on-demand* **in cooperation with Trafford Publishing.**
On-demand publishing is a unique process and service of making a book available for retail sale to the public taking advantage of on-demand manufacturing and Internet marketing. **On-demand publishing** includes promotions, retail sales, manufacturing, order fulfilment, accounting and collecting royalties on behalf of the author.

Suite 6E, 2333 Government St., Victoria, B.C. V8T 4P4, CANADA

Phone	250-383-6864	Toll-free	1-888-232-4444 (Canada & US)
Fax	250-383-6804	E-mail	sales@trafford.com
Web site	www.trafford.com	TRAFFORD PUBLISHING IS A DIVISION OF TRAFFORD HOLDINGS LTD.	
Trafford Catalogue #03-0411		www.trafford.com/robots/03-0411.html	

10   9   8   7   6   5   4   3   2   1

This book is dedicated to

Burnis and Harold
Catherine and Robert
Frances
Janet
Mike, Amanda, Calvin, and Timmy
Chris, Jeff, Jacob, and the next one

I wish to thank my editor, Kathryn Robinson. Her many suggestions and technical corrections have made Last Lorry to Mbordo both more readable and more understandable. She is responsible for all that is correct usage on the following pages and is not responsible for things I was too stubborn to change.

My thanks to Erica Stoll for her design of the cover and Richard Veloso for the lorry illustration.

My thanks also to family and friends who read earlier versions of this book and provided support and advice.

And thanks to my backyard basketball friends who keep me healthy.

John C. Kennedy was born in Lumberton, North Carolina.
He completed a BA at Ohio Northern University in Ada, Ohio, in 1965.
He taught:
Secondary school mathematics in Peki, Ghana, 1965-68, as a Peace Corp volunteer.
Mathematics in Bell Vocational High School, Washington DC, 1968-70.
Mathematics in Northwest Junior High School, Charlotte NC, 1970-71.
He completed a Masters degree at the University of Illinois, 1971-72.
He retired from the Antilles Consolidated School System in Puerto Rico in December of 2000, after twenty five years as a mathematics teacher and computer coordinator, to become a paperback writer.

LAST LORRY TO MBORDO
(MISADVENTURES IN NATION BUILDING)

PROLOGUE

No nation can match the United States in good intentions. In the glory times of the Kennedys and even for a while after the assassinations, we believed everything was possible. We knew the world could be a better place. We were certain life could be better for people in developing countries and we could be a part of making that happen. Volunteers from the United States, England, Canada and many other nations acted on that belief by working as teachers, agricultural specialists, community developers, and just about anything else Third World countries would allow them to attempt. They went to live in places most of us did not know existed.

This is the story of a few of those who volunteered and were assigned to the West African nation of Sakra. They came to the town of Mbordo in Sakra looking for experiences they did not think they could find in their own countries and looking for an opportunity to somehow become a part of the effort to turn Sakra into a modern nation. What they found and what they did were both less and more than any one of them could have anticipated.

CHAPTER 1
Frogs, Drums and Powdered Milk

"Damn, alone again," Alice mumbled, "some place in the middle of West Africa. Four months, twenty three days. Done! Eighteen months, five days left. Hmm, haven't gotten it down to hours yet. What ever happened to joy, excitement, hope? Must be somewhere, back in the kitchen with the powdered milk, dried soup, corned beef. Can't find anything good any more. How the hell can you get excited about powdered milk?

"Christ it's quiet. Noise is quiet. Damn drums on and on and on. No more real than the rain on my tin roof or the crickets and frogs. God, I wish for just a moment I could hear real sounds - - people, traffic, airplanes, even garbage trucks.

"It's Thursday. Oh my God. The weekend is coming. I don't know how many more Saturdays and Sundays I can bear.

"Goddamn it Alice, stop it! Weekends are bad enough without thinking about them. Sit, read, sleep, eat, drink, sit, read, eat, drink, sit, nothing more. Nothing more but my own thoughts.

"The alternatives, think of the alternatives. Start again. What am I doing here? How did I get to this place?

"Did I actually want to do this?

"Start again! Start again! Start again!

"You will feel better. You will feel better.

"Think of all the other wonderful things that you could be doing now. Right now. Doing right now. Go back, go back. Let's go lady. Go back. Go back.

"Sixty-two and nothing to do. Husband long dead. No children to worry about. Nothing to do. I remember. Join the Peace Corps. Do something useful. Don't rot. Too young to retire, but another year in DC? No. Couldn't take another week. Better to walk out than be carried out.

"Come to Atlanta, they said, and learn about Africa. Come to Atlanta and get ready to teach in the marvelous new nation of Sakra."

Alice shifted a little in order to rest a different part of her back against one of the posts that held up the porch roof of her bungalow. (She knew that it was impolite to sit on the floor of one's porch. But she liked to sit there and she knew that any Sakraians who might happen to pass that way would excuse her odd behavior.) The yellow cotton dress she wore was comfortable in the dry air. And it was just thick enough that no half slip was needed. Alice had eliminated the use of other than the most basic undergarments soon after arriving in Sakra. After all, who would care about seeing someone's bra in West Africa?

"It's dry, very dry. No rain for more than a month now. Miss the sound of it on my roof. The sun's red from the sand blown south from the Sahara. My skin is so damn dry and brittle. My lips feel terrible.

"Mrs. Manati! Whatever are you doing in this place? Look at yourself. What a fine condition you're in. Your skin may not last as long as the rest of your body. God, it would be unfortunate if my skin gives out. Imagine what that would look like!"

The thought was so morbid that it brought a series of chuckles from deep in her throat.

"Still a good question, Alice Manati. How in hell's name did you end up in this place?

"Sixty-two and nothing to do so I wrote a nice letter to the Peace Corps informing them that the services of a skilled and dedicated mathematics teacher were available."

Alice's thoughts returned to Atlanta.

"Training was good, or at least accurate; everything late, schedules messed up, unannounced changes, unanswered questions. Just like here. I bet they didn't know they got it right.

"All that stuff doesn't bother me anymore. Not much anyway. There was that six-hour wait for a visa to the Ivory Coast. I would still be sitting in their embassy if Gil had not bribed the official. No, bribed is the wrong way to think of it. Gilbert Adwin, our esteemed art teacher, would never bribe anyone. He only gave the gentleman a 'dash' in recognition of his lofty official position and in order to show friendship. Certainly not a bribe. At least in Washington they would try to keep it a secret. They're so damned obvious here.

"This ungodly dryness is depressing. It's cooler but it doesn't seem right. Sand in your lungs must be bad for your health. Ah, yes, yellow lung. That should mix well with white lung from chalk dust. I can see headlines in the *Post*, 'Teacher Found Dead in African Jungle with Lungs Full of Mathematical Symbols Written in Chalk Dust and Sand.'

"God, getting morbid again. Better find someone to talk to. It's four o'clock. Most people will be up and about.

"It's odd," she mused, "there are not many people I feel comfortable talking to about anything more than the weather. Maybe there is nothing to talk about. Or maybe I just don't fit in. The Americans worry about their health and bugs in their houses. The British talk about standards. The Indians and Pakistanis are always after you to buy something for them out of mail order catalogues. As for the Sakraians, it's just so easy to get into trouble. You talk about your room not being clean or nightsoil not being removed and you insult some tribal group or another.

"My goodness," Alice said out loud. "Nightsoil! What a wonderful name for shit. The English did themselves proud with that one.

"Of course, you can always talk about what it is like to live in America. But, if I have to listen to one more conversation about what Americans eat, I am going to throw up.

"Stop that," Alice muttered, "it isn't that bad. I am really beginning to work myself into a good state of depression. Everybody isn't like that. I wonder if Ian and Beth are home. I do have some questions about exam papers. I think I will go there. The walk will do me good."

Ian and Beth Harris lived in a bungalow on a part of the University-College compound that was separated from the classroom buildings and dwellings of most staff members by a few acres of forest and grasslands. That area had been a part of an agricultural experimental station whose functions had been assumed by the new Mbordo University-College. By road the distance from Alice's home was a little over three miles. However, a trail through the forest, less than a mile in length, connected the old experimental station with the rest of the University-College. Alice preferred the trail to catching a ride on the road. She found hitchhiking somewhat undignified and she disliked feeling undignified.

Alice walked back into the living room of the little house that the University-College provided. She moved down the short hall and into the bedroom she used for sleeping. She used the other bedroom as a small office in order to keep the living-dining room area free of school clutter. Alice took off her sandals and put on tennis shoes. She decided to stay with the yellow dress since its looseness was good for walking.

"Exercise is good for me," she told herself as she started for the Harrises. "This path may be the only reason I haven't shriveled up and blown away."

The trail was six feet wide in most places and lined with rocks to prevent vegetation from encroaching. Not that vines and grass had much of a chance. Early in the morning and in the late afternoon the trail became a living stream of farmers with machetes and women and children with headloads of food and wood. Alice remembered how afraid she had been her first time on the trail when a huge man carrying a machete came toward her. His bare shoulders glistened in the fading sunlight. The machete seemed to dangle at his side, relaxed but ready for instant use. The man had sensed Alice's fear. He had grasped the tip of the machete between his thumb and index finger to show her he intended no harm and stepped quickly to the side of the path. Her fear had changed to embarrassment. Even worse, she later met a pregnant woman with a child on her back who, in the process of shooing several children off the path to clear the way for Alice, nearly fell down. She had stopped using the trail until Beth taught her a few greetings in Bordo, the local language. She also taught her how to say, 'There is plenty of room on this path. Do not be afraid for me.'

The Sakraians who used the trail had soon gotten used to seeing her walking and seemed happy to be greeted in Bordo by the white-haired one.

"They probably thought I might complain about them," she mused as she moved from the savanna into forest. "What a marvelous place this is. It has everything that is beautiful in Sakra except the ocean."

The forest seemed alive with its own moods; when dark or cloudy it became somber and forbidding, but with sunlight it was a bright happy place with a thousand dancing shades of green and brown.

"Those who walk this path reflect the mood of the forest," Alice mused as she walked deeper into the forest. "Cloudy weather brings grim looks and a hurried pace, children quietly following. Sunshine brings smiling faces and children laughing and playing back and forth across the trail.

"Fiddlesticks," she muttered, "I have too much imagination. People just want to get home before it rains or gets dark."

Traffic was light on the trail. The few women she met wore the traditional wrapped skirt of bright printed or woven cloth that reached to the middle of the calf. Those with young babies used another cloth to wrap around under their arms and hold the baby on their back. Alice almost envied the women without babies who wrapped the second cloth around their heads turban style and left the rest of their bodies free of the heat and restriction of clothing. She amused herself as she walked by contemplating what would happen if she adopted a similar style.

Within the forest the trail was covered by layers of overhanging branches that formed a canopy twenty to thirty feet above Alice's head. Little sunlight penetrated to the level of the trail, and the vegetation on either side of the path was a rich, moist, dark green. Alice felt surrounded by birds and small animals. One staff member claimed to have seen a six-foot ape on the trail. However, Eric Thornton was not known for his moderation in the consumption of alcoholic beverage. Mr. Pordoe, the Sportsmaster, had assured her that no one else had seen an ape of that size in this part of Sakra in fifty years.

"The Sportsmaster should know," Alice thought. "He grew up here. Seems to know everything about all of the trails from being on them as a boy. He still uses them a lot from what I can see. Maybe that's why he is in such good condition. I'm glad I don't have his job. He seems to coach everything. Out there every afternoon in the sun. I love that name, the Sportsmaster. I guess he is master of all sports. It's interesting here how sometimes your job becomes your name. I wonder if they will start calling me the Mathsmaster or maybe Mathsmistress?"

Even on the hottest days Alice had found that she could maintain at least an illusion of coolness within the shelter of the forest trees. She paused halfway across a footbridge that crossed a stream fed by springs deeper in the forest. Mist from a small waterfall just above the bridge seemed to lower the temperature a few degrees.

The trail was at its best in the early morning and late afternoon. Springtime was available any morning at the footbridge if she reached there by six.

"Unfortunately, springtime disappears by seven even in the forest.

"Thank God it's cool on this part of the path in the evening too," Alice mused, as she sat down on a rock near the footbridge to enjoy the droplets of water sprayed in the air by the stream as it tumbled down the small rock ledge that formed the falls.

"But," she reminded herself in a spoken and firm tone, "I am never going to take a chance on being on this trail when it's getting dark. What happened to Jason was no fun, no fun at all."

Jason Wills had been on the trail at dusk and stepped a little too close to a cobra. The sandals and khaki shorts the younger, male Peace Corps volunteers usually wore provided little protection from the snake's bite. She had seen them bring him in. Alice chuckled now at the thought of how afraid he had been. She had been frightened also but Dr. Grasinski said that Jason would probably have survived even without the serum as long as he didn't die of fright.

"Well," Alice thought as she looked more carefully at small movements in the leaves around her, "he did survive and was back at work in a few days so the Doctor must have known what he was talking about. I don't know how much a Polish doctor would know about tropical snakes but he has been here long enough to see a lot of them. Anyway he is the only doctor in this area. It's a long ways to get to the Peace Corps Doctor in the capital."

Another thirty minutes of walking brought Alice to a second stream. Only a trickle of water flowed over the small rocks that formed the stream bed. Since this stream's major source of water was runoff from rain, it all but disappeared during harmattan.

"It should rain soon," she thought, "it's been more than a month. Gil said it would rain at least once a month. The Harrises claim that by April it will be raining so much that I will long for the dry season. Impossible. Don't believe that at all. This bridge seems ridiculous. Even a child could step over this stream with little danger of wet shoes."

Alice had asked Jason about the bridge. He had explained that during the rainy season the stream could become waist high. The bridge had been constructed after several expatriate members of the University-College staff had contracted schistosomiasis after wading the stream.

"The two S'es," Alice mused , "snakes and schisto. Otherwise a perfect walk."

Fifty yards beyond the stream the trail emerged from the forest. The Harrises' bungalow was on the far side of one of the fields used by the University-College to experiment with local food crops.

"Uh oh!" she thought, "they have a visitor. That old Puegot belongs to Mr. Thornton."

Alice had no desire to talk to Mr. Thornton, or for that matter to be anywhere near him, but she decided that she might as well say hello to the Harrises and sit down for a few minutes before starting back.

As she raised her hand to knock she heard the loud, raspy voice of Eric Thornton.

"The standard of work in this school is bloody atrocious. This should be a secondary school, not a pompous University-College. Maybe even a middle school."

She heard Beth's reply, "If the students are that awful, then we should all resign in protest and return to England."

Ian continued, "Better yet, we should all request that our salaries be lowered to the level of middle school teachers. After all, if that is the level of work we are doing that is the level at which we should be paid."

Ian noticed Alice standing at the door and said, "Don't be shy Alice. Come in."

Beth stood up and moved to open the door for Alice. Alice noted that Beth wore shorts very well. But then Beth seemed to look quite nice in almost anything she wore.

"Alice, how nice to see you," she said. "Please do come in. Would you like something to drink?"

The others were drinking beer but Alice thought, "I'm still not quite ready to start at four, at least not on a Thursday."

Instead she asked Beth, "Do you have Coke?"

Beth replied, "I am very sorry, Alice, we don't. The only soda we have is cherry, awful stuff, but it is all that we could get this week. Some sort of bottle shortage in the capital."

"That will do just fine," Alice replied as she thought, "awful stuff is right, like drinking Kool Aid with far too much sugar. But if I don't drink something I will dehydrate altogether."

Alice noticed that her presence seemed to cause Eric Thornton to fidget in his chair and look down at the floor. A few weeks after Alice had arrived in Mbordo, Thornton had expressed a rather overt romantic interest in her at a staff social event. Alice did consider herself well preserved for her age, attractive and even somewhat "with it." But her tastes in men, such as they were, did not include middle-aged alcoholics. She had not been impressed by Thornton's clumsy efforts. Her final rebuff that evening had been rather harsh.

Thornton finished his drink and nearly dropped his glass on the floor when he attempted to return it to the low table in front of him.

He stood up, slipped on his gray blazer and excused himself with a half mumbled, "Must return to the bungalow and begin preparing next term's lectures. The work load here is heavier than any place that I have ever taught. One has to do a lot of searching about to find something easy enough for our so-called students."

Beth sighed when she heard the grumbly motor of Thornton's old Puegot turn over and strain as the car crawled back toward the road that connected the village of Mbordo with this part of the University-College.

"Thank God, he's off," she said. "You remember when he couldn't get the damn thing started? He visited us every three hours, to be sure that no one made off with that bloody piece of junk."

"Better you than me," Alice said. "I hope his car never stalls in front of my house."

Beth laughed and said, "He probably would want to spend the night at your place, Alice."

"Well I will say this for Mr. Thornton," Alice mused as she forced down some cherry soda, "he certainly is ambitious. It's a minor miracle if I even get as far as working on next week's lessons, much less next term's."

Ian started to laugh as he spoke, "Thornton hasn't worked on a lecture since 1960. His lectures on British history stop with Queen Victoria, the last truly great ruler of the British Empire, even though she was a woman. On the history of Sakra he stops with the '52 riots and the beginning of what he labels the 'great tragedy.' He doesn't believe anything worth discussing has happened in Sakra since then."

"Don't exaggerate dear," Beth said in mock seriousness, "you told me yourself that last year he did include two lectures on the subject of the development of political institutions in independent Sakra."

"Ah, most certainly," Ian replied, "they were entitled 'The Tragedy of Modern Political Institutions in Sakra - Part I'; and 'The Tragedy of Modern Political Institutions in Sakra - Part II.'"

"Why do they put up with him?" Alice asked.

"I don't know," Ian replied. "He is ridiculous. It's bloody awful to be in the same department. You're lucky to be spared that. The students never stop complaining about his attitude."

"I suppose Sakraians are kinder to old fools than Western cultures are," Alice theorized. "After all, I should know."

"Alice," Ian snapped, "if you ever become even the slightest bit like old Eric, I will personally buy your ticket and see to it that you get on the plane. We couldn't stand another Thornton here."

"Thornton has been in Sakra for more than thirty years," Beth explained. "In one sense he is a helpless old man with no place to go, but I do believe that he does harm to this school and to our students. Imagine what it must be like to be told that your country is a piece of shit and that in the order of things you rank slightly higher than the baboon but lower than an Englishman and a drunken one at that."

"It's possible," Ian reflected, "that they keep him around as the token colonist. Someone to remind them of how it was in the good old days so they don't forget. They have given him several honorary titles. One means 'Man who should have been his own grandfather.' Another is 'Ocean.'"

"Ocean?" Alice asked.

"Yes," Ian replied, "into which great rivers of liquids flow."

"That is terrible," Alice said as she tried to suppress her laughter. "I wonder what names they have for me?"

"I have heard one," Beth answered, "but I am not quite sure what it means. But you can be sure that it is something that conveys respect. The students here are totally in awe of your mathematical ability. Most of our students, including the women, had never even thought of the possibility of a woman of your age knowing anything about mathematics."

Ian sensed that Alice was uneasy as the subject of praise and returned the conversation to Thornton.

"The students also understand that Thornton has a certain prestige value. When he is sober he dresses very well, even a full suit and tie if appropriate for the occasion. And, he is, no matter his other problems, an Oxford graduate. That looks good on their records and goes down well with visiting dignitaries."

"OK, OK, then it's agreed," Alice responded, "we will allow him to remain on the staff if: first, no one takes what he says and does seriously, and second, I don't have to be within three miles of him after four o'clock."

Alice, over the sound of the Harrises' laughter asked, "Did he leave here because he is still embarrassed about that night?"

"If he did," Beth sputtered, "we are going to send a student for you every time he comes to visit."

"That was rather remarkable behavior on his part," Ian said. "If he isn't still embarrassed he definitely should be."

"Well, enough about Mr. Thornton," Alice said, "I did have a purpose in coming over today. The upper level students that I teach seem quite concerned about their end-of-year exams. They ask almost every day whether or not the material we are covering is on the exam. They actually get upset when I tell them I have never seen the end-of-year exam and am not particularly concerned whether what I am teaching is on it or not."

Ian's laughter was spontaneous and uncontrolled.

Beth remarked, "Alice, if you continue that line, they won't be just upset by the end of the year, they will be hysterical."

Alice wasn't convinced that what she had said was worthy of the humorous reception it received and asked with a touch of irritation in her voice, "All right, all right, so what in the hell is this exam, and why are the students so worried about it?"

Ian asked, "Didn't your university have comprehensive exams, Alice?"

"I did have comprehensive exams at the Master's degree level," Alice replied in a defensive tone, "but few American universities continue to believe that the archaic tradition of comprehensive exams on the undergraduate level adds much to the quality of education or provides any realistic measurement of what the student actually knows."

Alice knew before she finished her last sentence that she had blundered into the 'standards' argument.

As she expected Ian replied, "Exactly how do your universities judge what you have learned without comprehensive papers? I don't suppose that they give degrees on the basis of attendance?"

"Stop that Ian," Beth chided, "you know quite well how the American system works, and I think it's super. Much better to test as one goes than to pretend that a silly paper can measure what someone has learned in three years."

"Nevertheless," Ian replied in a deep, pompous voice, "the measure of a civilized man is his ability to bullshit over a period of time longer than three..."

"Oh shut up," Alice said half jokingly, "I didn't come over here to argue about the same crap that comes up in every staff meeting. I just want to find out what's on those exams before the students start complaining to the Vice-Chancellor."

"Yes," Beth replied with a slight smile, "and I will be happy to tell you about the papers as soon as Ian Harris, the defender of our educational system and culture, is finished extolling the merits of his super British education, every moment of which, he has personally assured me, he loathed."

"All right, all right," Ian said, "maybe it wasn't perfect, but it did have its good points and as soon as I remember any of them I will tell you what they were."

"Marvelous," Beth remarked looking toward Alice, "he may be totally silent for several weeks just from the effort to think."

Before Ian could frame a retort Alice interrupted, "You two can carry on your discussion of Ian's thought processes at some other time. But now Beth, please, about the exam."

"I am sorry, Alice," Beth said, "it's just that we don't get much company with whom we are relaxed enough to argue in front of. The paper that our students have to write in mathematics is the same as the paper used by the University of Sakra. I have copies of old exams that you can look at. The questions are for the most part just standard material. The four years of maths that we offer all of our students in the University-College Mathematics Teacher Education Program theoretically prepares them for the university level mathematics paper as well as the paper that one needs for certification as a secondary level mathematics teacher."

"Thank you," Alice remarked, "now I know why students in my advanced level mathematics course call it the papers' course. Judging from what you have said about the importance of the exam, I think I had better take every test you can spare."

"Damn right," Ian said. "Only two conditions could lead to student violence in Sakra. First, if they believe that someone is stealing their food from the school store. And second, if they believe that a teacher is not getting them ready for their papers."

"Oh!" Alice asked, "You mean that I will be sacked if I don't teach for these tests?"

"That would be the least of your problems," Ian replied. "You would probably be subject to all sorts of curses courtesy of local jujumen hired by the students to get even with you for ruining their chances of getting soft government jobs. Perhaps, something like, 'May the chalk crumble in your hand as you attempt the demonstration of an important problem,' or, 'May you carry all sorts of tiny plants and small animals within your body when you return to your home in America.'"

"I really hope you're joking," Alice responded.

"Oh don't worry," Beth said, "you must already be following the syllabi of your courses reasonably well and that is what the papers are based on. The students would have told you if you weren't. Take these exam papers and glance through them. I would be surprised if you felt the need to make anything more than minor changes in what you are doing now. Why don't you stay for dinner and we will look at them afterwards?"

The offer was tempting but Alice did not wish to overburden a friendship that had become both comforting and useful.

"After all," she thought as she prepared to leave, "an old lady is an old lady. Can't be that much fun to be around."

She made her excuses about having something planned for supper (if one could consider yam and corned beef a plan), thanked Beth for the examination papers, and started back along the forest trail. Dusk turns to darkness quickly in the tropics and snakes move to more open areas to absorb the last stored heat of the day. Alice could still see the outline of the sides of the trail as she crossed the little bridge near her house, but details were less clear. She jumped quickly when she noticed a black slithering movement a few feet ahead and nearly fell.

She regained her balance and thought, "Damn, that was way too close, whatever it was. I could have fallen down, too. Double whammy, bitten and broken. Glad it heard me. Probably long gone. Will move to the other side of the trail but not too close to the edge. Better make some noise. Sing something. Sing what? 'The Saints Go Marching In.' That will do."

Others within hearing distance on the trail that night might have found what they heard a bit strange, but 'The Saints' did get Alice home safely.

CHAPTER 2
Hard Time

Alice arrived for morning assembly at 6:44. The Vice-Chancellor would appear promptly at 6:45 and the day's program would officially begin. (No one quite knew how the Vice-Chancellor managed to sit down in his chair in the hall every school day precisely at 6:45, but the students had carefully checked his timing with Radio Sakra and found him never late nor early.)

"Nothing else in all Sakra might start on time," Alice thought as she took her customary seat next to Mr. West, the head of the United States Agency for International Development (USAID) group from River State University, "but morning assemblies at the schools do."

A prayer, two Biblical selections, the pledge of allegiance to Sakra and its leader (Alice found that part a little hard and usually tried to just move her lips when it came time to pledge eternal loyalty to President Agyenkwa, the 'Savior' of Sakra), a religious song, the day's announcements, and another school day would be off to a proper start.

"Wouldn't do that religious part in Washington," Alice thought as the Vice-Chancellor dismissed the assembly. "Mr. West is Jewish. Guess he chooses Old Testament stuff to read when it's his turn. Must be even more difficult for the Muslim staff and students. They just sit in the back and keep quiet."

Alice's classroom was in the mathematics block, a building about one hundred yards from the hall in which the morning assembly took place. Her first class of the day was scheduled to begin at 7:05. As she walked from the assembly hall toward her classroom, the cooler morning breezes of the harmattan season reaffirmed the wisdom of her choice of a white long sleeve blouse and calf length blue skirt.

The mathematics block was a monument to the mass builders of the early colonial period of Sakra. The floor was a cement slab one hundred fifty feet long by thirty feet wide. Exterior walls were cement block up to four feet and ply-board the rest of the way up. The roof was corrugated tin. The building housed five rooms, railroad style, separated by ply-board partitions. Alice was fortunate to have been assigned one of the end rooms. She had only to compete with one other teacher and the cooks in the school kitchen area just to the south in making herself heard.

Five of the other six buildings used for instruction were identical to the mathematics block. The exception was the building that housed the science division. It was modern both in exterior style and in the design of its laboratories and teaching spaces. The construction of a science building had been a necessary factor in the University-College's ability to gain permission from the Ministry of Education to offer degree courses in agricultural sciences, science education, and the traditional scientific fields. The other buildings were leftover from an institution that had been known as the Mbordo Teacher Training College.

As the bell for the first class of the day rang, Alice walked down the ramp in front of the mathematics block and into her room, M-5. At the signal of the class prefect, thirty-six students, dressed in khaki shorts and white shirts, stood and greeted her in unison.

"Good morning Miss Manati," they said managing to sound almost cheerful.

She returned the greeting and the students sat down. Most of the other American staff members were not enthusiastic about this customary greeting and several openly discouraged it in belief that the standing students represented a colonialist tradition. But Alice enjoyed the deference paid by Sakraian students to teachers. In fact, it was a real treat. Sometimes she had trouble keeping a straight face if she let herself think about what one of her classes in DC would look like with students getting up altogether to say good morning to the teacher.

"The prefect would probably say something like, 'Come on you turkeys, get your asses out of those chairs,'" she thought. "That would be followed by comments from the rest of the class like, 'Go to hell man, she ain't the pledge or the national anthem.'"

Alice's thoughts returned to her class.

"Oh no," she muttered as she counted empty chairs, "one absent. Have to call the roll. The Biblical names I think I am getting right, but I will probably still be mispronouncing the others two years from now. Maybe I can figure out who is missing by just looking around the class."

Alice realized after scanning the room that she would have to call the roll. She was just beginning to learn to distinguish the faces of individual students in some of her smaller classes. In a class of this size it was still hopeless. She had convinced herself that someday she would be able to associate a name with every face, but this unfortunately was not that day.

The absent student was number thirty-two on her roll. When she reached the name she stopped with a sigh of relief. Alice was certain that she had made at least a dozen serious errors. She would have worked more on names if she had been able to find out what the correct pronunciations were. However, this was not an easy matter. The students were so completely agreeable. If she said, "Mazoon," and asked a student if that was correct, the answer was, "Yes madam." If she asked the same student if his name was 'Matson,' the answer would still be a polite and crisp, "Yes madam." She was tempted to pronounce one of the names 'Baboon' and ask if that were correct, but she already knew the answer would be, "Yes madam."

"My God," she thought, "these students are polite. So damn polite I almost miss those arguments that I used to have with my students in DC.

"Almost, but not really. This is better; much, much better. Some of it may very well be phony but it certainly makes teaching more pleasant."

Alice began with a small mathematical puzzle related to the day's lesson. She wrote the outline of the problem on the board. The students attacked the puzzle with a gusto that Alice still found remarkable. As she watched them work her thoughts wandered. The Vice-Chancellor had scheduled her highest level mathematics course, Maths 406, during the first hour of the instructional day to avoid forcing students to test their minds against differential equations during the hotter part of the tropical morning. Although he had been a geography and history teacher, he professed great respect for the disciplines of mathematics and science. Alice remembered that her first reaction to her teaching schedule had been to wonder why she had not come to Mbordo ten years earlier. Her last class of the day was over at 11:30. That, she had thought, would leave her the entire afternoon: to read to her heart's content, explore the African countryside, do projects, or just sit on her porch and contemplate the beauty of the tropical savanna and forest near her house.

Unfortunately, reading becomes boring after you try it four or five hours a day over a period of weeks. The grass and trees outside one's house become less interesting rather quickly. As for exploring the African countryside, Alice had found that old adage about Englishmen, mad dogs and the noonday sun was not frivolous. One afternoon she had marched off to the village from which the University-College took its name to find out more about life in Africa. Her collapse by the central market area had caused a near riot. The Vice-Chancellor had been summoned. He came quickly, picked her up and drove her back to the University-College in his personal car. He had explained quite clearly that if she wished to have something from the market, the only proper procedure was to send one of her students or the Vice-Chancellor's nephew to purchase the item. He further explained that if she wished a sight-seeing tour for cultural purposes, he would be very happy to transport her. He had stated in no uncertain terms that, as a teacher, she was far too valuable to the University-College to be risking her health by walking through areas of questionable cleanliness and exposing herself to the possibility of catching God-knows-what awful diseases.

Alice had been less than totally convinced about the part concerning her 'great value.' ("Probably just don't want an old lady to die on them," she had thought.) However, the rest of the Vice-Chancellor's lecture had been very effective. She had been embarrassed and frightened to the point that she had not left the University-College compound since, except to walk on the trail between her house and the Harrises.

That long block of time from 11:30 to dusk had become an unpleasant and difficult part of her daily life. Even now in the middle of her first class of the day she found herself thinking about the afternoon.

"Sleep, sleep," she thought, "that cuts down the time. But if I sleep too long, I won't be able to sleep tonight, and that's worse. Twelve, thirteen hours a day is too damn much, even for me. Only a zombie could sleep that much."

Several impatient hands waving in the classroom brought an end to her wandering thoughts.

"Stop this nonsense right now," Alice told herself. "You will never get through this lecture if you don't. This is a tough one."

She had never taught anything at this level of sophistication before. However, in DC her salary had been dependent on experience and level of education. Alice had completed course work equivalent to that necessary for the Ph. D. in mathematics at most universities. Teaching Maths 406 was challenging. She used at least forty-five minutes of every evening to prepare for this course alone.

"That time," she reflected, "stands between me and mental retrogression. It keeps me sane after supper. My God, saved by mathematics. I always thought it would work out the other way round."

Eight minutes had passed since the completion of the roll call. Most students looked puzzled. A few looked desperate. More hands waved.

Alice called on a student whose first name she could pronounce, "Yes, Moses, do you have the answer."

"No madam," Moses replied, "I do not. I believe the problem to be impossible. I can find no way to do it."

"Because you cannot find a way to do the problem, does that mean that it is impossible?" Alice asked.

"For me, yes," Moses Abene replied, "for you probably not. I believe you work them all whether impossible or not."

His reply brought smiles to the faces of other students. Alice smiled also.

She replied, "I am not a mathematical juju woman. But you are right about one thing. I can do this problem and you will be able to do it if you listen carefully."

Alice now had the full attention of every student.

She thought, "Teaching is so damn easy here, just like those mythical classrooms in teacher education courses."

Alice then explained a particular quirk of differential equations that made possible the solution of the puzzle. She did several examples that used of the same principle and helped her students as needed to get started with the assignment for the next day.

Alice's next class was Elementary Calculus, otherwise known as Maths 251.

"These students are not quite so beautiful," she thought as they quietly entered the classroom. "They try very hard but they just don't know basic algebra and trig well enough to handle calculus."

Alice had several arguments with this class concerning the best method of mastering the material in the syllabus. She thought that it was better to master material in a thorough manner, and not worry about completing the syllabus. The students in Maths 251 disagreed.

"But madam (or "sir" if really upset)," David Atar, the spokesman for the class, would say, "if we don't cover the material in the syllabus it will be a large disadvantage for us. Others who take the test will be able to do problems that we will not be able to do. How can we do as well as they do? We must be able to try all of the problems. The problems on the exam from the last part of the syllabus are the very easiest. You can do them even if you don't know the material well. If we can't do those easy problems it will be a very serious thing for us."

Alice had to admit, after looking at some of the tests, that what the students were saying was true. Problems from the first part of the syllabus were often quite difficult. Those from the very last parts of the syllabus required only a straightforward application of basic principles.

Alice had thought the dilemma of having too much material could be solved by extra classes. Unfortunately, the only time available in the students' day was between 3:00 and 4:00 p.m., just after the compulsory work period and just before practice for sports competition. Alice had learned something very important about three o'clock in West Africa. It was hot, very hot. She knew if she set a time, every student from this class would be there. But she could not face the afternoon heat, not yet anyway. One week of afternoon classes had convinced her that dedication had its limits.

Alice's third class of the day was a course in basic mathematical processes and how to teach them. The mathematical knowledge of students in this class was quite limited. Maths 131 was one last effort to prepare them to teach mathematics at the elementary school level. Alice tried to re-teach arithmetic from the point of view of understanding rather than a series of memorized steps. She was now in the process of explaining decimal and common fractions. Her students seemed to take genuine pleasure in learning about some of the basic logic underlying mathematical processes.

Alice hoped their new-found joy of learning would carry over into their own teaching practices. Some of the techniques that she had seen employed in her observations of practice teachers had been rather frightening.

One teacher, in attempting to teach a child the times table for the number seven, had stood over the child pounding his head with a thin stick while shouting, "Learn, learn, learn, learn....."

"Even allowing for cultural differences," Alice remembered thinking at the time, "this method does not seem likely to produce too many outstanding mathematicians."

Most of the students in Maths 131 really did seem happy to find a teacher who was willing to explain some of the mysteries of arithmetic.

"They are delightful," Alice thought.

She remembered how the class had reacted to the explanation of why only common fractions with the same denominator could be added.

Mr. Jarte had said, "We have always wondered why the denominators must be the same. We thought the whole thing was just some stupid procedure brought about by government decree. Now at last we know. This thing of mathematics is full of wonderment. It is beyond our best dreams that you should come here to explain these things to us."

Alice did suspect that perhaps students who made such speeches were looking toward future recommendations, but it was still a treat to have something like that said about your work.

As Alice completed this day's explanation on decimal fractions she heard the word 'wonderful' muttered by several students. (The use of that word had confused Alice until Jason had explained that students used 'wonderful' in what must be some old English form to mean something that was full of wonder.)

The syllabus for her fourth period class was to Alice a strange mixture of algebra, geometry and arithmetic. The Vice-Chancellor had explained to her in one of their early curriculum discussions that the students in this class were middle school teachers. If successful in their two-year program, they would be entitled to an advanced teaching certificate in maths, science, or agricultural sciences. In addition, if the quality of work done by any of these students was deemed to be excellent, they might be admitted to one of Mbordo's degree programs.

As students entered the room, Alice found herself panic stricken.

"Is it algebra day or arithmetic day," she mumbled.

She knew it wasn't geometry day because the students didn't have their protractors and compasses.

"I better remember," she thought. "These students are a little harsh. They don't want to mess around at all, ever."

"Today is Thursday," she reasoned. "Must be algebra day, let's see; Monday - arithmetic; Tuesday, Thursday - algebra; Wednesday, Friday - geometry. Yes, by God, it must be algebra day."

The class stood in unison at the signal of the prefect. "Good morning teacher."

"Good morning," Alice replied. "I hope everyone is feeling well. Today we have a very important topic in the field of algebra to discuss."

Alice surveyed the class for surprised, pained or angry looks. She saw none and decided that it must indeed be 'algebra day.'

Then she continued, "Today we discuss the solution of quadratic equations using the technique of factoring."

As she picked up a piece of chalk to write a sample equation on the board, thirty-eight pencils were raised in preparation to record whatever magic symbols she chose to place before the class.

"What power," Alice thought, "I could write anything and they would copy it. I should write something really foul."

But of course she wouldn't and she didn't. Instead she continued with the lecture. After ten minutes of explanation she called for questions. There were about a dozen questions all related to quadratic equations.

Then one brave student, William Ageman, had the courage to ask, "Is this the type of problem done by mathematics students in America?"

Alice replied, "Yes, students in some mathematics courses in the United States would probably be studying problems of exactly this type. Indeed . . ."

17

She noticed a hand waving wildly in the back of the room.

"Oh well," she thought, "better give him a chance to speak. He is the official class spokesman."

Mr. Kwame Aduma stood and said very slowly, "What you are saying about Maths in America is very, very interesting. It is so interesting that we believe that the entire school, everyone, even the other teachers, should have an opportunity to listen to you talk about this most important topic at an assembly. Perhaps, if you would ask the Vice-Chancellor, that can be arranged. But for now, in this time, we must learn maths. And perhaps, if we can have some further explanation of these equations or more examples, we will be able to do better when the time comes that we must do such problems on the exam."

Alice glared at the student and thought, "You son of a bitch. You'd squeeze every last number and mathematical operation you could out of an old lady, wouldn't you? Just to pass that damn exam."

Then she returned to the quadratic equations.

At 11:30 Alice was done for the day, really done. That last class was a real old-lady killer. Exhaustion and lunch time. Alice had once inquired about eating with the students in the dining hall. Everyone had discouraged the idea, even the students. The other expatriates said the food was terrible. The Vice-Chancellor said in no uncertain terms that she would become very sick. He was quite kind in his explanation.

He had said, "We know how much Peace Corps teachers want to understand our customs and foods. I did not understand this myself at first, but Mr. Henderson, who was the first Peace Corps volunteer that I had the pleasure of working with, explained all of this to me. The idea of getting to know the manner in which people in another culture live is very, very good. Marvelous in fact. But, if you eat with the students in the dining hall, the food will be strange to your stomach and will make you quite ill. If you are sick, you will not be able to teach. If you are not able to teach, you may have learned much about the customs and foods of Sakra, but you will be unable to help our students. And that would be a great tragedy for them."

Alice had decided to eat with the students anyway. She had been very careful to eat only well cooked foods and provide her own beverages. On the third Sunday of September the national dish of the Atan Tribe, *fufu* with groundnut soup, was served. It certainly had looked well cooked. In fact the yam looked as if it had been beaten to death. Unfortunately, as Alice learned later, the last step in the preparation of fufu involved the use of cold water. For a full week Alice was afraid to get more than twenty yards from a bathroom. She left her bungalow only once during that time to see Dr. Grasinski at the local clinic. After a week with the help of Paregoric, Lomotil, and several other rather disgusting medicines, she was able to stay away from the ladies' room long enough to teach one class at a time. A month had been required for complete recovery. Alice did not return to the student dining hall. Instead, she ate her lunches alone in her bungalow. A cheese or corned beef sandwich, some soup and a cup of tea was her usual fare.

"Not exciting," she thought as she sat eating, "but safe, damn safe. Yes, lunch is still one of the pleasures of the day, at least compared to what's left. A nap, a walk, some reading, the radio and then supper. For supper, rice and corned beef, rice and chicken, rice and tomatoes, or maybe just rice and rice. God, what I wouldn't give for a potato, a nice big baked potato. After supper, another walk, preparing lessons, some reading, bed. Dull but possible. Weekends are the worse.

"It's difficult, even for someone as old as I am, to take a nap Saturday afternoon after you have taken one Saturday morning. Maybe I should look at how other volunteers spend their weekends. Jason seems to have the problem solved. He found a girlfriend, even if she is a long ways away."

The idea that she might try Jason's solution caused Alice to chuckle, "I'm not even sure that I could handle a boyfriend, and I am damn sure I wouldn't find one worth traveling 180 miles to visit."

Alice decided it was time for her afternoon nap. She awoke at three.

"Dammit," she thought as she glanced at the clock, "too early."

She closed her eyes again in an effort to sleep.

"Too hot," her mind spoke as if to another person. "If you're exhausted you can sleep, but if anything less, it's impossible. The sheets get wet. They just get totally goddamned wet. It's hard to get up but worse to lay here in your own stinking sweat."

Alice sat up, stood up, then sat back down on her bed. Her thin pink nightgown clung to her body.

"I'll never make two years," she moaned, "Jesus, why in hell's name didn't I get a place in Florida? I could be sitting right now on some park bench feeding the birds."

That image always worked. The quickness with which she jumped out of bed surprised her.

"No damn bench sitting and bird feeding for me," she said out loud.

She took a bottle of water from the fridge and poured herself a glass.

"Good, very good," she mused, "water is the best thing when you are really thirsty. What to do now. The Karamazov Brothers are turning out to be a real drag. Who cares about their damn problems anyway? If I listen to Brahms's Third one more time I may smash the record player. Better go visit the boys. I've only been over there once this week. Don't want to make a nuisance of myself, but they do cheer me up."

The 'boys' were Jason Wills, Jeff Johnson, and Derrick Milson. Jason and Jeff were second year volunteers who had joined the Peace Corps a few weeks after graduating from college. Both were Americans who faced the option of the Peace Corps or the draft. Jason had a teaching license and could perhaps have found work in one of the big city school districts but choose Sakra instead. Jeff had known that work anywhere in the United States in his field of agriculture would leave him vulnerable to the whims of his draft board. Jason was a slender five feet ten inches tall. Jeff was a little taller and heavier than Jason. Derrick, from Wales, was the largest of the three, a good two inches taller than Jason, with broad shoulders and blond hair. He had completed the work needed for an advanced diploma in the fields of agriculture and soil management, and decided to sign up for a year with the British organization, Voluntary Service Overseas (VSO), just to be out of the British Isles for a while.

Alice put on a pink, cotton chambray dress she thought to be one of her coolest. As she walked toward the house in which the 'boys' lived, she met a group of five students returning from the compulsory work session. She recognized Mansa Kano from her third period class and then realized all five sat together in the back.

"They never say anything in class. I wonder if that is because they are from the North? Must try to involve the more."

"Good afternoon, sir!" Mansa greeted her.

She smiled and replied, "Good afternoon to you."

"Working in this heat would addle anyone's brain," she mused as she continued across the campus.

The ranch-style house occupied by the three male volunteers belonged to a Sakraian, Reverend Odum, who was working as an American supported missionary in Liberia. He and his wife had developed an admiration for American-style housing during their time as students in the United States. Since the Odums did not intend to retire for another twenty years, they were quite happy when the opportunity came up to rent the house to the University-College. The house was about half a mile away from the University-College compound in the direction of the village of Mbordo. Alice loved the atmosphere of the area. The small village that was developing near the Odums' place was an extension of the larger village of Mbordo. The town took its name from the Bordo tribe in much the same way that the names of Sakra and its capital, Nkra, came from the Kra river.

As she walked she thought, "If I make this trip very often I had better get a bicycle. I wonder if they make one I could ride."

When Alice approached the front porch of the house, she hesitated, wondering if she should call out or just go up and knock on the door. Derrick's familiar voice put an end to her dilemma.

"You don't have to stay out there. We allow everyone in this house."

"Even old ladies?" Alice replied.

"Ladies of any age," the voice answered.

"If you put it that way," Alice snapped, "I am not at all sure I want to come in."

"It's perfectly safe," Derrick replied. "We have all had our injections."

"Derrick, you are always safe," another voice responded.

"Enough of that," Alice said, "I didn't walk a mile to listen to a lot of talk about something I'm not interested in."

"Oh," Derrick said, "perhaps if you found the right person. Certainly, you must have had proposals."

"My, my," Alice said in a sad tone, "such impertinence in one so young. Jason, has he been drinking apeteshi again?"

"Speaking of drinking," Jason replied, "come on in and have something. With the fan it's a little cooler inside, anyway. What would you like, Alice? Beer, wine, scotch, rum? If you want palm wine we will have to send Kojo."

"It's not even four," Alice replied. "What are you two, a couple of drunks?"

"Hopefully, only on weekends," Jason chuckled.

"Well, I will have a glass of beer if you don't mind," Alice said as she wondered whether or not beer at this hour of the afternoon was a sign of impending alcoholism.

"I didn't need the whole bottle," Alice murmured, as Jason handed her a huge mug of beer.

"Local custom," replied Jason, "very impolite to serve less."

"Yes, I have noticed that nearly all of the local customs increase the quantity of whatever you happen to be drinking," Alice commented.

"Why Alice," Derrick said, "you have already developed insight into some of Sakra's most complex rituals."

"That's quite enough, Derrick," Alice replied as she took a sip of beer. "Where's Jeff?"

"He's in Kwim learning about local customs," Jason answered in a half serious tone.

"That's very ambitious," Alice commented. "Kwim must be at least forty miles from here."

Derrick laughed and explained further, "Miss Kanata provides an added inducement for Jeff to visit Kwim. That's her home village. Her father is paramount chief."

"Oh, now I understand," Alice replied. "Nevertheless, I do think it is good to learn more about Sakra."

"Certainly," Derrick added, "and when he is not acquiring knowledge of the culture of Sakra in Kwim, he does it here."

Jason, with a sigh, said, "Alice, I do my best to protect you, but it is impossible when you have a sick Welsh guy living with you."

Alice began laughing.

"Stop it, now," she commanded, "you will cause me to spill my beer. I know what your problem is. You two are jealous of Jeff's opportunity to learn more about local culture."

Alice decided that it was time to change the subject. Glancing upward she noticed objects on a shelf behind Jason.

"Whose carvings are those?" she asked. "The head figures of the man and woman."

"Those are mine," Jason replied.

"Where did you get them?" Alice inquired.

"I bought them on my front porch," Jason replied.

"Get serious," Alice protested. "I like them and I would like to know where to buy something similar."

Jason reasserted his previous claim. "I did buy them on my front porch. No one around Mbordo does this type of carving, but a Hausa man comes around about four times a year. I'll send him over to your place the next time I see him. If he knew an expatriate lived there, he probably would have already stopped by. Sakraians usually don't buy this junk."

"I don't think it's junk," Alice retorted, "but do you think it's safe?"

"What do you mean, 'safe'?" Derrick asked in a perplexed tone. "I never heard of anyone being injured by a statue. Except maybe those fertility dolls."

"You know damn well what I mean," Alice protested. "I live alone and having a strange man come to my house might not be very good idea."

Jason started to laugh and then thought better of it.

"I have heard of only one crime of that type in Sakra," he said. "Anyway, no one from the North would do something like that here. It would be suicidal. The Hausa and the Kroban have to be very careful outside their Muslim tribal areas."

"Well," Alice replied, "I just don't think that I should be careless. When this gentleman comes around, let me know and I'll come over here and see if there's anything I want to buy."

It did occur to Alice that Jason was probably right.

So, in spite of her doubts she continued, "Oh, what the heck. If you think he's all right send him on over."

"Don't worry," Jason replied, "if he causes you any trouble I will see to it that he suffers a fate worse than death. I won't buy any more of his junk."

"It's not junk!" Alice asserted again. "That old fertility doll is marvelous. I wonder how many babies it must have inspired."

"Well," Derrick remarked, "it is at least six months old and hopefully it hasn't inspired any babies yet.

"By the way Jason," Derrick continued, "is Karen coming this weekend?"

"Oh, shut up Derrick," Jason responded, "you wouldn't know an authentic carving from something done with a jigsaw. I scraped the bottom of that one and told you myself that it's not more than a few months old. And, no, Karen is not coming here this weekend."

The room was quiet.

Alice found the silence uncomfortable and said, "It is a long trip from Pandu. Jason, how long does it take?"

"It's 180 miles and the trip takes twelve hours," Jason answered, "unless you catch a ride with some crazy Syrian or Lebanese in a Mercedes. Then it takes maybe five or six hours, if you get there at all."

Alice, sensing that Jason was about to start on another of his lengthy stories about his epic struggles with lorry drivers, bad roads and crazy Syrians, diplomatically announced, "It's definitely time for me to get home. Send that Hausa fellow over if he has anything good left after you finish buying what you want. By the way, are you traveling next week or is Karen?"

"I am," Jason replied and then without thinking added, "Why don't you come with me?"

Alice almost laughed, "I doubt that I could make it that far, but I will give it some thought. It would be interesting. See you later."

As he watched Alice leave, Jason rethought his invitation.

"Strange that I did that," he mused. "That offer might not have been my best idea of the day."

Derrick's comment didn't help. "You will make a super threesome. Karen will be very pleased to see Mrs. Manati, I am sure."

"What the hell would you know about who Karen would be pleased to see," Jason snapped. "I think she would be quite happy to see Alice."

"Well, you don't have to worry," Derrick continued, "she would probably die of heat prostration or a heart attack before you reached Pandu. That certainly would be a big event in some little roadside village. They would be holding funerals and wakes for the next ten years, paid for by you of course."

"She's pretty strong for her age and I like her, and I don't give a shit what you think," Jason replied. "If she wants to go to Pandu with me, she damn well can."

"All right, all right," Derrick said, "don't get so excited mate. I was only joking. You are right of course, and it's damn decent of you to try and help her get off the compound. She does seem lonely."

Jason nodded and said nothing, not wishing to discuss the matter further.

That night he woke up in a cold sweat (a rare phenomenon in Sakra) after dreaming of being thirty miles from Pandu with Alice lying in his arms, gasping for breath while he argued with the driver of the lorry over the amount of fare they owed.

His first reflection on waking was, "How silly to worry. Of course they wouldn't charge me for her ride."

With that comforting thought he was able to sleep again.

The next night he woke after a more extended version of the same dream. The lorry driver was demanding extra money for the inconvenience of having someone sick on his lorry. Jason decided to get himself all the way awake and try to pull himself together. He got out of bed, went into the kitchen, poured a glass of Coke and decided a small self-lecture was in order.

"Listen Jason," he told himself, "she probably won't want to go at all, but if she says that she wants to go, then by God you invited her and by God you are going to take her."

He returned to bed and did not awake until well into Saturday morning.

23

Saturday passed with the usual reading, sleeping, eating and walking about a bit. Sunday at the 'boys' bungalow was much the same as Saturday except on Sunday they found that they had a bit more energy.

"It's damn unfair," Derrick explained to Jason as they ate a late Sunday breakfast. "On Saturday, when you could begin a reasonable trip, you're too goddamn tired. On Sunday, when you have had more rest than you can stand, it's too late to go anywhere. What we need is ten days of uninterrupted work and a double weekend."

"Why don't you bring that one up in a staff meeting Derrick," Jason suggested. "It might get through."

"Yes, quite possibly," Derrick replied. "You and Jeff could be counted on for support."

"Me, maybe," Jason responded, "Jeff, I don't think so. He's already figured out a way to have a four-day weekend after working three days. I don't think he would vote for ten days of work."

"Oh, yes," Derrick replied with a laugh, "I forgot American ingenuity. Everybody else hates observing student teachers in little villages, but Jeff has turned it into a rather good thing. Are all his student teachers in Kwim?"

"I don't know," Jason replied in an irritated tone.

"Sorry mate, didn't mean to offend you," Derrick replied. "How about popping down to the commons for a beer after breakfast?"

Jason groaned, "Other than the fact that drinking beer at ten in the morning is a little decadent, which I guess doesn't really matter, the place doesn't open until two.

"You know what I really miss? A good, big, thick Sunday newspaper with funnies and everything. With a Sunday newspaper you always have something to do on Sunday. Sunday papers have everything. Even sexy pictures unless it's the Christian Science Monitor. I remember some really fine bra and panty ads."

"Jason," Derrick protested, "you've been here too long. I didn't know you were that bad off. I will try to locate some *Playboy* magazines or something else with female pictures for you."

"That seems a little stupid," Jason remarked, "I've seen more bare breasts here in a year than even a doctor would see in a lifetime. Anyway, where would you get those magazines in Mbordo?"

"Mr. Whitland has a subscription to *Playboy*," Derrick replied, "I'm sure that if he heard of your dreams of newspaper advertisements he would try to help out."

"I take it you noticed those magazines on one of your trips to the Whitland bungalow?" Jason asked. "You seem to be spending a lot of time over there."

"He has a very fine library," Derrick answered, "perhaps the only really good collection of material in my field in this entire country."

Fun and games in the Whitland library, Jason thought, as he murmured, "So, you really enjoy the library? I thought perhaps the house had some other attraction for you."

Derrick answered with a shrug and picked up a book.

As he pretended to leaf through the pages, he thought, "Perhaps I should discuss what happened with someone. Matters really developed quickly. That first night seemed so spontaneous. Betty did invite me over to use her husband's library. That seemed completely normal. After all, I had asked Bob about the possibility, and I just assumed he told her to go ahead and do it. I just don't think he meant go ahead and do what we did. Anyway, how was I to know that Whitland was away in Nkra. Nice now, but no experience in what happens next. Could ask Jason, but he would probably just tell me to run like hell. No point in that. Too much fun the way it is."

"Heavy reading?" Jason asked half seriously. "Is it two o'clock yet?"

"No," Derrick replied, "let's have a beer here first."

The two men gently slipped into weekend alcoholism. Lunch was bread, cheese and a beer. After lunch, Jason tried to grade a few papers, but a second beer convinced him that work could wait. At two, Jason and Derrick opened the commons. By four, they had been driven out by the true alcoholics. Somehow, after that, they became involved in a game of football (soccer in the United States) with a group of students and found themselves stone-cold sober by six.

Supper, rice and corned beef stew fixed by Kojo, their houseboy, was dull but edible. They decided to go into one of the little bars in town for a beer, but knew they would have to hurry. The moon was in its first quarter and would provide little light once the last reflected rays of the sun were gone. Everything would close by seven-thirty.

"It's not big time," Jason thought as he sat drinking his lukewarm beer in Tango's tiny dark bar, "but I can live here."

The bar did close at seven-thirty and they made their way back to their house. They were surprised to find that Jeff had not yet returned from his trip to Kwim with Enata Kanata. No Benz buses or mammy wagons traveled the roads between Kwim and Mbordo after dark, unless delayed by mechanical failure or accident. However, Jeff and Enata had borrowed the Assistant Principal's car for the weekend trip to Enata's home village. The village of Kwim, or more precisely the collection of villages over which Enata's father presided as paramount chief, was in a wealthy area of Sakra. That wealth was entirely the result of the American and European taste for chocolate. The cocoa bean had made Chief Kanata a man of considerable influence. In addition to being paramount chief, his farms were among the top five in production of the cocoa bean in the nation of Sakra.

Enata's appointment as a teacher at the University-College was most probably made by an Mbordo administrator, or someone higher up in the educational bureaucracy, eager to comply with the edicts of the central government concerning sexual balance on academic staffs. Few women graduates were available. (Only two Sakraian women were staff members at the University-College this particular year.) The fact that her father was the Paramount Chief of Kwim was certainly not a negative factor, but his position was not the reason for her appointment.

Unfortunately, as much could not be said for the weekend loan of the car to Jeff and Enata. The Assistant Principal was an Atan living in a Bordo area and would have been unlikely to loan his car even to the Vice-Chancellor unless the Vice-Chancellor were willing to post a rather large bond. Enata, understanding well how the Assistant Principal felt about his car, had refused all offers of its use in the past. She was not sure whether the Assistant Principal's interests were in terms of some future favor from her father, or whether they were more directly related to her, but either way she wanted no part of it.

Jeff was less scrupulous, or perhaps had less to worry about in terms of the return of future favors. He had suffered through the trip from Mbordo to Kwim by lorry many, many times and was quite happy to accept the Assistant Principal's offer.

Enata had warned him, "If you damage this car you will not leave this country until you are a very old man. At your salary it would take 100 years to earn enough money to pay for it.

"But," she had laughed and continued, "that would not be so bad. Maybe it would be nice if you just stayed here forever. If the opportunity comes, I will cause you to wreck the car."

Nothing of the sort had happened. The car was running perfectly when they returned. Jeff was slightly apprehensive as he drove back through the University-College compound after dropping Enata at her apartment. He never quite knew how he would be greeted by Jason and Derrick. Much depended upon their degree of inebriation.

He drove the Datsun wagon onto the front lawn of the house and was greeted by Derrick: "Well, well, what have we here. It would appear to be a wealthy American. What fine long trousers you have on. What an excellent automobile. But, I'm very sorry, sir. You have come to the wrong place. My humblest apologies. You will have to seek lodgings elsewhere. We have no hot water tonight or any other night for that matter, and but one bathroom. I know that would not be satisfactory for a gentleman of your means and taste."

Jeff replied in his best Tennessee accent, "Don't worry about the damn hot water and bathroom, I don't need a bath. If you need one just sleep on the porch. That will keep the snakes and mosquitoes away."

"Come on," Jason said, "let's have a beer."

"What's the matter?" Jeff asked. "Both of you can still make coherent sentences. There a beer shortage in town?"

"If there was a beer shortage, mate, we would not be offering you one," Derrick replied. "Our weekend just possibly was not quite as enjoyable as yours."

After the three men were seated with beer in hand, Jason asked Jeff about his weekend in Kwim. Jeff began by talking about Chief Kanata.

"Enata's father was studying at sixth form level when he was asked to be paramount chief of Kwim. In those days if you became a paramount chief you had to return to your village immediately and live there. He had to make a choice between his schooling and becoming a chief."

"Couldn't he just have gone through the enstoolment ceremonies and then returned to school?" Derrick asked.

"No, not really," Jeff explained, "I asked him about that. He said that until the middle fifties a chief, and especially a paramount chief, had real power and had to decide many matters of importance."

"What about commuting?" Jason asked. "Go to school during the week and return to the village on weekends."

Jeff laughed and replied, "There were only three schools that had sixth forms. He was a student at Da Mota near Nkra. If you think the roads are bad now, would you believe it took him four days to make the trip from Kwim to his school?"

"That would do in a weekend," Derrick commented.

"Anyway," continued Jeff, "he lives there in Kwim pretty much as his father did, except that he has at least a dozen transistor radios. Enata did convince him to build a concrete house with a tin room, but he absolutely refuses to pave the courtyard. Says he likes the feel of dirt on his feet."

"He's right about the courtyard," Jason declared, "it's a lousy idea to pave it. It would be hot and kids would always be getting hurt when they fell down.

"Do you and Enata have separate accommodation?" Derrick asked. "Maybe the Chief's interested in some grandchildren."

Jeff, making no effort to hide his annoyance, replied, "Not that it's any of your business, but yes we do. The Chief would not consider an arrangement that involved an unmarried couple sharing the same room in his compound."

"Time for me to get to bed," Jason said as he finished his beer. "Full week ahead."

****

Monday morning the entire staff drifted into the staff room a few minutes before the start of morning assembly. The entire staff, that is, except the Vice-Chancellor and Mr. Thornton. The Vice-Chancellor had made the trip from his bungalow to the double classroom that served as an assembly hall so often that his timing was near perfect. The one instance that he could remember being late was on a day that an announcer for radio Sakra had given the incorrect time.

As he drove, the Vice-Chancellor thought, "Thornton, Thornton. Not much chance he will be at assembly today. Lucky if he shows up for his first class."

One task the Vice-Chancellor was not fond of was the need to periodically remind the old Englishman of his responsibilities to the University-College. He knew he should take decisive action and forcibly retire Thornton.

"The type of thing," he thought, "where one has a big celebration, thanks the retiree for his many years of valuable service, hands him a ticket back to England, and sees to it that he gets on the plane. No watch here of course, maybe a fertility doll with a gold belly button just to make sure he gets the message that he's not to come back."

However, it was not that simple for the Vice-Chancellor. Thornton had been his history master in secondary school many, many years before, at a time when there were few schools of quality in Sakra and even fewer teachers with any semblance of academic qualifications. The boys in his class, himself included, had hated Thornton. He had been tough and demanding academically and terribly pompous. But he had been effective. Most of his pupils did well on their O-level exams. The Vice-Chancellor had been able to continue his education at the university level and eventually do graduate work in the United States.

"Old loyalties die very hard," the Vice-Chancellor thought, "and Thornton is not at all reticent about reminding me of the good old days and all that I owe him. But this man is a problem. Some day one of our boys is going to kill him. If not for what he says, then for messing around with the female students."

As the car neared the assembly hall the Vice-Chancellor sighed and said aloud, "If he could find a job at all, he would not last more than three months anywhere but Sakra. Perhaps it is our kindness for the old. Maybe it is for the best. We will all be old someday."

The Vice-Chancellor arrived at morning assembly at 6:44. He was immaculately dressed in crisply pressed gray trousers, blue blazer and matching tie. He said good morning to Mr. West, and sat down beside him on the raised platform at the front to the hall. Mr. West was the Vice-Chancellor's counterpart in USAID jargon. His official title was "Chief of Party." The Vice-Chancellor had never been able to understand exactly what Mr. West's function was at the University-College. He even suspected that Mr. West himself was not very sure. In the Vice-Chancellor's mind, West was only a pale shadow of the first head of party from River State, Dr. Black.

"Ah, Dr. Black," the Vice-Chancellor mused. "There was a man who could get the attention of everyone in the room just by clearing his throat. I am not sure there would be a University-College without his help. He took on those people from the University of Sakra who wanted us to be just a teachers college, he helped me keep peace within the faculty, he got the River State people to complain less and work more, and he even got the students to work together. But most of all he helped me understand what I had to do. But no more, and maybe just as well. We have to begin to do this on our own. If you judge by their titles, the role of the Americans has been continuously changing. Once they were advisors, then professors, then co-workers and now counterparts. About all Mr. West seems good for is rewriting the plans for projects so that USAID will approve them. I think I just about have that figured out. Fifteen references as to how the project will help the common farmer raise more food is usually enough to insure acceptance. The Americans love that stuff. Not that they have any real idea of what would help the common farmer. Five hundred acres of bottom land in Illinois: that's what would help the common Sakraian farmer."

With that thought, the Vice-Chancellor chuckled. The other members of the administrative staff were startled by the unexpected noise since Mr. West was at that moment beginning the morning service.

"Better watch it," the Vice-Chancellor thought, "someone will accuse me of sacrilege. Speaking of sacrilege, Mr. West is the leader today. I suppose he uses Old Testament stuff when he can. Must be difficult for him when they start singing about Jesus. I wonder how long we will continue these services. I am surprised the Muslim students haven't demanded equal time. Then there are the Animists. We could do all three services together at the same time. Have a fight every morning. Oh, the pledge: better concentrate, disloyalty to the 'Savior' could have even worse consequences than sacrilege."

When the assembly ended, students and teachers moved toward classroom blocks. Alice walked rapidly. She liked to be in her room before the students arrived. That Monday, for Alice, was much the same as other days in Mbordo. The usual routines of work and rest were faithfully repeated. However, she was aware that something was different. She felt an excitement that touched her senses more than her mind. Chalk brought a tingling sensation to the tips of her fingers as she wrote on the board. The dried vegetable soup that she mixed with boiling water for her lunch seemed improved in body and flavor.

She wasn't sure exactly when she made up her mind to go with Jason to Pandu. It was probably Tuesday night as she sat correcting papers and listening to Beethoven's Ninth Symphony. Something in the strength and joy of the third movement told her get on with her life. That it was no good to be in Africa and sit in her bungalow day after day. That life had to be met. If that proved fatal, well no matter, one was just as dead either way.

She had slammed down her fist and said, "Jason invited me and by God I will go."

Wednesday morning at assembly she asked Jason to see her in the staff lounge after the day's classes were over. They met at noon.

"Jason," Alice said, "if you haven't changed your mind, I do believe I would like to make that trip to Pandu this weekend."

Jason's face went blank.

She continued quickly, "Of course, if it would be inconvenient or if you think that Karen would be upset by an uninvited guest, you need not feel obligated."

Jason recovered somewhat and replied, "Alice, if I didn't want you to go with me I would not have asked you."

He smiled slightly and continued, "If you want to ride a lorry for 180 miles then it sure would be a pleasure to have your company. We will leave here Friday at eleven if you can arrange for someone to take your last class."

Later that afternoon Alice asked the Vice-Chancellor for permission to leave Mbordo early on Friday.

He smiled and said, "Ah, going to make a trip to Nkra. The school lorry is going there Friday morning. Why don't you give your students a day off and take advantage of the ride."

"Oh boy, it's going to hit the fan now," Alice thought, as she replied, "I am not going to Nkra. We are going to Pandu."

"Pandu?" the Vice-Chancellor said very slowly, "Pandu? Who is taking you to Pandu?"

"Jason," she replied.

"Jason?" the Vice-Chancellor repeated. "Oh yes, Mr. Wills. He is famous for that trip. The students say that no European could make that trip except Mr. Wills and that no African would ever have sufficient reason to go that far and back in three days. Did you know that the Assistant Principal's wife lives in Pandu? He sees her only at the midterm and end of term breaks."

"That," replied Alice, making a major effort to sound dignified, "is the Assistant Principal's problem. Are you suggesting that I stay here and try to solve his problem in some manner?"

The Vice-Chancellor knew he had been bested.

Every part of his body seemed to be trying to laugh as he answered, "Good heavens no. God forbid that I would ever have such a thought. You Peace Corps people are all alike. Sooner or later you have to make yourselves ill somehow whether from the food or travel or whatever. Go on to Pandu. Have a good time. It's a lovely place. If I didn't have a University-College Council meeting this weekend I would transport you there myself. Why don't you wait until next weekend? I have business in Pandu and we could go together."

"No," Alice replied, "absolutely not. You want to drive to Pandu about as badly as our students want to do manual labor."

"Not so loud," the Vice-Chancellor said in a mock whisper, "if word is spread about that our students don't like manual labor we will lose AID funds.

"Just give that eleven o'clock class the day off. Forgive me if I seem overly protective. We do need you. Make the driver give you the front seat. You outrank everyone except perhaps a paramount chief and a chief would give you his seat out of politeness. The people on the lorry will be surprised to see you join them."

Alice almost blushed. She thanked the Vice-Chancellor for his concern and left his office.

Jason found himself thinking of the trip at odd times; in the middle of demonstrating an algebra problem, eating lunch, grading homework.

"If Alice collapses in the first hour or two of the trip, no problem. We will be near the hospital for the people working on the Kra dam. Admasi must have some kind of a hospital. Pandu must have several hospitals."

Jason was not the only person concerned about Alice's planned adventure. On Thursday the Vice-Chancellor was still in his office, well past the normal hour for the evening meal, working on the final aspects of an AID proposal that was already a week late.

"Working late," he mused, "must be an American invention. I had better talk to Mrs. Manati again. Her students will be very unhappy if she is unable to teach after this trip."

The Vice-Chancellor drove from his office to Alice's bungalow. Alice was alarmed when she heard the car. The only person that she could imagine who would be visiting her in a car was Thornton. She moved quickly to the door, hoping to keep him off the porch. She smiled and almost grinned as she recognized the stiff, erect frame of the Vice-Chancellor.

"Good evening Mrs. Manati," he said, "it's very good to see you in a happy mood this evening."

"Just laughing at myself," Alice replied. "For a moment I thought you were somebody else."

"Well, I am sorry to have disappointed you," the Vice-Chancellor said.

"Oh no," Alice said, "much better that it was you. Won't you come in and have a cup of tea."

"I will come in," replied the Vice-Chancellor, "but no thank you on the tea. I'm already late and my wife will be upset about supper."

They sat down in Alice's small living room.

She asked, "Now, to what do I owe the honor of a visit by the Vice-Chancellor?"

"Yes," the Vice-Chancellor said, "I want to.... that is I was hoping or wanted to ask you to reconsider the trip to Pandu. I really do have to go the weekend after next and believe that trip is much easier by car."

"All right, I will make you a deal," Alice said without a trace of humor, "I will go to Pandu this weekend with Jason. If I enjoy the city then I will make the trip the next weekend with you."

The Vice-Chancellor looked totally disconcerted.

"Look," she continued, "I am sorry if this business bothers you. I really am because I know how serious you are about keeping the University-College running smoothly. But, it will be all right. Nothing bad is going to happen, and even if it does it won't be your fault."

"Ayi," muttered the Vice-Chancellor, "you really are going."

"Yes," replied Alice, "and coming back, too."

"I sincerely hope so," the Vice-Chancellor said.

"You are really worried about me, aren't you?" Alice asked quietly.

"Well," the Vice-Chancellor replied, "you are a good teacher. No, not just good, excellent or whatever word like that one would use to describe the very best. You are exactly what our students need."

"I'm sorry," Alice replied, "it's just something that I need to do. I can't just sit here. If I don't get out and do something, I won't be a good teacher very long. I can't just teach mathematics all day and grade papers all night. I have to try, to grow, to participate, to somehow become a little more a part of things."

"I think I understand," The Vice-Chancellor replied, "I should have been more alert. I'm very sorry that I did not become aware of your needs more quickly. I should have made more of an effort to help you."

"That idea seems a little odd to me," Alice replied. "I do not wish to be impolite or critical but I don't think it's your responsibility to take care of me. I doubt very much that you would be able to do so even if for some crazy reason it was your responsibility."

"I don't understand," the Vice-Chancellor said.

"Well," Alice continued, "the first problem is that you lived in the United States so you know a lot about how we live. This knowledge effects how you think we should be treated. For example, if you took me to the house of an uncle who had never attended elementary school for the evening meal, you would provide a plate and silverware for my use. Would your uncle have provided these things if you were not there? Or would he have expected me to eat with my fingers like everyone else? It is comforting to find people who understand how things are done in America, especially at first. But it's time for me at least once in a while to try things the African way. And I can only do that by myself."

Before the Vice-Chancellor could respond, Alice continued, "Anyway, the Peace Corps has a very efficient process for sending useless bodies home whether dead or alive. If worse comes to worse, the evidence will be quickly removed."

The Vice-Chancellor replied, "Yes, I am sure they are very efficient, but I have heard it said that the Vice-Chancellor who loses one volunteer is never sent another. Nevertheless, I retreat before your eloquence and logic. I really don't understand why you people in the Peace Corps have this compulsive desire to travel. But I wish you good luck on your adventure. If you will permit, I will have the school truck take you to the junction. I must leave now. See you tomorrow."

Alice said good-by at the door and watched the Vice-Chancellor drive away.

"What a totally decent human being," she thought. "Hope his worry is meaningless. What is the worse that could happen? Just dying would not be so bad, but what if I got really sick and just had to lie here for weeks or months? No, stop that. It won't happen. I really want to make this trip."

CHAPTER 3
Pandu

Friday at eleven Jason was ready, Alice was ready, the school truck was ready. But the driver of the school truck was not ready. Something about saying good-by to a girlfriend. By eleven fifteen, the driver was ready.

Alice and Jason placed their small traveling bags in the back of the truck and climbed into the front seat by the driver. The driver backed the truck out of its wooden shelter and drove toward Mbordo at just a little above the maximum possible speed given the condition of the road and the truck. He slowed ever so slightly as he passed through the town. The street was narrow. Shops and houses sat back only a few feet from its edges. The road served as front yard and sidewalk. Children played on the street. Jason wondered how they avoided being hit by lorries and cars. Perhaps the small ones developed a sixth sense that warned them when to jump out of the way.

Alice sat quietly, content with her own thoughts: "The view from the front seat of this lorry is certainly different than from a car. I can see more of the town. Never realized how rectangular it was. But it's not quite regular. Something, a house, a tree, a clump of bamboo, a path out of place always seems to upset the symmetry. It almost seems deliberate, as if something or someone doesn't like the pattern and is determined to sabotage it one way or another. No separate neighborhoods here, instead two-story concrete block houses big enough for an army surrounded by small homes made of wood and mud."

Jason's concerned voice interrupted her thoughts.

"Uh oh, the driver is slowing down."

"What's wrong?" Alice inquired.

"I'm afraid to ask," Jason said. "Oh, he is offering someone a ride. Oh no, they have a load of firewood. This may take a while."

"My goodness, this is interesting!" Alice exclaimed. "Do they always stop like this for someone who wants a ride?"

Jason seemed near tears.

"Real interesting," he mumbled. "We could be here an hour."

The driver turned to the window on the passenger side of the truck and asked Jason in an apologetic tone, "Sir, it OK if I give my brother some help? He good friend but cannot get wood to his home."

"Where is his home?" Jason asked.

"Alum," replied the driver.

"Only four miles out of our way," Jason said quietly to Alice before he turned toward the driver and said, "OK, but got to be done quick, quick." Then he whispered words that were for the driver alone, "But got to be done really quick. Old lady here might get tired and die. Vice-Chancellor would be very unhappy."

The driver and his 'brother' began working hurriedly to load the wood. When they finished, the driver started the truck and was soon driving very rapidly on the laterite road. Dust billowed around the lorry in huge, angry, red clouds. Alice tried to fasten a scarf around her head to protect her white hair from the small red particles of laterite, but quickly decided it was not worth the effort.

The truck swayed back and forth as the driver tried to dodge potholes. Several times she was sure that the truck would end up against a tree or in one of the deep ditches along the sides of the road. She could hear her teeth grinding but couldn't stop the motion of her mouth.

Jason glanced sideways at Alice. Then he knew the true meaning of white. White as a ghost his mother used to say.

He leaned over and shouted to the driver, "It's OK, OK, slow down. We want to see more of the land."

He muttered to himself, "Dead either way I guess. The first rule of travel in Sakra, never tell a lorry driver you are in a hurry."

The house of the lorry driver's 'brother' was two miles beyond Alum on a bad, bad road. However, they did eventually get there, unload the wood and start again in the direction of the junction. According to the driver's watch, it was one o'clock when they got down from the school truck.

"Oh well," Jason thought, "so much for the great start. Thirteen miles in two hours, about average."

He turned to Alice, and said, "Last chance to turn back." As an afterthought he added, "I wonder if the Vice-Chancellor arranged our little side trip to be sure that you knew what you were getting into."

"I am not going back until Sunday," she replied.

Jason quickly added, "I wasn't serious about the Vice-Chancellor. He wouldn't do something like that. This business with the lorry drivers happens all the time."

"Really?" Alice asked with raised eyebrows. "You mean the whole damn trip is going to be like this? When will we get to Pandu? Sometime tomorrow morning?"

"No, no," Jason said with a small laugh. "Now that we are on the main road the drivers will not vary their routes for just one or two people. Look, the school driver is ready to return to Mbordo. Last chance to go back."

"Jason," Alice said sharply, "tell me the truth. What do you really think about me making this trip?"

"I think," Jason replied, "that we had better get ourselves over to the other side of the road and stop a lorry or it will be midnight before we see Pandu."

Alice was smiling as she followed Jason.

As they stood by the road she asked, "Would it help if I held up my thumb?"

Jason burst into laughter.

"What is the matter, Jason?" Alice asked in an annoyed tone. "If I've done something stupid please tell me what it is."

"No, no," Jason replied, "you haven't done anything wrong yet, but please, please don't try to thumb a ride. In Sakra 'the thumb' is equivalent to a sign made with one of the fingers in the United States."

"Oh," Alice said quietly, "I think I know which one."

"Wave your hand up and down like this," Jason instructed, "and don't worry, you will be a big help. We might even be able to stop a car and get to Towa in reasonable comfort."

Jason spotted a Mercedes. He waved his hand up and down slowly. The car's speed seemed to increase as it approached. When the man riding in the back seat saw Alice, he signaled his driver to pull over. The car skidded to a halt about two hundred feet down the road.

"Yes," Jason concluded, "it's a Sakraian. They would never pass up a white-haired European lady."

Alice and Jason walked toward the rapidly backing car. It stopped beside them. The rear door opened and a well dressed African stepped out.

"Madam," he addressed Alice, "has something happened to your car? Where are you going? Can I help you in any way?"

Alice replied timidly, "I don't have a car, but we are going to Pandu, and if you are going in that direction you could be of help to us."

"No car?" the African asked rhetorically. "Then you must be in the Peace Corps. I am quite sorry, but I do not go to Pandu today."

Jeff interceded quickly, "Nevertheless, you could be of much help to us if you would transport us as far as Towa."

"But of course," he replied with a slight smile, "exactly what I was going to suggest. You take the back seat and I will have the front with the driver."

The owner of the car did not speak for several minutes once the car was in motion again. Jason thought that perhaps he was annoyed at having been conned by an old lady into picking up two Peace Corps people. The sophisticated suspension and soft cushions of the Mercedes were a welcome change from the school truck. The voice of the African after perhaps fifteen minutes of silence startled Jason.

In a remark addressed to Alice he said, "The Ministry of Education should provide you people with some form of transportation."

Alice smiled but said nothing as she thought, "Yes, something like what we are riding in now would do very nicely."

The African continued looking directly at Jason, "I suppose it's all very well for you to be out on the road trying to find a lift, but madam you are very, you are eh. . ."

"Quite old," snapped Alice, "but tell me, sir, how do old ones of your own travel? Do they have their own transport?"

The man laughed and replied, "I am sure that you are a teacher. Only a teacher can sound like that. Oh, very well. I suppose that nearly all of our old ones must ride a lorry when they wish to travel."

"Well, that is exactly what we have planned to do," Alice replied, "and if you do not wish us to ride with you, please have the car stopped and let us out."

Jason gently pushed his elbow into Alice's side and said loudly, "Please Alice, it was very kind of this gentleman to offer us a ride. He is only expressing respect for your age. He is not being critical of your conduct."

"Indeed sir, that is correct," the African responded in a pleasant tone. "I do apologize if I have offended you, madam. I was not implying that your actions were in any way unacceptable. My only regret is that I will not be able to transport you to Admasi. The road from Towa to Admasi is not at all good."

Alice, still upset over the man's previous comment, managed to control an impulse to insert a malicious remark about what he could do with his ride. She decided the conversation was better left to Jason.

"However," the African continued, "I have to be in Nkra at three this afternoon for a meeting. Why don't you travel with me to Nkra and go by plane to Pandu?"

"Thank you very much for that kind offer," replied Jason, "but we find the Admasi route both a little quicker and quite a bit less expensive. Also, this is Mrs. Manati's first trip in Sakra other than to Nkra and she would like to view more of the countryside, close up."

"There is an old saying," the owner of the car reflected, "with which I am sure you are familiar, about mad dogs, Englishmen and the noonday sun. But when we were a British colony, I don't believe I ever remember seeing any of those Englishmen on a lorry. We will need a new saying about the Peace Corps people and lorries. How about, 'Getting there is half the fun,' eh?"

The reference to the old Greyhound advertisement surprised Alice.

"You lived in America?" she asked.

"Oh yes, of course," the African replied, "I was over there as a student in the early 50's and then back again for graduate studies in the 60's. It has always been difficult for me to understand how you people are able to adjust to our country."

"Some don't," Jason replied, "they leave quickly or become alcoholics. Others do. How did you find Sakra when you came back? Could you have stayed in America?"

"Hmmf," the African mused, "returning my question to me. I do not know. Some students stayed, but this is my home. I have a sense of belonging in this land that I could never achieve in America. I do not know how to explain exactly, but my family, my people, my country, they are all here. It is not possible to transfer such things as one transfers funds from one bank account to another."

After a brief pause he continued, "Also in America you have what is referred to as a racial problem. It was not so bad the last trip as the first but we do find it painful to see our brothers suffer. Of course such things do not affect us much. Here in Sakra I am a whole man, and as long as I am complete here in my home it mattered little to me what I was thought to be in America. Here I am comfortable as a person, in America it was something less than that; here my children will become Africans,

36

there they would be Blacks. For you this may be the same, for me it is quite different."

"I understand what you are saying," Alice commented, "I taught in Washington DC for more than thirty years."

The African smiled, "Ah yes, Washington DC. I was a student at Howard University from 1951 to 1955."

"My goodness," Alice responded, "many of the teachers that I worked with attended Howard."

As they talked, they found a number of mutual acquaintances and the tone of conversation in the car warmed.

After they had exhausted the topic of mutual friends, the owner of the car asked, "Where do you teach in Sakra?"

"Mbordo," Alice replied.

"My sister also teaches there," the African responded. "Perhaps you are acquainted? Enata Kanata is her name."

"Really!" Alice exclaimed, "Enata is your sister?"

The man laughed, "No, not really my sister. I believe in America you would say cousin or perhaps second cousin. She has gotten to know one of your people rather well. He visits Kwim."

The African turned in his seat to see Jason better and said curtly, "That's not you, is it?"

Jason replied, "No, that is not me. Enata and I are well acquainted but not friends."

Alice was startled and said, "Jason, what do you mean you are not friends?"

"Alice," Jason replied, "the term friend has a much stronger connotation here than in the United States when it is applied to a relationship between a man and a woman. If a man asks you to be his friend best be careful how you answer."

The African laughed lightly at Jason's explanation of the term 'friend,' but then spoke in a serious tone. "I really am not sure that I approve of Enata's relationship with this American. I don't know if that sort of thing can lead to any good. Her father is very liberal. Educated her and all that. I suppose she will learn much about America and if she travels there she will have useful contacts. But it is difficult for me to see much value in such a matter."

Then he spoke directly to Alice, "What do you think?"

Alice started to reply but thought better of it. The sudden appearance of the tall struts of the Towa bridge as they rounded a curve gave Alice the opportunity to avoid the African's question.

"Only a few more miles to Towa," he continued, "I do wish that I could transport you to Admasi."

"Absolutely not," Alice responded quickly, but with a smile. "Thank you very much for the ride to Towa, but from there we will travel by lorry."

Now the African's smile was very broad and he spoke with no little warmth, "You Americans are very strong, very strong. Not in America, of course. There you are weak. No one would even go fifty yards by walking, even every small trip is done by car. I don't really understand why you travel by lorry here. But it has truly been a great pleasure to have you as my guests for this short time. My name is Boark. I am in the Ministry of Health. My office is in the government services building in Nkra. If at any time you are in Nkra and have need of any type of service please come by that place and ask for Boark."

The car stopped at the Admasi junction in Towa.

Boark extended his hand and repeated, "It has been a great pleasure. Good-by for now."

Alice and Jason said good-by and thanked Mr. Boark and the driver.

As they walked toward the Admasi lorries, Jason said, "I must travel with you more often. That was my type of ride. You and Mr. Boark sounded like long lost friends. In an hour or so you will be sorry that you did not convince him to take us to Admasi."

The type of old truck they had found a ride on was known to everyone in Sakra as a mammy wagon since the women who bought and sold goods in the markets of Sakra, often called market mammies, were the only people who would ride in them by choice. It was little more than a motor, windshield, and a platform for wooden benches in the back.

In even less than an hour Alice fully understood Jason's prediction. She could not remember a time when she had hurt more. From her seat, a wooden plank on which she, another passenger and the driver sat, she looked back at Jason.

"At, least," she thought, "I have a back to lean on. His seat is just a board."

The road was laterite, more potholes than surface. The driver avoided those more than a foot deep by maneuvering the vehicle from side to side, creating a boat-like motion. He ignored those less than a foot deep. The truck seemed to have no springs. Each shock from the potholes was transmitted from the wheels through the body of the truck to the board on which Alice sat. She felt even the smallest jolt from the bones in her hips to the top of her head. Judging from the manner in which the passengers were bouncing, Alice decided that the ride in the back must be even worse. She glanced back at Jason again.

"Wonder how he stands the pain?" Alice thought.

Jason appeared to be in a near daze, head down, shoulders hunched with one hand braced against a two-by-four beam that supported the roof of the open-sided lorry. His eyes focused on nothing but the dust as he swayed between the board he held onto and a woman with a child on her back who sat half asleep beside him. They met a lorry coming in the opposite direction and a cloud of dust engulfed them. Alice pulled her scarf up over her nose but still found herself choking.

"My God," she thought, "some of those holes look three feet deep. I don't know how but the driver always misses the big ones. Oh God, this hurts, it really hurts. Where is that man with his car?"

The other passenger in the front seat was a large woman. She wore a wrap-around skirt and a matching fitted blouse. Another bright cloth of the same design protected her hair from the dust. Alice had attempted conversation with a 'good morning' at the beginning of the lorry ride. The woman had nodded and said nothing. Alice assumed that she spoke no English. During the early miles of the journey Alice had clung to the outside supports of the lorry as far away from the woman as possible. As pain and fatigue grew worse, she found that her body moved closer to the large woman and they now swayed back and forth together. The woman's body seemed to cushion the worst jolts. Alice relaxed to the point that she was near sleep. The large woman gently jostled her.

She waved her finger sharply and said, "No sleep in lorry, *Obroni*. In front seat you fall out. Get hurt bad, very bad."

Alice shook herself awake and managed a smile when she heard herself addressed as 'Obroni,' the name many Sakraians use for a White or European person.

"Thank-you," Alice said, "I would have probably bounced right out if you had not warned me. Do you travel this road often?"

"Yes," replied the woman, "too often, it is a terrible road. The government should repair it. Are you a teacher?"

"Yes I am," Alice replied, "I teach at Mbordo University-College."

"You are a Peace Corps?" the woman asked.

"Yes," Alice said, "how did you know?"

"No Obroni but Peace Corps ride this mammy wagon," she replied. "My name is Otan. Krago is my village, the next one on the road. Please stop for some little time at my house if it is possible."

"I don't know if it is possible," replied Alice as she glanced back at Jason. "I am traveling with my friend."

Although Madam Otan said nothing, her facial expression clearly indicated disbelief. Alice realized that her choice of words in describing their relationship had been unfortunate. She made an effort to correct the large woman's initial impression.

"I mean I am traveling with my brother in the back."

The women chuckled and shrugged her massive shoulders.

"It makes no difference," she said. "We just do not understand your American ways too much."

"We are going to Pandu," Alice continued. "I don't know if we have time to stop and still be able to reach there tonight."

"Pandu is far. To travel from Mbordo to Pandu in one day is difficult," the woman said. "But don't worry. Get down for a while and my brother will take you in his car to Masi. From there the road is not so bad as here."

"I do believe my brother would approve of that idea," Alice said.

Then she smiled slightly and thought, "And this old lady's bones think that is a damn good idea too."

Ten minutes more on the crater-scarred road brought them to the village of Madam Otan. Three hundred houses, more or less, some cement, others adobe, two bars (not counting palm wine places), a primary school and a middle school: that was Krago to Alice's eyes. When the lorry stopped, she got down and walked back to where Jason sat. The mention of a car to Masi brought a wide grin to his face. One of the other passengers in the back of the lorry explained to Jason that Madam Otan was the Queen Mother of the subtribe of the Atan nation that lived in and around Krago. Without further hesitation, Jason climbed down. Alice introduced him to Madam Otan.

She pointed toward one of the houses near the road and said, "Please, come out of the sun."

Jason was surprised that her house was not concrete block but adobe. The walls were at least a foot thick. Alice found the coolness of the room they entered in remarkable contrast to the heat of the afternoon sun. She sank into a cushioned chair. Her eyelids seemed made of lead as she tried to concentrate on what Madam Otan was saying.

"My God," Alice thought, "gin or beer. One drink and I'm stuck here for at least a week."

Alice heard Jason say that beer would be fine.

Madam Otan clapped her hands and a small girl came into the room with three bottles of beer and glasses. She poured the glasses full and placed them in front of Alice, Jason, and Madam Otan.

"Thank you," Jason said in Atan.

The girl smiled in a small, frightened way and left the room.

"It is very kind of you to have us here for some refreshment," Jason said to Madam Otan.

"Oh, don't mention it," she replied. "It is a difficult trip you try. Tell me what is of such great interest in Pandu."

Jason answered without equivocation, "I have a friend there."

Madam Otan shook with laughter.

She looked at Alice and said, "Then he is your brother. But why are you traveling to Pandu?"

"That's a good question," Alice thought, slightly flustered by Madam Otan's curiosity.

After a few seconds she replied, "The trip will help me see more of Sakra."

Madam Otan shrugged and commented, "But I think this way is difficult, too difficult."

She then spoke to Jason with a hint of mischievousness, "Your friend must be a very good friend for you to make such a trip."

"Yes, quite a good friend," Jason agreed.

Jason had no wish to discuss his relationship with Karen further and changed the subject.

"Tell me," he said, "you speak English quite well. Did you study English in school?"

"Yes," she replied, "I was one of the first graduates of Abusua Secondary School for girls. At that time unfortunately there was little work for educated women to do. Today, if I were again a young girl, I might look to become an engineer or lawyer. But what I am is all right for me. I do some small trade in Nkra and here. I like living in this small village. Sometimes I go to the primary school to help the teachers there, but I don't think I could be a teacher all the time. The pupils make me too angry. There is one thing that you might help us with. We would like our school to be part of the Mbordo University-College teacher education program but the Ministry of Education is saying that we are too far away for the students and professors to travel."

"I will find out if it is possible," Jason responded. "It is really a long trip, though."

"That would be very kind," Madam Otan replied. "The reputation of the program is excellent, especially in maths and science. That is what we need in Krago, much more than history and dancing."

"Thank you for your kindness," Jason said to Madam Otan, "it has made our trip much lighter. But Mrs. Manati and I must now continue our journey. It is still a good distance to Pandu."

"Of course, but sit a moment and finish your beer," Madam Otan replied. "I will see to the car."

Several minutes later they said good-by to Madam Otan and climbed into the roomy back seat of the 1949 Chrysler owned by Madam Otan's brother.

"No car ever dies in Sakra," Jason explained to Alice as the Chrysler eased away from Madam Otan's house. "Sakra has a scrap iron reprocessing facility. Another of the brilliant ideas of the 'Savior.' It's a beautiful place. Symbol of the industrialization of Sakra. It was in operation a full two weeks before they ran out of scrap. No junk yards here. Everything is used and used until it just disappears."

The car quickly passed the last houses of Krago. The driver said little as he gave full attention to avoiding the worst of the potholes. At one point the road came within a hundred feet of the edge of the first of the great scarps of Sakra. The geography of this part of Sakra could be described as a series of three extensive plateaus that formed giant steps beginning at sea level and separated by scarps as one moved northward. The scarps were broken only by the Kra river. The geography of this ancient continent made possible the Kra lake, one of the largest artificial bodies of water in the world. The vast Nkra Plain lay over six hundred feet below. To Alice's eye the arid, desolate land stretched beyond the ability of her mind to perceive distance. The drab browns and grays of the plain blended with the reddish brown dust of the harmattan.

Jason interrupted her thoughts.

"On a clear day," he said, "you can see the ocean. But of course this time of year the dust cuts down the visibility."

"But," Alice mumbled, "it's so dry down there. It's almost a desert."

"It would be a real desert," Jason explained, "except at the beginning and end of the rainy season some rain falls there. About twenty inches in a year. In Mbordo we will have more than eighty inches of rain in a year."

"Strange," Alice mused, "I can't believe it will rain that much."

The road moved away from the scarp toward the town of Masi. The road between Masi and Admasi was paved and generally smooth, providing both Alice and Jason with an opportunity to doze. Jason awoke near the outskirts of Admasi. This little city was considerably larger than the other towns in the area. It could boast of numerous local government offices, a police department, many schools, what seemed to be thousands of small business, and a wide variety of personal dwellings jumbled together on every available piece of suitable and not so suitable land.

"Activity everywhere," Jason thought, "not rapid but continuous. People walking around buying and selling stuff to each other. I wonder if anyone actually buys anything for their own use or if everything is just continuously sold back and forth. Almost five-thirty. People should be on the way home for the evening meal before long."

The driver took them to the lorry park and started to make arrangements with a lorry driver to transport them on to Pandu. Jason 'dashed' (tipped) the driver of the old car four shillings and indicated that he would make the arrangements for the trip to Pandu himself. He decided to try the same driver the man from Krago had talked to.

Jason asked, "When do you go for Pandu?"

"Quick, very quick," the man replied, "you and your sister get into the lorry and we go."

Jason motioned toward the entrance of the lorry park and said, "When you reach that gate then we board your truck."

"OK, Obroni," the driver replied holding his hands up above his head as if to say, 'If that is what you want.'

The driver added, "We leave for sure in one-quarter hour. Don't worry, you see. Put your bags in lorry."

Jason turned to Alice and said, "Throw your bag on the front seat of this Benz bus and let's get something to eat. I think he will leave in about half an hour."

Alice looked skeptically at the ragged appearance of the food shops that lined the front of the park.

"Is anything safe to eat here?" she asked.

"If it's not, I am in trouble," Jason replied. "I have been eating here for more than a year. Some foods are definitely safe. Nothing could really be wrong with boiled eggs still in the shell and there isn't likely to be a problem with those donut holes. They are cooked in boiling lard.

Jason purchased five eggs. At another little shop he bought two cokes and three donut holes. They walked back to the lorry and began their small feast.

"My goodness, I never realized that boiled eggs and coke make such a nice combination," Alice said almost merrily.

"It's all in where you are and how hungry you are," Jason responded.

Alice noticed an argument in progress near the front gate of the lorry park. She asked Jason what was going on.

"Looks like an argument between a Kroban driver from the North and one of the Atan drivers from Pandu," Jason answered. "The Atan drivers don't like it when the Kroban lorries take local passengers. They believe they should take only Kroban passengers traveling to the North."

"That doesn't seem right," Alice said. "Can't people ride whatever lorry they want to."

"You could try it, but I won't," Jason explained. "I don't want to be involved in any tribal disputes. The consequences can be painful. The Atan driver will win this one. This is Atan land. Anyway, our bags are already on an Atan lorry.

"Speaking of which," he continued, "Our driver looks like he wants to leave now and his lorry is only half full. His wife must have promised him fufu and groundnut soup tonight."

"It will be nice to ride on an uncrowded bus," Alice commented.

"I'm afraid," Jason explained as he helped Alice into the front seat, "every good thing also has its bad side. We may be more comfortable, but the trip will take longer. The driver will pick up and let off passengers everywhere since his bus is not full."

The time required to travel the 80 miles from Admasi to Pandu would stretch to more than four hours. Alice had tried to amuse herself by counting the number of stops. After twenty she lost track. At first she had found the forests and the small roadside villages of some interest. But once into the second hour, she found herself almost praying that no one would be standing by the road looking for a ride.

Jason sensed her mood and said, "This is the worst part. Pandu seems to slide further to the north. There are times when I think it's somewhere near the Algerian border. But, when this ride is over the trip itself is over."

Alice tried to smile but found that she could not.

"Don't you worry," she said, "I will be all right. I am going to make it. I'll be all right."

As they neared Pandu, Alice's bladder began sending her brain emergency signals.

She glanced toward Jason and thought, "It's no problem for men. They can go wherever they please. Must definitely remember never to drink beer on a trip again. Better to be dehydrated. I have got to hold out to Pandu."

It was a little past ten when the Benz Bus passed through the gates of the Pandu lorry park.

"Thank God, thank God," Alice mumbled.

"Well, we did it," Jason said, after paying the lorry driver. "And your spirits are brighter already, aren't they? Let's get a taxi."

Alice said nothing but thought, "My spirits will be a lot better after I find a bathroom."

They rode in silence, in a small Datsun taxi, to the area of Pandu in which Karen lived.

Karen's residence, a three bedroom cement block house rented by her school, was on the edge of the Zongo (newcomers' area) of Pandu. The residents of that area were Africans from neighboring countries who had migrated to Sakra to find work. Most of the houses in the Zongo were little more than shacks or huts made of adobe, wood, or even cardboard if nothing else was available. The people who lived in this area spent as little money as possible in order to save for the time they would return to their own countries.

As the taxi stopped in front of Karen's place, Jason's thoughts focused briefly now on how she would react to Alice's presence.

"We are late. Hope this doesn't turn out to be too much of a shock."

He paid the driver, and helped Alice, who moved stiffly but quickly, out of the back seat. Jason opened the squeaky gate on the small fence that kept animals out of the paved area in front of the house. Karen opened the door.

"Alice!" she exclaimed, "how in the world did you get here? You didn't come with Jason on those awful lorries? Oh, yes you did. I can tell by the way you look. Come in and have a seat."

"Oh God!" groaned Alice, "if I look anything like I feel, I am sorry to frighten you so. I must look like death warmed over."

"No you don't," Karen replied. "In fact, for someone who has been on a mammy wagon for the last twelve hours you look great. Come on in. You must be hungry. I have food ready."

"Right at this moment," Alice answered, "the only thing in the entire world that I want is a bathroom."

"Of course. I know how that can be," Karen replied. "That way, second door. It's British style. All by itself."

Karen had started for the kitchen when Jason wrapped his arms around her from behind, enclosing her in a bear hug.

She glanced over her shoulder and said, "Be careful, your new traveling companion will be shocked."

Jason dropped his arms and replied, "I'm sorry I didn't let you know. I would have sent a telegram but she didn't tell me definitely that she wanted to make the trip until Wednesday."

Karen smiled and said, "Don't worry, I'm not angry, Jason. I'm willing to share. I'll pick up one of my local suitors and we'll make it a foursome for the weekend."

For a moment, Jason considered a retort, but as they embraced desire born of two weeks apart swept aside any further thought of a response. After a number of lingering kisses, they heard the flushing sound from the water closet.

"Let me get the sandwiches," Karen whispered. "Alice must be starving."

"What about me?" Jason asked in a plaintive tone.

"Silly," she replied, "you will have to wait. I would certainly look rather strange attempting to serve sandwiches to Alice and trying to do something about you at the same time."

"OK, OK," Jason said, "that's not really what I had in mind. Maybe, could I have some sandwiches, too?"

"Certainly you may, that is, if there are enough to go around," Karen replied as she walked toward the kitchen.

Karen returned with sandwiches and Cokes. Alice managed a few sentences and about half a sandwich before she fell asleep. Jason and Karen roused her enough to guide her into the bedroom of Karen's housemate who was traveling that weekend. They left her in a deep and restful sleep.

Jason tried to guide Karen toward her bedroom.

"Don't you want to finish your sandwich?" Karen asked.

"Perhaps later," Jason replied. "Right now, other things are more important."

"What about Alice?" Karen asked. "Shouldn't we wait until we are sure she's asleep? She might just be faking."

"I only hope she wakes up sometime before Sunday morning," Jason replied as they sat down on Karen's bed. "I don't think I've ever seen anyone that tired."

"Yeah, she did seem to be really exhausted," Karen said as she fell backwards on the bed and pulled Jason down on top of her.

A little later that evening, Jason and Karen sat on her bed, sharing a beer and what was left of the sandwiches.

"Tell me," Karen asked, "why did Alice want to make this trip? She doesn't look too well."

"She looked fine when we left Mbordo," Jason replied. "Hope she's feeling all right by Sunday. My God, it would be terrible if I had to stay here the entire week and take care of her."

"Ah ha," Karen exclaimed, "a plan. I knew you had a plan. You always have a plan. Yes, yes, I think that I could put up with both of you for a week. But that still doesn't answer my question. Why did she make this trip?"

"She wanted to travel," Jason explained. "I think, for the same reasons that I did before I met you. Just to avoid sitting in Mbordo day after day. You better believe she wanted to make this trip in the worst way. The Vice-Chancellor was really against it. The guy even offered to drive her here himself next weekend. Can you imagine driving 360 miles just to keep your mathematics staff alive and well?"

"For Alice, maybe," Karen responded, "for the rest of the math department, no, I don't think so."

When Jason awoke the next morning, his eyelids and back muscles told his mind that it was early, much too early to be awake.

Karen looked in the door of the bedroom and said, "Up already. I'll bring some tea."

She returned with two mugs of tea and sat down on the side of the bed.

Jason put his free arm around her and said, "I hope you don't mind having Alice here."

"Oh silly," she said as she pushed him away slightly, "of course I don't mind. She is a wonderful person and we will have a marvelous time."

"Hey, I really do appreciate that," he said gently. "She did want to come. And so far she has not affected, eh . . what we do."

"That's true so far," Karen replied, "but I think that we may have to vary somewhat the things that we usually do in the afternoons."

Jason smiled and said, "Then we'd best make up for it now."

"Let me check if Alice is still asleep," Karen said as she pulled away.

Karen returned quickly and slipped into bed.

Bright sunlight woke Alice. She found herself confused.

"Couldn't be in Mbordo," she thought. "Always keep my bed away from damn morning sunlight. Maybe DC. Taken ill on trip and sent home. Trip, what trip? Trip somewhere. Trip to Pandu. Yes, with Jason to Pandu. Yes, big trip. Maybe last trip. Better wake up and enjoy it."

She felt good, very good at just the thought of still being alive. That is, until she tried to move her arms and legs.

"Oh my God," she thought, "instant arthritis, a new meaning for the word 'stiff.' Well at least they all seem to work."

The sound of a bed in motion somewhere and the occasional hint of a sigh or moan brought a slight smile to Alice's face. She decided that it would be wise to stay in bed just a bit longer.

She lay quiet until she heard someone in the kitchen. When she pushed the sheet back, she realized that she was still dressed.

"OK," she thought as she swung her legs stiffly over the side of the bed, in a week or two I'll be ready for the trip back. My God, we have to go back tomorrow. Try to forget that, Alice. Might as well enjoy today. Worry about tomorrow, tomorrow."

She stumbled down the hall and into the living-dining room area. Karen had eggs, toast and coffee on the table.

"Sit down. Help yourself," Karen said with an infectious smile.

"Thank you," Alice replied, "but I don't think I am ready for any food yet. Could I just have a cup of coffee?"

"Are you all right?" Jason asked as he poured the coffee.

"Of course," Alice replied, "well, as best I can tell I'm all right. No broken bones or anything like that."

"I'm glad for that," Jason responded. "You certainly look much better."

46

A few sips of coffee improved Alice's appetite, and she found herself eating more than she ordinarily would have in Mbordo.

"I say, old girl," Jason mumbled in a British accent learned from Derrick, "traveling seems to have done wonders for your appetite. Now, how shall we amuse ourselves today?"

Alice replied, "First, you may call me girl, but not old. Second, please drop the accent, it reminds me of Mr. Thornton. And third why don't you two just do what you normally would on a Saturday?"

Jason laughed sheepishly and replied, "Number one and two I agree to fully and unconditionally. Number three will work pretty well until the late afternoon, then. . ."

"Don't be a bore, Jason," Karen grumbled. "Usually we go to Kingsway department store in the morning and then over to the City Hotel for lunch and dancing in the afternoon. When we are tired of dancing, we come back here for a rest. In the evening we go to a Lebanese restaurant for supper and then go see a movie."

"That sounds marvelous," Alice said happily. "I will start with you and just quit when I wear out. Any chance we could go to the market?"

"We could go there instead of the department store," Jason replied.

"That would be good for me, too," Karen added. "I need to buy sandals. Mine are about to fall apart."

"Just give me a moment to fix my hair and change clothes," Alice said.

When Alice was ready Karen locked the house and they walked to a main thoroughfare to catch a taxi.

Their taxi stopped near the front entrance of the Pandu market. Jason and Karen introduced Alice to the market by taking her to the second level of a small building near the front entrance. Alice was amazed at the size. Before her lay row after row of shops. The walking areas between shops were full. She had never seen that many people together in one spot in Sakra. To the far left she saw a collection of meat shops. Patrons would point out the section of meat they wished to purchase, and the butcher would hack it off a freshly butchered carcass. Vegetable shops were in the row adjacent to the meat section. Clothing shops were next and after that beds, pillows and anything else that one might need for a comfortable night's sleep. Rows of cloth and sewing shops were close by.

"My Goodness!" Alice exclaimed, "the ultimate supermarket and department store combination. Is there anything they don't sell here?"

"Yes," replied Jason, "I have never seen a TV set or a washing machine."

"Come on," Karen said, "let's go down to the sandal shops."

They found a small establishment that could accommodate them immediately. The owner provided a chair for Alice.

"Alice," Jason suggested, "while we are here why don't you get a pair of sandals, too?"

"That's a good idea," Alice replied. "How long does it take, and how much do they cost?"

"Ten minutes and twenty shillings," Karen answered. "They aren't fancy, just a piece of leather or tire rubber with a Kenti strap for your toes."

"Regardless of style, the price is right," Alice said. "I definitely want a pair."

The owner of the shop measured, cut, and sewed sandals for Alice and Karen. Both were pleased by the end results.

As they wedged their way back toward the front entrance of the market, Alice asked, "What's next? I think I am ready for something exciting."

Jason laughed and replied, "Ladies, it's about eleven. Alice wants to do something exciting. It must be time for the City Hotel."

"Let's go then," Karen agreed.

A half hour later their taxi reached the City Hotel.

They found a table near the dance floor and ordered beer and club sandwiches. The band played an assortment of American pop tunes and highlife, a popular type of West African dance music with an irresistible double beat. The band completed a highlife number and moved into the opening notes of one of Jason's favorites, 'Satisfaction.'

"Come on, Karen, let's dance," he said.

"And leave Mrs. Manati to the vultures," Karen responded. "They are beginning to gather over there."

"I do believe," Jason replied, "that Alice is quite capable of taking care of herself."

"Damn right!" Alice said decisively. "Now go ahead with your dancing. Away! Off!"

The band's version of 'Satisfaction' lasted well over ten minutes. When Jason and Karen returned to their table they found Alice trying to control her laughter.

"You were right, Karen," she said, "the vultures did swarm. Seven requests to dance and four proposals of marriage. Must be some type of a record I would say."

The band moved comfortably back into highlife as an elderly gentleman approached their table.

"Oh no," Alice said in mock distress, "not another one."

"Don't worry," Karen said, "he's an acquaintance."

"Good afternoon," Karen said turning toward the gentleman, "Mrs. Manati, it's my pleasure to introduce Mr. Anasa. He is the Headteacher of an elementary school near my house. Mr. Anasa, I believe that you already know Jason."

"Of course," Mr. Anasa responded to the greeting, "so good to meet you again, Mr. Wills, and Mrs. Manati, it is indeed a pleasure to make your acquaintance."

"Please, have a seat," Jason suggested.

Mr. Anasa sat down and asked, "Do you also teach in the Mbordo University-College, Mrs. Manati?"

"Yes, I do," she replied.

"Which subjects?" he continued.

"Maths," Alice responded, "only maths."

"The same as Miss Wilson," Mr. Anasa commented. "I am sure that you are aware that Miss Wilson helps us with the maths program in our small school. Some of the things that she does are wonderful, truly wonderful. Of course we also have two teachers who passed out of one of your programs at Mbordo. They do very well with their children. They use the cane even less than I do."

"We really appreciate knowing that the University's efforts do help," Jason interjected. "Sometimes it's difficult to know if anything that you are doing is worthwhile."

"Oh, that is so very, very true wherever you teach," Mr. Anasa responded. "We teachers know the results of our work only many years later, sometimes even after we are no longer of this earth. But no matter, that is the way of our work."

"Mr. Wills," he continued, "would you object if I ask Mrs. Manati to accompany me in the next dance?"

"It most certainly is all right with me," Jason replied, "but of course Alice will have to decide whether or not she wishes to dance."

Mr. Anasa turned toward Alice.

She hesitated then replied, "I will try but I have had very little practice."

"I am sure that you are being overly modest," Mr. Anasa said as they moved toward the dancing area.

At first Alice felt stiff and out of place, but the easy to dance to, rhythmic double-beat of the highlife soon caused her knees to forget the reluctance of her mind. When the band switched back to 'My Boy Lollipop,' Mr. Anasa returned with Alice to where Jason and Karen sat. He excused himself with the explanation that it was time for him to look for his wife who was shopping in the nearby stores.

Alice spoke first, "You know that dancing did help. I feel much better. It takes away some of the muscle tightness."

"It affects me the same way," Jason said, "but enough is enough. Let's catch a taxi back to Karen's place. I could use a nap before we go out on the town tonight. How 'bout you Alice?"

"If you need a nap, you must already know how I feel," Alice replied.

Alice was in bed within minutes of their return to Karen's house. Karen looked in on her.

When she returned to the living room she said, "I guess we don't need to change our afternoon routine. I don't think an earthquake would wake her up. But if you are tired maybe you should just take a nap."

Jason needed no further encouragement. He guided Karen toward her bedroom. Their playful lovemaking seemed to wash away the fatigue of the morning.

Afterwards Jason said, "I think I want a beer. Shall I bring you a glass."

"That sounds like a nice idea," Karen replied.

Jason returned with the beer.

"What's this about your wonderful work at the elementary school?" he asked. "Just teaching twenty-five classes a week isn't enough?"

"I don't really do much," Karen replied. "It's the school where Babeta, the little girl I know from the Zongo, goes. I try to play math games and work with the teachers on the use of concrete stuff to teach math. The teachers are astonished that children can learn about mathematics by doing something that is fun. That must be what the Headteacher meant by 'wonderful.'"

"But how do you have the time and energy?" Jason asked.

"Actually, it helps me keep my mind off some of the shit that goes on at the secondary school," Karen replied.

"Yes you probably do need some sort of diversion," Jason agreed. "If I may ask without causing too much pain, how's your Headmaster these days?"

"Oh, he's just fine. Doing very well in fact," Karen responded. "He and the bursar have all sorts of creative ways of making money from student fees. For example, as part of the boarding fee, they charge each student nine pence a term for toilet paper. The bursar distributes four pieces to each student and that's the allotment for the entire term."

"Four pieces!" Jason exclaimed. "They are doing well with that."

"Yes, in a year about three shillings per student," Karen said. "I guess they just split the profit."

After more small talk, they slept. Jason woke about ninety minutes later.

"Cloudy sky to the south," he thought as he looked out of the window of Karen's bedroom, "probably rain on Monday. Cool and dry tomorrow. That will be good for Alice on the trip back."

Jason looked at Karen as she lay beside him still half asleep.

"How beautiful she is," he thought as she opened her eyes and smiled a quiet, lazy smile. "Some women are attractive only after they work at it. But Karen, she is beautiful all of the time. I wonder if I am losing my sense of perspective."

"Why are you looking at me that way?" Karen asked in a puzzled tone.

"If I tell her the truth," Jason thought, "she will call me a liar or break my neck."

He replied, "Obviously, because I enjoy looking at you. I do hope you don't find that offensive."

"Look all you wish, I guess," Karen replied. "I wonder if Alice is awake. I heard someone outside, but it might be Babeta."

What Karen heard was Babeta and Alice deep in conversation. Babeta was providing a list of her likes and dislikes in primary school. Her feelings were easily summed up; she liked the teacher and some students, but there were other students that she did not like and of course she hated the cane.

She explained to Alice, "If you late, the cane; if you don't learn spell words proper, the cane; if maths no good, the cane; if you look at teacher wrong way, the cane. I very good girl, still the cane."

Alice commented, "It does not sound like a very good place to go, that school."

"Oh, no, no," Babeta cried, "school very good place. Want go to school. Cane no hurt too much. Miss Wilson help me go to school. No help from Miss Wilson, no school. She talk to Headteacher. Much talk. No school for Zongo."

Karen joined the conversation and explained that Babeta had been refused admittance to primary school because the schools were already overcrowded with Sakra children and her father was not Atan or Ave but from Upper Kra. She had been able to convince one Headteacher, Mr. Anasa, to accept Babeta by reminding him that Sakraian law required that all children have the opportunity to attend primary school and assuring him that money would be available for a school uniform, books and other incidental fees. Karen had provided the money (about $10.00 per term), and Babeta's parents the uniform.

At seven years of age Babeta was fluent in three languages: a language of Upper Kra spoken by her parents at home, the Atan language of Pandu, and English. She was the next to youngest child of one of the men employed by Karen's school as a night watchman. The family lived on a small compound in the Zongo, a quarter mile from Karen's house. Babeta's extended family numbered more than thirty people.

"It's remarkable," Alice commented after Babeta had gone, "that you are able to make that type of contact with people."

Jason laughed and said, "Karen's problem is not making contact. She always has three or four men and a dozen children following her. Or haven't you noticed."

"You are just jealous," Karen answered, "but it can be a problem. A lot of people hang around because they want money or some of them because they believe it's some weird form of prestige if they can say they know you. But, once in a while you do meet people like Babeta and her family. They actually become your friends and you help them and they help you without anyone really thinking it's a big deal."

Jason couldn't resist a comment and said, "Actually, all they want is your clothes and your dog for chop when you leave."

He covered his head as both Alice and Karen tried to hit him.

"That's a horrible attitude, Jason," Alice said. "That little girl is the sweetest thing I have seen in years."

"All right, all right, peace," Jason said. "I like her, too. I was only joking, only joking. It's time to think seriously about the evening meal. Alice, are you up to dining out?"

"I've made it this far, and I am determined to do the rest of the weekend," Alice replied.

Jason and Karen's Saturday night restaurant was a Lebanese establishment that featured hummus as appetizer and beef kabob as the main course. Alice found her meal of reasonably tender beef, the first she had tasted in four months, something like a combination of Christmas and her birthday.

The choice of movies was limited to a very old John Wayne film or a subcontinent Indian movie. They chose the John Wayne film.

"Hope the Daily Globe was correct," Jason mused as they left the restaurant.

Their taxi driver confirmed the newspaper's listing.

"Too much people here tonight," he said. "American Western movie. Bang-bang all the time. Very crowded."

The ticket booth was detached and about twenty yards from the theater entrance. As they approached, the ticket queue -- stretching for thirty feet like a snake whose head had been removed -- dissolved completely, and the ticket seller's small booth was suddenly surrounded by people massed four or five deep, all attempting to reach forward and somehow gain the attention of the small man inside. He retreated to the center of the booth and dropped to a crouch. After five minutes, Jason decided that he was making no progress in moving closer to the ticker seller. All he could see was a hand that rose from the center of the booth, grabbed money and returned tickets.

He had almost given up when he was approached by a husky young Sakraian who said, "Please sir, if you wish to have tickets, I will go for you."

He handed the Sakraian thirty shillings and said, "Buy three. If you wish, buy one for yourself or keep what is left of the money. We wish to sit in the balcony."

The young man shouted, "Four balcony tickets for the Obronies."

The ticket seller immediately took his money and handed up the tickets. When the young man returned, he explained that the problem at the booth had been caused by a near sellout of the lower priced floor level tickets. They moved quickly through the entrance of the theater and upstairs to the relatively empty balcony.

"This movie," Alice thought after watching the opening scenes, "is not one of John Wayne's better efforts. I don't even care for his better efforts. Then why am I enjoying it? Could Sakra be making me into a John Wayne fan?"

She glanced in Jason's direction.

"I'm sorry," he said, "but if you think this is short on artistic merit, we'll take you to one of the Indian films next time."

"What makes you think I don't like this one?" Alice replied.

"When you're at a movie like this, the audience puts on the best show," Karen commented.

During fighting scenes the people in the seats below, mostly young men, would leap to their feet and scream in Atan, "Destroy him, hurt him, knock him out, destroy him!"

A chant of "Kill them, kill them, kill them!" grew so loud in the middle of the final shoot-out that it overwhelmed the audio system of the theater.

Jason noticed Alice's look of concern.

"Don't worry," he shouted, "it's all just some form of emotional release. Very well controlled, I hope. Everyone is always very polite once the movie is over."

"I'm sure that's true," Alice replied. "It's just not the way people here usually act."

The movie ended. The bad guys were all dead or in jail. Big John had said good-by to the heroine and ridden away into the sunset. They decided to remain in their seats a few minutes in order to allow the crowd leaving the theater time to thin out.

"You don't think much about violence here," Karen mused, "that is, until you see the reaction of an audience to a movie like this. Still, it does seem out of character."

"I'm not sure how true that is," Jason said. "Have you ever seen a 'hue and cry'?"

"I don't really know," Karen replied. "What's a 'hue and cry'?"

Jason explained, "It's an old Anglo-Saxon term. One you see in history books and old novels. They were raised against those believed to be enemies of the people or the nation. Witches, thieves, murderers. If a person was caught in the act of stealing and ran away, everyone would start yelling and chasing him. That's the cry part. I guess they hued when they caught up with him. If he was lucky, he would only be beaten to a bloody pulp and thrown out of town."

"Sounds like an effective means of crime control," Alice mused. "Can't believe you've seen that type of thing here."

"But I have," Jason answered. "Once in Nkra near the central market I saw a thief grab something from one of the small shops. At first only the owner of the shop chased him, shouting as loud as she could that she had been robbed. Five or six others joined her. In a few minutes the street was full of people shouting and chasing the thief. Other mammies came out of side streets ahead of the thief and trapped him. The women formed a circle. When he tried to break out, the mammies knocked him back in. People on the outside were picking up rocks. Children were throwing pebbles. The man looked completely desperate. I walked down the street. I guess I had some thought of doing something, but I don't know what. When I was about a block away one of those tall policemen from one of the Northern tribes came out of one of the side streets. He pushed his way through to the thief, grabbed what was left of his shirt. He shoved the man into the taxi and got in beside him. The taxi managed to inch its way through the crowd and got clear of the area."

"The thief was lucky," Alice commented. "Would they have killed him?"

"If they didn't plan to kill him, they did one hell of a job of faking it," Jason replied. "Might have depended on where he was from. I don't think a Kroban or someone from Upper Kra would have much of a chance without help."

"Now that you brought up the subject," Karen added, "I remember an incident on the road to my house about five months ago. I heard a lot of noise early in the morning. Must have been before six. I got up and looked out the window. About fifty people were chasing a man down the street toward the Zongo. They were screaming and throwing stuff. I didn't see them catch up with him but in the next morning's Globe I saw a story about a man who was found beaten to death near my house. The newspaper indicated that there were 'rumors' of the man having been a thief."

"Oh my God," Alice gasped, "you two don't need to see movies. Remind me never to steal anything in Sakra."

"Let's get out of here before we get morbid," Jason said. "There aren't many people left."

They caught a taxi back to Karen's house. Alice went to bed immediately, but Jason and Karen decided to share a beer and talk for awhile.

"You look worried," Jason said.

"Not worried," Karen replied, "just perplexed. I can't imagine beating someone to death."

"Oh, still worried about that," Jason replied. "I'm sorry I brought it up."

"It just doesn't seem like people here," Karen continued.

"I know," Jason mused, "it seems so totally out of character. I once got into a discussion with Mr. Pordoe, the Sportsmaster at the University-College, about violence in Sakra. He is Bordo but his wife is from Nkra. When I mentioned my impression that little violence occurred in Sakra, he found the idea humorous. When he was young, serious fights were commonplace in Nkra. People moved from all parts of Sakra to find work in the capitol. They tended to live together in tribal groups and subgroups. He said fights could start over anything or even nothing. All the neighbors and relatives would join in. After one outbreak of fighting that caused the death of a child, the government decided to put an end to it. Whenever a fight of any type occurred everyone involved or even near the area was arrested and thrown in jail. According to Mr. Pordoe, the plan worked. Those big fights just don't happen in Nkra anymore."

"That business of the man in front of my house still bothers me," Karen said. "I never really thought much about it until you started talking about your 'hue and cry' business. It seems so terrible."

"I'm sorry, if I had known it would worry you so much, I would never have brought it up," Jason replied. "No one is allowed to carry or even own modern guns in Sakra except the army and special policemen. That probably limits violence a lot. But it is also probably why thieves are beaten to death. I am sure that people would agree to shoot them if they could. Though, I do think a knife or machete would be more efficient than fists and stones."

"Enough of this," Karen protested. "Let's just enjoy what's left of our time together."

****

By seven the next morning everyone was up. Jason wanted to be on the Admasi road by nine-thirty in order to reach the Mbordo junction before dark. They took a taxi to the outskirts of Pandu. Karen stayed with them until a Benz bus responded to their hand signals.

The trip back was painful but otherwise uneventful. They reached the Mbordo junction shortly after five and stopped a small lorry that was returning from one of the little villages along the main road.

Alice glanced at the old mammy wagon named 'Jesus is With Us,' then said quietly to Jason, "This looks worse than anything we have been on today. I am not sure I can stand one of these things."

"I'm afraid this is the last lorry to Mbordo tonight," Jason replied. "We will get you the front seat. That's the best we can do."

A brief explanation of where they had traveled that weekend convinced the driver that Alice should not only have the front seat but should also be delivered to her doorstep.

Alice found her legs unreliable as she climbed out of the front seat. The driver and Jason supported, then almost carried Alice to her bungalow. She made it up the steps and sat down on the small chair she kept on the porch.

"Go on home," Alice said with what bravado she could still manage, "I'm fine."

Jason hesitated, then decided that he didn't really feel much like making the long walk back to his house. He said good-by and left with the lorry driver. Alice managed to push herself up out of the chair and limp through the doorway of her bungalow. She found a container of water in the refrigerator and poured herself a glass.

As she drank she thought, "Home never looked this good before, and the water is better than I ever remembered. Think I'll lay down for a few minutes before I worry about supper."

When she awoke, the room was filled with sunlight.

"I do still seem to be alive," she mused. "That's something positive."

"My God," she thought as she looked at the clock, "it's almost seven. The emergency squad will be here any minute."

As she pushed herself up into a sitting position on the couch, she recognized the sound of the Vice-Chancellor's Volkswagen.

She heard a voice call, "Mrs. Manati, are you well? Can we come in?"

"I'm a little wrinkled but still fully dressed," Alice thought. "Sleeping in my clothes is getting to be a habit."

She moved stiffly toward the door and replied, "I am quite well, thank you. And yes, come in, come in by all means."

Both Jason and the Vice-Chancellor had come. The Vice-Chancellor suggested that she take the day off. Alice refused.

She said, "If one of you will be kind enough to inform my first period class not to go away, I will be there in less than half an hour."

"If you insist," the Vice-Chancellor replied with a slight smile.

"Alice, are you sure you're all right?" Jason asked.

"Yes, I am," she replied decisively. "Now if you gentlemen would be kind enough to leave me alone, I will prepare myself for work today."

"Amazing," was the Vice-Chancellor's only comment to Jason as they left the bungalow.

Residual excitement from the trip sustained Alice through Monday's classes. Her students seemed even more courteous and helpful than their usual high standards of behavior. Tuesday, however, was different. Delayed fatigue enveloped her Monday evening, and she found that the effort to get out of bed Tuesday morning caused her more pain than she wished to deal with. The Vice-Chancellor sent word that she should remain at home until she felt completely well.

Jason and Jeff came to visit as the sun was setting.

"So, how is the famous African traveler?" Jeff teased.

"I'm fine, more or less," Alice replied, "and you can just cut out that bull about this famous African traveler."

"It's too late to stop it," Jeff continued. "Jason is spreading rumors that you crossed vast deserts, climbed mountains, and endured hour after hour of painful lorry rides"

"Bull, all bull," Alice said, "except, of course that part about painful lorry rides. Jason, what are you telling people?"

"Only that you made the trip to Pandu with me," Jason replied. "It wasn't necessary to say anything more. Our students know the route. They say that many have made the trip on a Friday but few return on Sunday. You have become the local 'Wonderful Woman.'"

"Enough," Alice said, "I definitely do not feel wonderful, whatever meaning you choose. Yesterday afternoon I thought I was going to die. How long before the pain goes away?"

"I hope you are fine tomorrow," Jason replied, "but it varies. Karen claims she is stiff as a board until at least Thursday."

"Oh no!" groaned Alice, "if she's stiff that long, I won't be right for a month."

Alice managed to return to work on Wednesday. She did have to assign more of the difficult problems as special homework in Maths 406, and in the other courses she did spend more than the usual few minutes of class time discussing life in the United States. Much to her surprise, she found that students were interested in her trip to Pandu. On Thursday she decided to try the student dining hall again. Her arrival there caused the meal to come to a near halt. She was quickly ushered to the head table and served.

But the final realization that the trip had permanently changed student perception of her as a person did not come until Friday in her fourth period class. It was 11:45. Fifteen more minutes and her work week was over. She was more than tired. She found it difficult to concentrate on even the relatively simple quadratic equation in front of her.

"One more of these damn things and my mind is dead," she protested to herself.

She saw, out of the corner of her eye, a hand go up.

"There it is," she groaned inwardly, "Kwame's going to ask me to do another one."

She thought about ignoring the hand, but realized with fifteen minutes to go if Kwame didn't ask a question, someone else would. She nodded in his direction. Kwame Aduma stood.

"Oh no," she thought, "it's always a tough one when they stand."

He began very slowly, "We understood that you took a journey this weekend past. Did you enjoy the trip? Why did you go?"

"My God," Alice thought, "Kwame never asked a question like that before. I know the class reaction to his one: sit down, shut up, etc. But why not have a try at it anyway."

She told the class, in some detail, about the pleasant aspects of the trip: Madam Otan's hospitality, sandals in the Pandu Market, the city hotel, dinner and the movie. After about five minutes of extolling the virtues of traveling in Sakra, Alice realized that the class seemed entranced. A few were even taking notes.

"My God," she thought, "one lorry trip did this. Damn well should have gone long ago."

Alice said nothing for about half a minute.

The spokesman for the class broke silence and said, "Could you please continue?"

"I don't believe I have anything more to say," Alice replied, but quickly added, " I could answer questions if there are any."

Several hands went up.

"How does traveling in Africa compare to traveling in America?" was the first question.

"That's a tough one," Alice thought. "Better be a little careful or I will get myself into hot water."

"Well," she replied, "some Americans do travel by bus. Only the buses used are all large ones."

"Oh, I think I understand," a student volunteered, "buses like those in Nkra or the ones used by the government transport service between Nkra and Pandu."

"Yes, I think so, pretty much like that," Alice answered. "Of course many people travel by airplane and a few by train. But most people use their own automobile when they wish to go somewhere."

"Is it true," another student asked, "that every American has three cars: a big one for long trips, a small one for short trips, and a sports one to drive a friend in?"

Alice swallowed her laughter and replied, "No, a very few families have three cars, some have two, but most have only one. And it is also true that some families in America don't have a car at all."

"Did you own a car in America?" Kwame asked.

"Yes," Alice replied, "I had only one, and it was very small."

"What did you do with it, when you came to Sakra?" another student asked.

"I sold it," Alice said.

Only the class spokesman was brave enough to ask the crucial question, "Why did you not bring that car with you to Sakra so that you could drive it to Pandu and not have to ride the lorry?"

"Several reasons," Alice replied as the bell rang.

She hoped they would all now leave and go to the noon meal, but no one moved.

Alice decided to enumerate the reasons.

"First," she said, "it is not difficult to find transportation here in Sakra. Since few people have cars, the lorries go everywhere. Second, I have no idea about how to repair cars, and if mine broke, I don't know if I could find anyone to fix it. Third, the Peace Corps director in Sakra has told all of us volunteers that we are not allowed to have a car while we are in Sakra. Let's go to lunch."

In the weeks that followed, Alice was content to rest, relax and recover. Her life settled into a routine of teaching, sleeping, reading and making occasional small trips to the shops and local market. She became friends with the Vice-Chancellor's wife, Peace. When Alice bought vegetables in the market that looked good but that she had no idea how to prepare, she would invite Peace over for the afternoon. They would cook Alice's bargain of the day, then share a meal of what they had prepared.

However, her fourth period class was a still a pain, afternoons were often empty, and her weekends could not really be considered enjoyable once her Saturday morning trip to the market was over. But small elements of quality had been added to her life, and they made what she was doing seem at least tolerable and often much more.

She enjoyed occasional lunches in the student dining hall until she made the error of trying to sit at one of the student tables instead of the head table reserved for teachers. The problem was not that it was a student table, but a Kroban student table. Alice had thought since the students from the North seldom asked question or spoke in class, lunch might provide an informal opportunity to get to know them better. The Atan and Ave students immediately objected and requested that Alice sit at their tables or move back to the head table. The Kroban students were offended. Only the intervention of the Sportsmaster, Mr. Pordoe, prevented a fight.

"These students cause this kind of trouble all the time," he explained. "If something is good in anyway for one group then it must be bad for the others. They will argue over anything, the amount of food, the quality of the silverware, the placement of tables, and now even where you sit. The Vice-Chancellor has ask me to be here to prevent trouble. Could you sit at the head table? They won't hurt you, but they will hurt each other."

"I really am sorry," Alice said. "I just didn't know that where I sit is that big a deal. I will move to the head table. I don't want to be a problem. I hope that is the end of it."

"There is no end to it," the Mr. Pordoe replied, "but it is not your fault. If they don't fight over this, it will be something else."

CHAPTER 4
I Am from the University

One Thursday evening late in February, Alice had Jason and Jeff over for dinner.

"Marvelous meal," Jeff commented as he sipped after-dinner tea. "If you get tired of teaching math, please let us know. We'll find another position for Kojo."

"I'm afraid," Alice replied, "that I would get tired of cooking a lot faster than I get tired of mathematics. Come on, bring your tea and let's move to more comfortable chairs."

After they were seated Alice commented, "Professor Whitland must have a very good library. Derrick said he was going there tonight and didn't have time to come for dinner."

Jeff glanced at Jason.

Jason shrugged, as if to say, "Why keep secrets from Alice?"

"He isn't just interested in Whitland's books," Jeff remarked, "but then perhaps he and Mrs. Whitland do a lot of reading together."

"Oh," Alice mused, "so it's like that."

"Yes," Jason added, "it's like that. Hope for everybody's sake the whole thing doesn't blow up."

"I work with Whitland quite a bit," Jeff said. "I guess in some American context he might be an all-right guy. But here he comes across as a jerk. If the farmers here take his advice and do it the American way, in just a few years he could have them all on the brink of starvation."

"Aren't you being a little harsh?" Jason commented. "At least he actually leaves the campus and visits farms. That's more than most of our other 'agricultural experts' do."

"Maybe they know their limitations," Jeff replied. "For a person to come to Sakra from Middle America and believe that he can teach people something about farming in the tropics is ludicrous. What the hell does Whitland know about soils here, about seeds, rainfall, kinship systems, inheritance?"

"I suppose you know a good deal more than Whitland about these things," Jason responded.

"At the very least," Jeff replied patiently, "I've got a much better idea of what I don't know. Some solutions to Sakra's agricultural problems reoccur in cycles. Plowing is the most notorious. Like the locust, it keeps coming back every fifteen years or so. Chief Kanata told me of a project in 1941. He said it was related to the war effort in some way he never understood. Four thousand acres near Admasi of the richest lands in Sakra were plowed and planted in corn. The first year there was beautiful, tall green corn. The second year the land was as hard and brittle as the laterite road between here and the junction. Without natural cover, the rains leached the land of the few nutrients and decaying material that the corn crop had not already used. The second wave of mechanization came in 1957, when the 'Savior' decided that Sakra's agriculture had to be modernized. He bought more than a thousand Russian tractors. Twenty thousand acres in different parts of Sakra were chosen. Some of the most fertile lands were destroyed by plowing. Food production dropped drastically. The government blamed the decrease in production on the British, political opponents, the weather, and just about anyone or anything else they could think of. Some of those places still don't produce much. The forest does heal the scars but it takes time. The only good part of this was the Russian tractors were poorly made and most stopped working in a few years.

"Now here we go one more time. Mbordo University-College wants to get into the plowing business to help reduce the poor farmers' work load and increase his production."

"Wait a minute," Jason said, "what is the alternative, bush-fallow? That method does appear to be wasteful. I mean to farm a patch of land a few years, let it grow up in brush, and then clear it off to farm again. That's a lot of work. How would you like to have to farm like that?"

"Not very well, I'm sure," Jeff replied. "That's why I am an agricultural 'expert,' not a farmer. But how I feel about it doesn't mean a damn thing. The truth about farming in Sakra is that no one has come up with a more efficient method than the old bush-fallow technique. Tropical soils are thin. Trees may grow more than a hundred feet tall but their roots stay near the surface. Topsoil is seldom more than a few inches thick. A few years of crops depletes the soil. Then it won't grow much of anything until it is abandoned and nature is allowed to replenish nutrients and humus."

"Well, what about the people from Indiana who do understand the difficulties involved in tropical agriculture?" Alice asked. "There most be some. What do they do?"

"Most just vegetate," Jeff replied. "They sit here and count the days until they are allowed back into paradise. Whitland's new. He'll get tired of being ignored and fall into the same pattern. The sooner the better. Who knows, once he stops trying to modernize tropical agriculture and starts working in areas where he is competent, he might even do some useful research. He's supposed to be a good seed breeder."

"Farming here is complicated," Alice mumbled. "Are you trying to say that we have nothing much to offer?"

"I wouldn't put it that bluntly," Jeff replied. "It would be unwise to admit that we are completely useless. If they found out they might tell us to pack up and go home. Anyway, maybe the University-College can develop into a legitimate research facility where some future possibility might exist of developing better methods. But you have to be careful. Your mistake is somebody else's hunger."

"But then what do we have to offer now?" Alice asked.

"Very little, perhaps nothing," was Jeff's quick reply.

"So what are you doing with your time here?" Jason asked.

Jeff thought for a moment, shrugged, and then replied, "Offering my friendship and that of the people of the United States of America."

"Yes, we know all about that," Jason replied good naturedly.

Jeff laughed as he tried to frame a retort, "Ah, what the hell, I spend a lot of time cleaning up Whitland's mistakes. I follow him around and 'translate' the meaning of what he says. You know, stuff like, 'Don't worry about the big U.S. turkey. He may be wearing expensive trousers and a nice shirt, but he can't have your fingernails pulled out. Try not to do anything that he tells you because he doesn't know much about farming in Sakra.'"

"Bet you will be glad when he stops trying," Alice commented.

"I know this is going to sound weird," Jeff replied, "but when he does give up there's going to be a void in my life. I don't know how I will use the extra time. I am working on a curriculum for a course in agriculture for teachers at the middle school level. The one in use now is 'wonderful.' It should be titled 'Farming in England during the Middle Ages.'"

"So what's with this curriculum?" Alice asked.

"It's no big deal," Jeff replied. "It's not even official. Just my own small effort. I hope to work up a program using some of the better research ideas on preserving soil nutrients that would enable a school or an individual student to grow what you need for a good diet. Enata and her father have been of tremendous help in providing practical information. They saved me a lot of mistakes. We've started an experimental plot behind one of the middle schools in Kwim. I am working on one here in Mbordo, too. That way, anything that we put in the curriculum will be tested. Once Whitland gives up, I will probably devote most of my time to it."

Alice interrupted, "I am still curious about what happens when someone like Whitland is sent here. If he is as bad as you say, that must cause a lot of difficulty. How does his African counterpart react? After all, Whitland is only an advisor, isn't he?"

"Well, his counterpart is Mr. Oganda," Jeff replied. "Let me tell you about something that happened on a farm near Tongo a few weeks after Whitland arrived. A farmer had agreed, three years ago, to allow the tractor driver from here to plow his land. His crop was really pitiful. About fifty waist-high stocks with about half a dozen small ears of corn. Whitland spent ten, maybe fifteen minutes looking at the farmer's plot. Finally he turned to Mr. Oganda and asked, 'What the hell has happened here? This land is in terrible condition. Why would anyone try to raise corn on land like this?' Mr. Oganda smiled and replied, 'Don't worry, sir. There is no problem here. This was only an experiment. It doesn't have to be successful.'"

"Oh come on," Alice remarked, "you can't be serious."

"I swear it's true," Jeff replied.

"Doesn't Oganda care about what happened to that man's land? How is he feeding his family?" Alice asked.

61

"I don't know how he is feeding his family," Jeff mused. "Hope he has relatives with good land. As to how Oganda feels, I don't know about that, either. But what would you do in his situation? Being an agricultural expert is not a bad job. Sure beats farming. You get to wear nice clothing, even a tie if that's what you want. Your salary is reasonable and you get a government car. So why get upset about destroying some farmer's land? After all, everything for the last twenty years has been an experiment."

"But Jeff, that's people's food," Jason commented. "What are they supposed to eat while we are 'experimenting' with their farming?"

"Ah yes," Jeff replied, "therein lies the beauty of the whole thing. To keep this man and his family from starving we provide food from America under the food for peace program. Now, if we muck up their agriculture enough, they will become totally dependent on the United States for food and we will have another permanent market."

"Wait a minute," Alice interjected, "you don't seriously believe that the U.S. government is supporting Mbordo University-College in order to destroy agricultural production in Sakra so that we will have a better market for our surplus food?"

"Keep your voice low, Alice," Jason whispered, "someone might hear you. I can see the headline in tomorrow's Globe, 'Elderly Peace Corps Worker and Cohorts Confess to Being Agents of C.I.A. Bent on Destruction of Agriculture in Sakra.'"

Alice laughed, but not convincingly, then continued, "All right it does sound ridiculous to say it that way. But have I really misinterpreted what you were saying, Jeff?"

"No," Jeff replied. "It almost seems that way sometimes. But I know that I am definitely not in the C.I.A. Jason, though, I'm not so sure of. Those trips to Pandu are a little suspicious. Only someone who is crazy or who is carrying secret documents would make a trip like that."

"He's crazy all right," Alice said, "crazy about Karen. But you avoided my question. What do you think we are doing here? You brought the whole thing up. Now you tell me what you really think."

Jeff sat with his chin resting on his hands for a few moments.

He noticed the perturbed look on Alice's face and said, "I don't think any of us were actually sent here to destroy the agriculture of Sakra. I couldn't accept that. I would be on my way home tomorrow if I believed that. Of course, if we do harm their ability to produce food the result will be the same whether we intended to or not. I do find that disturbing. When I really get upset, what I find comforting is the thought that maybe, just maybe, we are much, much less important than we would like to think. It's entirely possible that we have little or no effect on the way most food in Sakra is produced."

"But how do you justify being here?" Alice asked. "For me, I have my classes. I can see what the students are accomplishing and I can see pretty clearly what I am doing well and not so well. Even though my work may not be important to Sakra's future in some cosmic sense, it is very important to our students right now. Isn't it difficult to work with people like Whitland when the best that can come of it, is that you won't leave anyone worse off then they already are?"

"Do you have any rope, Alice?" Jeff asked without even a flicker of a smile. "Now that you have laid my life out before me so clearly, I think I might as well be done with it all here and now."

"My God," Alice said, "I didn't mean that's the way it really is. I just wanted to see if I understood what you were saying. Now see here, there is always hope."

Both Jason and Jeff were laughing.

"Don't worry," Jason said, "he's well adjusted. And he has heard much harsher descriptions of his efforts from others."

"Seriously," Jeff said, "and I am now going to be serious. It was very difficult. That first year I was as close as I ever want to be to alcoholism. But some good things happened. The middle school project is important to me. And of course Enata and I became friends. Beyond that I don't worry much about the value of my existence. In Sakra, perhaps it is enough to just exist. The longer I am here, the less I worry."

"Well I am happy that you have managed to adjust," Alice commented. "It's really quite remarkable that our students aren't completely cynical with examples like your buddies, Whitland and Oganda. I still don't understand how Mr. Oganda can be so little concerned about a family losing its food supply. Doesn't he care about his own people?"

Jason smiled ever so slightly and replied, "Alice, Mr. Oganda is Kroban. The people in this area are Ave and Bordo. They are in no way his 'own people.'"

"Does it make that much difference?" Alice asked.

"More than you can imagine," Jeff answered. "Black is 'Black' only in the United States. Here Black is Atan, or Black is Kroban, or Black is Ave or Bordo or a hundred other names."

"I can't even tell people of one tribe from another," Alice mused.

"Yes, I know," Jason said, "I'm not very good at it, either. But there are differences in facial characteristics, facial and body markings, body build, color, customs and of course language. I doubt that Oganda has any interest whatsoever in what happens to the Ave and Bordo farmers. In fact he would probably just as soon see them all starve."

"That's a little harsh," Alice said sharply. "Doesn't education modify tribal feelings at least a little bit."

"We would all like to believe that," Jason replied. "But as they say, actions speak louder than words. Look at the way your students sit in your classroom or in the dining hall. Or check out the way in which dormitory assignments are made. It was the policy of the University-College to mix students from different tribes in our dorms. But that ended when all the Kroban students threatened to leave. Now we don't mix Kroban students with any other tribe. Even the Ave and Atan are pretty much separated. "

"But why?" Alice asked. "The people of Sakra seem so much alike in so many ways."

"Only superficially," Jeff replied. "The Kroban are Muslim, but the Ave, Bordo and Atan tend to be Christian. Most of the people of the smaller tribes in the middle of the country are Animist. The authority structures within the tribes are very different. Attitudes vary a great deal towards work, the definition of success, obligation to family and just about anything else."

"However, one thing is constant," Jason said. "One's position and influence within the tribal structure is the single most important thing in the lives of most Sakraians. Everything else they are or hope to be is secondary to that."

"Thank you for the lecture on life and leisure in Sakra," Alice added in jest. "I doubt that I will be able to remember more than a tenth of it."

"There are just too damn many things that divide this country," Jeff mused, "economics, religion, education."

"Why education?" Alice asked. "I would think that education would lessen tribal conflict, not contribute to it."

"Yes, it could work that way," Jeff replied, "but it doesn't. It's not really the process of education, but the past pattern of educational opportunity. The British ruled by taking advantage of the natural divisions and animosities among the tribes. The Atans, who lived near the coast, had the first British schooling. They were then given some of the lower level civil service positions that the British were willing to entrust to Africans. The Atans worked not only in Sakra but also in other British colonies on the West African Coast. When the Aves saw what was happening, they asked for more schools. When the British ignored their requests, they started their own schools. The Atan had a big head start and still have the best positions in government service. The Aves never get the top jobs. But they bust their rear ends to get a lot of lower level positions that require specific skills such as teaching or store clerking. They will take any type of job that turns over cash. Look in the driver's seat of a taxi or lorry anywhere in Sakra and the chances are pretty good that you will find an Ave. And he will either own it or be trying to earn the money to buy his own vehicle. Most bricklayers and carpenters are Ave."

"So what about the Kroban?" Alice asked. "Where do they fit?"

Jeff continued, "In the North the British found it easier to switch than fight. The power structure of the Kroban is not exactly democratic. The Sultan rules. What he says is law. The British left that system intact. The Sultan was entrusted with the internal government of the Northern territory, the British handled external affairs and trade. Before the fifties, one of the Sultan's policies was not to allow any Christian mission schools in the North. The British had no interest in spending money on schools there, either. Without government or mission schools, Western style education was effectively excluded from the North. A new Sultan allowed a few mission schools in the fifties, and the first government secondary school in the Northern territory started in 1960. A few Kroban had been sent south to secondary school before that time, but not many. They were pretty much left out of the economic development of the southern part of Sakra before independence. And these days they don't like being left out of anything. Of course they are only about half the population; 46 per cent was the last figure I saw."

"What about the Middle Tribes?" Alice asked.

"The Dowin, President Agyenkwa's tribe, are doing quite well at the moment, thank you," Jeff replied. "How the others have done I think depends on their traditional relationships with the North and South. Those who follow the pattern of the South have better opportunities. But I don't think there is any real pattern, except there is usually less of everything in the Middle Belt."

"So what holds this country together?" Alice asked. "If even education divides, what keeps the whole thing from flying apart?"

Jeff shrugged, "You know, I'm not really sure. Perhaps President Agyenkwa, the 'Savior.' You know, our supreme, invincible leader."

"But Agyenkwa is hiding most of the time," Jason remarked. "It's rumored that someone attempted to assassinate him in October near Nandu."

"But he still is quite popular," Alice said almost emphatically.

"Well, nobody speaks against him in public," Jason said, "but just how popular he is right now is a little difficult to find out. I heard that he has a very efficient system of informants at universities and secondary schools. One of my best students disappeared last year. He had been criticizing the 'Savior's' economic policies. When I tried to find out what had happened, the Vice-Chancellor called me in and said it was better I didn't ask."

"That's not good!" Alice exclaimed. "I didn't know that type of thing was happening. Do you think some type of secret police killed him?"

"No," Jason replied, "he's probably in a detention center or prison. You have to be careful. I'm sure you remember the meeting with the director the first week your group was in Sakra."

"You mean the one in which the director locked all the doors, closed the windows and told us we were suspected of being C.I.A. agents," Alice replied. "Then he gave us the 'return to Nkra' code word and told us never to discuss politics with anyone from Sakra."

"That's the meeting," Jason said. "I found the ban on discussing politics with Sakraians amusing because everybody here is afraid to talk about politics."

"Anyway," Alice said, "not much good I've ever seen comes out of talking about politics. I hate to be impolite, but if I don't get to bed soon, I won't be able to teach tomorrow."

"Planning a trip at midterm break, Alice?" Jeff asked as he and Jason moved toward the door of the bungalow.

"No," Alice replied, "I thought about going to Nkra, but I really don't have any reason to go there."

"Why don't you come with me to Kwim?" Jeff asked. "There's plenty of room and I think Enata's family would enjoy having you as a guest."

"I'd love to," Alice replied. "Are you sure that Enata's family would not mind?"

"I think they would be honored," Jeff said.

"After all," Jason added, "who could fail to be pleased at having the opportunity to entertain 'wonderful woman,' the famous American traveler, from Mbordo?"

CHAPTER 5
Kwim

Alice informed the Vice-Chancellor of her intended trip to Kwim on the Wednesday before midterm break. She did not understand his amused expression until he spoke.

"I know you will find this a little hard to believe, but I am planning a trip to Kwim on Saturday. I do hope that you will accept my offer of transport. Also Miss Kanata and Mr. Johnson, if they are traveling with you."

"I don't believe you!" Alice replied. "If I was able to survive the trip to Pandu, then I most certainly will have no trouble on a trip to Kwim."

"Please, I meant no insult," the Vice-Chancellor said. "Please, go to Kwim any way that you wish. Go to Khartoum if you so wish. That is your business, not mine. But the truth is I do have to go to Kwim and will go on Saturday regardless of whether or not you accompany me. Chief Kanata and I are related, as you Americans would say, by marriage. There is some family business that must be formally taken care of. I will also conduct a bit of University business while I am there. I wish to examine the agricultural and educational programs of the University in the middle schools of Kwim and discuss those programs with the Headteachers."

"I am sorry I jumped to conclusions," Alice replied, "Let me talk it over with Jeff and Enata."

"Certainly," the Vice-Chancellor answered. "Just let me know if you need a ride."

Jeff and Enata decided to leave by lorry on Friday for Kwim, but they encouraged Alice to accept the Vice-Chancellor's offer. Not that Alice needed much encouragement. Her bones still held the memory of the Pandu trip.

The Vice-Chancellor called for Alice the Saturday morning of the planned trip at six. Paul Kwame Onanga was a tall man by Sakraian standards, a shade over six-feet. His father was a minister of the United Protestant Christian Mission Board of Sakra. In his own youth, the Vice-Chancellor's father had little opportunity to obtain a formal education in his home village in the Middle Belt. However, through a combination of persistent self-study and short courses offered by the Mission Board, he had, at the age of thirty-six, qualified for ordination. After being ordained, he was asked by the Board to return to his home village. There were few Christians in that Middle Belt community at the time of his father's return, and even after forty years of effort Christians were still in the minority. However, the Vice-Chancellor's father, through his efforts to improve material conditions and educational opportunities had won the respect and gratitude of most of the people, whether Christian or otherwise. The Vice-Chancellor had been named after the Christian missionary, Paul of Tarsus. Whenever possible, he ignored his Christian name and used Kwame.

At six o'clock the temperature was not yet 70 degrees. Alice had never been in the village this early. The low mountains to either side were now a lovely blue-green that would be lost to the bright sun of midmorning. Alice was amazed at the activity. Farmers were hurrying to plots on the hillsides. Children dodged back and forth in front of the car, moving to the public water taps with buckets of all types. They moved quickly since this time of year water was scarce. The pumps would soon be turned off and the water taps dry until evening. Occasionally the village wells would dry up completely and the children would have to walk into the forest behind Alice's bungalow to the stream that was never dry.

When they were out of Mbordo, the Vice-Chancellor relaxed a bit and asked, "Mrs. Manati, is it all right if I address you by your given name?"

"Given name?" Alice asked.

"Oh, I'm sorry," the Vice-Chancellor replied, "I mean your first name. I forgot that is the way you say it in the United States."

"You certainly may" Alice replied. "Frankly I do become a little weary of the formality here, Mr. Onanga. The students are almost too polite, but it is nice."

"Please," the Vice-Chancellor said, "call me Kwame."

"All right," Alice said and then continued. "You know it really is marvelous to have students who are all polite."

"Well, yes, it is true that our students are polite to expatriates," the Vice-Chancellor said quietly. "It's unfortunate that they are not equally polite to everyone else."

"Wait a minute," Alice said in a puzzled tone. "I don't remember any student ever being impolite to you. I can't believe they ever would be."

"Of course not," the Vice-Chancellor replied as he swerved to avoid a chicken, "they wouldn't dare, at least not to my face. It would go against our cultural values, everything they have learned since they were very small children. But what I was really referring to is the way they treat each other. Animosity between students is becoming worse. I am very worried that some of our students from the North may soon choose to withdraw. I don't think they even trust me anymore."

"I don't understand," Alice remarked, "I haven't noticed anything unusual."

"No, you probably wouldn't see much of it," the Vice-Chancellor replied. "This type of thing is kept out of sight of expatriates. Students are embarrassed to admit tribalism to Europeans, but let me give you an example. Two days ago a Kroban student found one of his best shirts on his bed cut into a dozen pieces. He reported the incident to me and even named the person he thought responsible. But there was little I could do since no one would admit to having seen the act committed."

"Why was it done?" Alice asked. "It seems stupid to destroy someone's shirt like that."

"I know," the Vice-Chancellor replied. "We can't afford to throw away things like you do in America. In our culture, short of murder, the destruction of that shirt was one of the worst things that could happen. If you bloody a person's nose or cut his skin, he will be quite angry and no doubt retaliate in some manner. But it will be a thing of the moment and quickly forgotten. Not so if you rip his shirt or trousers. That kind of incident can lead to permanent animosity."

"But why did it happen?" Alice asked again.

"Some Ave students believe that the University should be only for them" the Vice-Chancellor explained. "They are willing to allow a few Atan and Bordo to attend, but they want the Kroban out. Tribalism tied to religion is a very bad mixture. You know religion in this place is a very sad thing.

"Alice," he continued, "I really do believe from what I know of several religions that they should bring those who believe a sense of peace and happiness, not only within but also with their fellow man. But in my country they bring only conflict."

"Kwame, you talk as if you've had some personal experience with religious conflict," Alice commented.

"Yes, unfortunately so," Kwame answered, "I grew up in a village in which the Christians and the Muslims fought continuously for the souls of the pagan. My father was one of the 'generals' on the Christian side. It seems so ridiculous now. All that effort to change people without really changing anything. I now think that the only truly 'religious' people in my village were the old people who were Animists. They always listened politely but ignored what was said by both the Christians and Muslims. They had no interest in converts. The truth of what they believed was evident to them; the trees, rocks, rivers, everything of the earth was a part of their faith. Whether anyone else cared to believe as they did was of no importance to them."

"Are you an Animist?" Alice asked bluntly.

"You mean one of those evil pagans," Kwame answered. "No, I am not. Didn't you know that we don't educate Animists in Sakra? Even the government schools won't admit you unless you profess to be a Christian or Muslim."

The Vice-Chancellor continued speaking as much to himself as to Alice. "Running the University-College is very complicated. Each group believes that I favor the others. They all think that I favor the people of my own village, the Damis. Of course the irony is that I do try to balance everything. That's how I am able to get them all angry. Even the people from my village are often angry with me because they feel that I do not favor them enough."

"Well, anyway, teaching certainly is easy here," Alice said. "I guess that some aspects of the life of an educational institution are always going to be difficult, no matter how good things are otherwise."

"Unfortunately, it is becoming increasingly difficult," Kwame continued. "If it were just the University-College, one could resign and go elsewhere, but the problems of the College are not much different than those of the nation. It is sad, very sad. I find it difficult to accept what is happening. At first, after independence, we seemed near paradise. Money flowed from the cocoa tree. Everywhere there was new construction, new industry, improved roads, and schools, schools for all of our children. Then the world market for cocoa beans went sour, very sour. As the price of that bitter bean fell, our prices on everything else went up, at first only 20 to 30 per cent a year. But now prices on some goods double and even triple in less than half a year. The man who led us in the fight for independence now hides. Not many dare to speak against him, but the whispers increase."

Kwame noticed that Alice was starring out a side window.

He chuckled and said, "I'm sorry, Mrs. Manati. I know that you Peace Corps people are not allowed to discuss politics. I will not embarrass you further."

"Also," he continued in an amused tone, "when that special word comes from Nkra, I know that you will be up and instantly away. Every morning I expect that I will come by and find your house empty."

Alice could not restrain her curiosity.

She asked, "How do you know all that?"

Kwame replied, "In Sakra, there are no secrets."

"But, enough of gloomy things," Kwame continued, "let's stop and have something to drink. We are more than halfway to Kwim."

"My goodness, already halfway," Alice remarked. "Riding a lorry certainly helps you appreciate a car."

Alice's comment brought a smile to Kwame's face as he stopped the car near a bar in one of the small villages near the road.

"It certainly is a pleasure having your company," he said. "I hope that my rambling on and on is not too boring."

"Certainly not. I don't mind the least bit," replied Alice. "But, I am beginning to think that I may not want to know everything about the University-College or Sakra. It's a bit frightening, some of the things you said."

"Don't worry," Kwame answered, "at heart I believe that most people of Sakra are kind and peace loving."

"From my personal experience that is certainly true," Alice replied.

But even as she spoke, thoughts of Jason's story of the stoning of the thief lingered in her memory. After drinking Cokes purchased at the little bar, they returned to the car and continued toward Kwim.

Alice noted changes in the nature of the land and vegetation. Enata's village was forty miles southeast of Mbordo on the outer edge of traditional Bordo lands. Although Chief Kanata was Bordo, his wife and perhaps half the population of Kwim were Ave. In spite of their relative proximity, the villages differed in many ways. Mbordo was located in a valley on the edge of forest lands, between two low mountain ranges. The village itself was at the valley's narrowest point, the University-College at its widest. Kwim was on a plateau, near the eastern end of the second of the great scarps of Sakra. Its elevation was several hundred feet higher than the lowest points of the Mbordo valley. The area around Kwim was ideal for the production of cocoa. By comparison, drainage in the Mbordo valley was for the most part too poor to grow the valuable trees. Kwim had, by Sakraian standards, become wealthy during the high cocoa demand era of the late fifties. Those who had taken the money made from cocoa and invested it in transportation ventures or durable goods were now growing even richer.

As they neared Kwim, Alice noted that nearly all available land was devoted to the production of cocoa. The only food crops she saw were those planted between and under cocoa trees that had not yet begun to produce the pods in which the cocoa bean develops. The Vice-Chancellor stopped by a field of mature trees and called to a laborer who was cleaning the area between the trees. The man quickly pulled a pod from one of the trees and brought it to the Vice-Chancellor. He pulled the sides of the pod apart and handed it to Alice to inspect.

She laughed and said, "So this is where a Hershey chocolate bar starts."

"Yes indeed," the Vice-Chancellor replied, "Hershey buys 70 percent of Sakra's cocoa crop. We produce the very best beans in the world. Other countries measure the quality of their crop against our standard.

"But it does give one pause," continued the Vice-Chancellor, "to think that the economy of Sakra should depend so much upon what to you people is just a luxury. Our economy would be destroyed if you stopped eating chocolate."

"My God," Alice said, "I will never be able to pass up another chocolate bar. Is it really that important?"

"Yes and no," the Vice-Chancellor answered. "Certainly if people stopped using chocolate, the government and cocoa farmers would have a lot less to spend. I would be out of work for sure. But most of the people of Sakra don't have much to do with what is called the 'national economy' or what you might call the 'money economy' of Sakra. They will continue to plant, harvest, and eat their own food crops as they have always done. Sociology textbooks call them subsistence farmers. They participate in the money economy in only minor ways. Perhaps they sell a few yam in order to earn money to pay school fees for the brightest or oldest child or to purchase a radio."

"Are you saying that if money just disappeared from Sakra, most people would not be affected?" Alice asked.

"I think for most people it would be their attitude toward the future that would change more than their immediate economic well-being," Kwame replied. "Without money the schools would close. We would certainly be out of work. Or I should say that I would be out of work and you would return to the United States. Our roads, such as they are, would deteriorate completely. The cities would disintegrate. People would have to return to their villages."

"Anyway," Alice said, "it won't happen. Chocolate has become an American necessity, not a luxury. Nothing short of conclusive findings that chocolate causes the immediate onset of stomach cancer would convince Americans to give it up."

"God forbid," the Vice-Chancellor exclaimed, "you know that I did not acquire a taste for chocolate until I studied in America. Ridiculous, is it not? Most Africans really don't care for the taste of a chocolate bar. Too sweet I think."

"Strange," Alice said, "it grows better here than anywhere but you don't care for it."

"That's right," the Vice-Chancellor replied. "Dr. Agyenkwa has tried to push the development of a chocolate candy industry. Unfortunately the results have not been promising. The students say that one bar of Nkra chocolate will give you a three-day headache."

Alice noticed the sun's reflection off tin roofs in the distance.

"Wonder if that's Kwim," she thought. "Great trip. Don't think it's even nine yet, but the sun is getting warm."

"This is Kwim," the Vice-Chancellor said as the car neared the first of the houses. "What do you think?"

Alice did not answer. Kwim looked much like other villages that she had seen. She did notice that more of the houses were made of concrete block and had tin or zinc roofs.

Chief Kanata had ordered a formal welcome. Most of the elders and other important personages of Kwim had assembled in the courtyard of the Chief's home. The Vice-Chancellor parked the car. They were escorted to the Chief's compound by one of the younger men of the village. He was formally dressed in silk Kente cloth. Alice did not recognize him as one of her fourth period students until they were within a few steps of Chief Kanata's home.

"Amazing," she thought, "that William Ageman should look so much more dignified in that cloth than he does in University-College dress."

She complemented his appearance. He replied with a modest 'thank you' and added that he believed that she would have quite a good lesson today in the customs of Kwim.

Chief Kanata sat on a carved stool in the corner most distant from the entrance. He was protected from the sun by a huge, colorful umbrella held by a man Alice judged to be not yet thirty. The village linguist stood a few feet to the right of the Chief. He held himself erect, as vertical as the carved staff in his right hand. The staff was the symbol of his ability to speak many tongues and of his special function as an intermediary between the Chief of Kwim and the rest of the world. The elders and the Queen Mother, who was an elderly relative of the Chief, were seated behind Chief Kanata. When Alice and the Vice-Chancellor entered the compound, the linguist greeted them in English.

"Chief Kanata, the Kwimohene, bids you welcome," he said. "He is very pleased to have the Vice-Chancellor of Mbordo University-College and the teacher of mathematics visit our humble village. Will you join us for some refreshment?"

"Most certainly," the Vice-Chancellor replied, "it gives us great pleasure to return to this excellent village of Kwim. We have been away too long. We look forward to the enjoyment of our time here. We greatly appreciate your hospitality and generosity."

The linguist returned to the side of Chief Kanata and spoke loudly in Bordo. The Chief nodded his approval. At once small boys appeared with chairs for Alice and the Vice-Chancellor. Two men came with umbrellas to provide the visitors shade. Jeff and Enata emerged from one of the side rooms of the compound. They were seated next to Alice and the Vice-Chancellor. Alice was amazed by the beauty and quality of clothing around her. Enata had chosen to wear an outfit of blue and gold woven cloth that accentuated the strength of her tall slim frame. Even Jeff had given up his usual khaki shorts in favor of perhaps his only pair of full-length pants. Women distributed glasses for the beer and gin carried into the compound by several young men. The Chief was served first. He used the traditional calabash drinking gourd to pour a libation in honor of his ancestors and the other ancestors of the people of the village. Enata whispered to Alice that the purpose of the libation was to satisfy the thirst of the spirits of the dead and to ask their blessing on the day's events. After everyone had time to consume a glass of beer or gin, the Chief spoke to his linguist again. The linguist then approached Alice and the Vice-Chancellor and asked if they would be willing to accept personal greetings from the elders, the Queen Mother and her attendants.

Alice replied, "Of course, it would be a pleasure."

She, the Vice-Chancellor and Jeff formed an impromptu reception line as the linguist brought each of the Kwim dignitaries who wished to be introduced over to where they were standing. This process required almost an hour and Alice was not unhappy to be escorted back to her seat when they had finished the introductions.

Once again Chief Kanata spoke to his linguist. The linguist turned and spoke to the elders.

Enata nudged Alice. "He is telling them that the time has come for you to rest. That your journey was long and that it is time for everyone to leave."

After speaking to the elders the linguist turned and walked to where Alice and the Vice-Chancellor sat.

He said in a formal and almost grave tone, "We are very happy that you have come. Chief Kanata requests that you spend this night and tomorrow night with him here in his home. He will come to be with you in a few minutes. Please follow this young man into that room so that the sun will not be on your heads."

Once inside, Alice remarked to Enata, "I did not expect to be treated as a dignitary."

"I hope it was not too tedious," Enata replied. "This village has few important visitors. When someone does come, everyone wants to meet them."

A man in slacks and a European style shirt entered the room.

Alice did not recognize him until Enata said, "Father, I think you frightened Mrs. Manati with your formal welcome."

Chief Kanata smiled broadly and said in a merry baritone voice, "It is not often that we have such distinguished visitors to our humble village. The Vice-Chancellor and Mrs. Manati have done us a great honor by their visit."

The Vice-Chancellor replied, "Chief Kanata, you have never had such a ceremony when I visited this village before."

"Nor have I seen such a ceremony in honor of one of my visits," Jeff could not resist interjecting.

"But it is the combination of your visits that has given this day such great importance," the Chief protested. "I know, Mr. Vice-Chancellor and Mr. Johnson, that both of you have honored our village with your presence before. However, this time you brought with you the distinguished American woman mathematician.

"The elders have been astounded by the accounts they have heard of your ability with numbers and your strength in travel," Chief Kanata continued as he looked in Alice's direction. "Frankly, it was all that I could do to prevent them from asking you to do a few sums and products on the spot."

"All right, all right," Alice replied, "I know I'm a freak."

"I'm sorry," the Chief answered, "we did not mean to be discourteous. You really are an illustrious person in this village."

"I didn't mean that like it sounded," Alice responded, "only trying to be humorous at my own expense. The welcome was marvelous."

"Ah yes," the Chief replied, "my daughter has often told me of this remarkable trait that you have of 'being humorous at one's own expense.' I did not immediately understand what it meant. But after I gave the idea some thought I decided that perhaps that sort of humor would be a good thing for all of us. I am very glad that you found some pleasure in our welcome. I find them more duty than pleasure.

"I have long wished to meet you, Mrs. Manati. Enata is my major source of information for what happens beyond the streets of these villages. I do believe that in this short time you have been in Sakra you have become a model for her."

Alice blinked rapidly and bit her lip. She was surprised by Chief Kanata's comment. It had never occurred to her that her life would or even could serve as a model for anyone.

The Chief turned to the Vice-Chancellor and spoke, "My friend, it is good to see you again. How are things with your family?"

"Quite well, sir," the Vice-Chancellor replied, "and how does the cocoa crop look this year?"

"The crop is excellent. As good as I have seen," Chief Kanata replied. "Unfortunately as much cannot be said for the price. The more cocoa we grow, the lower the price.

"But enough of this moaning," the Chief continued. "Mrs. Manati, did you know that your Vice-Chancellor and I attended the same secondary school? He, of course, continued his education and became the leader of a great institution of higher education. I left before even completing secondary school and became chief of this humble village."

"Now father," Enata interjected, "you have many times said that it was a choice freely made and never regretted. Why do you now take this opportunity when we have guests to mourn the past?"

"And," added the Vice-Chancellor, "for you, my friend, to call yourself the humble chief of a small village is a bit ridiculous. Actually, Alice, the man who sits here with us is the chief of six villages whose lands are among the most fertile in Sakra. His wealth and influence far exceed anything that I might even dream of acquiring."

"Enough, I believe you," Alice protested, "but it does no harm to consider where other paths we might have traveled could have taken us. At my age I find that a growing obsession."

"From what I understand," the Chief replied, "you have taken not only many paths in this life but also all roads, no matter how rough."

"Please," Alice replied with a grin, "I'm afraid that my reputation as a traveler has been exaggerated."

"Nevertheless," the Chief said, "I have heard that your students and even your colleagues find you rather astonishing. But enough of what I am sure you already know. What would you like to see of our village?"

"Well," Alice replied hesitantly, "I prefer not to have anyone go to a lot of trouble on my account. Maybe I could just walk around some by myself."

"Alice," Enata said, "tell my father what you wish to see. The whole village is at your service whether you want it to be or not, so you might as will take good advantage of the opportunity."

"Yes," Chief Kanata said, "we will go to much trouble no matter how you feel about it. You cannot stop us. However, you can help us by telling us those things in our village that you are most interested in."

"If that's the way it is," Alice replied, "I would like to see a cocoa farm, Jeff's project, and meet a jujuman, not necessarily in that order, of course."

"Would you mind, also, Mrs. Manati?" the Chief asked, "if we had some small drumming and dancing?"

"I would enjoy that very much," Alice replied.

A late lunch was served. Alice was exhausted from the morning's activity and her stomach was in revolt. Chief Kanata had anticipated her fatigue and had planned nothing for the afternoon. Alice found the room, set aside for her in one corner of the compound, very comfortable and fell asleep quickly.

****

In a small bungalow located about twenty yards behind the main compound, Jeff lay resting on a large double bed. Enata sat beside him. Chief Kanata had constructed the little two-bedroom house (with its own bathroom and kitchen) to accommodate his grown children more comfortably when they visited Kwim.

"It is good that Alice came," Enata said. "I hope the celebration tonight is not too tiring for her."

"Her!" Jeff exclaimed. "What about me?"

"Perhaps," Enata mused, "if you are concerned about preserving your strength, we should sleep in different rooms tonight."

Jeff answered quickly, "That's not what makes me tired."

"Oh, superman?" Enata joked.

"Very close," Jeff replied then continued, "now, tell me the truth, did you really tell your father that stuff about Alice being your model?"

"Not exactly," Enata said, "my father tends to exaggerate to make guests feel welcome. That is a tradition here. We also say that for a person with white hair no praise can be too extravagant."

"That's really a contrast," Jeff commented, "in the United States someone Alice's age is usually retired and often more or less ignored. We put them out to pasture."

"Put them out to pasture?" Enata asked. "What does that mean? That you boil them?"

"No," Jeff replied as he tried but failed to control his laughter.

"Damn you," Enata replied angrily, "if you laugh at me because I don't understand all of your silly American sayings, I will just go somewhere else."

"Please," Jeff replied, "I didn't say pasteurize. A pasture is a field in which cows or horses graze. That is what I meant. When a horse is 'put out to pasture,' it means that it will never be used for work again. It will just wander around eating grass until it dies of old age."

"Not much better than being boiled," Enata reflected.

"No, not really I guess," Jeff remarked, "but why so much respect for the old here?"

"I never really thought about why, there just is," Enata replied. "That is our custom. We would be very uncomfortable if we did not treat our elders with respect. As children we are told that the old are wise because they have lived many years."

"Certainly no one could dispute that living many years is definitely necessary to become old," Jeff added a bit sarcastically.

"Your education has not been completely wasted," Enata teased. "Maybe it also has something to do with older people being nearer to the spirit world and we want to be sure they leave with happy memories so they won't cause us problems from over there."

"I wonder if that will change as Sakra becomes more developed? If more people are educated and move to the cities?" Jeff asked.

"I don't think so," Enata replied, "as for me, wherever I am or whatever I am doing, I will see that my father is comfortable in his old age."

"Even if that meant returning to this village to live?" questioned Jeff.

"Yes, I think if that became necessary I would do so," Enata replied.

Jeff decided not to pursue the subject further. Enata's answers troubled him. He had for several months tried to find some way in which to discuss the future of their relationship but feared that might lead to the end of their time as 'friends.' Enata's thoughts were not much different. She too feared that careful analysis of their relationship would not have any good effect.

"You look worried," she said. "Is something wrong?"

"No, just thinking about the project," Jeff improvised. "It sure takes a hell of a long time to find out whether or not the instructions we have written actually work. You read the manual. How do you think we are doing?"

"It will never work. You left out the part about pouring the libation before planting and having a jujuman sprinkle the field with the proper powders," Enata replied.

"Please," Jeff said, "I am trying to be a little bit serious. What do you really think?"

"I think," Enata replied pretending to be serious, "that you will have to wait and see whether or not the vegetables grow, and if you agree to wait until they grow before you leave this place, I will poison the ground so that you will have to wait here forever."

"I surrender," Jeff replied as he pulled Enata down on top of him. "While we are waiting for the vegetables to grow, perhaps we can find some way to pass the time."

"I thought you were exhausted by this morning's ceremonies," protested Enata.

"Two different things," Jeff replied. "That had to be done standing up, this can be done lying down."

"You are quite right my love, it is different," Enata whispered as their lips met.

****

Dinner that night was served on a huge table in one corner of the compound. A constant flow of boys and girls from the kitchen assured that no plate or glass was ever empty. The main course was plantain fufu served with groundnut soup. Chief Kanata noticed and understood Alice's questioning glances in Jeff's direction.

"Don't worry, Mrs. Manati," he said, "we made Jeff ill only three times before he told us that we must boil the water used in making fufu."

Alice sighed, "I am sorry to be such a bother."

"Please do not apologize again," the Chief said. "To go to a bother for you is a pleasure for us. The boiling of the water is better not just for you, but for all of us who eat this fufu. Jeff explained the problem with the small organisms in the water to us in great detail and with color slides."

The Chief's remarks led to laughter around the table. Alice found that plantain fufu was lighter and easier to deal with than the yam fufu that she had sampled in the student dining hall. The soup was a combination of chicken, okra, onion, and tomato cooked in groundnut paste.

"A marvelous meal," Alice said, as after dinner tea was served, "simply marvelous. Why don't we have food like this in the University-College dining hall?"

To Alice's surprise and embarrassment, the Vice Chancellor answered, "Two reasons, Mrs. Manati. First we would have to triple school fees to provide food of this quality, and second, we would have to kidnap half of Chief Kanata's family to prepare it properly for us."

Alice was astonished by the Vice-Chancellor's last remark and spoke without thought, "All of these people are part of your family, Chief Kanata?"

"Certainly," Enata said, "my father is a powerful man. He has thirteen wives and seventy-three children."

Alice looked perplexed. Jeff bit his lip.

The Chief spoke in a tone of mock resignation, "My daughter exaggerates the number of my wives by 12. I have only one wife, now deceased, and three living children. The others that you see around you I believe would be called cousins and nephews in your country."

The Chief continued, "The memories of my wife often bring me much happiness but always, at the same time, sadness. In my poor libation much of what is poured on the ground in honor of our ancestors is for her. I know that it is not in the Christian tradition, but I hope that God will forgive me for the small comfort it brings. But enough of the past. If we are ready, the dancing and drumming will begin."

When no one objected, he called one of the small boys that always seemed to be wandering about the compound and sent him to inform those who were to dance that the Chief and his guests were ready. The drummers came first. They demonstrated how the quality and pitch could be varied by changing the shape of the hand or the place struck on the drumhead. Skilled hands made the drums talk. Alice would have called the instruments played by three others cowbells had she been in the United States. They were different sizes with different tones and were played by striking the side of the bell sharply with a stick. Other instruments were made from large and small gourds. These were used to produce the distinctive background double beat that characterized Sakraian music.

At the Chief's signal, the drumming began. The overall effect was remarkable. Each man seemed to be playing almost in some form of splendid isolation. And yet the end result was a unified, rhythmic, and beautiful composition, a pleasant yet exhilarating sound. Alice found it increasingly difficult to concentrate. She realized that what her mind now perceived through her ear was much more than a simple combination of sounds. The drums spoke together in one voice out of many. They invited the listener to put away the cares and problems of the day and to become with the musicians a part of the music itself. Alice's mind perceived that her body had relaxed. Sound and feeling moved from the hands of the drummer down into the drums, on into the ground on which they rested, then up through her sandals and feet into her bones and finally took possession of her very being. Her head now moved gently up and down with the double beat of the drums.

Most of the people of the village had gathered behind the place where Alice and the others were seated. The Chief's expression was impassive, showing little emotion, as was proper for a man of his station in life. The Vice-Chancellor looked a bit bored. Jeff and Enata were paying more attention to each other than to what was happening in front of them. But Alice's attention remained concentrated on the performers. The sudden entrance of the dancers seemed completely a part of the drumming so skillfully did they blend the movements of their bodies to the sound of the drums. The interaction between drum and dancer, at times cooperative, at times competitive, produced a remarkable but always changing synthesis. Next, elders of the village performed a slow but beautiful dance symbolizing the time of planting food crops. Near the end of the elder's dance, the drums called on the Chief to rise. Chief Kanata moved toward the drummers in the slow pace symbolic of his important office. He stopped about six feet in front of the drummers, made several slow but graceful movements, then turned and walked slowly to where Alice sat.

Much to Alice's surprise, the Chief said, "Would you be so kind as to dance for a few moments."

Enata whispered, "Go and do a few steps. It is the traditional manner for a guest to say thank you. Don't worry, it is not quality but effort that is important. Everyone will be happy even if you just walk toward the drummers."

Alice out of the corner of her eye could see the beginning of a smirk on Jeff's lips. She sighed deeply, got up, and almost tripped over her chair. She did her best to shuffle around a bit. Alice could hear but not understand comments from where most of the people of the village were standing, and she found herself wondering about the possibility of a hue and cry for ruining the evening of dancing. As she moved closer to her seat she thought she heard the Bordo expression, "She is trying, she is trying."

She looked at Chief Kanata and was greeted with a broad smile.

"Thank God," she thought, "it looks like I didn't ruin the evening completely."

Suddenly the entire courtyard was crowded with dancers. The entire village joined Chief Kanata and Alice in front of the drummers.

The Chief said, "You dance very well, Mrs. Manati."

"You needn't lie to protect my feelings," Alice replied, "I know exactly how I dance and that is very badly."

The Chief was amused by Alice's bluntness.

"You are a very honest person," he told her. "However, and now I am being completely truthful, your performance was admirable. Let me assure you that the people of this village are very grateful. Now come, we have danced long enough. We can sit down."

"Yes, I would like to sit down," sighed Alice. "Tell me, did I really look as terrible as I thought I did? Don't answer that, please. I want an objective opinion. I will ask Jeff."

The Chief had difficulty containing his laughter as he spoke, "If Mr. Johnson says you were anything less than magnificent, he will sleep in the road tonight."

"Let's find out," Alice replied as they made their way back to their chairs. "Jeff, what did you think of my efforts to dance?"

Jeff replied without hesitation, "Alice, you were magnificent."

Alice sighed, shook her head and said, "This old lady's been taken in again."

Then she joined in the amused laughter of the others.

CHAPTER 6
Alice Explores Kwim and Meets a Jujuman

Early the next morning Enata entered Alice's room with a small candle. She squeezed Alice's shoulder gently.

When she saw Alice's eyes partially open she said quietly, "Alice, if you feel strong enough, we should go now to look at the cocoa farms before the sun is high and it becomes too hot to be walking about."

"My God, what time is it?" was all that Alice could think of to say.

"About four-thirty," Enata replied, "are you sure you wish to do this?"

"If I can get dressed and have a cup of tea," Alice mumbled.

"Of course," Enata said, somewhat bemused by the awakening confusion of the usually precise Alice. "You have nothing to worry about. This is not America. We do not starve our elders here. We don't even put them out to pasture."

"Thank God for that," Alice replied. "Enata, you sure do know how to bring a person wide awake. We will save that famous pasture for another day."

"Good, very good," Enata said, "I will have the tea sent to this room so that you can enjoy it as you dress."

"That would be very nice," Alice commented as Enata left the room.

A few minutes later a small girl brought Alice a tray that held a teapot, cup, a plate of bread, and a small jar of jam. After Alice had dressed and eaten, she joined Chief Kanata, the Vice-Chancellor, Jeff, Enata and several other members of the Chief's household in the courtyard. By five, the village was no longer quiet. Everyone seemed awake. It was Sunday, but even devout Christians would visit their farms before morning services in order to check the progress of their food crops and perhaps return with something for the day's meals. Others less devout or non-Christian might work until midmorning on their vegetable and yam plots or at clearing brush from around cocoa trees.

Chief Kanata decided to show Alice one of his own farms. The place they were to visit today was approximately half a mile from the village by footpath. Alice found the early morning walk invigorating. Chief Kanata expressed surprise and delight at Alice's strength. The Vice-Chancellor commented dryly that Alice would never accept a ride anywhere in a car if she were able to walk or find a lorry going in the same direction. They were accompanied by about twenty people from the village.

"Perhaps," Alice conjectured, "they had come along to scare snakes away or to carry me back if I can't make it on my own."

What Alice had from a distance thought to be one hill, she realized as they approached, was actually two. A small valley between the two hills provided an ideal location for growing cocoa trees. The Chief explained that this farm had both mature producing trees and young trees that had not yet produced any cocoa pods. Food crops were grown between the young trees. They reached a part of the farm where the cocoa trees were mature enough to produce bright green cocoa pods. The Chief removed a near ripe pod from one of the trees and broke it apart for Alice to examine. (She did not mention, out of politeness, that it was her second pod of the weekend.) The size of the trees and the symmetric pattern in which they were planted reminded Alice of cherry orchards.

"It must be very difficult work to clear this land," Alice commented.

"Yes," the Chief responded, "it is painful work. When I was a youngster, I did occasionally help to clear the land. Now most of the work is done by laborers from the North. When my sons lived here, I would send them to work with the laborers."

"A good lesson," chuckled the Vice-Chancellor. "None of them will ever wish to become farmers."

"It may well have had that effect," mused the Chief. "I don't think either of them wishes to return here. But, be that as it may, I do believe that work of this type is good for a person at least in moderation.

"Time to eat breakfast," the Chief announced. "Mrs. Manati, are you hungry?"

"Yes, I am," Alice replied, "but what do we eat?"

"Don't worry," Jeff responded, "we brought it with us."

The reason for the large number of people who came with them was now evident. One man set up a table. Small stools were provided for them to sit on. The breakfast menu consisted of yam slices cooked in hot tomato sauce with small bits of beef. Ordinarily Alice would have in no way been able to force down that sort of food at eight in the morning. However, the walk from Kwim had given her good appetite. She ate well and found the food delicious.

By nine they were moving back toward the village. The heavy breakfast and the morning heat combined to make Alice's earlier thoughts of needing assistance to make it back nearly come true. However, with the help of the terrain (mostly downhill) and stubborn pride she made it to the Chief's compound on her own. She politely refused Enata's invitation to attend church and returned to her room to rest.

When the Chief and his daughter returned from services, the midday meal was served. After lunch Chief Kanata suggested that everyone rest until the cooler part of the afternoon. Alice was more than happy to have further time to recover from the morning's hike. The other adults and even the children retreated to the coolness of the thick-walled rooms. The Chief and the Vice-Chancellor were left sitting alone in the courtyard.

"Old friend, good friend," the Chief said to the Vice-Chancellor, "I know that you did not make this journey only to become informed of our local customs or to investigate Mr. Johnson's project. So tell me now, why do you honor us with this visit to Kwim?"

The Vice-Chancellor sat quietly for a moment, then spoke in measured tones, "Events do not go well for our country, Sakra. The 'Savior,' our Dr. Agyenkwa, is isolated. He seems to know little of what is happening beyond his own doorway. Everything is becoming costly. Food is the worst. They say that even people starve in

Nkra. It is worse for the small people than for us. They are unhappy, even more than unhappy.

"I believe he is making a big mistake in looking to the Chinese and Russians for help. Especially those Chinese who came to build the cotton mill. I understand they live by themselves in specially built housing near the construction site. No African is allowed anywhere near them. Even when they go to the beach on Sundays, a portion of the most popular beach near Nkra is always sealed off by the police. People say that the equipment is just old stuff from China that no one there wanted any more. I have even heard stories that my friends say come directly from dockworkers that the boats that unloaded the equipment for the cotton mill returned to China loaded with Sakraian yams. True or not, these stories make people really angry. The price of yam has increased fourfold since they arrived."

"Do you think the Chinese like yam?" the Chief asked with a half smile. "I thought they favored rice. But it doesn't matter. I have heard the same stories. The Russian guards of the 'Savior' are also disliked by nearly everyone. In fact, I tried not many weeks ago to visit Dr. Agyenkwa in order to tell him some of what you say. I never passed beyond those Russians. They keep everyone away except those who tell him only what he wants to hear.

"We chiefs have no power outside our own villages now, and for that matter very little within the village gates except that given to us by the traditional respect of our people. The Assembly of Chiefs that is charged with advising the 'Savior' is a farce. It is never consulted. But perhaps rightly so. They are a bunch of doddering old fools. You could not believe the debates. One man will say, 'Let us endorse President Agyenkwa's statement that he should be the supreme leader of all of Africa.' Another will say, 'No, no let us commend the "Savior" for making such a brilliant statement.' Still another old fool will shout above the others, 'I have a better plan. Let us declare that Dr. Agyenkwa is the supreme leader of all Africa.' I don't know the final result of the debate. I left after two hours."

"What do you think will happen?" the Vice-Chancellor asked. "Sakra cannot continue in this way."

"I do not know," Chief Kanata replied. "I hear whispers of plots to bring an end to the 'Savior's' government and even his life. But what would come next? Nothing good can be the result. Whatever happens will bring trouble."

The Vice-Chancellor nodded in agreement and said, "Yes, it seems as if the Atan, the Ave, and the Kroban are already preparing to battle for power if Dr. Agyenkwa is removed. At the University-College tribalism is now a very difficult problem. It seems to be in everything. Worse than I have seen in any of my other schools. I don't know how to deal with it anymore. If we catch those who are guilty, they are severely punished. But we do not often find the guilty ones. On one day a Kroban student's shoes will be splattered with paint. The next day an Ave student's shirt will be cut to ribbons. Rough play on the football field often will develop into fights between students of different tribes, even those on the same team. It is everywhere and it never stops."

"The same problems come to us here," the Chief replied. "The people who live in this village are Bordo or Ave for the most part, but the workers who do most of the hard labor on the cocoa farms are from the North. A few come from beyond the borders of Sakra, but most are Kroban. I have several times had to stop Sunday football matches that degenerated into fights between the laborers and young men of Kwim. Problems have developed in our schools. Many of the masters are Atan. The Ave students come to me with many complaints of their mistreatment at the hands of the Atan masters. One middle school girl needed three days in hospital to recover after a caning. Her offense was a tribal slur against one of the Atan masters. Little can be done in such a case. I have no power in the schools. If the girl wishes to continue her education she must go back to that teacher.

"But, old friend," the Chief continued, "you still have not explained how I may be of service to you. I cannot even help with the students from this village who attend the University-College. Once they have traveled to Mbordo they no longer pay any attention to this little educated Chief. I have no influence with them."

"I am sure they still respect you," the Vice-Chancellor replied, "but that is not the reason for my visit. What I have come to ask is that, in the time of trouble we both know must come, we help each other as best we can. We are both from small tribes. Whatever evil befalls Sakra, it is our people who will suffer most."

"What you say is very true," the Chief replied. "When the large animals fight, they may be injured and badly scarred but they live to fight again. It is the small animals that are trampled underfoot and destroyed in the battle. Yes Kwame, we must do our best for each other."

Chief Kanata grasped the Vice-Chancellor's hand and continued, "Whatever help I can render you and your family is yours."

"And I pledge all help that is within my power to you and your family," the Vice-Chancellor responded.

The Chief spoke again, "But, old friend, it was unnecessary for you to seek that which was already yours. My feeling for you is as deep as for my own family and village. You have already done much for us in rendering assistance to my daughter."

"Her value to the University-College is not as your daughter, of course, but in terms of her own abilities and accomplishments," the Vice-Chancellor answered. "However, that we were able to employ your daughter as a lecturer at the University-College gave me great happiness."

The Chief was amused by the Vice-Chancellor's effort to explain that their friendship had played no role in the decision to hire Enata but was nevertheless a matter of some importance.

"Spoken like a true friend," was his diplomatic comment.

"Now," the Vice-Chancellor said, "what is your opinion of Mr. Johnson's project?"

"He is a very intelligent and decent person," the Chief replied, "but if he were to attempt to live on what he could grow on his farm behind the middle school, in time he would become thin, quite thin."

The Vice-Chancellor chuckled.

He decided to press the point with a blunt question, "Do you mean that the project will not succeed?"

"No," the Chief replied, "I did not mean that at all. In my lifetime I have seen many manuals written by people who had experience in growing crops only in England. Those who followed the advice of such manuals found only disaster. Of course, the manuals that tell how to grow cash crops such as cocoa from which the English also benefited were much better than the corn and yam manuals. They were often based on the actual production of the cash crop on experimental farms. Now, as I see it, Mr. Johnson is also attempting to use this same method. The instructions that he writes are tried on his small farm. If they fail, the instructions are corrected. This procedure alone makes the project of some value. However, time is his enemy. In one or two years it is impossible to learn enough about farming even in this one village."

"Perhaps, if we could find someone to continue his work?" the Vice-Chancellor remarked.

The Chief replied, "You know very well what happens. The next European has to learn again for himself. By the time he understands that he knows nothing, it is also time for him to leave."

"You don't sound very optimistic," the Vice-Chancellor said. "Why not have a Sakraian replace Jeff on the project?"

Chief Kanata sighed, "My oldest and dearest friend, you have been with the University too long. Even the students from your school will not dip their hands into the soil when they return to this village. I know about your work program, but in truth, it only makes those students more determined than ever not to perform any type of manual labor again for the rest of their lives. I cannot even begin to imagine any distinguished Sakraian member of your staff doing anything that so closely resembles actual work as Mr. Johnson's project. Did you know that when Mr. Oganda comes, if he is feeling strong and if the sun is not too hot, he might visit one of the farms on the edge of the village? Otherwise, he uses his time here to drink with a Kroban who has a small store at the north edge of Kwim. He does not represent the University-College well in this place. The Kroban who come here to clean our cocoa plots are good people. They are very respectful and usually cause no trouble, but this man Oganda is a problem. When he drinks he talks about the Kroban being a superior tribe and how much he wishes he could be assigned to work somewhere in the North. I am afraid that one of our younger men will take action against his car if he continues with this behavior."

The Vice-Chancellor said nothing, but Chief Kanata could read the frustration caused by what had been said in his countenance.

The Chief continued, "I know, my good friend, that you are sincere in your belief that Mbordo University-College should contribute to the development of agriculture in the villages. But don't worry. This project is not bad, anyway. It will do no harm and perhaps it may prove beneficial. We old ones sometimes become set in our ways. We have seen too much to believe in anything. Please, I ask you sincerely, do not give up on this project because of my words. And most certainly bring the government and the AID people to visit. They will love it. This is what they dream of in their offices. Have no fear of my comments. I will carefully explain that Mr. Johnson's project is the most wonderful event that has occurred in this village since the gift of the stool of Kwim from our most honored ancestors. And that it will change the nature of agricultural practice and triple agricultural production in Kwim within five years."

"Just a simple country chief," the Vice-Chancellor said, placing his hand on the Chief's shoulder. "You should be the President of Sakra. You could take care of everyone."

"God forbid," the Chief replied. "But do not mistake my intentions. I would not say these things to the officials only out of friendship for you. I have watched carefully your efforts to build the University-College. What some others have chosen to call expediency, I would call statesmanship. What the University-College can do for my family and my village today or even tomorrow is not so important. What is important to all of us is that it be strong. If it is strong then perhaps someday it will be able to help. If it is not strong, it will die quickly and there will be nothing. Yes, yes, my friend, I talk often with Enata, Mr. Johnson and the others from this village who are students at Mbordo. Many times they find it difficult to understand your actions. But I never find it so. You need never fear my tongue. I will do nothing ever to harm Mbordo University-College, and I will do everything within my power to protect its good name."

"My deepest and most sincere thanks," the Vice-Chancellor said. "I could ask for no greater gift. I wish that I could remain here with you and your family longer, however with your permission I will return to Mbordo today. I have much work to complete before classes resume on Tuesday."

"We are disappointed that you must leave us after such a brief stay, but we understand well why it must be so," the Chief replied. "Should we awake Mrs. Manati?"

"No," the Vice-Chancellor said, "I believe that she will return with your daughter and Mr. Johnson on Monday. I had almost forgotten to thank you for the hospitality and kindness that you have shown her."

"It is entirely our pleasure," replied Chief Kanata. "She is indeed a remarkable woman."

"Quite," the Vice-Chancellor said. "The improvement that she brought to our mathematics department at the University-College in only six months is really unbelievable. Student morale in that area has changed from poor to exceptionally good. But she is sometimes a bit of a burden. I did honestly fear that the trip to Pandu might well have been her last journey."

"But certainly it was not," the Chief said. "I think perhaps that she is easily as fit as you or I. Will you return for her on Monday?"

"Certainly not," the Vice-Chancellor replied, "Mrs. Manati would never forgive me. They will all ride the lorry back to Mbordo and I will worry until I see Mrs. Manati in morning services on Tuesday."

"We all have our burdens," the Chief commented, "and I am quite sure she is not one of your heavier ones."

"Quite right," the Vice-Chancellor said. "Were all my problems so easily handled, I would be a very relaxed man. I would say good-by to Mr. Johnson and your daughter but don't wish to intrude on their privacy. If you will forgive the question, what do you think of the relationship that has developed between them?"

"That is my burden, old friend," Chief Kanata replied. "Anyway, in this time of the liberation of women my opinion in this matter is of little importance."

The Chief paused, then continued, "Of course, what I have said is a little untrue and certainly unfair to my daughter. If I were to object strongly I am sure that she would not see Mr. Johnson again. But I cannot find it in my heart to do so. I hope that somehow it ends well, but who can tell about such a thing."

"No one," the Vice-Chancellor said quietly.

Chief Kanata accompanied the Vice-Chancellor to his car and watched until the car disappeared from sight. He turned and walked back toward the compound. Alice's efforts to greet him in Bordo from the courtyard entrance did not at first register. She repeated the greeting a bit louder. He heard and smiled at her efforts with his language.

"Good afternoon," he replied in Bordo and then continued in English, "I did not know that you spoke the language of this village."

"Only a few words," Alice explained.

"They will be useful this afternoon," Chief Kanata said. "The Jujuman speaks very little English."

After the extraordinary display of dancing and drumming the previous evening, Kwim no longer looked to Alice as other villages she had seen. Now she noticed the different shades of orange and brown of the walls for mud brick houses, the pleasantly arranged plants and small trees along the roads and paths, and the careful almost geometric pattern of the sweeping of the dirt areas used for work and play. Whole families greeted the chief and the mathematics lady from almost every compound as they moved through the village. Little ones peeked out from behind parents or siblings and smiled shyly.

"What a wonderful treat just walking around Kwim is," Alice thought. "This would make the trip worthwhile even without anything else."

The house of the Jujuman was a rather ordinary, small, mudwalled bungalow set about fifty yards behind and apart from other houses in the village.

The Jujuman (or Wizard, which is perhaps a better translation of the Bordo name for the 'man who does magic') greeted them at the door. Alice's immediate problem was that she had no idea how to greet a wizard. After a moment's hesitation she offered her hand and said good afternoon in Bordo. The Wizard looked at her curiously then accepted her hand. She found his hand soft, softer than any Sakraian hand she had ever shaken.

"Perhaps one does not even touch a jujuman without some horrible result," she thought in a brief moment of panic.

By his gestures, the Wizard indicated that Chief Kanata and Alice should enter his home. One room, in the back, served as a place for the Wizard to sleep. The larger front room was lined with shelves of jars that contained leaves, powders and a number of things that Alice did not care to ask about. A small circle of rocks had been carefully placed in the center of the room. Alice noticed a circular hole in the roof above the rocks.

She turned to Chief Kanata and asked, "I don't suppose that he would be willing to do something for me?"

Chief Kanata talked with the Wizard then spoke to Alice.

"He would be very pleased. He has heard of your 'mathematics' and considers you something of a fellow wizard. He wishes to know what problem you need help with."

Alice was befuddled.

"I can't think of any problems just at the moment," she replied. "Couldn't he just do something in general."

The Chief spoke to the Wizard again. The Wizard seemed puzzled. He shrugged, as if to say, why come to a wizard if you have no problems. A few moments later the perplexed look disappeared. He spoke rapidly in Bordo to Chief Kanata.

The Chief translated for Alice, "He will use a mixture of powders to bring you general good luck."

Alice smiled and replied, "That would be marvelous. I can think of nothing better than general good luck."

The Wizard nodded and began removing powders from different jars on the shelves. He worked quickly mixing the powders together on a small table.

"What are those powders?" Alice asked.

When the Chief translated Alice's question into Bordo the Wizard looked shocked and replied sharply.

"He says that it would not be proper for him to explain the secrets of his family," Chief Kanata translated. "He also asks that he not be interrupted again since that might well destroy the power of that which is being prepared."

"Then, I shall not interrupt again," Alice murmured.

"Yes, that would be the best course of action, especially if you wish good luck in the future," the Chief replied.

When the Wizard was finished mixing the powder he used a small brush to sweep everything into a copper urn about the size of a man's head. He placed the urn in the center of the rock circle, closed the door to the room and lit the mixture with a match. The powder mixture smoldered but did not flame. The room filled with smoke.

Alice thought, "The fragrance is pleasant enough, but I wonder how much longer I can stand this."

Chief Kanata sensed her plight and suggested that they sit on small stools to one side of the room since the smoke was less intense closer to the floor. In a few minutes the powder was consumed and the room began to clear of smoke. The Wizard rose from a squatting position near the rock circle and moved to open the door. They followed him out of the room. Alice thanked the Wizard and started to walk away when she noticed that he had assumed a stance similar to that of a bellboy who had just carried your bags.

She asked Chief Kanata, "Is there a problem? Is something wrong?"

"I forgot," the Chief replied. "We offered him no presents in return for the service that he provided."

"I didn't bring anything special. Would two shillings do?" Alice asked.

"Quite well," Chief Kanata replied, "two shillings is special in this village."

She offered the Wizard the money.

He smiled and said, "Jesus be with you."

They moved quickly away from the Wizard's house before they both started laughing.

"I really don't want to laugh," Alice said, "but I can't help it."

"Yes, I understand perfectly," the Chief agreed. "That could be the only phrase of English that he knows."

"Or maybe he was just being polite," Alice thought out loud.

"That might be the case," Chief Kanata said, "but perhaps he was attempting to cover all of the possibilities of good luck."

"You know a strange idea keeps popping into my mind," Alice replied. "Your Wizard reminds me of Oral Roberts. That mixture of powder that brings overall good luck is a heck of a lot like the way that Oral tells his followers Christ will bring them good health and good fortune."

"Oral who?" the Chief asked.

"I'm sorry," Alice replied. "Oral Roberts is a famous American faith healer."

"You have them, too?" Chief Kanata asked. "I thought with so many doctors you would surely have no need of such people. In Kwim no one visits a jujuman if a doctor is available. But, Mrs. Manati, how do you understand this healing in America? Do you believe that it is possible?"

"It has," Alice replied, "in my opinion about the same success as the efforts of your Wizard to bring me good luck."

The Chief broke into a merry laughter.

Alice continued, "But how do you see the efforts of this Wizard of Kwim? It does not seem that you are completely serious about what he does."

The Chief replied, "That Wizard I think well of. In so far as I know, he has never tried to harm anyone of this village. It is even true that some of his small jars do contain effective remedies for some problems. He has a very good medicine for the stomach. He also has several for fever. Some sickness will simply go away with the passing of time. Other types are not of the body but of the head. With this type the Wizard is sometimes even more effective than the hospital. But, it really does not matter. He is the best we can do. It would be better to have a doctor in every village, but that is not possible."

"I did read something about the jujuman as the African substitute for the psychiatrist," Alice remarked. "Can he really help people with mental problems?"

"I do believe so," the Chief replied, "a little incense, a small libation, and a good chat can really do wonders for worry. The Wizard you just met does very well with this sort of thing. But one must be careful. Not all of them are helpful. Some wizards are truly evil. Not many years ago a man died in this village as the result of the actions of a Jujuman."

"Did the Jujuman give him poison?" Alice asked.

"No," the Chief said, "but wait until we reach the compound and have some refreshment. I will tell you the entire story."

Back at the compound they sat down and were quickly served beer by two of the ever-present preteen children.

After half a glass Alice said, "Now Chief Kanata, about the story of the Jujuman."

"Ah, yes," the Chief replied. "Those unhappy matters occurred some four years ago, about this time of the year. I must explain first that we Africans must be extraordinarily careful in dealing with custom. There are those who believe that by attending the schools of the government we will be able to wash away our superstitions and beliefs. But it is not so. They are still within us. When we do not understand this and we fail to respect the customs that were a part of our childhood, we often find more trouble than our minds and bodies are able to bear. Such is the story of the man that I will tell you of. He completed fifth form of secondary school in Admasi, but did not do well enough on his exams to be permitted to enter sixth form. He returned to this village to teach in one of the middle schools.

"Of course young men of this age always know more about the nature of life and the world than all the other people in a village such as Kwim. His ideas about how life in Kwim could be improved were as numerous as the grains of rice in a pile the height of a tall man. Some of his thoughts were indeed reasonable and we used them to the advantage of the village. This, unfortunately, did little to improve his attitude. Instead, he became even more insufferable.

"In that same year a Jujuman from one of the Middle Tribes decided to settle near Kwim. The place that he came from is known in Sakra and even throughout West Africa for the quality and strength of its magic. Men from that tribe often become traveling wizards. They move from town to town, depending on the demand for their skills. Most of the people of this village believed that the power of the Wizard from the Middle Tribes was much greater than that of the Wizard we visited today.

"One market day this Wizard came to the market in search of certain substances he needed for his magic. The young man and several of his friends had also decided to walk through the market and make small talk with the sellers. As usual, the young man was explaining to anyone who would listen how the market could be improved.

"One of his companions sensing an opportunity to provide amusement for the group said, 'Over there is the Wizard from the Middle Tribes. If you know so much, explain how he is able to cause evil spells to fall upon people.'

"The young man replied, 'He has no power. His only strength is with the fools of this village. He can hurt no one unless they believe he is able to do so. I know that what he does is all trickery. His spells are harmless. He can do nothing to hurt me.'

"The young teacher's companions were shocked. They would not have said such things even in the privacy of their own compounds out of fear that the Wizard's magic would enable him to hear anything said in the village.

"One of them said, 'If what you say is true, then you will not be afraid to walk over to where the Wizard stands and tell him that he has no power over you.'

"The man who spoke had intended his remark only to cause the young teacher to stop talking about such a dangerous subject, not as an actual challenge. His companions were stunned when the young man said that he would do exactly as his friend suggested.

"He moved to the place where the Jujuman stood and said, 'You, Wizard, you are nothing more than an old fool. You have no power over anyone or anything. You take our money but for nothing because you can do nothing.'

"The Jujuman was silent for a moment, then spoke in a low but clear voice.

"He said, 'It will not be well with you,' then turned and left the market.

"The entire village did little for several days but wait in anticipation of the evil that they were certain would befall the young teacher. To call a jujuman a fool was the greatest possible insult. The implication of the word was that the man from the Middle Tribes was insane or had at the very least lost control of his mental faculties.

"But a week passed, then two, and three, and still nothing happened.

"This caused the Wizard to lose respect. Fewer people consulted with him. His food supply must have been running low. I began to think that he would soon have to leave or starve. The young teacher grew more and more boastful. Only now most of the people of the village listened with respect.

"During the fifth week after the events of the marketplace, in a time of heavy rains, the young teacher began to feel pain in his chest.

"In the beginning the pain was not severe. But the young teacher found that the memory of the Wizard's voice made sleep difficult and even on some nights impossible. His condition grew worse. He stopped eating and soon was unable to leave his bed for more than a few minutes without feeling faint.

"His friends and family began to insist that he visit the Wizard from the Middle Tribes to seek forgiveness and help. No one believed that any other jujuman in this part of Sakra would be able to prevail against the Wizard's curse. When his condition continued to deteriorate, the young teacher decided that he must see the Wizard. His friends carried him to within thirty yards of the old man's hut but were afraid to move closer. His weakness was so profound that he could no longer use his legs. It took him more than an hour to cover the short distance using his arms to pull himself over the rough ground.

"His reward for that effort was the taunts of the Wizard, 'Why have you come to this place? You who do not believe in juju. Go away, I cannot help you.'"

"The young teacher exhausted by his efforts to reach the Wizard's door burst into tears. He cried out, 'Please, please, I beg your forgiveness. I am sorry that I spoke as I did. I was a complete fool. I believe in your power. Please, please, forgive me. I will do whatever you say.'

"The Wizard answered, 'I will help you but not in this place. Because you insulted me in the market that also must be the place of your deliverance. Tell me more of your pain.'

"'My chest,' the young man cried, 'My chest hurts more than anything I have known in my life.'

"'Very well,' the Wizard replied, 'Tomorrow night, when darkness has come, be in the place where the insult occurred. I will remove the cause of your pain.'

"The next night it seemed as if the entire village gathered in the marketplace. The young man was carried by his friends to the spot where he had insulted the Wizard. The Wizard of course kept us all waiting. He appeared about eleven.

"Once there, he lit his pot of incense. It exploded into bright yellow and blue flame.

"Then looking upward, he spoke, 'Tell them, you fool, that my magic is powerful.'

"'Your magic is powerful,' the young teacher said in a near whisper.

"The Wizard turned his head slowly until his eyes met those of the afflicted man. For a moment he stared intently then suddenly screamed, 'Say it louder, so loud that even your ancestors might hear and know well what a fool has come from them.'

"The young man rose on one elbow and in a loud but pitiful voice cried out, 'I am a fool. Your magic is powerful.'

"Then he collapsed. The Wizard instructed two of the young teacher's friends to hold him upright.

"The Wizard took a razor blade from his bag and quickly made five vertical slices on the young teacher's chest. Then he placed his mouth on the cuts and sucked blood. The blood that he spat from his mouth into a flat pan contained small metal pellets.

"When he had finished the Wizard looked at the pan and said, 'These pieces of metal were the cause of the pain in your chest. Now you are cured. Your chest will pain you no more. Never, never again make light of the power of juju.'

"The young man fell to the ground. The Wizard quickly repacked his equipment and moved away in the direction of his hut.

"By the time I reached the place where the young teacher had collapsed, his eyes were glazed. They saw nothing. His breath was rapid and shallow. His skin was not just warm but hot and dry. His pulse was strong but very, very fast. We put him into a lorry. I accompanied the driver to the hospital in Mbordo. He was dead long before we reached there. The official record listed the cause of death as pneumonia. Of course, no one in this village gave any credit to that report."

"My God," Alice commented, "that was it? That was all? Couldn't that Wizard be punished or was everyone too afraid? I hope he is not still here."

"Wait, wait," Chief Kanata replied gently, "I shall answer your question in good time, but let me continue the story in its natural order.

"The next day I returned to Kwim with the body of the young teacher. The anger of the village was indeed great. The young man had been arrogant. But no one could see any good purpose in his death. I am sure that the Wizard never had any intentions of killing the young teacher. However, by his actions the man was now dead. The people of this village, led by several of the elders, made plans to drive the Wizard out of Kwim. (I was not consulted because they feared I would not approve of any plans that might lead to violence. They need not have worried.)

"Shortly before noon, men surrounded the Wizard's hut. Members of the family of the dead man entered the hut and dragged the Wizard out. They threw him on the ground and screamed insults. One man found the ceremonial pot that he had used in the market place. They put the pot over the Wizard's head and made him walk in front of them toward the village.

"Within minutes, it seemed as if the everyone was following him. Children would run up and throw sticks and stones. Their parents shouted curses and spat. They took him to the compound of the dead man's family. The mother of the young teacher began to scream when she saw the Wizard coming. She tried to throw a pot of boiling water on his head. I thank God that someone was able to stop her. The mood of the others became even more intense. It was an ugly thing. The Wizard seemed to be trying to shrink back to within himself to avoid the pain inflicted by the pebbles and sticks thrown by the children. When I saw the older ones fingering bigger rocks, I knew that I must intervene. I moved through the crowd to where he stood. When he recognized me a little of the fear left his face. I grabbed his shirt roughly and twisted it so that it wound tight about his neck. He gasped but did not complain.

"I half pulled, half dragged him toward a trail on the northern edge of the village.

"In the loudest voice that I could find I shouted, 'This is the trail to the north. Go back to the place from which you came. We have no use for your evil magic in this village. Your power in this place is gone, finished forever. Destroyed by your own evil deeds. Never, never pass this way again.'

"He started running down that trail as rapidly as someone of his age could move. Several of the men wanted to follow the Wizard in order to further punish him. I managed to prevent that. I saw no good reason for two deaths. One had been more than I cared for. I did send two men that I had great faith in to follow the Wizard in order to be sure that he did not return. Later that night they told me that he did not stop until he collapsed from exhaustion at a distance of no less than twenty miles from this place. I was not at all unhappy to see the last of that man. A bad wizard brings only trouble."

"I can certainly understand that," Alice said. "But tell me, what do you really think killed that young teacher?"

"A combination of pride and fear," Chief Kanata replied. "That would be from your American scientific point of view the correct answer, would it not?"

"Yes," Alice mused, "the irreversible mental involvement syndrome."

"Pardon me," the Chief replied, "I don't understand what you just said."

"I'm sorry," Alice said, "just something I studied in a psychology course long ago. The body reacts to a frightening situation by increasing the flow of adrenaline and other stimulants into the blood stream. The rate of heart beat increases. The body is ready for action. An excellent preparation if one has to fight a lion or run. Unfortunately, if there is no lion to fight or no place to run, the mind receives signals from the body only that something is very wrong. Confusion results and even more fright. That feeling builds to terror. The body pumps more adrenaline, the heart beats even faster. The process accelerates until the life support systems of the body self-destruct and the individual dies."

Very interesting," the Chief remarked, "but why not just say that the Wizard was responsible. The young teacher would have liked your explanation. He would have found it quite satisfactory, until he became involved with that Wizard. But as I said earlier, we are all Africans. We cannot ignore what we learned from our elders. If we do the results can be very bad."

"Even fatal," Alice commented. "I am quite happy that your Wizard from the Middle Belt is no longer here. I don't think I would want him to do anything for me."

"Neither would I," the Chief replied. "Would you care for another beer?"

"Yes, thank-you," Alice replied.

She took a sip of beer the Chief had poured for her then said, "Last night you mentioned that you have three children. I am sure they are all as nice as Enata."

"They are two boys and Enata," the Chief explained. "My youngest boy, Joshua, is studying engineering in America at River State University."

"That is an excellent university," Alice commented, then asked, "When will he return to Sakra?"

"In less than two years time he will complete his first course, but I do not know if he will then return. From his letters I can tell that he is not unhappy in your country. My oldest son, Joseph, is in the army. He grew tired of university and decided to try the soldier's life. At first I was quite disappointed, but now I must admit that he has done well with it. The government even selected him to attend military college in England, and he now holds the rank of Major. But I worry about what the future holds for him. His mother was Ave. If trouble comes, the decisions that he may be forced to make will indeed be painful. He is loyal, even more than loyal to the nation, but if he has to choose it will not be an easy matter for him to turn against his mother's people."

"Yes, I think that I can understand," Alice replied hesitantly. "We can hope that choice will never have to be made."

"Yes, if God is with us perhaps not," the Chief continued. "But that worry is never far from my door. I am a Bordo Chief, but many Aves live here and also we have quite a number of people from the North. I can't imagine how Kwim would survive if trouble comes. I can only hope that we will be simply left alone."

Alice, ever mindful of the Peace Corps sanction against discussing the politics of Sakra, replied, "Yes, I am certain that it is a very difficult problem. Of course, I know little of these troubles."

The Chief chuckled and said, "Of course, Mrs. Manati, officially you know nothing of our problems here in Sakra. Jeff has explained why you Peace Corps people do not discuss politics with the 'natives.' But perhaps when your time as a Peace Corps person is almost complete, you will revisit this village and do us the honor of sharing your wisdom with us concerning how we might deal with these problems."

"It is true," Alice said, "that I have lived many years and perhaps know something of life. But, that was in a different place. What I know might be useful in that place, but of course few people there would care to listen to someone as old as I. In this land, I am but a small child. I did not even know Sakra had any serious problems until a few weeks ago. You know, in the few months that I have been in this country, people have been kind to me whether they were Kroban or Ave or Atan or Bordo. It is difficult for me to understand how they can be unkind to each other."

Chief Kanata sat quietly for perhaps a full minute, then spoke slowly.

"Enata told us that you knew all things about mathematics. She did not also tell me that you have the true wisdom of the old. Even when you speak of having no knowledge, you demonstrate wisdom. It is so completely true that were we all wise enough to bury the past in history books and treat our fellow countrymen as well as we treat strangers there would be no trouble. Did you know that less than eighty years ago Ave and Atan were at war? A crucial battle was fought in the hills around Mbordo. The Atan were the most powerful tribe in all of West Africa. Their lands stretched far beyond the borders of Sakra to the east. In that war Bordo and Ave fought as brothers. My grandfather died in that battle. Ave and Bordo were victorious, but it cost the lives of almost half the men of this village. That day brought to an end the westward expansion of the Atan nation. They have never forgiven the Bordo people for aiding the Aves in that battle. In fact, the Atan place most of the blame for their loss on the wizards of the Bordo villages who made much magic in preparation for that battle. In Africa, the past is never forgotten and never forgiven. That same battle has been fought a thousand times over in every Atan, Ave and Bordo village. But enough, it is almost time for the evening meal."

The next morning, Chief Kanata took Alice, Jeff and Enata on a tour of the schools of Kwim, which numbered five, three primary and two middle. Alice was amazed at the beauty and order of school compounds. Each schoolyard was a perfect rectangle enclosed by a dark green hedge perfectly trimmed. The patterns created by trees, shrubs, and flowers growing within the hedges varied by school but all were pleasing to the eye. As they walked toward the middle school where Jeff had his experimental garden, Alice remarked, "I really find the beauty of school grounds remarkable. How do they manage to create such beautiful places?"

"With a great deal of student labor," Jeff commented. "These compounds are beautiful, but I sometimes wonder if the students' hard work would not be better spent in the classroom or even on the farm."

"Perhaps," Chief Kanata replied, "but to create something of beauty is its own reward. The school buildings themselves are usually something less than beautiful, but in our school yards we have something that requires little money, only labor. These schools were not constructed by the government. The materials are humble. Only mud brick for the walls. The local cocoa buying board was able to provide money for the purchase of tin for the roofs. But all of the construction work was done by the people of this village. They would be very unhappy if the students did not maintain their yards well."

The area in front of the middle school they now approached was not as well attended as those of the primary schools.

The Chief commented, "The older the students become, the less willing they are to work on their school compounds. Also, the experimental farm requires much of the time set aside for work outside the classroom."

Alice smiled a bit as she listened to Jeff explain the purpose of the garden behind the middle school. More than a half the quarter acre plot was bare. The reason, Jeff said, was that cabbage, lettuce and okra seeds had been planted too deeply. The teacher who had supervised the student workers had not known what 1/4 inch deep meant in any practical sense. He had simply told the students to plant the seed at the same depth as he had seen Jeff instruct the students to plant corn seed.

Jeff continued to talk about the problems that he had with students and teachers following directions, with insects, with local plant diseases, and on and on for what seemed to Alice to be a very long time considering the small size of the plot. When Jeff began to explain how seed depth, rainfall, and resistance to wind damage were interrelated, Alice could no longer stifle her yawns.

"Jeff, I think Alice is growing tired of standing in this hot sun," Enata said politely. "Perhaps we should return to the compound for a rest before we start for Mbordo. We do all have to teach tomorrow."

Jeff shook his head slightly and smiled as he said, "I am sorry. I get so worked up about this project that I forget it is not quite as interesting to everyone else as it is to me."

"That's quite all right," Alice answered. "It is interesting and important. I wish I could help in some way, but I can't even raise flowers."

They returned to Chief Kanata's compound, rested awhile, then had lunch. At two, they boarded the lorry that would take them to the Mbordo junction. They reached the junction at four. Alice and Enata stood in the shade about twenty feet away from the right side of the road. Jeff stationed himself next to the road on the left side in order to get the attention of any traffic moving in the direction of Mbordo. He spotted a Puegot slowing to make the turn from the main road. Mr. Oganda looked straight ahead as he passed Jeff but slowed to a halt as he past Alice and Enata. He jumped out and opened the door for Alice and Enata.

"Get in quickly," he said. "I don't like to stop here. It seems there are people in this area who don't like those of us from the North.

"Mr. Johnson, come quickly," he called back to Jeff.

"Has something happened here?" Alice asked.

"Sometimes they throw rocks as I go by," Mr. Oganda replied. "I don't know what would happen if I stopped by myself."

As Jeff slipped into the front seat, Alice noticed several people gathering in the yard of one of the houses near the car. They seemed to be picking up something but did nothing more. One man was obviously pointing out the Obronies in the car.

"He's probably run over a lot of chickens and a few goats here," Jeff whispered to Alice once the car was in motion.

CHAPTER 7
Easter in Mbordo

The third term ended the Wednesday before Easter. Alice had been told by both Americans and Sakraians that Easter in Mbordo was special. She had not fully understood the meaning of 'special' until the afternoon of Good Friday when she went into Mbordo with the Harrises to buy a few things in the market. Lorries that she had never seen before were parked along Mbordo's main street. Three government transport buses, normally used only between the larger cities of Sakra, were parked in front of a middle school. Several taxis from other cities passed as Alice, Beth, and Ian walked toward the market. When Alice had finished her shopping, she could not resist the impulse to catch a cab back to the University-College. She asked the driver why he had come to Mbordo.

He replied, "Easter here very good. I was small boy in this place. My family is here. I come back every Easter. I bring others from Nkra. If anyone needs taxi here, I take them."

That evening, by hand courier, senior members of the University-College staff (everyone with a college degree) received invitations to a Sunday afternoon cocktail party.

Saturday morning Alice awoke to the sound of what she thought might be firecrackers or gunfire. For a moment, she wondered if some tribal conflict between the Kroban, Atan and Ave had gotten out of hand but then remembered that all but the Bordo students had left Mbordo for the Easter break. Then she heard banging on her door.

Jason's familiar voice called, "Alice, come on! You'll miss the best weekend of the year."

"Just a minute," she replied as she got up and slipped on a robe.

Jason, Karen, and Gilbert Adwin, the art teacher, were waiting at the door.

"Come in," Alice said, "and have a cup of tea."

"No thanks," Jason replied, "but if you have a cold beer, that would do just fine."

"Beer?" Alice said grimacing. "It's only eight o'clock."

"It's Easter, Mrs. Manati," Jason replied. "Tea this late in the day would turn my stomach."

"Karen?" Alice asked in a slightly worried tone.

"Beer for me too," Karen replied. "It really is Easter in Mbordo. But I will fix tea for you while you are getting dressed."

"And what about you, Gil?" Alice questioned.

"If it does not cause you too much embarrassment," Gil said smiling broadly, "beer would also be best for me."

Alice was still shaking her head in disbelief as she placed two bottles of beer on the table.

"I don't care if it is Easter," she said, "at eight in the morning I still drink tea."

By the time Karen finished brewing the tea, Alice was dressed.

"What in heaven's name is all that noise? Firecrackers?" Alice asked Gil.

"Those are guns," Gil replied. "But don't worry. They are only being used to celebrate Easter. Those guns are very old. Left over from World War I or maybe before. They have to be reloaded after every shot. Today, of course, they are being fired with only the blasting charge."

"Not exactly your latest in weapons," Alice mused.

"No" Gil continued, "but they are very accurate. I have seen the hunters shoot small snakes in very tall trees."

"How many people do you think are in Mbordo this weekend?" Alice asked.

"Many," Gil replied conclusively, "it is very crowded. In my own small house we have ten visitors. Maybe the town has altogether four times its usual number."

Jason mumbled, "Sixty thousand people! My God, where do they stay?"

"Everywhere," Gil said almost laughing. "On the couch, under the couch, behind the couch. The floor of my house is full. Nowhere even to step. That is why I left. No more room for me."

When they had finished the two bottles of beer, Jason suggested that they go into the village. They caught a ride on one of the many lorries that now seemed to be continuously moving through all parts of Mbordo. The driver charged them nothing for the ride since he was a brother (distant cousin) of Gil's and staying at his house for the weekend. Once down from the lorry near the center of Mbordo, they found even the palm wine bars crowded. Some friends of Gil made room for them in Tango's bar. Although Alice had heard much of it, she had never sampled Tango's special. It was a drink that would, according to Tango, cure baldness, infertility, general tiredness, and even old age (or at least make you forget you were old for a little while).

Alice decided that one her age could ill afford to pass up such an opportunity. They ordered four shots. Alice choked on her first sip.

"Hold your breath as you drink," Karen advised.

She followed that guidance and was after many small sips finally able to finish her Tango's special. The drink left a pleasant sensation in her mouth and throat. Even her chest and stomach began to feel warm.

"This is ridiculous," she said, "I feel good, really good."

"Maybe even younger?" Jason asked. "Unfortunately it won't last unless you repeat the treatment every fifteen minutes."

Gil's friends had been discussing, in Bordo, some aspects of life in the capital city Nkra. When they turned again to speak with Gil, he introduced them to Jason, Karen and Alice.

They were Mr. Ungar, a teacher in a secondary school in the capital city; Mr. Bedun, the manager of a department store, also in Nkra; Mr. Andre, a Ministry of Health official assigned to the Pandu region; and Mr. Smith, a captain in the army of

Sakra. ('Smith' was not a common Bordo name but one of the Captain's great grandfathers had been English.) Their light banter about the past revealed that they and Gil had all attended the same middle school in Mbordo in the fifties.

An intended jest turned their conversation to serious matters.

Mr. Ungar had said to Mr. Bedun, "I was in your store last week. The price of everything has gone up. Some things are double from not a fortnight ago. I can no longer even afford batteries for my flashlight. Some night I will be bitten by a snake and have to go to one of Andre's hospitals. I will then be very poor, but you and Andre will be wealthy."

"What wonderful dreams you have for me," Mr. Bedun replied. "If I could keep all of the money that comes to the store and not have to pay the suppliers, and not have to dash all of the government officials who approve my import quotas, then I would be wealthy. But for a short time only. Because whatever money I would have would soon be worth little if prices keep going up. There seems no end to it. My clerks complain constantly that they cannot live on what I pay them, even though I doubled their wages in less than six months. The only prices that remain low are on those items controlled by the government such as rice and canned milk."

"It is good that the prices of a few important goods are low," Mr. Andre commented, "but you will never find any milk or rice in the large stores. Only the market mammies have these items, and they will only sell at three or four times the controlled price."

"That is quite true," Mr. Bedun said sadly. "The last time we got a shipment of those small cans of milk, I limited the number that each person could purchase to three. The mammies just sent their fourteen children to buy two or three each over and over again. Forty cases of milk did not even last one full day."

"These prices are not good for anyone," Mr. Andre said. "Only a year ago, my salary was quite all right. My family and I could live decently. Now I instruct my wife to take care in what she purchases or the money is finished before the end of the month."

"You think that matters are difficult in the Ministry of Health," Gil's friend, Mr. Ungar from Nkra, said. "Consider the plight of the poor teacher. Our salary was never sufficient to meet the needs of a family. Now it is much too expensive to live in Nkra but we are paid the same as last year. My three rooms, less than one-third of a full house, eats half my salary. We can no longer afford any good food. If prices continue to go up, I will be forced to send my wife and children back to their village where at least they will be able to farm and have something to eat."

"If you find life difficult, my friend," Mr. Bedun addressed Mr. Ungar, "think of the man who must feed himself and perhaps a family by day labor in our capital city. Five years ago the six or eight shillings that he earned for a day's work would pay for a room, lorry fare to get to work, gari, rice, milk and perhaps even a little meat. He might even have enough left to have apetishe or palm wine in the evening and still save a shilling or two to send to his family. Now perhaps, if he is fortunate, he makes ten shillings per day, but just his room and food will cost more. And God help him if he has to pay lorry fare to get to his place of work."

"And all that is true only if he is one of the lucky ones to have any type of job at all," Captain Smith added. "If you do not have work in Nkra, the choice is only between starvation and leaving. In the last few months we have been finding the remains of some of those unfortunates along the roads. They start too late and starvation overtakes them before they are able to reach their home villages."

"What a horrible thing," Alice said without thought, "to starve to death, alone without friend or family, but with food available in your own village, if only you could somehow make it that far."

"The government should do something," Gil said angrily. "People should not be allowed to die like that."

"The government will do nothing," the Captain said in a near whisper. "The big men are too busy with their great projects to worry about the small ones."

Gil asked, "How does the army fare? Is your salary sufficient?"

Captain Smith replied, "Most of our food is provided directly from government stores. We are not much affected by changes in price. Our wages are not what they should be, of course, but in that our complaints are all the same."

Alice's seat was on the side of the table facing the entrance of the bar. Both she and Gil noted the entrance of a short young man in a bright Kente cloth. Alice recognized him as a student at the University-College, who was active in student government.

She noticed that Gil moved the first finger of his right hand to his eye. Then he moved his hand to a part of his own cloth.

He whispered to Alice, "That student is suspected of being an agent of the 'Savior.' I told the others to watch carefully using the symbols on my cloth."

The table was silent for a moment then Captain Smith said, "But let us talk of happy things. We came this week to celebrate Easter and celebrate we will. Tango, bring eight more bottles of beer!"

By eleven Alice was famished. She was confused by her hunger until she remembered that she had skipped breakfast. Even Tango's special was no substitute for food. Alice, Jason and Karen excused themselves to look for something to eat. Gil remained with his friends.

They walked past the area where bamboo shelters had been erected to shade dignitaries invited to watch the dancing and drumming scheduled for the afternoon.

After lunch they returned for the performances. There were so many 'dignitaries' that most seats were already taken. Alice, of course, was provided with a chair just behind the Mbordohene. Jason and Karen found standing room near the edge of one of the shelters with Jeff and Enata. Jeff had invited Derrick to come with them, but he had excused himself, saying that he had work to do at the University-College.

"Probably in Whitland's library," Jeff commented.

"Jealous?" Enata responded.

The performances were long, very long. By three-thirty Alice was quite fatigued and excused herself to return to her bungalow.

That evening, Alice picked out her nicest dress. Gilbert had explained that everyone who attended the Saturday night Easter Dance would wear their finest clothing. Jason, Karen, Jeff, Enata, Gilbert and Alice planned to attend the dance together. Alice was not really surprised when a taxi arrived at her door at eight-thirty. The way people were dressed did surprise her. She had to fight an inclination to apologize for her attractive but plain white, knee-length dress. Both Karen and Enata wore floor length gowns sewn from beautifully patterned West African Cloth. She had difficulty recognizing Jeff in long trousers and bright tie. Gilbert wore a conservative but well tailored black suit with black tie. Only Jason looked his normal self in Bermuda shorts, open shirt, and sandals.

Alice's smile when she saw Jason getting out of the car caused Karen to comment, "Incorrigible, isn't he?

The price of admission to the dance was one pound per couple. Alice was amazed at the manner in which the half finished community center had been transformed into a very good replica of a quality dance hall. A bandstand had been constructed at one end. The unfinished concrete block walls had been hidden by carefully arranged palm branches and colored paper. The tables, which had been placed around the area reserved for dancing, were covered with white tablecloths. A bouquet of flowers was the centerpiece for each table. Everyone present (with the exception of Jason) was immaculately dressed. Men wore a suit and tie or the traditional Kente cloth. The women generally wore long skirts with fitted tops. Alice was thankful that she had at least picked the best of what she had to wear.

They found Beth, Ian, the Vice-Chancellor and his wife, and Mr. Pordoe and his wife at a table that still had empty seats. After Alice was comfortably settled, she surveyed other parts of the community center and noted that most of the University-College staff had come to the dance. With the exception of the Whitlands, all of the American professors from River State and their wives were there. She noticed the absence of both Derrick and Betty.

"Where is Derrick?" Alice quietly asked Jason.

"Said he had to do some important research," Jason replied.

"I hope not in Mr. Whitland's library," Alice whispered.

"I am afraid so," Jason said. "I believe that Mr. Whitland is at a special AID conference in Nkra during the Easter break."

The band arrived. To Alice's surprise, they were not only good, but also played a remarkable range of music: highlife, American rock, soul, waltzes, and some African music that Alice found difficult to classify but nevertheless pleasing to her ear. After about thirty minutes of attempting to be polite, she realized that she would have to start refusing invitations to dance or collapse. At the end of the band's first set, most of those sitting at the table went off to the bathrooms or to buy beer.

"It is really remarkable," Jason commented a bit sarcastically, "every Easter Mbordo is transformed from a rural village into a center of art, culture, and good social life."

"This time is very nice for those of us who live here," Gil responded. "We have a small opportunity to taste of the big city life."

"Yes," Mr. Pordoe continued, "for a few days we sample the life of the city without having to deal with the cities' problems."

"People do wear beautiful clothes," Karen said, "and that band is excellent."

"Only the very best," Gil explained. "This band is one of the most famous in Sakra. We have to pay them much money to convince them to make this trip."

"More than £100, I was told," Pordoe commented.

The other staff members returned with a generous supply of beer. The band also returned and conversation became impossible except in snatches between numbers.

In time, with the free flow of beer at the table, trips to the bathrooms became increasingly necessary. When Ian returned from just such a journey, Beth inquired as to the general condition of the rooms.

"A foot high and rising," was the answer Alice overheard.

Beth asked, "You are exaggerating aren't you?"

"Go and see for yourself," Ian replied, "but don't let your dress fall below your knees."

"My God," Beth exclaimed, "how disgusting. But I really must go.

"Excuse me," she said crisply as she left.

Alice nudged Karen and whispered, "I am not sure that I want to know, but what did Ian mean by 'a foot high and rising'? He wasn't really talking about the bathrooms was he?"

"There are no real bathrooms, just rooms," Karen replied.

"No bathrooms!" Alice exclaimed. "Where are all of these people going?"

"Well," Jeff interrupted, "the Community Center is not yet complete. One part that is not done are the sanitary facilities. You see those two rooms over there. They have been designated temporary urinals, one for the men and one for the women."

"You mean those rooms over there around where the floors look wet?" Alice asked.

"Correct, absolutely correct," Jeff replied. "Your insight is improving by the moment."

"At least they could drill a hole in the floor," Beth remarked dryly as she returned. "I thought you were joking about a foot high and rising."

"I take it then," Ian said, "that the ladies room is in no better condition than the men's."

"That's not so bad for men, but what in hell's name do we do?" Alice asked Karen quietly.

"I'll explain," Karen said.

She moved closer to Alice and whispered into her ear.

"You really do it like that?" Alice asked in a disbelieving tone.

Karen shrugged, "It's the only way on a trip or in a situation like this."

"I am not sure that I can," Alice replied. "My bones are not as limber as they used to be, but I will try."

Alice was a little pale when she returned to the table.

"Is everything all right?" Karen asked.

"As far as I can tell," Alice replied with a sigh, "but my feeling of elegance has almost disappeared."

However, Alice found that a few sips of beer quickly pushed thoughts of her trip to the 'ladies room' to the back of her mind.

The band stopped playing at three. Gil decided to walk to his house, which was near the community center. The others saw Alice home by taxi after she had declined an invitation to stop by the boys' house for further drink and conversation.

The two couples returned to the boys' abode. Derrick was home and still awake when they arrived.

"I am going to church tomorrow," Jeff announced.

"Congratulations," Derrick said without thinking, "sin tonight, saved tomorrow."

"If anyone needs to follow that advice," Jason commented, "it would be you, Derrick. How did your evening of research turn out?"

"Quite well," was the only answer that Derrick could manage.

"Perhaps we should all go to church tomorrow," Karen said.

"No, thank-you," Enata replied emphatically. "Jeff is attending church because one of the middle school students who works on his project is to be confirmed, and he asked Jeff to be there. Jeff is afraid that if he doesn't go, the boy will not work for him anymore.

"Of course," Enata continued with a giggle, "a little religious experience will certainly do Jeff no harm."

"What denomination?" Karen asked.

"I don't know." Jeff answered. "In fact all I really do know is that it is the church that you come to when you follow the path behind the house for about three hundred yards."

"What time do services commence?" Derrick inquired.

"The boy said to be there at nine o'clock," Jeff answered.

"Try not to make too much noise as you leave the house," Enata said.

Jeff set his alarm for eight the next morning.

When it sounded, Enata did not even turn over. Two cups of very strong coffee brought Jeff only half awake. By the time he reached the old church, it was already near full. He was quickly ushered to one of the seats near the front. The service began with a ten-minute invocation followed by three hymns. Next came an altar collection conducted by day-names. In Sakra many people do not know the actual date of their birth but everyone knows the day of the week on which he or she was born. The day of the week actually becomes a part of the formal name given to the child. There are seven day-names for boys and seven for girls. Kofi (Friday) and Kwame (Saturday) were the most popular. (Jeff had often wondered if women actually waited for those days to give birth.) President Agyenkwa, for example, was born on Friday and was known as Kofi before he became the 'Savior.' Jeff had decided rather arbitrarily that he had been born on Friday also, and adopted the name 'Kofi' for those occasions when he needed a day-name. The minister used day-names to call people forward to make their contributions. He began with the Kwasis and Ammas, men and women born on Sunday, and proceeded through the week. When the Kofis and Afuas were called, Jeff went forward with the others who were born on Friday and placed a ten shilling note in one of the plates on the alter. He noticed that after each day-name group made its contribution, the ushers would quickly dump all of the money into a bucket so that the plates were again empty when the next group was called. The buckets of money were immediately moved to a group of men sitting in one corner of the church. Each bucket was given to a different man, who began counting. It seemed a curious procedure, but Jeff decided that it was perhaps some well-thought-out theft prevention technique.

Five children were confirmed. The minister was very, very careful about the process. When the ceremony was over, Jeff noted mentally that those children were more confirmed than any he had ever known.

After that part of the service, the minister moved down in front of the pulpit. He clasped his hands behind his back and bent slightly forward. Then he raised his head and looked slowly around the congregation. When he spoke his words came slowly in a loud, but deep and sorrowful tone. He would speak first in Bordo then English to be sure that no one present missed the meaning of his words.

"Brethren," he cried, "we have counted the offering. Those of you who were born on Tuesday gave less than any other day. I too was born on Tuesday. I stand before you in shame that we should do so poorly before the Lord. But all is not lost. We will give you an opportunity to clear the good names of Kwabene and Abena. The plates lie empty on the rail. Those born on Tuesday come forward and make Jesus happy."

The minister himself led the way by dropping a five pound note in the most conspicuous plate. As the other worshipers born on Tuesday moved toward the front, Jeff was congratulating himself on the choice of the day-name Kofi. He reasoned that since those with Friday and Saturday day-names were more numerous their contributions had been larger.

The Tuesday people returned to their seats, the plates again were emptied and the money turned over to the men in the corner. The minister returned to the pulpit and led the congregation in a hymn. Near the end of the hymn, one of the men from the corner delivered a note to the minister. He glanced at the paper and smiled slightly. When the hymn was completed the minister again came down from the pulpit.

His sudden, joyful shout startled Jeff who had been close to sleep.

"Praise be to God Almighty," he cried out, "a wonderful thing has happened in this very place. Those born on Tuesday are no longer the last in giving. Nor are they next to last, not even middle. No, no my fellow Christians by the grace of God and his Son Jesus Christ they are now . . . . But wait you know that it is written, 'The last shall be . . . first.' Oh praise God, praise God, it is now true, those born on Tuesday were last and now they are first. They have given more than any other day-name, hallelujah, praise be to God."

"However," the minister continued with a dramatic change in tone and expression, "it gives me very great sorrow to announce that those born on Thursday are now the weakest before God in their contributions to his divine work. Brethren, my own mother was born on Thursday. It brings me the greatest of sadnesses that this blessed day should be so disgraced. Think of all the mothers born on Thursday. The plates are empty, come forward and praise the Lord. In honor of my mother let me be the first to contribute with those born on Thursday."

Once again the minister led the way with a five pound note. A long prayer gave the money counters time to learn that those born on Thursday were no longer in last place. That honor went next to those born on Wednesday. The minister seemed to have a relative or beloved friend born on every day of the week, and it was costing him plenty, Jeff thought, unless he was using the same five pound note over and over again. When the Kofis and Afuas dropped to last place Jeff dutifully went forward and contributed his last two shilling piece. Those born on Saturday were eventually declared the champion givers. Jeff had half expected a loud cheer to greet the announcement, but the congregation seemed too exhausted to take much note of anything being said.

The minister's sermon divided itself neatly into two parts. The first praised God's wisdom and mercy in having sent his Son to earth to die so that our sins might be forgiven. The second part exhorted those who visited Mbordo only at Easter to help their village (and especially this particular church in their village) during the rest of the year. The service was over by twelve-thirty. Jeff half walked and half stumbled back to the house. Once there he had a bowl of soup, half a sandwich and collapsed into a deep sleep on the living room couch.

Enata woke him at two-thirty to prepare for the cocktail party. The affair was in the dining area of the University-College. The two couples and Alice arrived at the same time. Alice was offered a place at the speakers' table by one of the ushers. Jason whispered that she should politely refuse and instead sit with them off to one side of the room. She asked why. Jason indicated that the reason would become apparent. A small printed program listed ten people scheduled to speak. Jeff was not at all sure that he could stand even one more sentence, but with Enata at his side he decided to persevere at least as long as beer was available.

The speakers were divided evenly; five who resided in Mbordo year round, and five who had returned for Easter. The Mbordohene spoke first. He implored those here only for the Easter celebration not to abandon interest in the village once they returned to the cities of Sakra. After twenty minutes, he turned the microphone over to a gentleman who was the first vice president of the National Bank of Sakra.

The first vice president began, "Mbordo is a wonderful place, which I dearly love but . . . ." and then proceeded to list all of the things that he thought should have been available in order that those coming to Mbordo for Easter might be able to make the visit without undue suffering. Cold beer and proper urinals in the community center were high on his list.

When the banker had finished, Alice nudged Karen and said, "I definitely agree with the cold beer and bathrooms."

The next speaker was an old man who was brief and blunt.

He said, "If you want things to be better here when you come to drink our beer and palm wine, then take an interest all year round. If you wish to see these improvements that you are suggesting, give us the money now and when you come next year these things will be done."

The fourth speaker's presentation (another nonresident) was much the same as that of the banker. By the time he sat down, no one in the audience was listening. Private conversations were only briefly interrupted by the applause started by those at the head table at the end of each speaker's remarks.

"Thank-you for keeping me away from the head table," Alice shouted at Jason. "Why don't they just stop?"

"What counts," Jason replied, "is not whether anybody hears what you have to say, but that you are important enough to have been allowed to speak."

The last speaker finished at four-thirty, the beer finished at five, and that ended not only the cocktail party but the Easter festivities as well.

On Monday, Jason and Karen started for Pandu, Jeff and Enata returned to Kwim, and Derrick left for Nkra. Alice was more than satisfied to remain in Mbordo for a week of rest. Very odd she thought, when she reflected on some of her more difficult moments earlier in that year, that she actually was looking forward to having time to read and listen to her records.

****

Derrick had decided on a few days in Nkra. The Ministry of Education provided a small hostel in Nkra at a rate of six shillings per night for teachers to use when visiting the capital city. Each sleeping room contained eight to ten sets of bunk beds and thousands of mosquitoes. Musa, the cook and manager, prepared the finest scrambled eggs and bacon in all of Sakra.

Of the volunteers stationed in Mbordo, Derrick was the most frequent visitor to Nkra. He and Musa had become friends. On some weekend trips, he and Musa had been the only occupants of the hostel. Derrick had come to realize that Musa was also very much a foreigner in Nkra, struggling to adjust and survive. Musa listened with much sympathy to Derrick's problems. But when Musa spoke of the quality of his own life, Derrick knew that much of what he said about his own problems must have sounded to Musa like the prattling of a spoiled, small boy.

Musa spoke of a family left behind in the North that, if God were merciful, he would see every three or four years. He spoke of returning to them one day with enough money to open a little chop house. He spoke of deciding to walk the eight miles from the newcomers' village on the outskirts of Nkra, both morning and evening, because the cost of the lorry had gone up by four times.

He did not speak often of such things. Musa considered himself a fortunate man. Many of his friends who had held jobs as laborers could now find work only as handlers of nightsoil. Others had started the long journey back to their home villages to the North. Derrick had been able to help Musa with the transportation problem. He found an old bicycle in Mbordo and with a few repairs made it rideable. He had given it to Musa.

Musa was always a willing listener, although he often had trouble understanding why Derrick did not simply take the obvious action needed to solve a given problem. One common theme of not just Derrick but others who stayed at the hostel was the problem of unruly students in the classroom. Musa could not understand how anyone in a teacher's exalted position could have problems like that, but he still tried to listen with sympathy. Once Musa became disgusted and had offered Derrick the following advice.

"These boys very lucky to be in school," he said. "My children no have good chance like that. If they be bad, beat them. If they still bad, beat more. If they no learn, send them away. Others come who want learn. If you don't beat, I go for Mbordo and beat for you."

The hostel was crowded when Derrick arrived Monday afternoon. It was not until Tuesday after lunch, when most of the other volunteers had either gone shopping or off to the beach, that Derrick found himself alone, sitting on the porch of the hostel. Musa finished washing the dishes from the noon meal and wandered out.

"Good afternoon, sir," he said politely.

"Hello, Mr. Musa, sir," Derrick said jokingly. "How are things in Nkra?"

"No be good," Musa said. "Money weak. Buy little chop. Everything cost too much. Small gari now be three pence. My room up one pound each month. Somebody sleep there now when I go work. That my chop money."

"So bad that you must share your bed," Derrick replied.

"Much, much bad," Musa commented, "but my friend. No see you long time. What you do?"

"Getting myself into trouble, bad trouble," Derrick responded.

"Your bad trouble easy for me," Musa said with a broad smile. "Me fix easy. What your problem?"

"It is difficult," Derrick said with a slight frown. "Please be sure to mention it to no one."

"Sir," Musa straightened his back as he admonished Derrick, "I no go speak about such things, even to wife if she be here."

"I am sorry," Derrick replied, "I already knew that. There is an American professor, very big man at the University-College. His wife is some years younger than he is."

"I understand now," Musa interrupted. "Professor a little old. Not make wife happy enough. You make wife happy. You have good time. She have good time. That no problem."

"Dammit Musa," Derrick thought, "you have such a wonderful way of simplifying problems."

"This situation is a bit difficult," Derrick continued. "This woman is becoming very bold. She wants to go to the bed even a few minutes before her husband is to return. It is almost as if she wishes her husband to find out."

"That not big problem," Musa interrupted again. "In this place if her husband find out, he not get very upset. Only since you Obroni, he make you pay much money for damage."

"Unfortunately," Derrick responded, "Americans do not handle this type of problem in such a civilized manner, at least from what little I know of them. I have heard her husband has a gun and is the type who might well use it."

"He crazy person," Musa said. "Nobody shoot somebody because of woman. What good that do? If he shoot woman, no man have her. If he shoot you, he go to jail and no have woman. If he shoot self, him dead. No good in that. African way better. Husband get both money and woman."

Derrick would have laughed if not for the serious tone in which Musa had spoken.

Instead he replied, "I believe that you are right. African way better. Unfortunately I do not believe that the man I speak of will agree."

Musa moved closer to where Derrick sat and said quietly, "My good friend, if I you, I no see this woman again. Plenty women here. I find you one. To be shot maybe dead for such a thing is a waste of life. No good for such a thing to happen because of woman."

"I know what you say is true," Derrick said sadly, "but it is difficult for me, very difficult."

"Ayee," Musa said with a slight smirk, "you no tell me everything. You not just have good time with woman. You like too much."

Derrick nodded his head and said nothing.

Musa shrugged and said, "My advice very good for most men, but maybe not for you. Such problems are inside. Musa cannot help. I go clean sleeping rooms now."

Derrick sat alone after Musa left. Musa's advice had been good. What he was now doing made little sense. At first he thought that Betty's need for sex was all that was involved. Now he suspected that her motives were more complex or at the very least confused. Upon reflection, he began to realize that very little of what had happened between them had been simply a matter of chance. That first time she had known that Whitland would be away for the evening. It was Betty, not her husband, who invited him over that night to finish preparations for a new course. She offered help in finding material. They had sipped Scotch and moved around the library selecting various books for further examination. The second time she half rubbed, half bumped his shoulder as she replaced a book, their eyes met. He kissed her lightly as if to test the depths of her emotion. She moaned and pulled his head toward hers. The force of her embrace had surprised Derrick.

In the ensuing weeks Betty had become increasingly demanding. She even convinced Derrick to visit when Whitland was scheduled to lecture. Her needs and motives became more and more confused. On a given night she might scream at him to go away and never return, that he would ruin her marriage and disgrace her husband. Within a few days, she would make some arrangement that would enable her to meet him alone somewhere on the University-College campus. She would cry, say that she needed him desperately, and ask him to forgive her. Derrick really began to feel that matters were spinning out of control when Betty demanded that he take her to the Easter dance.

"Everybody knows about us anyway except my husband," she reasoned "And he's not here, so what difference could it make?"

He had refused. They compromised and remained together in the Whitland home the evening of the dance.

"What madness," Derrick concluded. "Musa is right. This situation must end. The real problem is that I have become fond of her. I wonder if it is only pleasure or if there is something more. But if I really do love her, then what in the hell should I do? To think of love is ridiculous. Get your mind working correctly again, Derrick. What difference would the question of love make? I must put an end to it. I should find something else right now while I am here. Don't want to be any more vulnerable than necessary when I go back to Mbordo. Problem will be how to tell Betty. Can't write a letter, that's for sure. Betty might even get so angry that she would show it to her husband. Must tell her in person. God, will she be mad."

With that decision made, Derrick avoided thinking about anything of substance much the rest of the week. Musa's prognosis of the number of women available in Nkra had proved quite accurate. Nkra was certainly not a traveler's paradise, but compared to Mbordo it had certain charms. Two Lebanese restaurants offered reasonably tender filet mignon and excellent hummus. At the Ringway Nightclub one could actually buy a decent American-style hamburger. There were four established clubs, the Ringway, the Lido, the Metropole, and the Ali. On nights when a 'name' band played, admission might be as high as ten shillings. The area where patrons sat and consumed beer or other alcoholic beverages was sheltered from the rain, but the dance floor itself was open to the sky. The nightclubs were usually part of a larger hotel complex in which a room could be hired by the day or by the hour, depending on one's need.

By Friday Derrick was nearly out of money. He had also exhausted his emotional and physical reserves, and the thought of another prostitute in an 'hour' room made him nauseous. Late that morning he said good-by to Musa and took a taxi to the lorry park. He had come early to reserve a seat on Iron Boy, the lorry that ran between Nkra and Mbordo. The driver explained that Derrick could have a front seat unless someone of unexpected importance appeared. Derrick handed his single piece of luggage up to the driver's mate.

Iron Boy left the park at two. The front seat of a Benz bus is extraordinarily comfortable compared to a mammy wagon or even to the crowded seats in the interior of the Benz, where five and even six people were squeezed together on seats meant for four. The view from the front was much superior to elsewhere in the lorry. First came the long drive across the Nkra Plain, a barren strip that stretched from Nkra, west and north to the first scarp. Then on to the bridge that crossed the Kra river a few miles below the new dam. After that, through hilly land along the edge of the forest region until they reached the Mbordo Junction. The main road continued along the forest's edge, eventually reaching the regional capital of the western region, the ancient Ave city of Hunta. The road to Mbordo ran north and west into the forest.

But Derrick's eyes, even though open, saw little of what passed on the roadside. Rather, they seemed to look inward as Derrick thought of what he would say to Betty.

They met Saturday morning in the University Post Office building. Derrick had gone there to pick up his mail.

She spoke first. "Kojo told me you were back. I thought that you would never come by to get your mail. Don't you care about your mother? There must be at least three or four letters there from her by now."

She continued in a teasing tone, "How was your trip to Nkra? I have heard rumors of what you do there. Get into lots of fun things?"

Betty had prepared well for their meeting. Derrick could not remember when she looked better. Her skirt fell just above her knees and the blouse she wore accentuated her bust.

He replied, "The trip went quite well. How was your vacation?"

"Dammit, you know how it was," Betty replied in a horse whisper, "totally miserable, without you. Listen, Bob is in Nkra. He won't be back until tomorrow afternoon. Why don't you come over?"

On certain occasions the mind of the human being is capable of a process that combines both self-delusion and painfully accurate introspection. Meeting with Betty alone would provide an opportunity for Derrick to explain why he wished to stop seeing her. So much for self-delusion. Derrick also realized that it provided an opportunity to spend an entire day and night making love in a manner that buying a whore in Nkra was no substitute for. The halfhearted efforts of prostitutes, he now realized at a more primitive level of feeling, had not satiated his sexual desire but rather increased his need to be with Betty.

He replied, "Yes, I think it is important that we talk. I will come by in about an hour."

"Only on one condition," Betty replied.

"And that would be?" Derrick asked.

"We must do more than talk." Betty whispered.

"Unfortunately," Derrick replied, "that is exactly what I wanted to talk about."

"God, you are a strange one," Betty said. "Let's compromise and decide what to do first when you get there."

"An excellent idea," Derrick replied.

An hour later Derrick knocked on the front door of the Whitland bungalow. Betty greeted him dressed in a robe. She placed one finger on her lips and motioned for him to come in. Then she took his hand and led him to the room that served as a library. Once in the library she put her arms on his shoulders and clasped her hands behind his head. The robe fell open. Bare breasts and bikini panties ended Derrick's 'stillborn' efforts at conversation. They made love on the library floor, then moved to the bedroom.

Betty spoke first as she gently caressed his shoulders. "Do you think you might manage a third time?"

"Of course," Derrick replied, "but I am not sure when."

"Sometime before tomorrow morning, I hope," Betty said. "Now, what was it that you wanted to talk about that was so important?"

"I really can't remember," Derrick replied.

The next morning Derrick woke with bright sunlight in his eyes. He stirred just enough to wake Betty.

She opened her eyes and half screamed, "Oh my God, you have got to get out of here. Bob planned to come back early this morning."

Derrick reacted quickly and was behind the house next door when Whitland pulled into his driveway. A glance toward Betty standing half dressed at the front door convinced him that he did not have to worry about Whitland looking in his direction. In a moment of curiosity tinged with jealously Derrick hesitated just long enough to watch through the open bedroom window as Betty pushed her husband back onto their bed.

CHAPTER 8
The Rains

With the fourth term came the rains. Thunderheads, born in the oceans to the south, piled one on top of another, releasing torrents of moisture. At times water filled the space between land and sky. The winds of harmattan seemed banished northward forever. Alice found it difficult to even remember the uncomfortable dryness. Six, eight, even twenty hours a day it rained. After a few weeks even farmers had little use for the constant downpour. Only the mold and the fungus loved all of the rainy season. Alice found these unwelcome guests everywhere; on her clothes, food, furniture, records, books.

The trail through the forest became a channel of muck and slime. Once during a break in the rains Alice did try the path. She slipped and slid as far as the first bridge. Where once flowers grew and small frogs played, a small river now seemed to reach for the underside of the bridge, splashing onto its surface when its impetuous journey was interrupted by a branch or board. The trail looked no better beyond the bridge. The vision of herself stranded on the other side of a washed-out bridge with a sprained ankle was vivid enough to convince her to turn back.

As she left the forest, Alice felt both depressed and exhilarated. She could tell with only a glance toward the southern sky and the hint of raindrops in the air that it might be the next morning before she could safely venture out again. But the rains brought life not just to the forest but also to every living thing around her. The orderly patterns of lower school compounds in Mbordo and other nearby villages now became a profuse display of brilliantly shaded leaves and flowers that seem to leap from recently near-dead branches and roots. Around her own house flowers and beautiful green and white plants grew that Alice would never have dreamed existed there. She found herself content to sit on her porch and enjoy the strength and vitality of the tropical plants and animals. She found the small lizards delightful in their always alert posture, looking for food or perhaps a mate.

But the rains did restrict her movement. She admired the way in which the 'boys' seemed to ignore them, simply walking or riding their bikes wherever they wished, no matter what the weather conditions. More than once Jason or Jeff had arrived at her bungalow totally soaked, laughing at her concern and explaining that they were not so sweet that they would melt.

Alice had tested the strength of the heavy rains only once. She had gone to the senior commons room on a Sunday afternoon. The morning had been sunny. However, the clouds had converged again before she had finished half a glass of beer. She found herself sharing a table with Eric Thornton as the rains returned. She excused herself to the ladies room and exited by a side door. The distance to her bungalow was not more than a quarter mile. Alice had been confident at first. The rain did not seem heavy, but the effect was cumulative. The raindrops seemed to grow heavier and colder. They penetrated the light raincoat she wore, struck through her other clothing, and stung her body. As she passed the mathematics block, the winds became stronger. A sudden gust knocked her off balance and she almost fell.

"I might have been in serious trouble," she reflected, "if Moses and William had not been there somehow to help me the rest of the way home. God, they sure looked frightened."

The two students who aided Alice that day in the rain had performed an act of bravery, for they feared the effects of the rain even more than Alice did. The rainy season was a time of death as well as life. Students often wore sweaters and jackets to their classes even on days when the temperature never dropped below eighty. They avoided the rain, believing that the first step toward the dreaded 'fever' was the chill and dampness from being caught out in a storm. Death was common during the time of the rains. The rain brought new life but not food. Not until August, when the first of the new harvest was in, would food become plentiful. If the previous year's harvest had been good, then enough food would be available for all. If not, some would die, not of starvation of course. On the edge of the forest enough gari and cassava root was always available to fill the belly, but its nutritional value was close to that of sawdust. The weak and young, especially those three and four years old, just off the rich milk of the mother's nipple, would often die of the 'fever' during the rains. Of course, the expatriates of Mbordo knew little of this suffering. The people of the villages who had lived with the rains since their ancestors had settled on the edge of the forest would not talk of such things with visitors. They buried their young, bore others, and continued to survive as family and tribe.

Rain did effect the volunteer teachers in other ways. On Wednesday of the fourth week of the term Jason received a telegram:

COMING TO MBORDO FRIDAY STOP SEE YOU SOON STOP LOVE KAREN STOP

To be sure that Karen would not be stranded by herself at the Mbordo junction if she arrived late, Jason always met her there. That Friday he hitched a ride with Mr. West, who was on his way to Nkra, and was at the junction by three. He did not expect Karen before five. The rains of the previous week had been heavy. Five came and went. By six there was still no sign of Karen. A light rain brought early darkness. Jason climbed into the only shelter available near the road, an old mammy wagon named 'God's Will' that had been temporarily abandoned due to mechanical failure. He began to mull over the possibilities.

"First," he thought, "no one will hurt Karen. That just does not happen in Sakra. It is possible that the telegram was incorrect. They often are. The wind crosses the line and the little dots and dashes get all mixed up. A '3' gets changed to a '5.' Or a 'not' gets left out. Look at the telegram again. Maybe it should have been 'NOT COMING TO MBORDO FRIDAY.' No, she would not have said 'SEE YOU

114

SOON' if she wasn't planning to come. She must be on her way. Seven now. Remember that article from Time magazine. Two lorries near Pandu, head on at full speed. Fifty people dead. Couldn't face it. Dammit, quit being silly. Probably only delayed by rain. Might already be back in Pandu. Turned back by high waters. Safe and warm at home while I sit in this goddamn lorry freezing my butt. Shut up, Jason. Much better that than swept off the road someplace. I hope she is safe home. Maybe I should return to Mbordo. If I don't go soon I'll be here all night. No, better to stay. I wouldn't sleep anyway. Probably end up trying to walk back out here at midnight."

A lorry stopped. Jason ignored the rain and moved quickly to see if Karen was on board. She wasn't, nor had the driver seen anyone that fit her description. He did tell Jason that the Pandu-Admasi road was impassable due to high water. The driver suggested that Jason return to Mbordo with him since it was now impossible for anyone to travel from Pandu southward.

"Mine is the last lorry to Mbordo this night," he explained to Jason.

But Jason decided to wait. He watched wistfully from the old truck as the lorry moved away. The sand flies were thick that night and they dined in gourmet fashion on Jason's exposed skin, but he gave little thought to their bites. He had moments of anger at thoughts of spending the entire night alone. But memories of Karen would intrude. Old lorries continued to pass on the main road. Most were loaded with yam and other food produce and moved in the direction of Nkra in order to be there for the morning opening of the markets. Jason's hopes rose and fell with the few lorries that traveled in the opposite direction as they slowed for a slight curve near the junction. The sound of the rain on the roof of 'God's Will' and exhaustion finally brought sleep.

Jason was awakened by the groaning sound of lorry brakes. His eyes saw Karen in the front seat of the old mammy wagon but his body refused to move, believing that his vision was perhaps just a dream.

"This no good place for you," Jason heard the driver say. "Come to Hunta with truck. I take you to good school there. Headman very good. He find good place for you."

Jason decided it was no dream. He ran toward the road, slipped on the muddy pavement, and slid into the side of the lorry.

"Careful," Karen said, "I didn't make this trip just to nurse someone with a broken ankle."

"My God, am I glad to see you," Jason said as he helped her down. "I had just about given up."

"You should know," Karen replied with a half smile, "that neither wind, nor rain, nor snow could keep me from Mbordo."

"How about the lack of lorry," Jason said as they watched the wagon that brought Karen to the junction resume its journey.

They sat together in the front seat of the abandoned truck. Rain clouds covered the moon and the families that lived near the junction had hours before extinguished their kerosene lanterns and were asleep for the night. The darkness was near complete except for the dim headlights of an occasional lorry on the main road.

For minutes that seemed like seconds they held each other tightly in celebration of Karen's safe arrival. As their lips met desire overwhelmed inhibition. After a very short period of experimentation they agreed that the front seat of a mammy wagon was not one of the better places to make love. They quickly moved to the back of the old lorry.

Some minutes later they found themselves relaxed, holding each other tightly and laughing at their inability to wait. Their conversation turned to Karen's trip. The day had started well enough. Karen had the front seat of a Benz bus out of Pandu. Unfortunately, what had seemed a moderate rain in Pandu quickly turned into a horrendous downpour. At first puddles were only a few inches deep and the driver moved through them without slowing. Soon, however, Karen noticed that in places the water covered the entire road and the driver moved slowly in search of the side of the road with least water. As they moved southward, the water seemed deeper in each small valley. Gangs of men from nearby villages stood near the deepest spots waiting to pull stranded cars out of the valley waters, for a reasonable fee, of course. A few miles later they reached a place where a small creek ordinarily flowed through a medium sized pipe under the road. The pipe was blocked by debris and the 'small' creek was over the road and at least thirty yards wide. The depth and strength of the creek had been difficult to assess until a group of men attempted to push a Mercedes Benz car through the water. About fifty vehicles were backed up on either side of the water, their drivers carefully watching the progress of the Mercedes. The driver and his passenger had climbed on top with an umbrella and seemed almost in a holiday mood. All seemed to go well until the men reached midpoint in the stream. Suddenly the car began to slide. The driver and passenger slid off the back of the roof and were rescued by the other men in the water as the car floated away into the forest. For the other drivers, what they had just seen was sufficient evidence of the impassability of the road. The rain was heavy, however, and few passengers on Karen's lorry had witnessed what had happened to the Mercedes.

When Karen and several other passengers protested their driver's decision to turn back he explained, "You go in that water. You not reach Nkra. You reach heaven. We do not go today. Tomorrow maybe yes, maybe no."

Karen asked the driver if some other way could be found to reach Admasi.

"Not on one of these small lorries," he replied, "but army truck may reach there. Wheels very large. Good chance in water."

Karen had quickly gotten down from the Benz and walked toward the spot where the army truck was parked. The rain was still heavy and by the time she reached the window on the driver's side to ask for a ride she was soaked. The driver referred her to the Captain in charge of the small contingent of men who rode in the truck. His answer at first was a polite no. Karen had explained as best she could using both Atan and English why she had to reach Admasi that day.

The captain paused, then explained further, "The truck is very difficult to ride in. Very uncomfortable. There is no room in front. We may all die if the truck follows that car into the forest. But if you want to go through that water at the risk of your life you may ride in the back."

Karen had given the Captain's serious words little thought. The truck bed was at least five feet off the ground and she had no desire to return to Pandu and spend the night worrying about Jason sitting at the junction. With the help of a sergeant she climbed into the back of the truck. It seemed to Karen that every able bodied man in the area gathered around the truck to help push it through the water. She heard the Captain promise each one four shillings if and only if the truck reached the other side. New and stronger ropes were stretched across the water. The truck moved forward under its own power as the men moved with it. About one-third of the way across the channel the motor stalled. She heard the Captain yell at the men to push. She felt the truck slip sideways and noticed that the water level had reached the floor of the compartment in which she sat. A scream died on her lips as the truck lurched toward the forest. But the ropes held and she again felt and saw movement toward the opposite shore as the men in the water battled the current. In a few minutes the truck was out of the deepest part and making progress at a steady rate. When they reached the other side the Captain was more than happy to pay the villagers for their efforts. Karen climbed down and watched the driver dry the distributor cap and spark plug connections. She realized that she was not the only one frightened by what had happened to the big truck. The men from the villages along the road had decided to call it a day and told the drivers of other vehicles to turn back.

The engine of the truck had been cranky after its bath but did start. When Karen had left the truck near Admasi she thanked the driver and the Captain and offered to pay for her trip.

The Captain had laughed and said, "We take no money for what small help that we can provide. You are a very brave lady. I am sorry that we can not take you directly to Mbordo but the rains have made us late and we must report to camp Akokodur. If I can ever be of any service to you again please ask for Captain Mudua at Camp Akokodur."

Karen waved down the first taxi she saw. It was near dark when she reached the Admasi lorry park. She got on the only transportation moving in the direction of Towa that evening, a truly ancient mammy wagon. The weak lights of the lorry penetrated the darkness no more than a few feet as it crawled and bounced slowly along the rough road. After they turned on to the paved road that ran toward the Mbordo junction, the driver cranked up his old pile of metal and wood to its maximum speed, twenty miles per hour.

"Anyway," Karen said as she ended her story, "here I am, for better or worse."

"And" Jason replied, "here we may stay. If nothing comes by in the next hour going to Mbordo we probably should go on down the main road to Forfo and spend the night. There are Peace Corps volunteers at the secondary school, two girls. They won't mind much and even if they do it will be too late to throw us out."

"How far is it?" Karen asked.

"About ten miles," Jason replied. "But let's wait here awhile. There is some small chance that someone might come by."

They sat quietly and listened to the sounds of small insects until Jason broke the silence of the African night.

"I wanted to talk to you about something, but this seems like such a dumb place to talk about anything serious," he said.

"This may not be the best place for much of anything," Karen interrupted, "but we've already done most of the other things that we could do here, so what do we have left to do but to talk"

"I did want to talk," Jason said in a dejected tone.

"I'm sorry, I didn't mean to make fun," Karen replied. "What do you want to talk about?"

"I'm thinking about extending for another year," Jason said. "Do you think you could convince the Peace Corps director and the Ministry of Education to have you transferred to Mbordo or at least a little closer? It would simplify our lives a great deal."

"And if I can't, will you decide not to stay?" Karen asked teasingly.

Jason replied, "I've already made up my mind to extend. I don't care if they send you to Nandu, I am still going to stay in Sakra and come and visit you."

"I wouldn't want you to stay in Mbordo another year because of me," Karen said.

"Don't flatter yourself too much," Jason replied. "I probably would have extended anyway. I don't find teaching here unpleasant."

"In that case, I will try. I'll write a letter to the Director," Karen said. "I would not be that unhappy to leave my present Headmaster. Probably someone near Mbordo is completing their two years."

"God, I hope so," Jason said. "There is a certain element of interest to riding these lorries, but it all disappears after about the first thirty minutes or one hundred potholes."

"Listen my love, nobody in the world knows that better than I do right now," Karen said as she moved closer to Jason. "Are we going to spend the night here?"

Jason and Karen soon gave up on going to Mbordo that night and caught a lorry to Forfo. It was past midnight when their pounding on the door woke the two girls. The next day they made it to Mbordo around noon.

That Saturday at the evening meal when Jason announced his intention of extending his Peace Corps service, Jeff started to chuckle.

"What's so funny?" Jason asked.

"I've just about decided to extend, too," Jeff replied.

"I bet Enata convinced you that another year would be a good idea," Karen teased.

"Actually," Jeff replied, "I have never discussed the matter with Enata. My Agricultural Education Manual isn't complete and I would like to see it through."

"Then Enata has nothing to do with your decision," Karen declared.

"For all I know, Miss Wise Ass," Jeff responded sharply, "she may be transferred next year to the other side of Sakra."

"Oh my, aren't we sensitive," Karen said.

Jeff relented slightly, "I'm sorry. You must be a little careful about how you tease me. Of course Enata is involved in any decision I make."

Karen's return to Pandu the next day was uneventful until the mammy wagon she had boarded in Towa was within a few miles of Admasi. The roads seemed almost empty even for a Sunday and the driver reduced his speed to a few miles per hour.

"What is wrong?" Karen asked him. "Is the engine getting too hot?"

"No," he replied. "Lorry fine. My brother tell me on the road that big trouble in Admasi. Lorry drivers very angry about double in price of gasoline on Friday. They no drive lorry and stop everybody else."

As they neared the lorry park the road was full of empty taxis, Benz buses, and mammy wagons of all kinds. Even an empty government transport bus was parked a few blocks away.

The driver pulled the mammy wagon into an empty spot and said, "This is as far as we go today. No truck leaves this place."

"But how will I get to Pandu?" Karen asked. "I have to teach students tomorrow. Can I take a taxi?"

"Very dangerous to travel in taxi now," the driver explained. "If lorry drivers see them they stop and beat them, maybe passengers too. You better stay in Admasi tonight. Can't go anywhere now. You go to hotel six blocks that way."

Karen got down from the lorry, took her small suitcase, and started to walk in the direction the driver had suggested. She thought she heard someone calling, "Miss, Miss." She looked in the direction of the sound and saw the driver of a small car waving his arm for her to come. She was reluctant to move toward the car until she recognized Gil's friend Mr. Andre from the Easter gathering at Tango's bar.

"I am trying to go to Pandu," he said. "I don't know if they will let me through, but if you are going that way, we might even have a better chance together."

"Why do you think that?" Karen asked.

"They want to stop all traffic because they are angry about the cost of gasoline," Mr. Andre replied. "I am a government official but that won't help. But I can pretend to be your driver. I don't think they will want to bother you."

They were stopped four times before leaving Admasi. Each time Mr. Andre explained that he needed to get the Obroni to Pandu and each time the men smiled and waved them through.

119

CHAPTER 9
The Savior Cannot Save Himself – Derrick Leaves Mbordo

The next Friday Jason faced a weekend alone. During his third class of the morning he noticed a student who was also a close friend standing at the door, motioning for him to come. Jason finished his explanation of adding mixed numbers and gave the class a few examples to try before moving to the door.

As he drew near the student reached for his arm, pulled him closer and whispered, "The 'Savior' is no longer the leader of Sakra."

Jason gave the student an incredulous look and replied, "I don't believe it. Be very careful what you say."

"No," the student said loudly so that others in the class could hear, "we do not have to be afraid any longer. The 'Savior' is done. Finished. We heard the news on the radio and from lorry drivers returning from Nkra."

"I don't believe it," Jason thought as he returned to his desk. "It's just not possible. Dr. Agyenkwa is still popular. He is well loved by all the people of Sakra. At least most of them. I can almost remember the words of the director of our training program, 'Certainly Dr. Agyenkwa has committed some excesses and does, as all of us do, have some faults. But he stands unchallenged as the man who led Sakra to independence and as the most important leader of the Pan-African movement. In Sakra itself, he is perhaps the only man who can prevent the ethnic groups of that nation from fighting among themselves and provide the leadership needed to mold Sakra into a nation state.'"

Jason was so completely convinced that what the student had reported was untrue that he continued to teach his classes. He did notice that students seemed to be having more difficulty than usual concentrating on their work. At 11:45 the Assistant Principal knocked on the door of his classroom.

"I'm sorry to interrupt," he said, "but very important events have occurred today. There will be an important radio broadcast at twelve o'clock and we are dismissing classes now so that everyone will have the opportunity to listen."

"I do believe," he continued with a broad smile and a wink, "that we will be forced to make some modifications in our morning pledge."

The class burst into an uproar in at least five languages. The noise was very close to a cheer. Jason made no effort to restore order and waved the students toward the open door.

The noise in the senior faculty lounge was as loud or louder than it had been in Jason's classroom. It was packed with people who all seemed to be drinking and yelling. The noise stopped at twelve as someone turned up the radio.

"This is General Ali Musa of the armed forces of Sakra," a deep voice coming from the radio proclaimed. "Dr. Agyenkwa is no longer the ruler of Sakra. The myth of the 'Savior' is broken. All parts of the nation of Sakra are now under the control of the armed forces and police. A council has been formed of the highest officials of the police and armed forces. This council, which will be known as the Transitional Governing Council, will guide the nation of Sakra back to true democratic rule. There is no cause for alarm. Please remain calm and stay where you are. All elected government officials and members of Dr. Agyenkwa's political party, the SNP, should report immediately to their local police stations."

The General continued in an even more somber tone, "It is with the greatest regret that I make the following announcement. When troops of the First Army Division approached and surrounded the 'Savior's' residence, he ordered his Russian guards to fight to the death. Three of the Russian guards and twelve soldiers of the First Army died. During the battle Dr. Agyenkwa also received mortal wounds. I repeat, Dr. Agyenkwa is dead of wounds received during the battle for his residence. His body has been removed and buried in the national cemetery. No mourning other than the traditional rites performed by family will be permitted."

Jason thought, "So this is the way it ends. The man who had led the nation of Sakra through what had seemed an impossible time of dreams and hope to independence from Britain was no longer a living human being. The invincible warrior, the eternal leader, the savior of his nation was dead."

Jason gradually became aware that the voices around him gave no hint of anger or even sorrow. He saw not a single sad face in the lounge. Someone called for more beer. Outside he could see students gathering.

They were chanting, "No more 'Savior,' no more 'Savior.' Musa, Musa, Musa."

Jason could also hear sounds of celebration coming from the direction of the town of Mbordo.

"Yes, the people here would be happy," Jason reflected. "Agyenkwa was never popular with the Bordo or Ave. Many have friends or relatives in preventive detention."

He saw Alice standing near the door and walked over to where she stood.

"I don't believe it," she said. "The same man who yesterday was the supreme, invincible leader of this nation, today does not seem to have a single friend or supporter left in this room."

"I noticed that, too," Jason replied. "I wonder how much resistance there was in Nkra."

"I certainly have no idea," Alice replied. "The whole thing is a big surprise to me, and I don't think that sort of information is likely to be broadcast on the radio."

"I'm going to Nkra to see what is happening," Jason said suddenly.

"You are absolutely crazy," Alice countered in an authoritative tone. "You want to be killed. Just stay where you are and enjoy the celebration. We will know soon enough about everything that happened."

"I'll probably never be in a country that has a coup again," Jason replied. "It's my only chance to see the nature of one close up. I am going."

Jason went home, packed a few clothes and walked to the other side of Mbordo. However, he found that nothing was moving in the direction of Nkra that afternoon.

One lorry driver returning from Nkra explained to Jason, "You go that way today, you have big trouble."

Strangely, but perhaps out of economic necessity, the lorries ran as usual the next morning and Jason was at the Nkra lorry park by nine-thirty. All of Nkra seemed to be on holiday. The city's old buses were filled with people cheering and singing. They seemed to be moving, not on any regular routes, but aimlessly about the city, stopping to pick up anyone who wished to go for a ride. The streets were filled with people who were singing and dancing to the sounds of drums that seemed to have sprung up with their masters on every other street corner.

"Musa be praised, God bless Musa, Allah bless Musa. The 'Savior' is no more. Free of the Savior at last," were the most common chants.

"If Agyenkwa has a single friend left in this city," Jason thought, "he must be hiding in the innermost room of his compound."

Once he left the lorry park Jason was repeatedly stopped on the street by Sakraians and asked if he were an American. Each time he answered yes, the man or woman would grab his hand and tell him of the deep respect and love that all Sakraians had for his nation and how glad they were that the evil Agyenkwa was dead and would bring no more Chinese and Russians to Sakra. Other volunteers, staying at the teachers hostel, explained to Jason that stories about the Chinese cotton mill workers and the ships filled with yam leaving for China had been more than enough to quickly make everyone with even Chinese features unwelcome in Sakra after the coup. The new government had sensed the mood of the people toward the Chinese, and they were all on a plane headed in the general direction of Peking even before Jason arrived in Nkra that Saturday morning.

The role of the Russian Guards as protector of the 'Savior' had made Russians almost as unpopular as the Chinese workers. Getting them out of Sakra was a bit more complicated since a number of them had been assigned to teach mathematics and science in various places in Sakra, in positions similar to those held by Peace Corps volunteers. However, they must have had their own code word. A reliable source -- Musa -- brought word to the teachers hostel that every Russian in Sakra had already arrived at the airport to await transportation home.

Alter lunch Jason went out walking in search of signs of dissatisfaction with the coup. He found none. Only smiles and friendly greetings for the American, who now it seemed, was the special friend of all Sakraians. In time he made his way to the International Hotel and sat down to have a beer with a group of volunteers already there.

"Is there no one in this whole damn country who has even a little positive feeling left for Dr. Agyenkwa?" he asked.

One of the other volunteers chuckled and spoke, "If there is he ain't going to say nothing now, that's for damn sure. Not even his own mother would defend him now. Look, it's not really that strange. People were sick and tired of his arrogance. Tired of inflation, of corruption. Tired of his cars, big houses and all of those women. We can be very glad of one thing, though. He was a friend of the Russians and not our government. Otherwise, it would be our butts being kicked out and not theirs."

"That's for damn sure," another volunteer said. "In Africa much better to have a government in power that hates you. I hope the new government will not be too friendly."

"That's kind of sad," Jason commented. "Given the problems that a new nation like Sakra faces, no government or leader has much real prospect of anything like complete success. But from what is happening now you would think that Agyenkwa had been a complete failure. That nothing good had happened in this country in the last twelve years. It's as if he were a common thief or murderer. No one even seems to care that he is dead."

The first man spoke again. "If you attempt to convince people that you are a God or close to it, that can work pretty well as long as no one finds out that you are not. But when they learn you are but a man like other men, the reaction will almost certainly be unpleasant. People will think you not only evil but also a great fool. Have you heard the story that the `Savior' had a number of pregnant women murdered and buried under his statue at the Mankra Ideological Institute."

"No, I did not hear that story," Jason replied, "and I hope it's not true."

"Probably not," the other volunteer replied, "but true or false, it served the same purpose, to convince the ordinary Sakraian that Agyenkwa could live forever. Each pregnant woman was to give him an extra life."

"Maybe two if she had twins," another volunteer commented.

Nobody laughed.

The volunteer who mentioned the stories of the statue continued, "I have heard that the statue was knocked down and smashed into small pieces almost as soon as the first news of the coup was broadcast. You know that Agyenkwa's death probably came at least an hour after the destruction of the statue."

"You sound as if you believe those stories," another volunteer said.

He shrugged.

"Did they look for the bodies of the women?" Jason asked.

"I heard nothing about that," the volunteer replied. "And I doubt if we will ever hear anything no matter what they find under the statue. The government would suppress any news of the finding of bodies out of fear that people might believe that the 'Savior' was coming back. The people running the government might even believe it."

****

Jason returned to Mbordo the next day. It was not quite two when he got down from the old mammy wagon that had given him a lift from the junction. He found

Derrick sitting alone in the front room of the bungalow, staring at a half empty bottle of beer that rested on the table in front of him.

"What's the matter," Jason asked, "mourning the 'Savior'?"

Derrick replied quietly, "That bastard got what he deserved. But I may be no better off. The problem I have may prove just as fatal."

"So, what's the big problem?" Jason asked. "Don't tell me. That's the last beer in the house and every bar in town is completely sold out."

"My God, I do wish," Derrick replied. "Jason, I need some advice. There is nothing that I dislike more than involving other people in my problems, but this is really out of hand."

"All right, all right," Jason said, trying to reassure Derrick, who seemed near tears. "What's the problem?"

Derrick took another drink from the bottle of beer and began slowly to explain, "When I went to Nkra during Easter break, I gave a lot of thought to my relationship with Betty. I knew the whole affair was becoming a very bad idea and decided to break it off. She wanted me to take her places, to flaunt our relationship. Almost as if she wanted everyone to know. It had to stop. I thought if I had a few whores in Nkra, it would make everything easier when I got back. It didn't. But, to get to the point, I have the clap. I noticed some pain about two weeks ago. You try to be optimistic and hope that it will go away, but it got worse."

Jason interrupted, "That's no real problem. Just go to the dispensary. It's their number two specialty after malaria. The students say they have a big, long, dull needle that hurts like hell. But the treatment works."

Derrick almost smiled as he replied, "Unfortunately that's only a minor part of the problem. I have already been, and the needle is big and long and dull, very dull. I asked the technician how many times it had been used. He had no idea but said it was the only needle that he had ever used in the five years that he worked there. It's been three days and my ass is still sore. If that were my only problem I wouldn't be sitting here talking to you. What I did, like a damn fool, was to sleep with Betty after I got back and more than once."

"I'm beginning to understand," Jason mused. "This could cause some anger in the wrong places. Is it possible that Betty is not sleeping with her husband anymore? Then you can just tell her what happened. She probably will not want to see your pretty face again or any other part of your body, but that no doubt is to everyone's benefit, anyway. She can find someplace in Nkra to buy penicillin and take care of her problem if she's developed one. Then you both will be in the clear."

"There is not much chance of that plan working," Derrick replied. "I know her husband has screwed her at least once."

"How in the hell do you know that?" Jason asked. "You become a peeping Tom, too?"

Derrick shrugged and tried to explain, "Not really. I mean I don't normally. Look, I know it's hard to believe, but I saw them without really intending to do so. Betty and I were in the library together in what one might call a compromising situation. It was Monday morning and Whitland wasn't supposed to be home, but he must have dismissed his class early. He was already at the front door by the time Betty was able to slip on a robe. That woman is a true actress. I would have been jealous, if I hadn't been scared shitless. She got to him before he was three feet inside the door. She said that she had been waiting for him to come back all morning and couldn't wait another second. She pulled him to the bedroom. I waited until they got pretty well into it and slipped out the front door."

"Hey, you sure as hell do have a problem," Jason said. "Trying to have sex with somebody's wife during an hour class period is not really that great an idea."

"All right, all right, so tell me something that I don't already know," Derrick replied. "But right now all I want is out of this mess one way or another. Maybe Betty would marry me."

"That seems a rather desperate solution," Jason said. "Do you even want to get married?"

Jason almost laughed as he expressed his next thought: "You can tell her that she probably has the clap and that you want to marry her all in the same sentence. You know the old 'good news, bad news' routine."

"I don't know which she would consider the good news and which the bad," Derrick mused. "But as idiotic as it may sound, I really do think that I love her. I was going to stop the whole thing during the Easter break. But the next time I saw her, I just don't know what happened. I didn't seem to be able to stop."

"Good luck, old buddy," Jason said. "Any advice I would give you probably wouldn't help much. But you do have to tell her about the problem, whatever else you decide."

By Monday of the next week Derrick had decided to ask Betty to marry him. Tuesday morning he went to the Whitland bungalow. Whitland had gone to Nkra for the day on business.

Once in the bungalow, Betty had taken his hand and pulled him toward the library. He held onto her hand but did not move.

"We have something that we must discuss," he said sharply.

"All right," Betty replied with a coy smile and a hand squeeze, "but don't take too long. There are other things that I would rather do."

"Betty," Derrick said as quickly as he could form the words, "I have the clap and I want to marry you."

In the following moments Betty's unspoken demeanor, communicated by her facial expression, changed from a manifestation of lust and anticipation of pleasure to at first non-comprehension, then incredulity, and finally total, massive anger.

"You've got what?" she asked.

"Gonorrhea. I have Gonorrhea. You know, the clap," Derrick replied.

"If you have it, then I have it," Betty said slowly.

The full impact of Derrick's blunt revelation destroyed what was left of Betty's composure.

"You son of a bitch," she screamed. "You didn't have to go to Nkra just to get a piece of ass. I was here all the time. What's the matter with me? Don't I squeeze hard enough? Or do you prefer black pussy?"

"Dammit, Betty, try to calm down," Derrick replied as he tried to place his hands on her shoulders. "I really did think we should stop seeing each other. I thought if I slept with somebody else it would be easier. But it didn't work. Not at all. I couldn't stand the thought of not being with you again. I love you and I want to marry you."

"You forgot one small item, lover boy," Betty replied. "I already have a husband."

"I am quite aware of that," Derrick said. "Obviously we would have to wait until the divorce proceedings are over."

Betty started to laugh then said, "Whatever are you babbling about? What makes you think that I would divorce my husband to marry you?"

"I just thought . . . .," Derrick said as he struggled to explain his feelings.

"Well think again, child," Betty interrupted. "I happen to enjoy being married to a university professor. It's this place that I don't like. Do you know why we are here? Two or three years in this hell hole and River State will make my husband an Associate Professor with full tenure. I want that. Not you. What makes you think that I would ever want to marry a little boy like you and spend the rest of my life in some cold flat in England starving on a secondary school teacher's pay?"

"We could live in the United States or any place else that you wished," was the only thing that Derrick could manage to say in an effort to counter Betty's cold logic.

"And just what in the hell do you think you could do in America? Sell insurance?" Betty said coldly. "Or maybe teach in some stinking private school? I would probably have to become a prostitute to support us. Jesus Christ! Can't you understand that I like being Professor Whitland's wife? Screwing around with you was all right, but mostly I just wanted to cause enough of a scandal so they would send us back to Indiana a little early. God, I never wanted Bob to know."

Derrick said nothing, but his face betrayed a mixture of annoyance and confusion. His deflated countenance seemed to rekindle Betty's rage.

"Oh, I am so very sorry that I've hurt your feelings," she continued. "You make me fucking sick. I gave you the best you ever had and what did you give me? The goddamn clap."

"What are we going to do about Bob?" Derrick asked.

"Oh my God," Betty said, "He probably has it too. God, I can't stand this. I have to think. You just get the hell out of here. If I never see you again it will be too soon."

Derrick left and started on the long walk back to the boy's place. A combination of relief, deflation and apprehension made him insensitive to the heat of the tropical morning and the traffic on the road. Several times he stumbled as he moved to the rough berm in response to the horns of passing mammy wagons.

The affair was over, of that much he was certain. But he did have difficulty in accepting the full import of just how little he and his body had actually meant to Betty.

"Just a goddamn toy, less than a little pet dog," he thought.

Even before Derrick was out the door Betty was deciding how to deal with her husband. If he had the clap, she was sure that he would blame her. Her own ego would not allow her to consider the possibility that he had slept with other women. She decided on a full confession in the hope that Bob would forgive her. Of course she would explain that Derrick had very nearly committed rape that first time in the library and that Whitland's own actions in offering Derrick the use of his library had been a primary cause of her infidelity.

Betty told her husband of the affair that same afternoon. He did forgive her, but not Derrick. Fortunately, Mr. Whitland talked to Mr. West about how he felt. Mr. West in turn discussed the problem with the Vice-Chancellor. The illicit relationship between the American Professor's wife and the British 'boy,' that had for months been the subject of rumor within the Mbordo expatriate community, quickly became a full blown scandal, at least in the opinion of the European and American staff. When the Vice-Chancellor called a meeting of certain senior staff members, most of those summoned assumed that the agenda would center around what to do about the Milson-Whitland affair. Alice had been among those invited to attend the meeting scheduled for Wednesday after the completion of classes.

"What a mess," she thought as she walked toward the Vice-Chancellor's office. "Just remember to keep your mouth shut and don't get caught in the middle."

When they were all seated in his office, the Vice-Chancellor said, "I believe that everyone who was asked to be here is now present. Most of you are senior staff members or have been teachers for many years. I have included Mr. Pordoe, the Sportsmaster, in this meeting because he sees more of our students every day than any other staff member. I asked you to come to my office this afternoon so that we could discuss a problem that has existed here at the University-College for many months. But that has in the past few weeks grown to such a level of difficulty that we can no longer afford to ignore it or pretend that it does not exist."

"Here we go," Alice thought.

"The problem," he continued, "is tribalism. Tribalism among our students and even, much to my distress, I have reports of this disease among some of our junior staff."

The Vice-Chancellor, noting the surprised expressions on the faces of the expatriates explained further. "Some of you of course, who are not from Sakra, perhaps would not even have been aware that such a problem existed here on our University-College compound. Nevertheless, it is a problem those of us who are Sakraian have had with us all of our lives and since the coup matters have, I believe, gotten worse, much worse. I thought very carefully about whether or not to invite only Sakraians to this meeting or to include those of you from Europe and the

United States. It was perhaps unfair to include you without telling you in advance the purpose of this meeting. If you believe that you should not involve yourselves in these matters, I would fully understand and you may feel free to leave."

None of the expatriates in the room moved.

Mr. West spoke, "We are here to help the University-College. This problem affects the University-College. Speaking for myself, I will do anything that I can to help."

The others nodded their agreement. Alice felt like giving Mr. West a big hug. It was the bravest thing she had ever heard him say.

"Thank you," the Vice-Chancellor said. "Your support is much appreciated. Before the coup it seemed that most students were in agreement that Dr. Agyenkwa should no longer rule. But now there is no agreement on anything. Our students from the North view General Musa as a national hero who can do no wrong. The Ave and Atan students say that he will become a dictator and that his vote on the Transitional Governing Council is the only one that counts. There have been arguments between students that have ended in physical violence. Thus far we have been fortunate. No serious injuries have resulted from these fights. As long as blood comes only from the nose or mouth and no teeth are lost nor bones broken, we can probably keep the situation under control. But I am now afraid, very much afraid that if we do not take action, as you Americans say, to cool the situation, it will be only a matter of time until some students resort to the use of machetes or other weapons. If that happens, the University-College will never be the same again."

"What can we do?" Mr. West asked.

Thornton spoke up, "We should expel those involved in these ridiculous incidents. Get them out of here. They don't belong in a civilized institution."

"I have investigated each case that has been brought to my attention with great care," the Vice-Chancellor answered. "It is not an easy matter to place responsibility, nor for that matter even to find out which students were actually involved. Rumors are plentiful, but to find a student who will come forward as a witness is very rare. And mark my words, if a Kroban student is injured and I expel an Ave for inflicting the wound, the incident would still be far from over. No, the Kroban would still take revenge for his injury on another Ave student, and that student and his friends on another. And the friends of the expelled Ave student would probably take revenge on some other Kroban student to avenge the expulsion."

Mr. Pordoe, the Sportsmaster, spoke, "The government has outlawed tribalism. I don't think that we need to have it at this University-College. We should assemble all of the students and explain that by committing this type of act they are violating the laws of Sakra."

That suggestion caused some suppressed laughter in the back of the room until the Vice-Chancellor spoke harshly, "Perhaps those of you who are smiling have some better solutions."

The Sportsmaster, now somewhat emboldened, continued, "The students are not mixed in the hostels. All Ave stay in one part of a certain hostel, the Atan in another part, and the Bordo also by themselves. The Kroban even have a building entirely separate from the others. Perhaps if they did not live separately, they would learn to live together."

Gil spoke for the first time at the meeting, "I fear that mixing students will only cause more trouble. The Kroban students fear the Ave. They say that because they are few in number they must stay together. This plan was tried some years ago but had to be abandoned because of the complaints of the Kroban students."

The Vice-Chancellor let the matter drop for the moment and asked for other suggestions.

When none were forthcoming, he again spoke, "That decision to stop mixing our students in the hostels and to allow them to live segregated by tribe, looking back now, was probably one of the worst decisions that I have made as Vice-Chancellor. However, Mr. Adwin has a point. Reintroduction of such a policy now could serve to increase our problems rather than help to solve them. But, are there any other possibilities? We must take action. I would rather do something, even the wrong thing, than to sit quietly and wait for this problem to overwhelm and destroy us."

"Are matters really to that point?" Mr. West asked.

"Yes," the Vice-Chancellor replied quickly. "If we do not act now, we may lose whatever chance we have. Tomorrow, first period, we will assemble the students. I will explain the laws of Sakra that deal with tribalism and remind our students of their duties as citizens. I will also announce the new housing policy and ask the registrar to prepare a list of new housing assignments. I am asking each of you to speak to students in all of your classes during the day tomorrow. Please stress the importance of acting as a citizen of Sakra and not in a tribalistic manner. I will also call an emergency meeting of the entire staff for later this afternoon and ask the others to speak out against tribalism. The students should be made well aware that they are the ones who will suffer if tribalism destroys the learning atmosphere at this University-College."

The room was silent.

"Anything else?" the Vice-Chancellor asked. "If not, that is all I have for now."

As the teachers were leaving the Vice-Chancellor looked toward Alice and said, "Mrs. Manati, would you be so kind as to stay for a few minutes longer? I have another matter I would like to discuss with you."

"Certainly," Alice replied.

Once the room had cleared, the Vice-Chancellor said, "Alice, I am sorry to involve you a second time today in one of our problems, but I have to deal with it and frankly it's in an area where my experience is very limited. No doubt you have heard as much or more than I have of the difficulties between Mr. Whitland and Mr. Milson."

"Yes, I am afraid that I have heard more than I wished," Alice replied.

"Mr. West tells me," the Vice-Chancellor continued, "that Mr. Whitland is threatening to kill Mr. Milson."

Alice's calm tenor disappeared.

She muttered, "My God, it's worse than a soap opera."

"I also understand," the Vice-Chancellor said, "that Mr. Whitland has the means to carry out his threat. There is a rumor of a smuggled gun in his possession. Now, to be very frank, it is quite difficult for me to understand how one could make such a threat. In this place we would not even consider killing someone over such a dispute. Some reparation would have to be made, of course, but to kill someone, this I don't understand. However, I did read of such cases in the newspapers when I was a student in the United States. Your expression has already answered most of my questions. Obviously, you do take the threat seriously. Do you really think that Whitland would commit such an act?"

By the time the Vice-Chancellor had finished speaking Alice had regained her composure. In fact, she found herself smiling and had to repress a laugh.

"I'm sorry," she said, "the whole thing is, as you say, somewhat ridiculous. But to answer your question, yes, it is quite possible that a man would kill another man in this type of situation."

"Then, there is only one solution," the Vice-Chancellor said. "One of them must leave Mbordo and quickly. I have known for some time that Whitland's wife is unhappy in this place, but his work is of some importance to us. He is trying quite hard to develop seed for a strain of grass that would provide soil cover without competing with corn for soil nutrients. But I know that he needs at least another year to complete the project. It often makes no difference whether or not most projects are completed since they have the same value in a completed stage as they do in an incompleted stage - none. However, and it is ironic that it would have to be this particular case, Mr. Whitland's project is one of the few that I have been reasonably sure would have some value if completed."

The Vice-Chancellor paused, then continued, "Mr. Milson's scheduled year with us would have been completed in a few months. I do wish that he could have finished up here. Unfortunately, judging from the evidence available, for him to do so might be quite dangerous. Perhaps, if we are able to arrange a transfer for Mr. Milson to a location at a reasonable distance from Mbordo, the problem will be solved."

"Yes," Alice agreed, "the sooner Derrick leaves Mbordo the better. It's not a pleasant thing, but you are right, it must be done. But is it possible to make such arrangements?"

"Perhaps," the Vice-Chancellor replied. "I know the director of the British Volunteer Program quite well. We will send Mr. Milson to Nkra immediately. Would you be kind enough to inform Mr. Milson? Ask him to prepare his belongings and be ready to board the school lorry at six o'clock tonight. The lorry will come to his house. I am sorry to burden you with this but I know that I can trust you to tell no one else except Mr. Milson and the two men who live with him. I would go myself but if I were seen word might reach Mr. Whitland of Mr. Milson's departure and he might try to take some action before Mr. Milson is safe away from Mbordo."

"I understand," Alice said, "and I will go immediately."

Alice left the Vice-Chancellor's office, walked to the Mbordo road and flagged down a lorry moving in the direction of the boys' house.

As Alice rode, her thoughts turned to the boys. "They have been close. They will miss Derrick. I will miss Derrick. Still, no two ways about it, moving is better than being shot."

"I'm very grateful," Derrick said when Alice told him of the plan. "This is definitely one of those times when a prudent retreat is in order."

A slight tremor in Derrick's voice betrayed his true feelings at having to leave Mbordo.

Alice said, "I hope we get a chance to see you again before we all leave Sakra."

"Me too," Derrick replied as he kissed Alice on the cheek.

The school lorry was on time. The driver must have had very personal instructions from the Vice-Chancellor. Jason and Jeff helped Derrick load his luggage into the back. He and the driver were the only passengers.

Then Jason climbed onto the running board on the passenger side and said, "Let us know where you are once you get settled."

"You may have to ask the British Volunteer Director in Nkra," Derrick replied. "I have a feeling that if I am still in Sakra, they will not want me to post any mail to Mbordo."

"You're probably right," Jason answered. "Good luck. Have fun."

"Hey blokes," Derrick replied, "it has been super. Damn sorry to run out on you like this."

"Can't be helped," Jeff said as they shook hands all around. "Good-by Derrick."

The lorry made no stops. The Vice-Chancellor had instructed the driver in no uncertain terms that Derrick was to be delivered to the house of a certain gentleman (the VSO director) in Nkra. Derrick was knocking on Mr. Wilkins' door before nine.

"Come in, Derrick," Mr. Wilkins said. "We've been expecting you. Have a seat. I have heard from my friend the Vice-Chancellor that you are having a bit of difficulty with a certain American and his wife at Mbordo. Kwame called this afternoon to tell me you were on your way. He didn't give me the full details. Would you care for something to drink before you tell me about it?"

Derrick asked for a beer and then proceeded to explain with as little elaboration as possible the ramifications of his relationship with Mrs. Whitland that had led to his quick exit from Mbordo.

"Those Americans," Mr. Wilkins commented when Derrick had finished, "bloodthirsty lot, aren't they? But I must say, you were a bit indiscreet."

"Yes, of course sir, that's putting it very kindly," Derrick replied. "I am very sorry."

"Well, what's done is done," Mr. Wilkins continued. "We all do make mistakes from time to time. Would you prefer return to England or a change of post in Sakra? Normally I would not be able to offer you a change of post this late in the year, but one of our people from the North had to return home. She left today and will not be back. If you would like to try your hand at secondary school English, I think that we could arrange for you to fill her position. That would put you well away from Mbordo."

"It really is very kind of you to bother with my case," Derrick replied. "I don't mean to sound ungrateful, but could I have the evening to think the situation through more carefully?"

"Most certainly," Mr. Wilkins answered. "In fact, I was just going to suggest that you do so rather than attempt to decide immediately. What I am doing is no trouble, really. That school needs a teacher. The Vice-Chancellor spoke highly of your work at Mbordo."

"He is a fine person in every sense of the word," Derrick said, blinking his eyes to dissolve tears before they rolled down his cheeks.

"Now don't worry," Mr. Wilkins said, "whatever has happened, we will try to make the best of it from here on. Please try to decide before tomorrow noon so that I will be able to make travel arrangements. Would you like to spend the night here?"

"No," Derrick replied, "there is someone I would like to talk with at the Teachers' Hostel."

"Very well," Mr. Wilkins said, then added, with a slight smile, "and Derrick -- do stay out of trouble."

"Yes, most definitely, sir," Derrick replied.

Once away from the Director's house, Derrick stopped a taxi and gave the driver directions to the Teachers' Hostel. He arrived there just as Musa was leaving for the night.

"Hey, big man," Musa chided, "you no be teacher no more. Why you here on Thursday? Students run you all way to Nkra?"

"Trouble, very bad trouble, Musa, that's why I am here," Derrick replied. "The woman was a big problem. You were very right."

Musa laughed and said, "You leave town quick. Just like in movie."

"That is right," Derrick said as he started to laugh.

"You go back when not so hot?" Musa asked.

"No," Derrick said, "I don't go back ever. Man has a gun. I go home or I go to the North. What do you think is best for me?"

Musa's face broke into a broad grin, "You go North. That place good for you. No problems like this. Plenty women. Nobody get upset. Just be careful you no say bad things about Allah.

Derrick nodded and asked, "You think that I would enjoy life there?"

Musa shrugged, "I like you. You like me. There people more like me than here. People there like you. So you like it there."

Derrick said good-by to Musa. The hostel was empty that night. Derrick sat alone on the front porch and tried to bring some order to his thoughts.

"I would really rather not go back to England tomorrow. Too much to explain," he reasoned. "Musa was right about me before, almost dead right. Maybe he is right this time too. North it is."

****

Mr. Wilkins made the necessary arrangements for Derrick to leave for Nandu on Saturday. Space had not been available on the Alitalia flight that connected the two cities and continued on to Rome. The best transportation that he had been able to find was the government transport bus.

On Saturday the bus went only as far as Pandu, where it stopped for the night. Some passengers slept in the bus but Mr. Wilkins had provided Derrick with funds for a modest hotel room. The next morning he returned to the government transport station early enough to find a seat by a window. By seven the bus was full, completely full. It was of a type designed by the Germans (probably with the African market in mind) to maximize the number of passengers carried. Even the aisle was filled with passengers who sat on fold-down seats.

"An excellent design," Derrick thought as the bus moved away from the station, "unless of course you had an emergency need for a bathroom."

It had been raining moderately in Pandu, but after an hour and a half of travel northward the bus seemed to outrun the rain. Change in climate and ecology was gradual but obvious. Trees were smaller and more scattered. Still farther to the north there were only gnarled, twisted, stubby creatures, little taller than a man's height. Real trees grew only along a few dry streambeds. Another hundred miles and even the scrub trees disappeared except for an occasional clump. Vast plains of dry grass became the dominant feature of the landscape, so brown now before the coming of the rains that Derrick had difficulty in imagining that this land could ever be green and alive, much less produce grain. Before they reached Nandu, even the brown grass would disappear and all that would remain was sandy dry soil. Yet even that soil would yield a crop of groundnuts so plentiful that the harvest would be heaped into huge pyramids to await shipment to other parts of Sakra and Europe.

The rains would come. This far to the south they never failed. They might vary in intensity from year to year, but they always came. Only farther to the north did the farmers and herders living on the edge of the desert have to worry about the dependability of the rains. In the villages Derrick saw that everyone was preparing for of the rains.

"Planting in that sand is an act of faith," Derrick mused. "The ground looks incapable of even growing cacti, much less grain and groundnuts. It will be interesting to see the effect of the rains."

Derrick's first views of Nandu reminded him of stories he had read of mirages seen by travelers in the desert. The ancient town's minarets shimmered in the dry

133

heat and seemed to disappear and reappear as the bus rolled down through dips and up over small hills.

The secondary school to which Derrick had been assigned was outside the thick walls of the city proper. All Western-style schools and teacher training colleges established before the 1960's were outside the city walls. Nandu had been the center of government of the powerful Kroban nation centuries before the British had come to West Africa. The British had never conquered the Kroban nation. After a number of skirmishes in the early 1800's in which both sides claimed victory, the British and the Sultan reached an accommodation. The British agreed to leave the internal affairs of the Kroban nation to the Sultan, and the Sultan agreed to let the British handle foreign trade and other external matters for his people.

For a time the compromise proved to be of benefit to all. The profits from trade in groundnuts, grain and cattle products had made the Sultan, the British merchants, and their African agents all rich. The Northern region never really became a part of the British Bounty Coast. Only as independence of England's West African Colonies became inevitable was the North artificially grafted onto the rest of the Crown colony.

In the late 1930's a relatively progressive Sultan came to power. He had realized that lower level administrative positions in the British colonial presence in the North, even though few in number, were filled entirely by men from the South who had been educated in English style schools. Although the Koranic schools and universities of Nandu had an international reputation for quality which dated back to the 15th century, they were never designed or intended to prepare their graduates for participation in the political life of a British colony. In order to provide local candidates for civil service positions, he allowed Christian missionaries to establish a few elementary and secondary schools near but still outside the walls of several of the larger cities of the North. With independence, the number of civil service positions available to the educated mushroomed. Schools of all types had opened to meet the demand for Western-style education.

Derrick's bus stopped within two blocks of the school. An older man and six students were there to greet him.

"Welcome to Wesley Secondary School," the older man said. "I am the Headmaster. We are extremely pleased that you were able to come to us as a teacher. The students are very pleased and happy. They were quite worried that no one would be here to help them prepare for the examination papers in English after Miss Carson departed."

Derrick smiled and offered his hand, "Very good of you to meet my bus. I assure you that I will make every effort to help your students prepare for their papers."

"You will not find the appearance of our school much different than many others in Sakra," the Headmaster said as they walked through the school gates. "It was founded by the Methodists but is now a government school. We do try to maintain a part of our religious heritage even though many of our students are Muslim. Miss Carson lived in the girls' hostel and served as Headmistress there.

"You, of course," the Headmaster said with a noise between a laugh and a cough, "will not be given that responsibility."

"I should hope not," Derrick replied rather stiffly, wondering to himself just how much the Headmaster knew of the reasons for his transfer. "That would without a doubt be well beyond my educational training or ability."

"Quite so," the Headmaster said crisply. "We do have a small flat available for your use near the gate. Once you have made the acquaintance of the watchman, you will be able to go and come as it pleases you."

"I do have one request," the Headmaster continued reluctantly and then paused.

"What would that be?" Derrick asked.

"Let me explain carefully," the Headmaster said. "In this region of Sakra we very much appreciate the help of volunteers from England and the United States. Without you we would have no hope of maintaining a high standard of education. Few graduate teachers are willing to work here."

"Yes, I do appreciate your difficulty," Derrick said, "but what is your request?"

The Headmaster replied quickly, "I must ask that if at all possible you do not bring any sort of strong drink or beer onto the compound. We are in the midst of a Muslim community that forbids the use of alcohol to the faithful. We are also by tradition a Methodist community. I hope this will not be too much of a hardship."

"Hardship or not," Derrick replied offering his hand to the Headmaster, "I will abide by your rules."

The Headmaster relaxed visibly as he accepted Derrick's hand.

"Thank you, sir," he said. "Will you require a day of rest before you begin your duties or shall I inform the students to expect you in class tomorrow?"

"I will be in class tomorrow," Derrick replied. "No reason to waste a perfectly good school day."

The Headmaster showed Derrick his flat and had students move his baggage there. The day's journey had exhausted Derrick. But when he tried the narrow bed supplied with the apartment, soon after finishing supper, sleep did not come easily. His thoughts were a jumble of times, places, events, and the daunting prospect of no more beer until he went south again. When he finally did drift off, he found himself wide awake a few hours later from a dream that started with Betty answering her front door and then changing into an angry image of Mr. Whitland with his handgun.

"Wonder how he got that thing into Sakra," Derrick thought. "Either they didn't look at his stuff or he bribed someone. Oh well, that was a silly dream. He is not coming here, I hope. Might as well look at the books I will be using tomorrow. Nice of them to put copies here."

Thirty minutes with the English texts for secondary school brought Derrick back to the edge of sleep and a dreamless remainder of the night.

CHAPTER 10
Mrs. Manati's Anti-Tribalism Committee

By the time Derrick had finished the first two lessons of the day in his new school, the campaign at Mbordo University-College to eliminate tribalism or at least to alleviate its effects was well under way. The Vice-Chancellor's comments in full assembly that Monday morning had been well received, except for the mention of mandatory changes of quarters for some students. Even Alice had devoted a portion of each class to a discussion of the evils of divisiveness and the glories of cooperation. However, as Gil had anticipated, the reassignment of students to new hostels did not go smoothly. The Kroban students were vehement in expressing their discontent at not being allowed to live together. The problem was intensified by the objections of Ave students to having Kroban in 'their' dormitories. Representatives of both groups requested a meeting with the Vice-Chancellor. In the face of opposition to the quarter's reassignment plan by more than 80 per cent of the student body, the Vice-Chancellor decided to postpone that portion of the anti-tribalism campaign until the matter could be given further study.

That afternoon he called another meeting of the faculty and asked for further advice on the housing situation. Thornton was the first to respond.

"Those students unwilling to follow your directives should be sent home permanently," he huffed. "Call in the army if anyone refuses to leave."

"Mr. Thornton," the Vice-Chancellor replied, "your plan is admirable from the point of view of maintaining social discipline, but it is less satisfactory in terms of practical results. If 80 per cent of the student body is forcibly sent home, then 80 per cent of the staff will have to be let go, and that is a result that I am sure no one in the room really wants."

After a few more suggestions similar in nature to Thornton's, Alice waved her hand and was immediately recognized by the Vice Chancellor.

"Perhaps the students themselves might be able to work out a solution," she suggested. "A student committee on the prevention of tribalism could be set up and asked to develop a workable solution to the problem of where students should live."

The reactions to Alice's suggestion were mixed.

"Anti-tribalism student committee," the Vice Chancellor mused. "Yes, that might be a reasonable idea. Especially with the right leadership."

"Excellent idea," Mr. West volunteered.

"It will never work," Thornton mumbled.

Once the room had quieted the Vice-Chancellor said briskly, "If there are no further suggestions, I think that we shall try Mrs. Manati's Student Anti-Tribalism Committee. Mrs. Manati, would you be so kind as to stay a few minutes afterwards to discuss the plans for your committee in greater detail."

Alice started to protest that what she had said was not really a plan but only an idea. However, the Vice-Chancellor adjourned the meeting before she had the opportunity to speak.

"Alice," the Vice-Chancellor said after the others left, "thank you very much for that suggestion. If that meeting had gone on another ten minutes I really believe that some damn fool would have suggested that we hang three students, one from each major tribe of course, in order to show that we are firm in our opposition to tribalism. I shall begin working tonight on the membership of your committee. Perhaps you will be able to call the first meeting before the end of the week."

"Now wait just a minute!" Alice protested. "What do you mean my committee? I don't know the first thing about tribalism. Would it not be better to have a Sakraian advise the committee?"

"No, I do not believe that it would be better," the Vice-Chancellor replied. "I do not wish to take any credit away from you, but the thought of a committee of students had also been in my mind. However, the problem that I had been unable to solve was what member of the faculty could lead such a committee. No Sakraian staff member would ever be trusted by all of the students. Even if he was from one of the middle lands, he would still be suspected of ties to the other tribes by marriage, religion, eating habits, bribes or whatever. When you made your suggestion, I knew that I had the solution to the problem of who should lead the committee. What you consider your weakness is your strength. Your lack of knowledge is an advantage. The fact that you are an outsider and also have many years of wisdom is very important. All of the students can respect and trust you."

"But for how long?" Alice responded quietly. "They will very quickly find that no one is as stupid as an old person they once thought smart."

The Vice-Chancellor sighed and spoke slowly, "Alice, Alice, I very much dislike placing you in this unfortunate position, but there is no one else."

"What about Mr. Johnson, Mr. Wills or Mr. West?" Alice asked in an almost pleading tone. "They have the qualification of being outsiders and they know far more than I do about this problem."

The Vice-Chancellor replied after a few moments of thought, "Mr. Johnson would be suspect because of his relationship with Miss Kanata. Mr. West? Eh...No. A very nice man but you know how difficult it would be for him. But, Mr. Wills, yes, that might be possible. I am still convinced that you are best suited for this matter, but if you don't think that you can manage I will bring the matter up with him. But Alice, you must promise me that you will help even if Mr. Wills does accept."

"Certainly," Alice replied in a relieved tone, "I will do everything that I possibly can to help. But Mr. Wills would be much better. I am only beginning to understand just how serious this problem is."

"Alice," the Vice-Chancellor said, "serious is not even the correct word. What is now happening could bring disaster. I am very much afraid for my family, this university, for all of us if these matters once go beyond our control. Unfortunately, what happens here on our small compound is only a small part of the total. Dr. Agyenkwa was a poor leader in many, many ways, but when he was in the high place, we did have at least a symbol of our nationhood. That symbol is now gone. I can only hope that we find something to replace it and quickly."

Alice offered to explain the situation to Jason. She went immediately to the boys' house. Jason was at first reluctant to become involved but began to change his mind when Alice explained that if he did not, she would have to assume the sponsorship and that such a responsibility would probably be too much for her to handle. When asked later that evening to serve as sponsor of the Anti-Tribalism Committee by the Vice-Chancellor, he agreed.

Once Jason had accepted, the Vice-Chancellor began the difficult task of determining the composition of the committee. The process was complete Thursday afternoon and Jason was able to announce that the first meeting of the Student Anti-Tribalism Committee would occur the next day at 2:00 p.m.

After lunch on Friday Jason had dozed off and did not wake until two. He was ten minutes late in reaching the scheduled meeting place. He found the Kroban representatives standing about ten feet from the door of the room in which the encounter was to take place. The other students had already gone inside.

"Why don't you join the others inside?" Jason asked. "Don't you find the sun warm?"

"We would not feel comfortable inside," the student answered, then added quickly, "until you arrived."

"Why would you not feel comfortable?" Jason asked.

"It is difficult to explain," another student said. "Perhaps you would not be able to understand."

Jason decided to be direct and asked, "Are you afraid because the other students are not Kroban?"

The first Kroban student spoke again, "Not afraid, but uncomfortable. Because one does not enter the house of an enemy does not mean that he is a coward. It is rather wisdom to avoid a place where harm is possible."

Jason asked, "Will you go in with me?"

"Certainly," the student replied, "when you are here, it is your house. We are not uncomfortable then."

"A little United Nations," Jason thought as he looked around the meeting room, "three Kroban, three Ave, three Atan, one Bordo, and three from the Middle Tribes."

Jason sat down. The students waited quietly for him to speak.

"No point in beating around the bush," he thought, then said, "I believe you know the purpose of this committee. In the last few months trouble has come to the University-College. Far too much trouble. And much of it seems to be related to what is called tribalism. The staff of the University-College believes that tribalism must be controlled and eliminated from the life of this institution. Certain suggestions have been made toward that end. This committee is the result of one of those suggestions. I sincerely hope that each and every one of you fully understands just how important this committee is. If tribalism becomes a strong force on this campus, I fear that the Mbordo University-College will cease to exist. Now you may well wonder why I, an American, an outsider, have been chosen to advise this very important committee? You may ask what do I know of this thing called tribalism? The answer to that question is that I know very little about tribalism other than that its effects are not good. To be very frank, I was chosen to advise this committee because I have no tribe here, and the Vice-Chancellor believed that even though my knowledge was small, I would be trusted to favor no one. Do you have any comments?"

"Sir," the Bordo representative, William Ageman, spoke, "we appreciate your help and will do our best to be cooperative."

The other students present seemed to nod their assent.

"The first order of business will be the election of a chairman," Jason said. "We will conduct this election and other business in accordance with Robert's Rules of Order, if that is agreeable to everyone."

"Pardon me, sir," one of the Ave students, Benjamin Atue, interrupted, "we do not understand what you mean by Robert's Rules of Order. Perhaps you could explain."

Once the student representatives had realized that RRO procedures were similar to those used in legislative bodies, they had shown remarkable enthusiasm in understanding and mastering their use. By 3:30 Jason had been able to explain enough of Robert's Rules of Order for the process of the selection of a chairman to begin.

Mansa Kano was sure that everyone on the committee would agree that since his tribe was the largest by far in the nation of Sakra, that a Kroban student should automatically be chosen as chairman. When he noted the expressions of disgust on the faces of the non-Kroban students, Jason vetoed that idea without further discussion and suggested an open election. Jason's suggestion was put in the form of a motion by Joseph Agga (representative of one of the Middle Tribes), seconded and passed ten to three with only the Kroban students voting nay. Then came the nominations.

Musa Kwama nominated Mansa Kano and added an admonition that he should be elected without opposition since he represented the largest tribe.

Kwasi Mensah, an Atan student was nominated by, not surprisingly, another Atan Student, Kwame Aduma. Kwame claimed support for his candidate on grounds of the Atan Tribe's superior sophistication in the art of governing. David Atar, an Ave student was nominated by Moses Abene, another Ave, and supported on the grounds that the chairman should be from the dominant tribe of the area. Finally Jacob Nokumba, a student from one of the Middle Tribes, nominated William

Ageman. He supported this nomination by saying that the University-College was on traditional Bordo lands.

The Committee then proceeded to accept Jason's suggestion (which he was to regret a short time later) that the Chairman be chosen by majority vote rather than a plurality.

The results of the first secret ballot were:

Kwasi Mensah (Atan): 3

David Atar (Ave): 3

Mansa Kano (Kroban): 3

William Ageman (Bordo): 4

Jason suggested they drop all three candidates who had received the lowest vote totals and declare William Ageman the new Chairman. Unfortunately, the Ave, Atan and Kroban students would have no part of that suggestion. The only other thing that Jason could think of to do was to keep on voting. Through fifteen ballots and the dinner hour no one broke with their tribal group. On the sixteenth ballot the Ave students switched their support to the Bordo candidate, and Jason congratulated the new Chairman of the Student Anti-Tribalism Committee of Mbordo University-College, Mr. Abraham William Ageman. Mr. Ageman's first act as chairman was to call for adjournment until 10:00 a.m. Saturday morning.

The next morning Mr. Ageman reconvened the committee, and Jason formally presented the first major item of committee business, i.e. how the Vice-Chancellor's plan to integrate student housing could be implemented. Jason summarized the reasons for the Vice-Chancellor's actions, and the difficulties that had ensued. He then turned the meeting over to Mr. Ageman. An open discussion of the matter followed. The initial reaction of the committee was that the entire concept was a mistake and that students should be allowed to continue to live together in ethnic groupings. However, after an impassioned lecture by Jason on the subject of nationhood, the committee, by 12:30, developed a limited consensus that perhaps the Vice-Chancellor's plan did have some merit if implemented carefully. By 3:30 the committee (by then on the verge of starvation because the Chairman refused to allow a break for lunch) agreed to a plan that would begin the integration of student housing. Kroban students would be asked to live in hostels with students from the Atan and Middle Tribes. Ave students would be asked to do the same. But Ave and Kroban students would never be forced to live in the same building without first agreeing to do so in writing.

"This solution is not too bad," Jason thought as he watched the students congratulate each other on their success in coming to agreement.

The positive atmosphere was further reflected in a resolution passed unanimously just before adjournment that the committee remain in existence to handle future problems related to tribalism. After a quick sandwich, Jason walked over to the Vice-Chancellor's house to present the committee suggestions. The Vice-Chancellor invited him in and offered a cold beer that Jason gratefully accepted.

The Vice-Chancellor listened carefully to what the committee proposed and then asked, "How do you see this housing proposal, Mr. Wills? Is it the most our students are willing to do?"

Jason replied, "I don't think they are willing to go further. The Kroban students won't even enter a room occupied by Ave students unless others are present. And that feeling is mutual."

"I had hoped for some way to pull them all together. Hoped that if they lived together they might all learn that we are not as different as we now seem to believe," the Vice-Chancellor said as much to himself as to Jason. "However, what cannot be cannot be. But you have done well, very well. I will accept the student plan and instruct the registrar to develop new room assignments.

"I also like the idea of continuing the committee," he said with a slight chuckle. "That way every time something difficult comes along involving tribalism, I can turn it over to them, and I won't be caught in the middle. Mr. Wills, you will of course continue to help us in this area, won't you?"

"Then I will be in the middle, instead of you," Jason replied. "I would be willing to help, but as you know I often travel on the weekends."

"Then no more meetings will be held on weekends," the Vice-Chancellor replied. "I am afraid that the committee's work on this problem was much too good. To use an American expression, we can not afford to let you off the hook. If an emergency weekend meeting is necessary, Mrs. Manati has assured me that she will help as a substitute advisor."

"OK," Jason said, "but I have this strange feeling that I am putting my own head in a noose. I am not sure that one should do that sort of thing voluntarily."

"Pardon me," the Vice-Chancellor said, "I don't understand 'head in the noose.'"

"As in preparing to be hung," Jason explained.

"Oh," the Vice-Chancellor replied, "like in an American Western. Well, we shall do our very best to insure that the rope is never tightened."

The housing changes were completed by Wednesday. That experiment in partial integration, along with the verbal efforts of the Vice-Chancellor and most of the staff to lower tribal hostility, did appear to have the effect of reducing tension on the University-College compound.

The Wills committee, as the staff began to call it, continued to have more than enough business. Disputes arose from such diverse sources as broken pencils to treading on a foot in a soccer match. The most serious incident was a knife fight between an Ave and Kroban student. Fortunately the fight had been stopped before serious injury had occurred, but the use of weapons was a serious escalation of hostilities that had previously been acted out with words or fists. The committee recommended that both participants be expelled. The Vice-Chancellor agreed.

In the following weeks, submitting problems to the Committee became an increasingly popular method of resolving disputes. This is not to say that all problems were being solved. But both staff and student confidence in their own

141

abilities to find solutions was enhanced by the Committee's work. On the campus, tribalism was now accepted as an evil reality, but one that could with effort and goodwill be kept under control. However, no institution of education exists in isolation. When anger and passion dominate the political process at the highest levels, when discrimination and bigotry go unchallenged by a nation's leaders, when decision making appears based on ethnic instead of national interest, educators find themselves helpless. The history of a nation at times seems like the incoming tide. The individual of goodwill is as helpless as the man who would defy that tide by standing in the ocean with his arms spread wide.

On a warm Sunday in June, four weeks before the end of the school year, General Musa was murdered by a group of Army officers led by a certain Captain Roberts. An ambush had been laid on the outskirts of Nkra. The affair had seemed a simple matter. The road that General Musa always traveled between his home and office was blocked by army trucks. General Musa's car was stopped and then riddled with machine gun fire.

The attempted coup failed. The other members of the Transitional Governing Council maintained control over most of the other units of the armed forces and the national police network. The Captain responsible for the attempted coup and his known supporters were arrested and incarcerated. A mini-power struggle for control of the Council was over before Tuesday of the next week. General Jonathan Igon was selected as the new Chairman. He was immediately hailed by the press, both foreign and local, as a potentially great national leader who would return Sakra to a path of both political and economic rationality; a man with a brilliant war record in actual combat under the auspices of the United Nations in the Congo; a man who had stepped out of the barracks reluctantly to lead his country in a moment of national need.

Unfortunately, the appearance of national unity and support for a new leader in a time of crisis was not an accurate assessment of what had actually happened within the Council nor of the mood of the various ethnic groups of Sakra. The young Army Captain who led the attempted coup was Ave. General Igon was Ave. In the North only one conclusion seemed reasonable and logical. Belief in the North that General Musa's death was the result of an Ave plot was further reinforced by the post-arrest handling of Captain Roberts and his fellow conspirators. Although, according to an official announcement, they had been arrested and incarcerated, the government refused to provide any information concerning where they were being held. Rumors spread that Captain Roberts was not in jail at all but instead hiding in a house owned by General Igon. The press waited patiently for the announcement of the trials of the conspirators. The announcement never came. A new Kroban representative was appointed to the Transitional Governing Council as an ordinary member to fill the slot left by General Musa's death. However, General Igon reserved most power for himself. The Council seldom met, and when it did General Igon did not attend but instead sent a representative to explain to the Council what tasks he wished them to perform. It was rumored that the General did not even discuss what occurred in Council meetings with his representative. This is not to say that Sakra was not being effectively governed by General Igon. In fact, the efficiency of government machinery was as high and the level of overall corruption as low as that of any comparable period since independence. However, the full implications of the death of General Musa were apparent only to the most farsighted in the city of Nkra.

Indications of what was happening to the national fabric were perhaps more clearly felt on the University-College Compound in Mbordo than they were in the General's secluded home in the suburbs of Nkra. Within a fortnight of the coup five complaints had been presented to the Committee, three of them involving physical violence. All Kroban students moved back together into one hostel. They refused even the Vice-Chancellor's personal request that they return to their assigned rooms. Musa Kwama, one of the few Kroban students still even willing to discuss the situation, explained to Jason that he and other Kroban had been told that the Ave students were predicting that all Kroban at the University-College would meet the same fate as General Musa.

In spite of Jason's best efforts, ensuing meetings of the Anti-Tribalism Committee often degenerated into shouting matches. Robert's Rules of Order stood little chance against the passion of newly revived, but centuries old, ethnic rivalries. As the committee found fewer and fewer solutions, students began to lose confidence in its ability to help them and the number of matters brought before the committee decreased dramatically. However, on the Friday before the final week of instruction, the Vice-Chancellor asked the Committee to meet and discuss a particularly difficult case. It involved the destruction of the personal belongings of a Kroban student. His storage chest had been set on fire the previous day.

The discussion of the case quickly degenerated into a serious of angry accusations and counter accusations. Mansa Kano accused a particular Ave student of setting the fire because he said that he had heard of public statements made by the student that indicated that he planned to do so. David Atar denied that the student charged had set the fire but indicated that even if he had, the Kroban student had only gotten what he deserved since he had been talking a lot about what evil people the Ave were. This accusations continued for about thirty minutes until the Kroban members of the Committee walked out. They refused Jason's request to reconsider and indicated that they would not return to this or any further Committee meetings.

Jason reported what had happened to the Vice-Chancellor. They agreed that the useful life of the Anti-Tribalism Committee was over. No formal burial occurred. The Committee simply never met again that year.

After the death of the Anti-Tribalism Committee, the Vice-Chancellor decided that the best defense against further trouble was to end the term as quickly as possible. He called the staff together and announced that the yearly exams would begin on Friday, continue during the weekend and be over for all students by the next Wednesday. Students would be required to leave the campus after their last exam. The schedule was designed so that all Kroban students would complete their examinations on or before Monday.

In spite of these precautions three Kroban students were assaulted by groups of Ave students before they were able to complete their exams. Only Alice's intervention had prevented at fourth attack. After grading papers most of Saturday afternoon Alice decided to take a short break and walk as far as the first forest stream. She noticed a group of students standing to one side of the beginning of the forest trail. She saw that they were gathered around one student whose back was to a large tree. She realized he was Musa Kwama, one of her students and a member of what had been the Wills committee.

She heard one of the students say, "You are not in Kroban land. When you see us, get off this trail so that we may pass."

Musa said nothing.

The other student spoke again, "Perhaps we should help you in some way to remember this thing."

As he spoke he picked up a rock about the size of a golf ball. Alice had decided that she must do what she could.

She spoke sharply, "What is going on here!"

The student with the rock dropped it and said politely, "Nothing at all is happening here, sir. We are only discussing the proper use of this trail."

"If I understand the custom correctly," Alice said, "the trail is the property of no man or group but for all to use."

"You are, of course, correct," the student had replied.

He then had spoken to the Kroban student, "Use this trail as often and however you please. And I do hope that we will meet again for a further discussion."

After the other students were well away, Musa looked at Alice, shook his head slowly, and said, "Thank you. I don't know what might have happened without your help. I was very foolish to come here alone. I like to walk in this forest, but it is too dangerous. I am a stranger here, a Kroban. It is a time of great fear for us in this place. My greatest hope in life is to see my home and family again. The next time I leave Mbordo I shall not return. I stay now only to take the papers. I would leave but then the entire year would be wasted and the money used by my family to send me to school would be lost. My family is poor. My education is their only investment. If it were not so I would leave now before the sun sets this day."

The Vice-Chancellor asked local police to arrest the students responsible for the attacks on Kroban students. When police arrived other Ave students surrounded those accused and made it impossible for the police to take them into custody. All Kroban students left Mbordo by Sunday evening. Kroban laborers disappeared that same day. The end of the last examination on Wednesday morning brought a tremendous sense of relief to both administration and staff.

Alice mulled over events of the preceding weeks as she finished grading her exams on Thursday. Jason and Jeff had expressed some concern that the abrupt closing and quick examinations had been unfair to many students. She could understand their concern, but agreed with the Vice-Chancellor's decision.

"School is over for at least two months," she thought. "Perhaps time will help ease these problems and things will be back to normal by September. Next year will probably be exactly the same as the beginning of this year and I will be bored stiff. Anyway, I hope so."

CHAPTER 11
Two Journeys

Alice's thoughts during that first week after the hectic closing were not much on the problems of the University-College. She loved her summers. She had always found in the long vacation the opportunity to renew her spirit and regain her strength.

"That," she thought, "is especially needed after this year.

"That boredom I used to feel would be a relief," she mused as she moved toward the front door to answer a 'hello' from Jason.

Jason and Karen had convinced Alice to spend a few weeks with them in the Canary Islands before she began a volunteer assignment working with teachers assigned to Mbordo middle schools on the use of modern methods of teaching mathematics. Peace Corps volunteers were supposed to have only three weeks of vacation each year. Teachers were expected to find projects during the long break to fill in non-vacation time. Earlier in the year Alice had asked two Headteachers of middle schools in Mbordo about the possibility of working with their teachers after the regular school day. The response had been enthusiastic. A few days later Alice was approached by a delegation of primary school Headteachers. They made it very clear that Mbordo's primary school teachers were very disappointed that they would not have the same opportunity. Alice mentioned the problem to Karen. That led to a plan for Karen to provide classes for interested primary school teachers in Mbordo that summer while Alice continued her work with the middle school teachers. Volunteers who extended for a third year were granted home leave. Jason planned to fly from the Canaries back to the United States to visit his parents, leaving Karen and Alice to return together to Mbordo and their volunteer project.

"Come on in," Alice called to Jason. "Sit down and have some tea. I have been meaning to ask you, why all this interest in the Canary Islands?"

"I think half of the Peace Corps volunteers in Sakra are going to the Canary Islands this summer," Jason replied. "We can only travel in the Third World. They won't allow us to go to Europe. I guess volunteers on the French Riviera just don't fit the Peace Corps image, but the Canaries are still part of Africa."

"Most of the Canadian volunteers will be there too," Karen added.

"How about Jeff?" Alice asked. "Is he going?"

"I don't think he wanted to unless Enata could," Jason replied, "and with the turmoil at the top in government, the civil service has just about stopped issuing travel papers to Sakraians. The minimum time is three months, if you're lucky."

"That would be just in time for next term," Alice mused. "Are they going to spend the entire summer at Kwim?"

"Whoopee, summer in Kwim," Karen said with a giggle.

"There are worse places," Jason said quietly, "but I think they are planning a trip north to visit Derrick. His school is in session a month longer than we are, and I think Jeff would like to see him again before he leaves Sakra. After that, he's headed back to Tennessee. If everything works out we'll be on the same plane back here in August."

"I'm not at all sure I would want to go to the North right now," Alice commented.

"Me neither," Jason replied, "but Jeff thinks that knowing someone living near Nandu would take care of any problems they might encounter."

"I really don't think they should go, but I guess that's their business, not mine," Alice said. "Speaking of my business, when do we leave for the Canary Islands?"

"Tuesday," Jason replied.

Their flight lifted off from Sakra International Airport at 10:00 a.m. The route included stops at the Monrovia and Conakry airports to the west before the plane turned northward to fly across the western edge of the Sahara. Alice was fascinated by the vast size and seeming emptiness of the desert. She watched carefully for the coastline, assuming that at least small settlements would exist there. What she saw reminded her of an old joke about the desert being the world's largest beach. The only sign of human presence as the plane neared the ocean was a dirt trail that might have been a road, otherwise nothing but sand and water. Alice knew from looking at maps that Spanish Sahara had an official population figure, but how or where those people lived was impossible for her to imagine. Within a few more hours she could see the Canaries.

Geographically, the islands were a part of Africa, but in most other ways they were a part of Spain. Off-season prices at the little hotels along the beaches were low, very low. The plaza of Las Palmas was a thing of joy for Alice. One could sit for hours sipping a beer or a cup of Spanish coffee. The others made side trips to Tenerife and Morocco, but Alice was content to sit and relax in the plaza by day and enjoy the luxury of a hot bath and well prepared food in the evenings. She was quite aware of how much more enjoyable she now found these small matters of life. On the next to the last day of the trip, Alice saw two men arguing vehemently in front of one of the shops on the edge of the plaza. She could tell they were close to blows and wondered if she should intervene.

"Wait a minute," she thought. "You don't have any responsibility here for anyone's conduct but your own, thank God. This is not Mbordo. You will be there soon enough. Wonder what next term will be like? Wonder how Jeff and Enata are doing? Hope they're all right."

****

There was no hot water in the small hotel near the compound of Derrick's school in which he had found a place for Jeff and Enata. The owner was a Hausa trader who had accumulated a small fortune in the leather trade and decided to invest in property. The manager he hired to run the place was Ave. The hotel was not designed for the tourist trade. Most rooms were rented by the hour. Derrick had been able to convince the manager to let a room to Jeff and Enata, only if they agreed to vacate before the weekend. Friday, Saturday, and Sunday were the nights when short-term rentals were in greatest demand. The hotel was constructed courtyard style around a well that held water even in the worst of the dry season. Its single entrance was less than a quarter mile from Derrick's school. The well's water created an oasis environment of lush greenness within the courtyard, in contrast to the dryness outside the hotel walls. Derrick was amused by Jeff and Enata's reaction when he led them into the courtyard. He explained how he had found the place.

"I was looking for a bar," he said. "But there are no bars within a thousand miles of Nandu. Instead I found this place. Of course it doesn't have a bar, but if you sit long enough and make the proper signals, the waiter will bring you a bottle of ginger ale that tastes quite like Star beer."

Derrick enjoyed having company. His few months in Nandu had been difficult. He was the only volunteer at the school. His teaching load was heavy. Drilling students in preparation for the English O-level was a new experience and one that he did not wish to repeat. But for the first few days of Jeff and Enata's visit all of that was at least temporarily put aside as they sat together in the courtyard of the little hotel, drank beer and reminisced about the 'good old days' at Mbordo. During the part of the day that Derrick was forced to work, Jeff and Enata toured parts of the old city of Nandu. They visited the cloth dying pits (where workers who did the actual dying had both purple hands and purple feet), the leather works, and Nandu's vast market that made even the Pandu market seem small.

Both Jeff and Enata noticed that they were the subject of much curiosity. They were used to being watched. In the South people had been attracted to them by a mixture of curiosity and interest. But in this city of the North curiosity seemed tinged with hostility. Jeff at first thought that the hostility was directed towards him or perhaps towards Enata for being in his company. When he shared these thoughts with Enata she had replied that he perhaps was correct, but in her opinion the attitude of the people of Nandu might be more related to the fact that her features were very much like those of the women of the Ave Tribe. Jeff only began to understand the full measure of what Enata had been trying to tell him after a ride to the market with an Ave taxi driver on the fourth day of their visit.

As Jeff was paying the fare, the driver motioned for him to move closer and spoke as he placed one finger near his eye, "Watch carefully your wife. Alone she will not be safe in this place. Kroban very angry about everything. Hurt many Ave. Myself, I drive only on certain streets. Else I be dead man. Soon take this car, family back to Aveland. Great danger for Ave here."

Jeff thanked the driver and promised himself that he would stay near Enata.

In the market they found a small shop that sold material that had been tie-dyed. However, when they asked about the price of one cloth the owner of the shop refused to deal with them. He said that he would not sell to them no matter what they were willing to pay.

The next morning Jeff and Enata were awakened by a commotion on the dirt road near the hotel. Four policemen were half carrying, half dragging a man toward the entrance. Jeff recognized him as the manager.

One of the policemen yelled in the general direction of the hotel, "We found this fool near the wall of the old city. Come and get him before he dies on this street. He had better stay here and mind his own business."

Either no one else was awake or they didn't wish to become involved. Jeff pulled on clothes and went to help the beaten man. He dragged him into the hotel's courtyard. The man was unconscious but most of his wounds appeared superficial. A hotel cook appeared and offered to help dress his wounds. The manager came to as the cook was working on a gash along his left leg.

"I am a very lucky man to be alive," he said to Jeff. "Tomorrow I will leave this place. Yesterday, I went to buy tickets to fly with my family to Nkra. The airport is on the other side of the walled city. I tried to come back quickly through the city, but that short journey was nearly my last. Tomorrow we go. I left the tickets with a friend near the airport. If you are wise you too will go quickly from this place. Go by airplane. I have heard that the roads are no longer safe for the Ave. You yourself have nothing to fear but your wife. . ."

He shook his head as his voice trailed off.

"But she is Bordo, not Ave," Jeff replied.

"For her sake I pray that you will have the opportunity to speak if trouble comes," the manager responded. "These people are very vicious. They hit you with a club first, then they ask who you are. They are much too angry to listen. A month ago I would not have said this would happen. But the situation becomes worse each day."

Jeff and Enata decided to follow the advice of the hotel manager. After talking with Derrick they decided that he would go to the airport to buy tickets and that they would move to the school and stay there until he returned.

Derrick brought disheartening news.

"There are no tickets available on any flights out of Nandu for the next three months," he explained. "The airport buildings are filled with Ave, just camping there in hopes of finding a vacant seat on any plane going anywhere. When the term is finished at my school in two weeks my year of service will be over, but I won't be able to fly out of Nandu. I will have to travel south by lorry to Nkra for a flight back to London.

"The rumors of severe beatings of Ave within the walled city and on the roads are just too numerous not to be true," he continued. "There are even reports of deaths."

Jeff and Enata decided to leave Nandu as quickly as possible. They moved their belongings to the road by Derrick's school. Derrick was able to stop a Benz bus. Jeff looked carefully at the driver and decided he was a man of one of the Middle Tribes. At first the driver refused to take Enata as a passenger. He explained that he wanted no trouble with the Kroban people and that Enata would have to find an Ave driver. Derrick explained carefully that Enata was Bordo and that Jeff as her husband would be able to protect both her and the driver. The offer of four times the usual fare, in advance, also helped the driver make up his mind in favor of taking them.

"Thanks, for getting us on this lorry," Jeff said through the window of the bus. "And, good luck on your own trip to Nkra."

"I won't have a problem," Derrick shouted as the bus began to move. "But, I hope we are doing the right thing with you two."

"It will be all right," Enata said quickly. "This is my country. Good-by and best of luck in everything."

After an hour of travel to the south, Jeff and Enata began to relax. Judging from what they had encountered thus far, the rumors that were circulating around Nandu had little basis in fact. The small villages and isolated farm compounds seemed no different than on the northward journey. Preparation continued for the coming rains. The few light showers that had already fallen brought little bits of green from the earth. Jeff was awakened from a drowsy half sleep when the forward motion of the bus came to an abrupt halt.

He thought the bus had hit something until he heard a harsh voice say, "Driver open door."

The leader of the men who stopped the bus boarded and quickly selected two men from near the front that he believed might be Ave. The other men in the group helped drag them off the bus. The two passengers screamed the name of one of the Middle Tribes, trying to convince the armed men that they were not Ave. The leader of the group ordered them to strip. He screamed at them to pledge their lives to the Prophet. Fortunately, they knew the direction of Mecca and fell to their knees, heads bowed. After a close inspection of their bodies and the markings on their faces the leader decided they were not Ave and allowed them to return to the bus. Even in this moment of fear, Jeff was struck by their countenance. They looked to him as he would have imagined souls returning from the grave. Several bodies lay about one hundred feet from the bus in mute testimony to the fate of those unable to convince the men they were not Ave. Once the two released men had slipped quietly into their seats, the leader moved to stand beside the driver. As he spoke, he slapped a piece of wood carved into the shape of a club against the palm of his left hand.

"It is very important," he proclaimed, "that we deal with these dogs from the South. They come to our home, take money, take women, everything. Then go away. They have murdered our leaders in Nkra. They expect to do this and nothing will happen. They throw our leader's body to the dogs of the city. They come here to the North and defile our religious places. They have no respect for God and his prophet. Now they want to run away to escape punishment, but we will not let them."

As he spoke his eyes moved carefully through the bus stopping to rest on each passenger. They did not miss Enata's partially covered face.

As he moved to where she sat he spoke, "Why do you cover your face woman? If you be good Muslim, you would use proper veil, not those evil colors of the South. Come, let me see all of your face?"

Enata let the cloth drop away from her face.

"You are Ave," the man said in a sneering tone that reflected his pleasure in finding another victim.

"No," Enata replied quickly, "I am not Ave, I am Bordo."

"Every Ave is a Bordo when it suits his purpose," the leader replied sarcastically as he reached across Jeff and grabbed Enata's arm.

Jeff grabbed the man's arm and started to protest, but the man's club silenced him. The force of the blow left Jeff semiconscious. He was aware that Enata was struggling as he felt her being pulled across his body but was unable to respond. Her scream seemed very real but far away. Full consciousness returned in time for him to see her being thrown to the ground near the bus. There was only one last small chance. He took his wallet from his pocket, opened it, and pulled himself over to a window of the bus.

"Look, look," he shouted as he waved the wallet outside the window, "I be American Peace Corps. Look at this picture. She is Bordo. The daughter of a chief. This I know for sure. I no lie. She my wife."

He threw the wallet toward the men. One of the men picked it up and handed it to the leader. He looked at all of the cards very carefully. One was the picture I.D. that identified Jeff as a member of the Peace Corps. The leader walked over to the window of the bus and looked carefully at Jeff and then at the picture on the I.D. card. He then returned to the others. Jeff could not follow the conversation but he assumed that it concerned his status and the contents of the wallet. That discussion seemed to Jeff to take several lifetimes. Enata sat up but did not attempt to move. Finally the leader returned to the bus and spoke to Jeff through the window.

He pointed to the picture on the I.D. and asked, "You this man?"

"Yes," Jeff replied, "I am. That is me."

"We don't want trouble with American Government. Peace Corps' people all right with us," the leader said.

Jeff tried to smile but found his face frozen in fear.

The man continued, "You say that your woman is Bordo and not Ave. But she look much like Ave. Can you prove what you say in some way?"

Jeff removed a letter from his suitcase. The letter was from his parents. It had arrived the day before they began their trip to the North.

"Look," he said, "this letter is from her father, the Bordo Chief of Kwim. It is to give her permission to go with me on this trip."

Jeff said a small, silent pray begging that the man did not know enough English to call his bluff. The leader took the letter and looked at it carefully before returning it to Jeff.

Then he spoke in a low voice so that only Jeff could hear.

"This is very stupid, to try to fool me. Can you not tell that I be educated? But anyway, I want no trouble with American people. I believe what you say about your wife and this letter will convince the others since none of them can write their names even in Kroban."

Then he continued in a loud voice, "What he says is true. This woman is Bordo. You may get down and help her onto the lorry."

As Jeff moved around to the front of the bus to help Enata, he noticed that the leader still had the wallet in his hand.

He said, "My friend, our business here requires money. Our expenses are many. Even to keep our bellies full requires that we buy food from these poor farmers around us. We would be very grateful if you would aid our cause."

Jeff replied quickly, trying to remove a tremor from his voice, "Most certainly I would be happy to contribute. Whatever you find there is yours."

The man smiled broadly, removed all cash from the wallet, handed it back to Jeff and said, "May Allah be with you and your Bordo wife."

Jeff helped Enata back onto the bus. She maintained her composure until the bus was out of sight of the men, then broke into sobbing, choking sounds that convulsed her entire body.

"I was dead or worse," she said. "I can't believe this could happen in my own country, I can't believe it."

Jeff held her. He cursed himself for having endangered her life and prayed that they would reach Pandu safely. Fortunately, their lorry driver had extensive knowledge of the roads. With the help of information received from drivers of lorries moving north he used back roads to avoid other groups of men searching for Ave.

Even those on the bus who were Kroban seemed relieved when they crossed the Aba river, the southern boundary of Kroban lands, a little after the sun had set. But no one was happier than Jeff and Enata to leave the land of the Kroban behind.

The remainder of the trip was uneventful. They decided not to tell Enata's father the full story of their trip and shared with him only the conclusion that life in the North had become hazardous for the Ave.

CHAPTER 12
Return to Mbordo

Three weeks had been sufficient vacation time for Alice. She had had her fill of sitting in the plaza in Las Palmas and was eager to return to Mbordo and began working with the middle school teachers.

Both Alice and Karen's classes were enjoyable. The middle and primary school teachers demonstrated the same type of excitement and interest that Alice had found in her third period class at the University-College, and having Karen around to discuss each day's events was both helpful and comforting. The classes ended in early August with a fufu and groundnut stew dinner provided by the students.

On Wednesday of the next week, Jason and Jeff returned to Nkra. Alice, Karen and Enata met them at the airport. They ate steak together that night at a Lebanese restaurant and slept at the Teachers Hostel. The next morning they enjoyed one of Musa's fine breakfasts and later had ice cream while they waited for Iron Boy to fill with passengers. Alice, Jeff and Enata were going back to Mbordo, Jason and Karen to Pandu. Karen's request for transfer had been granted the week before. She had been asked to fill a vacancy in one of the two secondary schools in the town of Mbordo. The Vice-Chancellor, when he learned of Karen's transfer, mentioned that one of the University-College lorries would be in Pandu on Saturday and could transport Karen's belongings to Mbordo on its return trip. Karen had gratefully accepted the offer.

Jason sat quietly beside Karen, staring out the window of the lorry, as they passed through the outer settlements of the city of Nkra.

"Deep thoughts?" Karen asked.

"My mind was playing time and space tricks," Jason replied. "Strange things happen, when you travel between cultures, to the way you visualize how you fit in a particular place. I think that Sakra is now reality for me. The United States is the abstraction. The United States is there, it is still there, it hasn't disappeared. But it just wasn't quite like I remembered it. I really couldn't tell whether it had changed or the way I saw it had changed. I knew what to say and when to say it, but I wasn't comfortable. It was as if I could step out of myself and watch what I was doing. I could even grade myself on the quality of my cultural adaptation to those strange people. I know it seems crazy but this is where I am comfortable, not there. Sometimes I felt completely out of place. Split. Here I am complete. One person. If I want to go somewhere I know how to stop a lorry or a taxi. If I am hungry, I know how to get food. I really had difficulty functioning there. It started right away, almost as soon as I got off the plane in New York. Jeff and I were on the same plane from London to Kennedy. We both had a layover of several hours. Jeff bought me a hamburger. It was marvelous, all juicy with lettuce and tomato. It tasted so good that

I bought myself another one. The second one made me sick. I almost threw up. That was the last hamburger I ate."

Karen laughed and said, "You are going to be here a long time. You won't be able to go home until the U.S. government starts a program of lorries and outlaws hamburgers."

Jason chuckled then continued, "I guess it's really not quite that bad. But people there just seemed so unfriendly. I know people pay attention to us here just because we are different, a curiosity, but it's still really nice to be able to think of yourself as somebody, a meaningful person."

"There are times when it's nice," Karen answered, "but there are also plenty of times when it's a damn nuisance."

"I know, I know, but don't ruin it already," Jason replied rather sadly. "In a few weeks I will probably be sick and tired of Sakra. But right now I feel great. Sakra is beautiful, just beautiful."

****

Jeff's thoughts, as the lorry that he, Enata, and Alice rode (with Alice in front and Jeff and Enata in the third row back) crossed the Nkra Plain were similar to Jason's. When he tried to explain, Enata showed no patience or mercy.

"In a few days you will be complaining again about the coldness of the water that you must use to shave each morning, bad food, and even about me," she said. "You are probably not comfortable anywhere."

"I am comfortable anytime I am near you," Jeff said as he tried to work his hand up under the fitted top worn by Enata.

"Stop that," Enata said in a sharp whisper. "Our very proper English school mistress at Saburi Girls School taught us very well that there is a proper time and place for everything, and that one should never attempt to do a thing outside of its proper time and place."

"What fools those English," Jeff commented. "I bet for some things there was never a time nor a place."

Enata giggled, "They would have had us believe that, but we knew better. We watched their actions instead of listening to their words. Most of the younger ones had a friend or two. They were almost human in that way."

"No teacher is completely human, that is certain," Jeff mused as he again tried to move his hand. "Take you for example. Did you know that at this very moment you are being extremely cruel?"

Enata poked Jeff in the ribs sharply with her elbow. His groan was loud enough to be heard by most of the other passengers. The driver of the bus was so startled that he stopped the bus.

He turned and asked in a polite voice, "Sir, are you hurt? Are you ill? Do you need to get down a moment?"

Jeff was more embarrassed than any time that he could remember since he was five and had forgotten his lines in a Sunday school play. He mumbled that he was all right and thanked the driver for his attention. The driver restarted the bus and they continued the journey toward Mbordo.

CHAPTER 13
Human Rivers

The fall term began on the third Monday of August. After several days of teaching, Alice realized that she no longer had any Kroban students in her classes. She asked the Vice-Chancellor why. He replied that all Kroban students enrolled the previous year had either discontinued their schooling or requested transfer. He also explained that none of the Kroban students newly admitted in this school year had chosen to attend Mbordo. He indicated some hope that several still might enroll at a later date.

The Vice-Chancellor asked Jason to give the Anti-Tribalism Committee another trial. The workload of the committee was greatly diminished by the disappearance of the Kroban students from the campus. Only one minor complaint from an Atan student was received during the first three weeks of the term. A sense of calm prevailed across the campus as students seemed to realize that the time lost at the end of the previous school year would now have to be made up if good marks were to be had on the papers at the end of this school year.

In mid-September, another coup occurred. A group of Kroban and Atan army officers planned and executed the change of leadership. The official announcement stated that General Igon died in a firefight during a battle for control of his personal residence. However, rumors quickly spread among the Ave students of the University-College that the General was murdered as he tried to surrender on his own lawn. A new government was officially proclaimed on Monday, a little after three in the afternoon, by an announcement on the government radio station.

Jason again thought about making a trip to Nkra to personally gauge the effects of this coup. However, tales and rumors of what was happening in the capital city, passed on to him by both Atan and Ave students, in addition to Karen's strident objections, dissuaded him from attempting the journey. Nevertheless, by putting together bits and pieces of information gathered from different sources, Jason developed what he thought was a reasonably accurate picture of what had occurred.

On Monday afternoon the insurgents had captured the radio station and claimed victory. General Igon's residence had also been taken that day and the General killed. Most other members of the Transitional Governing Council were still at large. Certain units of the army, navy and air force, led by Ave officers, had continued to resist. By Wednesday all members of the Council had either surrendered, died in the fighting, or fled in the direction of Aveland. Without leadership, resistance to the coup collapsed. Ave officers, enlisted men, and police quickly realized the weakness of their position and also fled. Those who reacted too slowly found themselves either before a firing squad if captured by Kroban soldiers or placed in preventive detention if fortunate enough to have fallen into the hands of soldiers commanded by an Atan officer.

Major Mansa emerged as the new supreme leader. His first act was to promote himself to the rank of Major General, supreme commander of the armed forces of Sakra.

The immediate effect of the coup on the University-College community was not dramatic. This was due in no small part to the absence of Kroban students. Even though Atan officers had been involved in the coup, Ave students tended to place most of the blame for the deaths of General Igon and other Ave soldiers with the Kroban. But the reports brought back from the Capital city by lorry drivers and fleeing soldiers -- of Ave deaths, injuries and imprisonment -- seemed to roll across the campus, like shock waves, causing almost visible shudders of pain and anguish among Ave students. One could sense their anger and frustration as they gathered around one wounded soldier after another and listened to their bitter denunciations of the officers who led the coup and of the men they thought were friends who deserted them because they were Ave. At first the students would listen quietly. But as the men continued to recite long lists of atrocities committed against Ave soldiers, General Igon, and the Ave Nation, the student's anger seemed to rise, as water boiled in a pot, until their bodies could no longer contain their rage. Their indignation and wrath took on a life of its own that seemed to explode into exclamations of hate, into body movements that were frightening in the emotions they betrayed, and finally into near dances that, though spontaneous, resembled the ancient dances done by the Ave in preparation for battle.

All middle schools in the area closed the day after the coup. Jeff's project came to an abrupt halt. Both laborers and students stopped working in the University-College fields. American and British professors continued to meet their classes. Students came to class. They sat politely and even managed to give the appearance of listening. But any professor who asked questions quickly realized that no one was hearing much of what was being said.

On Thursday an argument developed in one of Alice's classes between an Atan student and an Ave. It degenerated into a fist fight. Alice's DC training proved its full worth. She picked up a well made yardstick and rapped both students sharply in order to embarrass them and command their attention. It worked. They stopped fighting. But Alice knew that the classroom truce did not mean the end of the disagreement. The more perceptive Atan students were already making arrangements for transportation away from Mbordo. This was not an easy matter since many lorry drivers returning from Nkra refused to go again in that direction. Moving west was not as difficult since every Ave with a lorry seemed willing to drive toward the Ave city of Hunta.

Bordo students found themselves in an ambiguous situation. Since Bordo lands were completely enclosed within the borders of Aveland, the Ave people tended to assume that Bordo land and the people that lived on that land were just another part of the Ave nation. And, indeed, many close ties did exist between the two ethnic groups. Much intermarriage had occurred in the last fifty years and many stories were related by grandparents to grandchildren of how the Ave and Bordo nations had fought successfully together against the Atan and the Kroban before the British came. But, there were also stories of vicious battles between the two nations. The most damaging stories came from those periods of historical time in which the Ave had used the Bordo Tribe as a source of human beings to sell to coastal tribes, who in turn sold them to Europeans and Arabs for shipment to other parts of the world. The Bordo nation had a much stronger collective memory of those periods in their history than did the Ave. Bordo people in no way considered themselves to be brother to the Ave. Nor did they react to the coup and the death of General Igon as the Ave communities had. Instead they felt that General Igon was an overbearing tyrant whom Sakra was well off to be done with, and that anyway these matters were between Atan, Ave and Kroban and they would be happy to be involved as little as possible.

On Friday of the second week after the coup, Jeff and Jason received an unexpected early morning visit from one of the Bordo students, Robert Bedu. His knock was so quiet that they would probably not have known that he was at the back door had they not been eating breakfast in the kitchen. Jeff let him in. He was so frightened that he had difficulty making himself understood.

But the message he brought was simple, "Please, let your eyes look on the trail behind the house of the lady mathematics teacher that leads into the forest."

He refused to explain further and left quickly.

Jeff and Jason found the place without difficulty. Moses Abene, an Atan student, lay in tall grass about five yards from the trail. Jeff held his wrist and found he still had a pulse. Nothing else about the way he looked indicated that he was still alive. They carried him to Alice's bungalow. Alice fought back a wave of nausea as she recognized Moses, and realized he was the young man involved in the fight in her classroom.

Jeff administered what first aid he remembered from Peace Corps training and Jason went to find a way to transport the student to the dispensary. The Atan student survived and was able to walk within a couple of days. He refused to discuss what had happened with anyone other than Atan students and teachers. Rumors spread that he had been forced by at least six Ave students to accompany them to the place in which Jason and Jeff found him. The incident destroyed the last vestiges of goodwill between the two ethnic groups. By Tuesday of the next week not a single Atan student was left in Mbordo.

The same pattern of migration was also developing in other parts of Southern Sakra. Atan fled east and Ave west. They passed each other on roads and paths. Human rivers flowing in opposite directions.

Rumors of Ave succession became incessant. They piled one on top of another, gaining a false reality by their frequency. A lorry driver brought word that a government had been formed in Hunta, another that it was not a government but a committee to negotiate. Still another brought word that units of Ave soldiers were regrouping to support the soon-to-be-made announcement of secession. Little else was discussed in the University-College staff room.

The Atan professors left with the Atan students. The only outsiders on the compound now were a few students and professors from the Middle Tribes and the expatriates. The Peace Corps Volunteers privately speculated as to when they would be called to Nkra. But the 'word' did not come. In the capital city General Mansa and the officers loyal to him had consolidated their position as the new rulers of Sakra. All signs of resistance had disappeared in the city proper and its suburbs. The Peace Corps Director, who lived in the city of Nkra, perhaps did not understand the full implications of the reaction to the coup in villages and cities in other parts of Sakra.

In time, the rumors of secession grew so totally pervasive that they reached even the ears of General Mansa. He decided that it would be wise to embark on a policy of national reconciliation. The National Council of Redemption was created almost overnight and a few prominent Ave were convinced or perhaps coerced to serve on the Council. Ave officers and enlisted men who had been arrested by troops under the command of Atan officers (and hence still alive) were released and permitted to resume their former positions within the armed services and police forces, provided they agreed to sign a pledge of loyalty to General Mansa and the National Council of Redemption. Those who refused to sign the pledge were released anyway, and, in what truly was a gesture of conciliation, allowed to return to their homes.

In the weeks that followed, General Mansa actually allowed the National Council of Redemption to develop into an organization that was of some importance in the governance of Sakra. Talk of Ave secession lessened. A few Atan students and professors even returned to the University-College. Secondary, middle and primary schools in the town of Mbordo reopened.

The Peace Corps Volunteers had developed a pattern of meeting together at Alice's bungalow once or twice a week to share what they had heard and seen. The British couple, Beth and Ian Harris, also participated in most of these discussions. On a Thursday evening during the sixth week of the school term they were again together in Alice's kitchen, trying to sort out the effects of the coup and General Mansa's efforts at national reconciliation.

"It's truly remarkable," Alice said as she poured the tea. "Even 'wonderful' as they would say here. I'm back to teaching my classes. The students are doing their work again. It's almost as if nothing had happened."

"Almost but not quite," Jason was quick to comment. "It's different. There are definite signs. The Anti-Tribalism Committee is very, very dead. No one dares to file a complaint. We did meet once. But no one would say a damn thing. I finally gave up and adjourned the meeting."

"What's happening is eerie," Ian said, "it's like everybody just agreed to stop for awhile. But people died. The hate is deep, very deep. It's not just going to go away."

"I remember a summer in DC like that," Alice mused with a slight laugh that reflected sadness rather than mirth. "Three people were shot to death by policemen

159

in a week. There was a mini-riot on Fourteenth Street that just seemed to disappear when police reinforcements arrived. A lot of talk after that but nothing happened. But the hate was still there waiting to explode. The King assassination did it. People's emotions just seemed to blow up. God, I don't think I could stand something like that again. It was weird. On Sixteenth Street, when it started, you wouldn't know that anything had happened except for the smell of smoke. Fourteenth Street was on fire from Pennsylvania Avenue to the second alphabet."

"Let's hope that reason will prevail," Beth said. "I think secession would be a disaster for the Ave and the rest of the nation."

"If things start to go bad, how long would the Peace Corps leave us here?" Alice asked.

"Probably until the government of Sakra asked for us to be removed," Jason replied. "My guess is that the United States will be very careful about any move that would antagonize the new government or indicate a lack of faith in its stability. After all, there is the oil to consider."

"Do you really believe there is oil off the coast of Sakra?" Beth asked.

"There probably is," Jason replied, "at least judging from the rumors. But the major oil companies and the Sakra government have been very careful in their comments and predictions."

"Yes," Ian continued picking up the train of Jason's thoughts, "if there is oil, most of it is in the West off the coast of Aveland. I think the government might be a bit afraid that they would try to take the oil for themselves and tell the rest of the country to go to bloody Hell. The oil just might have more to do with General Mansa's efforts at conciliation than any genuine desire to accommodate the Ave nation."

"You two are total cynics," Alice said sharply. "But you're probably right. Anyway, whatever the General's motives, I hope he succeeds in holding this country together. It would be a shame if it fell apart."

"I am not completely sure of that," Ian responded. "The Ave might be better off alone. They are very industrious. With the oil money they could build a prosperous little nation."

"And I suppose the rest of the nation could just go to hell," Alice said softly.

"I don't know if it's fair to put it that way," Jason interjected. "Maybe some of it is their fault. But the Ave have not been well treated at all in the North and sometimes not even in other parts of the South. Look what happened to Jeff and Enata."

"That's true," Alice said, "but in all fairness the students from the North and even those from the East have never been treated as equals on the University-College compound, and this school is not really on Aveland. What's worse is the Ave don't even treat the Bordo with any respect, and they consider them to be almost brothers."

"It really does not matter who is at fault," Beth said. "It would be an economic disaster for most of the people of Sakra if it broke up into small parts. Think of all of the new and worthless currency that would be printed. And not just one General Mansa as supreme leader and redeemer of his nation but perhaps a full dozen, each with hundreds of advisors and his own personal army, navy and air force. The entire place would be bankrupt within days."

They laughed together for the first time that evening at Beth's outburst.

"By the way," Alice said to Jason, "what about Jeff and Enata? Why didn't they come tonight? I haven't seen much of Jeff this last week. Is he all right?"

"Yes Jason, what about Jeff?" Beth asked. "He passed by me in front of the senior lounge yesterday. I said hello but I really don't think he even saw me. Seemed totally occupied by his own thoughts."

"No doubt worrying about the future of Sakra," Ian commented.

"I don't know what's wrong," Jason replied, "but I doubt that he would believe the future of Sakra to be in his hands. He said that Enata was coming over tonight and they needed to talk, alone. If not for Alice's hospitality I would be out roaming the streets."

"One would think they could wait until later in the evening and use Enata's apartment for that sort of discussion," Beth said.

Everyone laughed except Jason.

"Unfortunately, I'm afraid that it may not be so simple," he said. "I have never seen him like this. Jeff's really concerned, whatever it is. When something really bothers him, he drinks Scotch in the middle of the night. The bottle is almost empty."

CHAPTER 14
Jeff and Enata

The sounds of the argument carried in the African night to the small houses nearest the bungalow. Their occupants heard loud voices but took little notice. The Europeans did so many strange things.

"I will not marry you now," Enata said. "You Americans are all crazy. You think that because someone gets a baby in her belly that she must have a husband. What happens if the baby is not alive when it comes out? Then you will go away. No baby, no husband. Just wait. Be patient. These matters can be decided after the baby comes."

Enata had, two days before, confirmed what Jeff had suspected for several weeks. They had taken precautions, but the condoms available locally came with no guarantees of quality.

He had asked, "Are you going to have a baby?"

She had teased with a smile and said, "I thought you already knew." She had then placed his hand gently on her belly and said apologetically, "I really did think you already knew, but don't worry. I feel very well. Everything will be all right."

He had not fallen asleep that night until he had made a final decision to marry Enata. The purpose of their meeting this night was to inform Enata of that decision. Unfortunately, from Jeff's point of view, Enata was having nothing to do with the idea.

In reply to her arguments he said, "I want to marry you because I love you. Whatever happens with the baby, I still just want to marry you and be your husband."

Enata looked into his eyes and spoke in a sad, hushed tone, "Jeff, Jeff, my brave, kind, considerate, little boy. Would you really have wanted to marry me if this had not happened?"

Jeff did not know how to answer. He hated dishonesty. Because he did not know what or how to answer, he said nothing. Finally he decided to tell Enata his real thoughts.

"I don't know," he said, "I just don't know for sure what I might have done. I do think that I would have wanted to marry you anyway. But I can't say for sure. But it's different now. You are pregnant. You are going to have a baby. How can I know what I would have done if this had not happened?"

"The fact that I am pregnant is perhaps different for you but not really for me," Enata replied. "You still do not understand us well. I am an African woman of the Bordo Tribe. I would have become pregnant in time, if not by you then by someone else. It is part of our fate. We will have children. That you are the father is not so important as, I think, you have convinced yourself. The child will be cared for whether you are here or not. In Kwim all babies are loved and accepted. They are precious to us. He or she will have many fathers. There are no bastards here. It is much better that we wait until after the baby is actually with us and then you can search your mind to see how and what you feel, and I also can decide in what manner I love you.

"Aii," Enata moaned, "in your face I see the pain that you feel. I am sorry my love. It need not be so. You have not done a bad thing. For me to have a child is only good. My father will be so very happy. Can you please try to understand?"

Jeff said nothing, but the tension that had engulfed his body seemed to dissipate, not out of relief but exhaustion. His shoulders seemed to sink into the couch. His eyes rested blankly on the floor as he tried to comprehend the meaning of what Enata was saying.

"Perhaps," he thought, "what she said would be best. Just wait and don't worry. Let things work themselves out."

Enata interrupted his thoughts, "The baby is more than four months along now. In two or three months I will travel to Hunta. I have an uncle there who is a doctor. The hospital there is good and he will see that I am well treated.

"Jeff, Jeff," Enata continued in a pleading tone, "you know you are ridiculous. I will miss you so much when I have to go. Can we not enjoy the time that remains?"

Jeff had trouble finding words to express his jumble of thoughts and feelings that seem to pile one on top of another.

After a few minutes of silence he smiled a little sadly and replied, "I promise that I will do my best. I don't know how good that will be, but if I can't convince you to marry me now, I will try to be a good boy and just hope you will change your mind."

Enata made no further effort to conceal the fact that she was pregnant. This created something of a scandal in the minds of the American advisors and their wives, but the rest of the University community took little notice. As Enata had tried to explain to Jeff, for a woman to have a child in Sakra was an ordinary event.

In the following weeks Jeff threw himself into the effort of acting as if nothing out of the ordinary had occurred. He and Enata went to movies, to the market, to visit friends; all of the things they had done before the pregnancy.

However, Jeff did make one trip that he did not mention to Enata. One Wednesday he left school at noon. Telling no one where he was going, Jeff walked over the hill to the paved road and took a lorry to Kwim. When Jeff reached the home of Enata's father, he hesitated calling out, unsure if he would be welcome. He need not have worried. Before he had time to decide, Chief Kanata came forward to greet him as if he were expected. Jeff had never fully understood the talking drums, but he did know messages traveled faster than lorries.

The Chief's words confirmed the efficiency of the drums, "Welcome, you are, as always, welcome in my house. We have been expecting you. Please come in and sit down with me for awhile. How was your lorry ride? Uncomfortable as usual I suppose?"

Jeff thanked the Chief for his hospitality and mumbled something about the ride being no worse than usual. He found the silence of the compound unnerving. Usually the courtyard was a place of much activity with women working and children everywhere. Today the women were out of sight and even the children had disappeared. A small boy brought beer and glasses, then he too disappeared.

Chief Kanata, after at least a full minute of silence, spoke, "It is Wednesday. A difficult day for you to make this trip. You must have important business."

Jeff said, "I wish to marry your daughter, Enata."

Chief Kanata did not reply immediately but instead sipped his beer. The glass was half empty before he spoke again.

"I know that my daughter will have a child soon," he said. "Is that the reason that you wish to marry her?"

Jeff replied, "No, I don't think that is the reason. I love her very much."

"There are times," the Chief said, "whether we like to admit it or not, when love is not the most important consideration. But anyway, my good friend, no matter what I feel for you and my daughter, what would you have me do?"

Jeff's sentences seemed to tumble over each other. "Talk to Enata. Tell her that to marry me would be a good thing for both of us. Tell her that you know that I love her and that you approve."

The Chief sighed and said, "I think you already know that you are discussing this matter with the wrong person. Enata is very much to her own way. Whatever the outcome, it will be her decision, not mine."

"But she loves you and respects your judgement," Jeff pleaded. "She listens carefully to what you say."

The Chief rested his forehead in his right hand in a gesture of resignation and thought, then spoke in a quiet tone.

"My good friend, I don't think I have ever been able to tell you less than the complete truth even when it is painful. In my own heart I can very well understand and perhaps even agree with Enata's reasons for avoiding marriage. She knows very well that you will not stay here forever. This is not your true home and all men do in time return to their homes. It cannot be otherwise, no matter what you say now. She is not at all confident that she could live in America. In Sakra the fact that you and she are not really the same is not so difficult. But she has read much about the problems of Black people in the United States, especially since she met you. In Sakra she has and is as much as a human being could expect to be in this life. She has respect, dignity, authority. Would this also be true in America? Could she hold her head proudly and be considered the equal of any person?"

Jeff answered quickly, "As my wife she would be accepted. We would find a place to live where being African would make no difference."

"Perhaps what you say is possible. I do not know America well and what one reads is never the complete truth," the Chief answered. "But would she be accepted as a person for her own merits? Our society is not that kind to women. Enata has struggled very long already to achieve this type of acceptance. It was never easy for her. Often I wished to tell her to stop fighting so hard and just be a woman, but I knew that she could not. I don't think she could now be happy in giving up what she has achieved, no matter how much she loves you."

"I'm sorry, I did not understand," Jeff said in a strained voice near tears. "I thought only of myself. I never thought of Enata's happiness."

"Also," Chief Kanata continued, "what can you say of the child? What would its future hold in America? In this land he will be my first grandson, the grandson of a chief. True, he will have no father in this place unless Enata marries, but he will have two uncles that will provide for his education and see to it that he has every opportunity to succeed. He will be a lawyer, or a doctor perhaps, if God so wishes. Can you say that he will have the same opportunity in America?"

"Yes," Jeff responded quietly, "I would do everything that I could to see that he had such opportunities."

"That much I am happy to know," the old man said. "My feelings are very confused. I would truly welcome you as a son. But I also wish Enata and the child to remain here with me always. My heart tells me that once they leave, I shall not see them again and that the child could never be as we are, an African."

The Chief paused, then said, "When I was in school at a very young age the English masters taught us that for a woman to have a child before marriage was a terrible thing, a tragedy next to death. They said that the child would be a bastard, that I believe is the term used by the English, unwanted and unloved, looked down upon and despised all of its life. Did you know that in the Bordo language we do not even have a word like 'bastard'? Every child born to a Bordo woman is precious to us, is loved and wanted. If that matter has worried you, then rest your thoughts. As I have already promised, the child will be well cared for."

"But Enata . . . ." Jeff tried to put into words his fears of her disgrace as a result of the pregnancy but found it impossible.

As was often his habit, Chief Kanata answered the unasked question.

"Enata will return to teach at Mbordo after the birth of the child," he said. "It will be very much as it was. The English no longer control our moral standards. When Enata is at work, the child will have many mothers here in my home. The day may come when she will marry, perhaps you or perhaps someone else. But most important, Enata will continue to be Enata."

Jeff tried to speak but found no words to express his thoughts.

The Chief continued, "I very much believe that you are sincere in what you say. I will speak to Enata of this conversation. However, I must again be honest with you. If it were within my power to force her to marry you, I would not do so."

The Chief turned his head toward the center of the compound, looking away from Jeff, and said, "If things were as I would have them, none of this would have happened. It brings as much sadness as joy. We have as always a proverb, 'For a chief the most difficult subjects are those in his compound.' But the child will bring the special happiness that only someone new to this place we call earth can. I do look forward to that event with great anticipation."

Neither man had anything further to say. They finished the last of the beer and said the traditional farewells of the Bordo. Jeff stopped a lorry going in the direction of the Mbordo junction. Moisture in his eyes blurred his sight but he didn't notice. His vision had turned inward as his body absorbed the jolts from potholes in the road. Only now was he beginning to understand his relationship with Enata. Only now was he beginning to see that his assumptions about love, marriage, and children were exactly that, his assumptions.

CHAPTER 15
Emergency Trip to Germany

On the second Wednesday of November, the messenger from the secondary school in which Karen worked appeared at the door of Jason's classroom. The boy was in an agitated state and waved his hand wildly to indicate that Jason should come to the door. He handed Jason a note from the Headmaster.

It read, "Miss Wilson is not feeling at all well. Severe pains in side. Please come as rapidly as possible."

Jason dismissed his class. He was able to convince one of the University-College lorry drivers to transport him and the messenger to the secondary school. Karen had already been taken to her small bungalow a few minutes walking distance from the school compound. When she saw Jason, Karen attempted a feeble smile. Hello formed on her lips. She shrieked when Jason touched her stomach.

Jason sent messages to Alice, Jeff and the Vice-Chancellor (hoping that at least one of them would be found quickly) requesting that the Peace Corps Doctor in Nkra be telephoned and informed that Karen might have appendicitis.

The Vice-Chancellor had been the first found. He relayed telephone instructions from Nkra to Jason that Karen should be moved to the Capital City as rapidly as possible. Dr. Grasinski arrived at about the same time as the Vice-Chancellor's message. He also recommended immediate evacuation to Nkra. The Vice-Chancellor arrived and offered his automobile. Alice and Jeff came a few minutes later. The Vice-Chancellor insisted that Alice accompany them in case Karen needed help while Jason was driving.

The trip was made more difficult by road checks conducted by the army. Jason found himself near tears at their slow pace and the sound of Karen's shallow, pain-filled breathing. Near the Atan side of the Kra river bridge, checkpoints were never more than five miles apart. After waiting in line at the first roadblock for more than forty minutes, they developed a system for getting through quickly. Jason would swing the car around the line of waiting vehicles, either on the berm or on the wrong side of the road, and stop within a few feet of the soldiers. Alice would jump out of the car, wave their passports, and point to the back seat. Karen would moan loudly or scream in pain depending on how she felt. One glance at Karen and the three American passports was usually enough to get the car waved through.

Late that afternoon they reached the office of the Peace Corps doctor in Nkra. By seven that evening Karen was on a flight to Frankfort, Germany. Her destination was a hospital on a military base located near that city.

His good-by to Karen at the airport had taken what remained of Jason's emotional strength. She had smiled and even laughed a little. He had tried to maintain his composure but broke into open tears the moment her wheelchair was no longer in sight. He couldn't remember feeling that tired before, not ever.

However, neither he nor Alice wished to spend the night in Nkra. On the trip back to Mbordo they no longer tried to move to the front of the line at roadblocks. Soldiers still on duty from that afternoon inquired after the health of the young lady and expressed their sympathy and best wishes. They reached the village of Mbordo a little after two the next morning.

The next day the Headmaster of Karen's school received a call from the Peace Corps office in Nkra. Karen had reached Germany in time for the removal of her appendix before rupture. Recovery was proceeding normally and she was expected to return to Sakra in a few weeks.

****

Two weeks later, Jason and Alice returned to Nkra in the Vice-Chancellor's car to meet Karen. Her flight was due in at 1:00 p.m. They arrived at the airport a few minutes before twelve. The Peace Corps Doctor was also there to check on Karen's condition before she returned to Mbordo. The airplane landed smoothly. Moments later they could see the faces of the people who had been on the plane as they walked down the stairs that had been rolled to the plane's door. The first people off looked frightened and unhappy.

Jason's thoughts became words, "Maybe they had some problem with the plane. They don't look very well."

"Perhaps it was a rough flight," Alice speculated.

They saw Karen come out of the airplane's door. She had one arm around a stewardess' shoulder. The stewardess had her arm tightly around Karen's waist to steady her steps as they made their way down to the tarmac. Both women were crying. When they reached the bottom and the stewardess loosened her grip, Karen seemed unsteady on her feet and confused about which direction to walk. Jason climbed the four-foot retaining wall. He ignored the calls of airport security guards and ran the fifty yards to where Karen stood. Jason slid his arm under hers and around her waist to provide support. They stood holding each other. Karen found it impossible to speak. Jason noticed the left side of her forehead was swollen and discolored. A small patch of dried blood was visible just above the hair line.

Finally Karen sobbed, "I am so damn glad to see you. Thank God you're here."

None of the other passengers appeared to be hurt, but they seemed in a state of near shock as they moved toward the terminal building. Many of the women were weeping.

One elderly gentleman did stop and say, "I hope that your lady will be well soon. I am so very sorry this happened in my country. She is very brave. God bless you both."

Jason guided Karen toward the customs room of the airport.

The customs officer said, "I am very sorry that this terrible thing has happened. I hope that someday you will not think so badly of us," and waved them through.

While Jason helped Karen, Alice had tried to talk to some of the other passengers on the flight. She had not been able to learn much, other than that trouble had occurred in Nandu. The flight had originated in Rome but made a scheduled stopover in Nandu before completing its route to Nkra.

An hour later at the Peace Corps Doctor's house, Karen was still crying.

The Doctor suggested that perhaps a sedative and rest would be the best course to follow but Karen protested, "I want to talk now. If I don't I am not sure I will wake up. It's worse than I can explain. I can still see the woman. Her face was so frightened, then just sad, worse than sad. I held her as long as I could. I would not have let them have her. But he hit me. He hit me hard. I could feel her slipping away. I heard her cry out for help. Then it was dark, but not long enough. I saw everything. I still see it."

"All right," Jason said, "tell us what happened if you can. But if it's too difficult then stop, please stop. You can tell us the rest some other time."

"It's better done now," Karen replied. "I'll try to control myself. I had an overnight layover in Rome. That was nice. Had a beautiful pizza."

Karen smiled slightly, for the first time since getting off the plane, looked toward Jason and said, "Wish you had been there.

"The plane left Rome this morning at nine," Karen continued. "I sat beside a woman from Hunta. She was returning from a visit with an aunt in England. We got to talking about Mbordo University-College. She has a younger sister studying there."

Karen began to cry.

"Oh my God," she said between sobs, "I will have to tell her sister.

"I tried! I really tried!" Karen cried, "I really did, but I don't know if her sister will understand."

"What do you have to tell her?" Jason asked.

"That her sister is dead, dead," Karen replied in a barely audible monotone.

"How do you know that she is dead?" the Doctor asked. "Perhaps she was just injured."

"I saw it all, goddamn it, I saw it all," Karen screamed, then did her best to continue. "When the plane landed in Nandu the soldiers or police or whatever they were came right on board. I just couldn't believe that they would do that on an international flight. They acted like madmen screaming over and over again, 'We are here to avenge the death of the noble General Musa. Are there any of those worthless, foolish Ave dogs on this plane?' They walked up and down the aisles examining the faces of all of the passengers. They picked out fifteen people they thought were Ave and just dragged them from the plane. The men were forced to kneel near the plane and were just butchered with machetes. The women were taken further away. We could hear their screams.

"They missed the woman beside me but the killing seemed to make them worse. They came back again. They made each passenger stand. Some they stripped to the waist to check for tribal markings. When they looked carefully at the woman beside me they were sure she was Ave. She screamed like nothing I have ever heard. Two of them reached over me to grab her hair, a third tried to grasp her shoulders. I wrapped my arms around her waist as tightly as I could and tried to keep them from pulling her away.

"I did try. I tried so hard, but they hit me with something, I think a rifle. They kept hitting me. I felt her slipping. She stopped struggling. She felt like something already dead. They lay her down in the aisle of the plane. She must have fainted. They turned back toward me and picked me up. I thought they were going to take me too but they didn't. They threw me in the seat by the window. They looked back and laughed as they dragged her away. One man said 'Stay out of this thing that is not your business. You are very foolish woman. Go home to your husband. Perhaps he can teach you how to behave properly.'"

When Karen stopped for a moment the Doctor asked, "Then perhaps by some miracle she survived?"

"No," Karen sobbed, "I saw it. They didn't take her as far away as the other women, only a few yards from the plane near a mini-van. One man grabbed her breasts. Another had a stick that he began to probe with. She seemed to come suddenly awake, determined to resist. She kicked the man with the stick in the groin. For a moment he doubled up in pain. Then he cut off her head with his machete."

Karen's sobs filled the room. Alice moved closer and put her arm around her.

"Oh my God, child," Alice said, "to have to see such things. But it will be all right. You are safe. We are all here. You are among friends and that's the way it's going to stay."

Karen, though still crying, managed a half smile and whispered, "It's so good to be off that awful plane. It was a nightmare. Everybody was sick or crying. The place smelled worse than anything I can remember. I never want to get on a plane again. I want to go home. That's all I want to do now. I don't think I can stay here. Can I go home, Doctor? Now? Today?"

"Probably," the Doctor replied, "but wouldn't it be better to wait just a few days and see how you feel then? If you still think that you want to go home, I am sure the Director will agree to providing you with a ticket."

Karen's reply to the Doctor's comment was accompanied by the sound of a combined laugh and sob, "I didn't mean home, home. I meant Mbordo. I want to go back to Mbordo, tonight."

The Doctor shook his head and smiled.

"Sometimes I don't believe you people," he said. "I do think you will be fine, Karen. But that is a nasty bruise. I really do believe that you should stay here in Nkra just a few more days to be sure there are no complications, and I want to check the incision from your operation and see how it is healing."

The look of concern that crossed Karen's face caused the Doctor to continue, "I'll try to arrange for Jason and Alice to remain in Nkra for a few days if that would help matters."

Karen smiled and nodded her approval.

They decided that it was time for Karen to rest. She did try, but each time she slept the woman's face returned. Each time she held on with all her strength but lost the struggle again and again. The woman's body seemed to melt away, leaving her arms empty. She could see the blade of the machete moving. She saw laughter on the face of the men but heard no sound. Then a scream, she heard a terrible scream, her own scream. Awake again, on the plane, no the Doctor's house. Jason held her. Back to sleep again. The woman's head. She could still see the woman's head rolling over and over. Like a thing possessed it would not stop but keeps rolling towards her down the runway of the airport, into the plane. It moves toward her now, suspended freely in the air, back to her lap with those same frightened pleading eyes.

"I'm sorry, I'm sorry," Karen screamed in a half awake state, "I tried to hold you, I really did, but they hit me, they hit me so hard. I couldn't hold on."

It seemed to Karen that the woman's head nodded in understanding, then faded away as she came fully awake. She found Jason still at her side.

"What is happening to this country?" she asked. "People were never like that in Pandu or Mbordo. Is it that people are different in the North?"

"No," Jason said sadly, "it might be better if that sort of hate and violence was just a problem of the North. But I don't really think so. I traveled some in the North my first year in Sakra. People there were kind, friendly, even generous to me as a stranger, not very much different than people in the East or West. But something's happened to drive people apart. It's almost like a madness of some kind, a mass hysteria. God help Sakra and Sakraians and for that matter all the rest of us if it doesn't stop."

"But where does it go from here?" Karen asked. "You can't have people being killed just because they happen to be in the wrong place. There has to be some standard of trust and acceptance. Otherwise there is no country. Just a bunch of people who hate each other."

"I don't really know," Jason said. "What happens here looks very bad to us. But I suppose that a lot of Blacks in the United States died just because they were in the wrong place at the wrong time. I read a book once made up of newspaper accounts of lynchings and lynch mobs in the Southern United States. Usually the victims were drifters who happened to be in a town after a rape or murder was supposed to have occurred. Little effort was made to determine guilt. They just grabbed the nearest Black drifter and lynched him. Most of the time the man they hung had nothing to do with the crime.

"Anyway," Jason continued, "I suspect that doesn't help how you feel much. The Doctor left some sleeping pills. Like to try one?"

"Yes, I think I should," Karen replied. "I don't want to keep you up all night."

Jason laughed and said, "Don't worry, I'll sleep all day tomorrow."

Exhaustion and two sleeping pills kept Karen in a deep but restless sleep punctuated by moans and sharp but not loud screams the rest of the night. Every sound made by Karen brought Jason wide awake again and again.

After breakfast Jason fell asleep sitting in a chair in the living room. The Doctor left for his office. Karen's most pressing dilemma was how she would be able to tell the student at Mbordo University College of her sister's death.

"Don't you worry," Alice said in an effort to reassure her, "I will tell her what has happened."

"Would you mind terribly?" Karen said. "I don't think I can do it."

"Of course I won't enjoy telling her," Alice replied, "but she must be told. Otherwise she might never know what happened. It is better for me to do it than you."

"Thank you, Alice," Karen said, "I don't have any idea even what I would say. It's difficult to know what to say."

"That's because there is no right thing to say. Everything is wrong because what happened was wrong," Alice mused. "But the best I can do is to tell her the truth. That woman died with a great deal of courage. She must have been very brave."

Karen, near tears, replied, "Oh my God, she was. I have never seen anyone fight like she did. I wish that somehow or someway I could have done something to save her."

Alice put her arm around Karen's shoulders, and said gently, "Come on, now, stop that. You did everything that was possible. You risked your own safety. Your head shows just how hard you tried."

"I'm so ugly now," Karen said as she gingerly touched her swollen forehead. "I must look hideous. Probably leave a scar. I wonder what Jason thinks of me when I look this bad."

"Child, child," Alice said quietly, "how little you know about true beauty. Nothing could hide yours. It's not a quality that has to do with how you look. As for Jason, he is madly in love with you. He may not fully understand that yet, but don't worry. He is a very bright boy and he'll figure it out if you give him time. I only hope for his sake that you love him as much as he loves you."

Karen responded with a light laugh, tinged with hope and perhaps even happiness.

"Alice, Alice," she said, "whatever happened to that hard, cynical Washington DC teacher? The one that looked deep into human nature and saw it for exactly what it was. The one who was always able to look at the future clearly and wonder if any future existed."

Alice's laughter startled Karen.

"That person is still in here," she said pointing toward herself. "Don't you worry about that. But I have also been around enough to know that there is some good left in the worst of times and in the worst of us."

On Sunday they returned to Mbordo.

A UPI stringer had been on the same flight that Karen had taken from Rome to Nandu. The article he filed was front-page news in the United States, London, and most of the rest of Europe. The government of Sakra was extremely embarrassed. Military officers of the rank of major and higher were assigned to operate the airport. No one else flying into or out of Nandu was harmed. However, this positive action on the part of the government did little to stop the overall pattern of violence and intimidation directed against Ave living in the North.

Charges of government complicity in the attacks on the Ave or at least indifference to what was happening were also made, not only by the Ave themselves, but also by neutral observers. The government vehemently denied such charges. But whether or not there was complicity was irrelevant, since the results were the same either way. The stories heard in Mbordo of atrocities in the North were often worse than it was possible for some of the expatriate staff to believe.

Trains and lorries were stopped repeatedly on their way south. Particularly poignant were reports of families who had used their life savings to buy their way through one roadblock only to die at the next. The fate of those who did not flee was no better. On the streets of Nandu and other Northern cities, Ave were picked up at random, forced onto lorries with no names and hauled away never to be seen again. What had been a small but continuous stream of people flowing south turned into a massive wave. People flew, rode in anything with wheels, or if nothing else was available, walked back toward the lands of their ancestors.

Some Ave drivers turned their lorries northward in an effort to bring home friends and relatives. For several weeks the usual four lorries that made the regular run between Mbordo and Nkra dwindled to one every other day. Many of the drivers who ventured north never returned. Those who did spoke of narrow escapes and of traveling on back roads under cover of darkness. By the middle of November persecution of the Ave in the North had become so intense that few who fled escaped the armed bands on the highways. Those who did reached the South even more deeply embittered than earlier refugees. They came with the memory of loss of their possessions, their jobs, and most painful of all, with the memory of lost brothers and sisters. In their own bitterness they saw little reason for Sakra to continue as a nation and they swelled the numbers of those Ave who favored secession.

Those in power in the government were not completely unaware of the dangers inherent in the level of hostility that had developed between the North and West. Efforts to lessen the problem led to a mini-coup. General Mansa was forced to step down as Chairman of the National Redemption Council. A little-known Colonel from the Middle Tribes named Manta replaced him. However, it was widely rumored that power was still in the hands of army officers from the North (including General Mansa, who remained a member of the Council). When the newly constituted government did make efforts to provide safe transport south for Ave still alive in the North, every member of that ethnic group took advantage of the special trains and buses. By the first of December, not a single Ave lived north of the Aba river. The flow northward was equally as complete, and no Kroban remained in the West.

The process of ethnic separation developed a life of its own. Ave anger had began to spill over and poison relations, not just with Kroban but all other ethnic groups considered outsiders in Aveland. The type of disputes and anger that had characterized Kroban-Ave relationships now began to occur between Ave and students from the Middle Tribes and between Ave and the few Atan students left on the University-College campus. Students seemed willing to fight over food, shoes, chairs, even the way in which someone said their names or looked at them. Juju symbols began appearing on the doors of rooms inhabited by students of the Middle Tribes and Atan.

No Atan students and only a few students from the Middle Tribes returned to Mbordo in January after the Christmas break. A number of professors from the Middle Lands did not return. Keeping the University-College operating became the major preoccupation of the Vice-Chancellor. He used much of his time to calm River State personnel and reassure AID officials in Nkra and Washington that the University-College continued to function.

With most 'outsiders' gone, the Bordo students began to find themselves in a more and more difficult situation. The Ave students pressured the Bordo to join them in their declarations of support for an independent Aveland which, just incidentally, would also include all of the Bordo lands. Those Bordo who said they were against the idea of secession or refused to commit themselves were branded as traitors and made outcasts on the University-College compound. Cold food at lunch, the worst clean-up duty, torn books and dirty clothing was their lot.

In national politics, one of those strange lulls occurred. The entire nation seemed again to be in a holding pattern. Secession seemed both impossible and certain, depending on what one read or to whom one talked.

In late January the Vice-Chancellor called what was left of his staff together and spoke optimistically, "We have gone through some very difficult times. But I believe the situation is now improving. At least, let us hope and pray that it will be so."

CHAPTER 16
The Child

By Enata's own calculations, the baby was due in late January. One of her mother's brothers was a doctor who practiced in Hunta. He had suggested that she travel there and have the baby in the hospital in which he did most of his work. It was a new facility with modern equipment and both Enata and her father had liked the idea. Jeff decided to accompany Enata to Hunta and spend at least the time of his Christmas break there with her. When the Vice-Chancellor learned of Jeff's plans, he suggested that he remain in Hunta with Enata until the baby was born. Chief Kanata offered Jeff his car to drive Enata from Kwim to Hunta. The Chief's car was at least twenty years old. However, it had been well maintained and ran perfectly.

The pace of the trip was agonizingly slow. The check points on the road were so frequent that Jeff seldom managed to get the old car into its top gear before slowing down to wait in line at another roadblock. Most of the troops checking vehicles were Ave. The soldiers were always polite. When they noticed Enata's condition, they invariably waved the old car past the makeshift barricades without the customary search.

Enata's uncle met them at the front gate of the enclosed area in front of his home. When they asked about a place to stay, he insisted they stay in a small apartment that was attached to the side of his house.

The city of Hunta nestled just below the second great scarp of western Sakra which rose over a thousand feet just to the north of the city. Once settled, Jeff and Enata, to help pass the time during the days of waiting, often drove the winding road that led up to the top of the scarp. The road was a bit treacherous in some parts with sharp curves and not much more width than required for two trucks to pass, but the beauty of the hillside view made the drive both exciting and enjoyable. After some exploring they found a small church whose carefully tended grounds reached the very edge of the cliffs. From there one could see all of Hunta and its satellite towns. It was a beautiful city with tree-lined main streets and a small but well designed market area. On a clear day even the sparkling Atlantic, some one hundred miles distant, was visible. Enata explained that in times of danger the Ave had retreated up the scarp and used its steep walls as a natural fortification. Hunta was certainly not the largest city in the West. But the Ave Tribe had never, even in the worst of times, lost control of the scarp. Hunta was held sacred by the Ave nation in memory of past victories on the cliffs.

The minister of the church lived nearby. He graciously offered the grounds of the church as a place for them to eat their picnic style lunch the first time they asked and at any future time they might wish to do so.

They developed a Sunday pattern; up the scarp by car, services at the church, picnic on the lawn near the edge of the scarp, and a late afternoon return to the city.

175

Their fourth visit to the church was on the third Sunday of January. After services a number of church members dropped by to chat with them as they ate. A little before four, after they had finished eating and talking, Jeff and Enata decided to begin their return trip down the scarp. About one-third the way down the steep incline, Jeff realized something was wrong when he heard the horn of a lorry behind them and noticed in a glance at his outside mirror the vehicle's increasing speed. The driver's wild motions and shouts indicated a loss of all braking power. The truck, with what appeared to be a load of plantain, was still about one hundred feet behind them when Jeff yelled at Enata to lie down and brace herself. He moved the Chief's car as far to the mountain side of the road as possible without hitting the rocks that had fallen from the cliffs above. The plantain lorry caught up with them in a blind curve. Jeff caught a glimpse of the driver's face in the mirror as he fought to swing the old truck out around the car. At that moment Jeff heard the sound of the horn of a vehicle coming up the road. Out of the corner of his eye he could see the old lorry beside him; its driver desperately trying to avoid the passenger lorry coming up the scarp. His grip on the wheel tightened but he sensed that he no longer had full control as he felt the car being forced sidewise into the mountain. Jeff's last visual memory before the crunching jolt that brought the car to a sudden halt was the look of terror in the eyes of the driver of the passenger lorry as the plantain lorry bounced off Chief Kanata's car into the path of his truck. The car's abrupt stop threw him forward into the windshield. Jeff did not see the actual crash. He did hear the sound of metal meeting metal, of splintering boards, of cries and terrified screams, then the sound of crashing, bouncing, rolling down the scarp. The terror stricken yells and screams faded, then disappeared. All that remained was an eerie silence interrupted only by an occasional moan.

Jeff realized that the sound that he heard was very near. He shook his head to clear away the numbness caused by the impact with the windshield. A small amount of blood trickled down his face. He wiped it away and looked toward Enata. She lay, partially on the seat and partially on the floor, moaning quietly as she rubbed her leg. Enata's right leg appeared to have been caught under the seat as the force of the car's sudden stop had thrown her toward the center of the car. Otherwise she seemed unhurt. Jeff examined her hip and leg as best he could without causing further pain and decided that her hip might be strained or displaced. The car was just off the road but both passenger side tires were axle deep in a small ditch on the mountain side of the road. He told Enata not to move while he went for help. The sight of only the plantain lorry jammed against the side of the mountain confirmed his fears. He walked to the spot where skid marks indicated the other lorry went over the cliff. The drop was at least 300 feet. Trees and brush concealed the final resting place of the unfortunate truck and its passengers.

A child, not more than ten years old, sat by the side of the road gently swaying back and forth. He made no sound as he slowly rubbed his left forearm. Something in the way the child gazed at the place where the passenger lorry left the road made Jeff certain that the child had been on the lorry.

"Probably," Jeff thought, "the only survivor. Must have jumped or been thrown from the lorry as it went over the side."

Jeff motioned for the child to come back with him to the car. The child shook his head and looked again toward the cliff.

"His mother is probably in the lorry," Jeff muttered.

Several other trucks and cars arrived at the scene of the accident. Their drivers stopped and offered help. Jeff returned to the car with men from one of the trucks. He found Enata moaning again but this time holding her stomach.

"Oh my God," Jeff said, "is it coming?"

Enata nodded in reply.

The other men moved to the cliff side of the car and attempted to lift it out of the ditch. They succeeded on the third try. Remarkably, the car started the second time that Jeff turned the key. The left front fender was destroyed but the tire still turned freely with only a slight wobble. Jeff tested the brakes and found them still capable of stopping the car at least from low speed. He thanked the men who lifted the car out of the ditch and drove on toward Hunta. He could not remember a longer drive. With every series of moans that signaled another contraction, he had to fight the urge to shift into a higher gear. But he resisted the temptation since he knew that the brakes might have been damaged in the accident.

By the time they reached the hospital, Enata's contractions were less than five minutes apart. A messenger was dispatched to the house of the Doctor. He arrived quickly. Enata was moved down one of the corridors away from the lobby. Jeff was told to wait. About thirty minutes later her uncle returned. His expression was grim.

He spoke quickly but clearly, "The news is not at all good. The baby wants to come out, but Enata's hip is out of place and is preventing a natural birth. We will put her hip back into place, but I fear that labor will be very difficult for her."

"What about a Cesarean?" Jeff blurted out more loudly than he had intended.

Enata's uncle bit his lip and shook his head slightly before he spoke.

"We have no surgeon now who could perform such an operation," he said. "Once we had three. All were Atan. The last one took leave of absence only a week ago."

"When will one of them be returning?" Jeff asked.

"They will not be back to this place, ever, I fear," the Doctor replied. "It is not their fault. They too were afraid."

"Look," Jeff said growing more desperate, "can't we move her to another city where the operation can be done?"

"It is already too late to think of such things," Enata's uncle replied sadly. "The accident caused the baby to begin its journey toward life. It is impossible to reverse the situation now."

"Please," Jeff said near tears, "let me go to Nkra and get a surgeon. I could be back by this time tomorrow."

The Doctor placed his hand on Jeff's shoulder and spoke slowly, "My friend, even if you could convince one to return, it would be much too late. What will happen will happen in the next few hours. By tomorrow it will be over. Nothing that we do other than to pray will have any effect."

In the next two hours Jeff's emotions tested the outer ranges of human feeling, from hope and thoughts of future happiness with Enata and the child to an alternate vision of despair. He cried, he prayed, he waited.

In two hours, just as the Doctor had predicted, it was over. Enata delivered a baby boy, alive and well. Within minutes of the delivery Jeff was invited in to be with Enata and the child. He sat beside her as she held the baby in her arms. Her uncle, another doctor and a midwife continued to work in order to alleviate some of the damage that the birth had done to Enata's injured body. Enata looked tired and the pain of the delivery lingered on her face.

At first Jeff found that he could say nothing as she tightly held his hand. His only sensation was a warmth that seemed to engulf his body born of a feeling of total relief and happiness at the sight of both Enata and his son. When the doctors and midwife departed, they were left alone with the child.

They talked of many things and laughed gently at each other's happiness.

"Now," Jeff said, "I do know how very much I want you to be my wife. I will stay here until you agree to marry me. You must say yes now or later. I will become a great nuisance if you refuse."

"I think it is your son that you love," Enata said teasingly. "But we can't have you hanging about forever, can we?"

"I am not sure I understood what you just said," Jeff replied. "But it sounded very close to yes."

Enata smiled lazily and nodded her head as she spoke softly. "I have always wanted to be your wife. Forever and ever. But I was so afraid that you didn't really love me or that you would only love me here and not when you returned to your home. Sometimes love is difficult to understand. I think we Bordos are more realistic about these things than you Americans."

"So damn realistic, and probably right, too," Jeff said. "I have done a lot of serious thinking about what you and your father told me after I learned you were pregnant. But I know now that it is you I love. The baby is just the greatest thing that I could ever have imagined, but I would love you anyway. I couldn't leave you, not now or ever."

"Don't exaggerate," Enata replied as she started to laugh.

"What are you laughing at?" Jeff asked in a surprised tone.

"You, my wonderful husband, or at least husband to be," Enata replied. "If you are going to marry me, I am afraid that you will have to develop a little more realistic attitude toward the nature of life and love. We are not so romantic here in Sakra."

"I will work on it," Jeff replied. "I will do my best to fit in."

The baby fell asleep in Enata's arms and Jeff carefully moved the child to a basket that had been thoughtfully placed near the bed by Enata's uncle. In the hours that followed Jeff kept watch over Enata as she rested in a light sleep. When she woke they talked of the past, of Kwim, the Chief, Enata's brothers, of the garden project, of the University-College and the town of Mbordo. But even more they spoke of the future. Of many futures together in America, in Nkra, Mbordo, Kwim. The whole world became as their own. Hours passed as minutes. Neither paid any attention to the lateness of the hour or even noticed the first rays of the morning sun.

But with the morning light, Jeff noticed a sharp and sudden change of expression in Enata's face. A mixture of fear and panic. She gasped for breath. He called loudly for help. The midwife and Doctor came immediately. They worked rapidly, speaking to each other in Ave. Enata grasped his hand tightly. Jeff felt the fear and panic that he had seen in Enata's face transmitted to his own body. Pain replaced all other emotion in Enata's face. Then, suddenly, the pain seemed to dissipate.

She looked into Jeff's eyes and silently mouthed the words, "I love you. Good-by."

Jeff's eyes filled with tears. He was unable to answer.

Moments later Enata died.

A nurse guided Jeff out of the room into an empty waiting area. His emotions turned inward as he sat alone and tried to understand what had happened. He knew that the past could not be undone. And yet, if he and Enata had never met, or had been more careful, she would, that very day, be preparing to teach in the coming term.

Contemplation of suicide developed from random thoughts to a serious preoccupation. Only his sense of responsibility for the present and future needs of the child seemed capable of driving the dark clouds of self destruction from his mind. But even those emotions were mixed and confused. The child was their child together. All that seemed left of his relationship with Enata. But Enata's life had been sacrificed, and Jeff found himself wishing that Enata had lived instead of the child.

That wish brought such unbearable remorse that Jeff began to mumble, "Do I hate or love the child? My God, I would give anything to have Enata back. But would I give my own son? Stop being stupid. The choice was never yours. The child is what you now have. All that you have. If you have any love or hope left it must be shared with the child."

It was well past noon when Jeff drifted off into sleep in the hospital lobby. He had remained there, reluctant to return to the part of the Doctor's house that he and Enata had shared. Also, he entertained the notion that he might be needed to take care of some detail or another related to Enata or the baby. Of course that concern was unnecessary. Enata's uncle had already made arrangements to have her body returned to Kwim, and the child had been placed in the care of the Doctor's wife.

Late that afternoon Jeff returned to the Doctor's compound.

179

He spent most of that evening and the next morning simply looking at the child and repeating over and over the silent thoughts, "I must stay alive. I must stay well. I must be ready if the child needs my help, today, tomorrow or twenty years from now. Perhaps there is nothing else left for me. But this will be enough. More than enough. I must stay alive. He is beautiful. He will have a good life. I am sorry that his mother is not here to share with me but that is not my choice. The child is left and I must be ready."

Enata's body was transported back to Kwim, the place of her youth, by lorry. Jeff agreed to drive Chief Kanata's car to Kwim. Enata's uncle, his wife and the baby accompanied the lorry in the doctor's car. Because of the poor condition of Chief Kanata's car, the uncle and his wife reached Kwim several hours before Jeff did. When Jeff arrived near dusk, Chief Kanata walked toward the car to greet him. The Chief seemed years older, his head and shoulders held stiffly erect only through great effort and years of pride and habit. Jeff moved quickly to leave the car and walk toward the compound. They both stopped while still several feet apart. Neither spoke. Jeff's eyes filled with moisture.

The Chief, seeing Jeff's anguish, said, "My brother has told me of the tragedy. Our grief cannot be spoken in words."

All that Jeff could manage was a broken, "I'm sorry, so sorry."

The Chief turned quickly and motioned for Jeff to follow him into the compound. One of the women directed him to a sleeping room. It was in a corner of the compound far removed from the rooms that he and Enata had once shared. A quick glance told him that part of the compound was the reception area for those who came to view the casket of the Chief's daughter. The Chief returned there to greet those who came to share in his mourning. Jeff was unsure if he would be welcome in the mourning room. He heard the small cry of a newborn baby and followed the sound to another room. There he resumed his vigil at the side of his son's crib. Hours later a woman brought a kerosene lantern. Near midnight, Chief Kanata came into the room and sat down beside him. They looked at the small boy and not at each other.

In time the Chief spoke, "Jeff Johnson, I do not blame you for this matter. My dear wife's brother told me how it happened, everything. Was Enata happy when she died?"

"Yes, yes," Jeff cried, "I am certain she was. We had such happy plans. I am certain she was happy."

"That much is only good," the Chief said.

Then he continued talking as much to himself as to Jeff, "Tomorrow at the funeral much will be said about life eternal and Enata's entrance into the heaven promised by the Christ. I don't believe that very much. I much prefer our own beliefs about life and death given to us by our fathers from the most ancient of times. They learned these secrets not from the heavens but from the very earth itself that we live on. Do you know of what I speak?"

"No," Jeff replied, "but I wish to know."

The Chief nodded and then spoke quietly, "The earth itself is eternal, the soil, the water, the rocks, the small plants, the huge trees. These things provide life, not only for us, but also those who were before us and those who will come after us. Three communities of people inhabit the earth. All of those who have lived in the past as we do now are one of those communities. We pour our libations in their honor. Although the gate swings in only one direction they are always with us. We who are now alive form the second community. The third and most precious of all are those who have not yet joined us. They wait within the spirit of that which is the earth until their time and then join us. This child until a few days ago was a part of that community. Now he is with us. His existence and the existence of all of the others as yet unborn make this earth the true holy place for us. We must be sure that we do not destroy it. If we do so, those unborn will never have the opportunity to live.

"I go to the Christian Church, but I cannot accept the Christian heaven. It sounds like some terrible exile. I will not send my daughter there. Her home is here. This is where she must stay. She will be a part of all that is here in this village. Every tree and rock and flower will be a part of her spirit. I cannot bear the thought of her spirit being separate from this place and from me for all of the years until I die, or even for a few days. Here she will always be with us."

All of the staff of the University College arrived in Kwim the next day for the funeral. After last rites and burial in the small cemetery behind the Methodist Church, the Mbordo staff left quickly in their cars and the school lorry. The Vice-Chancellor had offered Jeff a ride. He declined. Jeff had decided that the baby should live with him in Mbordo and wanted to explain his plans for the child to Chief Kanata before leaving Kwim.

The celebration of Enata's death continued long after her burial. It was well past midnight before Jeff had an opportunity to talk with Chief Kanata alone.

Jeff spoke first, "We must discuss the future of the child..."

Chief Kanata interrupted, "The child will remain here. The spirit of its mother and its ancestors now reside in this place. To take him elsewhere would be to perform an act of great cruelty."

"But I am the father," Jeff answered. "I want to take care of my son. See that he has every opportunity to..."

Jeff's voice seemed to die in his throat. He could not find words to explain the depth of his feeling for the child and that he needed the child as much or more than the child needed him.

Chief Kanata replied in a stern but not loud tone of voice, "No, this cannot be. The child will remain here. He is our future and our past. All that remains to bind us to Enata. Do you not understand that we need him? He will be a strong man, a powerful man, a good man in this village and perhaps he will be known throughout all of Sakra. I will not allow him to be taken away. He is African. This is his home. We are his people and he is one of us."

Chief Kanata paused and then continued, "Jeff, Jeff, I do know a little of how you feel. I buried my only daughter today. But can you not understand? I know what you wish. But what you wish cannot be. The child must stay with its own people. Please come to Kwim often and stay long. You are and will forever be welcome in this place. The boy will call you his father if that is what you wish. But this is where he must stay. It cannot be otherwise. I will not allow it."

Jeff tried to find words to voice arguments that only minutes before had seemed totally persuasive.

The Chief continued, "Save your words, my good friend. I will not permit it. You have no legal claim to the boy. No proof that you are the father."

Jeff hoped that what the old man was saying about legal claim to the child was not true, but he stilled an angry retort before it reached his lips. Much of what the Chief said seemed all too reasonable. Could he really provide the love and care that the child was assured if he stayed with his grandfather? Could he provide his half-African child the opportunities that would automatically be his birthright as the grandson of the wealthy and respected leader of the village of Kwim? He knew the small boy was his son. But could this be demonstrated to the satisfaction of a judge in a court of law in Sakra?

Jeff sighed, then stood. The Chief rose with him. Jeff offered his hand. The old man grasped it with both of his. Neither spoke. Their hands dropped. Jeff turned and walked toward the entrance of the compound without looking again in the direction of Chief Kanata or the room in which his son lay sleeping. He fought back tears of anger and frustration. An empty lorry awaited him on the street. The driver motioned for Jeff to sit in front.

He started the motor and said, "We go now for Mbordo."

In the weeks that followed, Jeff's appearance and actions became a cause of increasing concern to Alice, Jason and his other friends. He seemed to them little more than a hollow shell of his former self. He ate, he slept and he met his classes. Much of his time was spent working in the middle school project garden, not on developing the written curriculum for teaching gardening, but just working in the garden, doing planting, weeding, and watering that ordinarily would have been done by middle school students.

Jason made numerous efforts to start conversations, but Jeff would never respond with more than two or three words. Several times Jason woke up in the middle of the night and realized that candles were burning in the living room. He would find Jeff sitting on the couch staring at shadows of the flickering flames.

"Are you all right?" Jason would ask.

"Yes," is all that Jeff ever replied, with a half smile that wasn't a smile at all.

Jeff knew his friends were concerned. But he found himself unable to react to their efforts to help. He had prescribed his own course of action. He was healing. He knew that by small changes that seemed to occur almost daily and by new insights into how he felt about Enata, his son, and of course himself that seemed to come late at night in the quiet of the African darkness. The manual labor in the garden helped. He knew the middle school students and masters found the sight of a professor working in their garden quite strange, even comical, although they generally were able to conceal their mirth behind the walls of the school building. But in working with the fresh seed and young plants, Jeff found a closeness with his beloved Enata. In the garden he often thought of Chief Kanata's belief in the three kingdoms of the earth.

A month passed. He gave no thought to returning to Kwim. He knew that before he left Sakra he would go back, but he was not yet ready. A student from the village kept him informed as to the health and progress of the child.

****

Enata's death had affected not just Jeff but also others who knew her. The realization that all things have an end as well as a beginning had caused Jason to think seriously about his relationship with Karen. On a Friday early in February he asked Karen to go for a walk with him on the trail behind Alice's house. When they reached the bridge, Jason suggested they stop and sit by the stream for a while.

"I've been thinking," Jason said.

"What about?" Karen asked.

"About us," Jason replied. "We should get married. Maybe we could get teaching jobs from the Sakra government and stay here in Mbordo." .

"Does getting married depend on getting the jobs?" Karen inquired. "That may be difficult with the current troubles. Would we get divorced if have to leave Mbordo?"

"Dammit!" Jason exclaimed, "I always screw things up. I didn't mean it that way at all. I love you no matter what. I want you to be my wife. I don't care what else happens."

"I don't know what to say," Karen said. "It still sounds like a two-part proposal."

"There is only one part," Jason declared, "Just one. I'm sorry if I got ahead of myself on the other stuff. Will you marry me?"

"Can I have a little time to think it over?" Karen replied.

"Or course," Jason answered.

Karen found herself knocking on Alice's door that evening.

"Jason asked me to marry him," she said almost before Alice had the door open.

"Well, good for him," Alice said emphatically. "It's about time he used his intelligence for something other than math."

"I don't know if it is good idea," Karen said. "He talked about wanting to stay in Mbordo next year with government contracts. I don't know if he really want to marry me, or if he just wants someone to stay here with him."

"Getting married would at least keep him out of that awful Vietnam thing," Alice said. "No good in going there."

"Actually, it would not keep him out of Vietnam," Karen explained. "They changed the regulations to include married men. Because he's been deferred so long he will be very high on the draft list."

"Then he really does love you and wants to get married," Alice mused. "The question is, what do you want? Do you love him?"

"For a long time now," Karen replied. "I just don't want to get married to someone who might not understand what he's doing."

Alice grabbed Karen's hand and said, "Listen my dear, from what I have seen, men never know exactly what they are doing. If you want to get married, go ahead and do it. Jason would never have asked if he weren't good and ready."

Karen accepted Jason's proposal of marriage the next day. On February twentieth, they announced they would be married on the first of March in Mbordo.

A week before the wedding, Jason asked Jeff if he would be his best man. Jeff at first looked away and said nothing.

Then with great effort he replied, "You know, it could have been a double wedding."

He began sobbing. The story of the events that led to Enata's death seemed to burst forth in a torrent of words and anguished sounds. Guilt, anger, and sense of loss swept together as he tried to explain what had happened.

Jeff almost smiled through his tears.

"Look at us," he said. "Did they tell you about people like me when you joined the Peace Corps?"

"Well," Jason replied, "some professor did say that we might find a tribe or two with strange customs."

"Enough," Jeff said. "I will be your best man. Wouldn't let anyone else do it. But I may ruin your wedding. I don't think it's traditional for the best man to cry."

Jason laughed and said, "Too damn much tradition already. No one would know the difference anyway. We'll tell them that it's an old American custom."

The next day Jeff traveled to Kwim. He had not sent a message, but word of his coming preceded him. Chief Kanata greeted him as he stepped down from the lorry.

"Welcome to Kwim. It gives us much joy to see you. How are our friends in Mbordo?"

"They are well, thank you," Jeff replied, "I am happy to be in Kwim again. Would it be possible for me to see the child?"

"Of course, that is possible at any time," Chief Kanata replied. "Please come this way."

The Chief guided Jeff to the room in which the child stayed, then left him alone. Jeff was surprised at how much the boy had grown. He could even wave his arms about. When Jeff touched his small hand the baby grasped his finger. He was enchanted and played with his son until the boy started to cry. Jeff was not quite sure what to do about the child's very apparent discomfort. He was relieved when the baby's wet nurse came into the small room. Both the woman and the child seemed unaware of his presence as she offered the child her nipple.

When the woman noticed Jeff watching, she laughed and said, "He be fine big boy, healthy, very hungry."

Jeff smiled but did not answer. He watched the baby eat for a while longer and then decided that it was time for him to leave Kwim if he wanted to reach the junction in time to catch the last lorry to Mbordo. The Chief was waiting for him at the entrance to the compound. They clasped hands and said a brief but warm good-by.

"Come back soon and often," were Chief Kanata's final words.

The wedding was a pleasant affair, at least from Jason's point of view. Karen was only a few minutes late, the ceremony was short, and the reception was over very quickly (just as soon as the food and drink were finished).

Jason moved into the house provided by the secondary school where Karen taught. That left Jeff alone in the large house as the last of the 'boys.' His first night was difficult. He thought of the Scotch, then decided work might be better. The middle school garden manual provided an outlet for his middle-of-the-night time.

"No end to this damn thing," he mused. "Don't care if I stay up all night. Sleep during the day if I need to. Just don't want to be incoherent in class. Sleep enough to avoid that. Got to hang on till the end of the year. Wonder if it will get better or worse when I leave here?"

CHAPTER 17

The University Closes

The January change of government brought a period of stability to the political and social life of Sakra. However, no Ave now lived in the North, no Kroban in the West. An even more ominous portent of the future of Sakra was the separation of Ave and Atan. The westward migration that began with the Ave soldiers who fled the capital during the coup led by General Musa had never really ceased. The number of people moving east and west varied with the political situation but the direction of the flow -- Ave to the west, Atan to the east -- was never reversed. Those who could, moved. Ave officers and soldiers did not come back from leave if they were assigned to units stationed outside the West. The government made little effort to force them to return. There were rumors that these soldiers had quietly reformed into unofficial units in the West. When Ave soldiers with units in the West were reassigned to other parts of the nation, many of them simply disappeared. Ave soldiers who did remain a part of the regular army in the West were said to be forming unofficial units under the secret command of Ave officers.

Bordo soldiers found their situation in Aveland precarious. The Ave had traditionally thought of the Bordo as one would a competitive half brother: a beloved and close kinsman when the Ave were in need of help, but a troublesome distant relative when that need was reversed. Ave soldiers tended to look upon those Bordo who refused to become a part of their secret units as traitors. Many Bordo did join with the Ave soldiers, a few out of honest conviction, but most out of fear. Since few Ave soldiers were left to serve in the armed forces in other parts of Sakra, Bordo soldiers often found it easier to serve in units in the North and East.

By the time Jason and Karen were married, Sakra was no longer a single nation. Only the people of the Middle Tribes were still in any real sense citizens of Sakra. The others were Kroban, Atan or Ave.

Weapon smuggling had become a major business in the coastal waters of Aveland. Anything that could be carried in small to medium size boats, from bazookas to portable antiaircraft rocket launchers, seemed to be available on the world market. Guns were not yet openly carried by non-soldiers but bulges under shirts and in pant legs often betrayed the unraveling of customs and laws that had in the past kept lethal weapons out of the hands of civilians.

Curiously, a sense of calm, even complacency, pervaded the atmosphere of the University-College and the village of Mbordo. To the expatriates and perhaps even to many of the Sakraians on the compound, the problems of the nation seemed solved or at least in remission. After all, if people could not get along with each other, what better way to solve the problem than to send them back to where they came from. Enrollment at the University-College had only temporarily dropped without the Kroban and Atan students. Their places had been eagerly assumed by

Ave transfers fleeing from universities in other parts of the nation. Tribal friction was reduced to the lowest levels in memory since the only ethnic groups still represented on campus were the Ave, Bordo and the Middle Tribes. Those students from the Middle Tribes who remained did so only because of their confidence in the Vice-Chancellor's ability to protect them.

Sentiment among Ave students at the University-College (especially those returning from other parts of Sakra) was generally in favor of Ave secession. However, few students made their views known in a way that would reach the ears of the expatriate staff members. The students did after all have a vested interest in keeping the college open and AID funds flowing.

In the capital city, the Peace Corps Director had been warned by friends in the Sakraian civil service that events were approaching a decisive stage. Negotiations within the National Council of Redemption concerning the nature and possibility of ethnic autonomy (primarily Ave autonomy) within the structure of a loose federation were on the verge of collapse, they confided. Ave secession seemed inevitable. He relayed that message to the State Department.

The reply came quickly: "Sit tight, do nothing, say nothing. Withdrawal of Peace Corps and other USAID personnel at present time would be interpreted as lack of confidence in government and future of Sakra. Might precipitate events that would be desirable to avoid."

The predictions of the Director's friends proved false, or at least premature. If negotiations within the National Council of Redemption were indeed near the breaking point, few except those involved knew. The Council continued to maintain the official posture that negotiations were progressing smoothly. More political and civic leaders of the West were invited to join in discussions that were directed toward finding a way to develop a form of government acceptable to all ethnic segments.

But no compromise was found. The West was in effect already a separate nation, in fact if not in law. Its people were isolated, frightened, angry and unwelcome everywhere else in the nation of which they were supposed to be a part. The Ave could not, in this time of pain from loss of employment, kin, and property, find value in continuing to remain a part of the larger nation. On the other hand the Kroban and Atan negotiators on the Council would not accept the creation of an autonomous Ave state. After many weeks of effort to reach a settlement, it became apparent, one Wednesday near the middle of March, that negotiations had ended when the Ave negotiators did not appear for the usual morning session. Messengers sent to inquire of their whereabouts returned with word that they had left for the West and would not be back.

On March 17, General Deton, highest ranking Ave officer in the army of Sakra, announced the secession of the West. He also announced the creation of a new nation to be known as Dadze. For that nation he claimed all of the lands that had formerly been known as the Western region of Sakra. This meant that, in addition to Ave lands, the General also claimed Bordo lands, the lands near the coast inhabited by two other small non-Ave tribes, and areas near the Kra river long occupied by peoples of the Middle Tribes.

On the University-College compound, most students quit their classes to listen to radio replays of General Deton's declaration of Ave independence. Within hours most Ave students, and those Bordo who could be convinced or coerced into joining with them, organized into a company of civilian soldiers. Most of the expatriate staff of the University-College found the first practice drills of these ragtag soldiers humorous, but the students involved approached the matter with a deadly seriousness. The Vice-Chancellor tried to convince the student who seemed to be in charge, an ex-sergeant, that classes should resume.

The student replied politely but firmly, "You are not from this place. This is our homeland. Our future, our very lives now depend on the success of our new nation. When the soldiers from the North come, your maths and English and history and farming will not protect us. We must prepare to fight. We hold no anger for you. You may stay or leave this place as you see fit. But do not bother us anymore. We must be ready within a matter of days, perhaps even hours."

The Vice-Chancellor nodded and walked away realizing that further efforts to continue normal work were hopeless. His thoughts turned to his wife and children whom he hoped were safe with his wife's family in the Middle Lands. He remembered his reluctance in allowing her to leave and said a small prayer of thanks that she had foreseen what would happen better than he.

"Perhaps it was her contact with the people of the market," he mused, "or perhaps my own bullheadedness made me blind. Anyway, it is good that she won the argument."

He decided to concentrate on helping those who might be in danger. His first thought was to check on the students from the Middle Tribes and the one teacher from that area, Professor Kamure, who remained in residence at the University-College. Without exception he found them all preparing to leave. Many Bordo students and teachers who did not wish to be involved with the Ave militia left to return to their villages. That afternoon, via messengers, the Vice-Chancellor called a staff meeting. When what remained of the staff had gathered in the cafeteria, the Vice-Chancellor spoke first.

"Ladies and gentlemen, it is with true sorrow that I have called you together today. Nothing I have done in my life has made me sadder than what I must now do. The situation in our nation, or what was our nation, is grave. I am forced to close the school immediately. I fear that all of you or perhaps I should say all of us may face some danger in these unsettled times. Word from north of Mbordo brought by lorry drivers indicates that travel there is already very dangerous. Gangs of renegades and bandits, claiming to be part of the militia of the North, are moving southward. They do not seem to be under any central command. Some are perhaps soldiers, but most are probably common criminals and scavengers who wish to take advantage of the confusion to enrich themselves. I have also heard that much the same thing is happening to the south, where many areas have been infiltrated by armed bands from the east. Areas further to the west in the direction of Hunta are apparently under the control of soldiers formerly in the armed services of Sakra, who are now loyal to the rebels. Indications are that these troops are organized and disciplined. As for those of you from Europe or America, no messages or instructions have come from Nkra concerning how or when you will be evacuated. In fact, all communications between this region and the rest of Sakra, from what I have been able to learn, have been disrupted. Do any of you have any method to contact your embassies?"

Mr. West shook his head slowly. No one else said anything.

"If that is the case," the Vice-Chancellor continued, "the decision about what to do must be made here. The decision on your own course of action will be left to each of you. However, I will share my thoughts with you. As I see it, there are three possibilities. The first would be to stay here on the University-College compound and hope that any fighting occurs elsewhere. We would simply wait until we are rescued by regular troops of the government of Sakra or Dadze or whoever else is able to establish control over this area. The second possibility is to travel west in order to reach an area under the control of Ave regulars. The third course is to move east toward Nkra in the hopes of finding troops of the regular army of Sakra. Of course, as I have already said, the final decision is left to you."

The Vice-Chancellor left the room abruptly. Bedlam ensued. Everyone seemed to be yelling.

After a few minutes, Mr. West climbed up on a chair and shouted, "This will do no good. Dammit, let's talk about this thing reasonably."

"Let's just get the hell out of here," Whitland shouted from the back of the room. "Those bastards at AID really left us holding the bag."

Another uproar followed. Five minutes passed before Mr. West was able to regain some semblance of control. Alice sat quietly with her hand raised. In desperation, Mr. West recognized her.

"It seems to me that just about the worst thing that we could do is to go rushing about like a chicken with its head cut off," she said firmly. "Judging by what the Vice-Chancellor said, the situation all around Mbordo seems very uncertain. We have no idea what we might find twenty or even ten miles away in any direction. But here at least people know who we are. I think it would be best to stay put at least until we have a better idea of what is actually happening. We might even get help or at least some information from Nkra."

Alice's statement served to lower the heat of the discussion. The group soon came to the same conclusion as the Vice-Chancellor, that each person should make his or her own decision. About two-thirds of those present decided to follow Alice's advice and for the time being remain in Mbordo. The others left the meeting to make preparations to leave for Nkra the next morning.

About nine o'clock that evening two students from one of the Middle Tribes returned to the Mbordo campus on foot. With them they brought a badly injured man, Professor Kamure. The only medical personnel left in Mbordo, two nurse's assistants, were called.

The students explained what had happened. An hour after the news of Ave secession was broadcast, the professor had packed his car and left Mbordo with the two students. Less than ten miles from Mbordo they had been stopped by men carrying guns and machetes. The leader of the group claimed to be a captain in the new army of Dadze. He demanded that Kamure donate his car and other possessions to the welfare of that new army. The professor had resisted. The 'Captain' had pushed him against a tree and with one swing of his machete cut to the bone on his back and hip. The students were left by the side of the road with the gravely wounded man.

Professor Kamure died a little before midnight. Those who had been considering leaving for Nkra decided that Alice had been right about staying in Mbordo.

The next day the Vice-Chancellor was faced with a problem that he had not anticipated. He had expected that all of the students would leave as soon as the school was officially closed. When he suggested as much to the leaders of the Ave students still on the compound, he received a polite but firm reply that they did not at this time intend to leave, and that since the school was now closed the Vice-Chancellor no longer had any authority. The Ave leaders further informed the Vice-Chancellor of their intention to take control of the University-College in the name of the new government of Dadze and convert the facilities into a military training base. They explained that a committee had been formed that would control the affairs of both the University-College and the town of Mbordo. The Vice-Chancellor gave the matter a few moments thought, then turned and walked away.

One of the first acts of the new committee was to establish a dawn-to-dusk curfew. The penalty for violation was the normal and obvious, shot on sight. On the day the curfew was announced, Jeff, Jason, and Karen moved in with Alice, during daylight hours of course.

The expatriates in Mbordo and other parts of Sakra had not been forgotten by their embassies. In fact, during the days that followed the announcement of secession, activity in the British, American, Indian, Pakistan and Canadian embassies and at the Peace Corps Office in Nkra centered around efforts to contact nationals and find safe passage for them to the capital city and from there out of Sakra. Communication had been established with the new government of Dadze. Volunteers and other expatriates had been evacuated from virtually all parts of the West without difficulty.

However, Mbordo was near the center of a triangular-shaped buffer region between government controlled areas to the north and east and rebel controlled areas to the west. Neither side had committed regular troops to the area. Roving bands of irregulars, most little better than bandits, had formed. They moved in as air or liquid moves to a vacuum. It made little difference whether a particular group of men paid allegiance to the central government or to the rebels. Indeed, if challenged, the loyalties of many of these 'soldiers' could change to meet the needs of the moment.

Information concerning what was happening around Mbordo continued to filter back to the University-College compound. Sometimes it came in a direct and brutal form such as the return of Professor Kamure, but more often it came in messages and warnings brought by Bordo students and people from the village who had ventured out on bush trails to see what was happening. News of the troubles around Mbordo also moved in other directions. By the time the Peace Corps Director and the United States Ambassador sat down to discuss the situation with the highest ranking official of the government still willing to talk with them, the Minister of Education, few alternatives were available. The six helicopters owned by the Air Force of Sakra were all being repaired. They decided against the use of one-way radio messages to avoid giving away the location of the expatriates. Besides, they had no advice to offer.

The days that followed were lonely and long for those who remained in Mbordo. Bordo students who had not joined the Ave militia had disappeared into the forests to live as their ancestors had in times of trouble, although several did risk early morning visits to provide their former teachers with information. The Ave and Bordo students who did remain on campus spent most of their time in drilling and drinking.

Anyone venturing out on the roads did so at considerable risk. Nominal soldiers were on all the highways ready to steal, maim, and kill in the name of Dadze, Sakra, the North, the West, the East, God, Christ, Allah or whatever else might come to mind when dealing with an unfortunate traveler. However, none of these armed bands had chosen to challenge the student militia's self proclaimed control of the town of Mbordo or the grounds of the University-College.

Radio news from the capital was depressing. The government of Sakra accused the rebels of hiring American and European mercenaries to train and lead their troops. As evidence, the government cited the capture of several mercenaries near the Kra river. These villains had been executed at the site of their capture. The broadcasters had shown no reticence in repeatedly assuring their listeners in colorful language that other mercenaries would meet the same fate and even suggesting that the public might save the armed forces time and effort by dispatching suspected mercenaries immediately, wherever and whenever they were found.

Ironically, or perhaps expectably, Radio Dadze, the radio voice of the rebel state, accused the government of Sakra of similar efforts to hire European mercenaries. The rebels also guaranteed that captured mercenaries would be subject to swift and fatal justice.

191

On the sixth day after the coup a small group of Ave men moving south passed through Mbordo. They brought disturbing information. Units from the North were massing on the north shore of the Kra just to the west of the Kra lake. A few hundred men had already crossed. The rains had not yet come and in many places above the headwaters of the lake the Kra could still be waded. Few of the men they saw were in military uniform. The leader of the Ave group estimated their number to be ten thousand. Several students demanded that the militia march northward and attack immediately before more of the enemy had crossed the Kra. Cooler heads argued that the students were too few in number. They pointed out that if the leader's report was wrong by even as much as half they would still be unable to deal with five thousand men. They argued instead that the student militia, along with anyone else who chose to join them, should move south and west in an effort to link up with troops of the army of Dadze.

A late afternoon meeting conducted by the Vice-Chancellor had become a regular feature of the lives of the remaining staff. The news brought by the Ave men had already spread before they assembled. The Vice-Chancellor attempted to state the alternatives.

"There are," he said quietly, "only two directions in which we can travel to safety. To the southwest, with or without the student militia, in the hope of reaching a major Ave city with an airport and flying out. Or to the east toward Nkra in the hope of finding the protection of troops of the regular army of Sakra. I do not believe it will be safe for any of us to remain here."

The Vice-Chancellor tried to continue but found it impossible to speak above the angry words that erupted from some of the expatriates.

"What the hell do you mean, not safe," he heard Thornton blurt out. "I have lived in this bloody pest-hole of a country for the last twenty-five years. It is the bloody government's job to get me out. This would not have happened while we were in charge."

Whitland's wife was near hysteria. "You stupid black bastard," she shouted in the general direction of the Vice-Chancellor. "You better get us out of here or it will be your ass. My government will take care of you. I am an American citizen."

Words addressed to her husband were even less kind.

She grabbed his shirt and cried, "You useless son of a bitch. Look at this goddamn mess. You drug me in to this hell-hole of a country. Now we are going to be killed by a bunch of niggers."

The Vice-Chancellor decided that he had better do something quickly to control the situation. He picked up a large vase, raised it above his head and brought it crashing to the floor. The sound of shattering glass brought a moment of silence to the room.

In a calm and deliberate tone he said, "This type of behavior will do none of us any good nor will it bring us any closer to safety. I have explained what must be done. There are no other choices. Go to your homes and think carefully about what is the best course for you and your families to follow. Tomorrow morning we will meet to work out details."

After the meeting the Vice-Chancellor went to see the leaders of the student militia. Whatever their previous disagreements had been, they were now settled and preparations were underway to move south and west. They planned to leave that same evening. The Vice-Chancellor asked the students to inform the teachers of their decision to leave Mbordo. They did so and invited those who wished to join them to be ready by 9:00 p.m. Mr. West, several other expatriates, and all of the Ave staff members decided to travel with the students. The other staff members considered the student's offer but tended to agree with Jason's observation that if the student militia encountered troops other than those of the new Dadze government, any expatriates accompanying them were going to have a difficult time explaining what they were doing with a group of armed soldiers pledged to the rebel government.

The next morning eighteen expatriates and three Sakraian staff members remained at the University College. The expatriates were the four Peace Corps volunteers, three River State University couples, two unmarried advisors, and six British professors. The Vice-Chancellor; Mr. Pordoe, the Sportsmaster, who was Bordo; and Gilbert Adwin, the art teacher, who was half-Bordo, half-Atan had also chosen not to travel with the Ave student militia. The Sportsmaster could have remained behind and survived in the forest. However, his wife was Atan. She had, with their children, moved to Nkra several months earlier and the Sportsmaster decided that it was best for him to join them.

Seventeen staff members and the three American wives made it to the early morning meeting called by the Vice-Chancellor. He had gone to Thornton's house in an effort to ensure his presence. But once there, he decided it was better to allow the old man to sleep off the obvious excesses of the previous evening.

After an hour of talking about interesting but not very useful ideas -- helicopters from aircraft carriers, dressing as members of the International Red Cross, digging caves -- the Vice-Chancellor suggested that little would be accomplished by the continuation of the discussion. He proposed instead that Mr. Wills, Mr. Adwin, Mr. Pordoe, Mrs. Manati and himself meet and develop evacuation plans for presentation to the group at four o'clock. He suggested that everyone else return to their homes and pack their most valuable items but no more than they could carry.

The Vice-Chancellor, noting no immediate dissent, adjourned the meeting. Jason, Jeff, Alice, Karen, the Vice-Chancellor, Mr. Pordoe and Mr. Adwin went immediately to Alice's bungalow.

Once there and seated around Alice's dining room table, the Vice-Chancellor explained one option, "If we consolidate the gasoline from the cars and trucks that remain on the compound and put all of it into the school truck, I believe we would be able to drive east at least as far as Towa. There I believe we would be safe and could easily find transportation to Nkra."

The Sportsmaster interrupted. "I am sorry to disagree, sir. But not one week ago I made a brief visit to a relative who lives in that direction. I did not use the road but traveled by bush trails that I learned as a small boy. There were places on the trails from which I could see the road. Armed men are in many places. Most are strangers. A few wore uniforms, most did not. No one will be safe on the road. I would not travel there myself. The situation is very confused."

"I agree," Alice said. "What happened to Mr. Kamure is evidence enough for me that the roads are not safe."

"So what are we going to do," Karen said only half seriously, "walk to Nkra?"

The room was silent for a moment, then the Sportsmaster spoke.

"That is the way that I will go," he said. "It is the only way for me. Others will have to decide for themselves. Most of the men on the road are strangers to this area. Some are from the Middle Tribes, some are Ave, and I have heard that even some Kroban men have come this far south. Strangers will stay near the roads. They do not know the trails and they fear the magic of the forest. On the trails I think that I have some very good chance. On the road I don't think that I will see my wife and children again. There are too many men there who don't care who or what you are. All they want is your money, and if you have none they take your life. There are rumors that the regular army of Sakra has moved troops across the bridge near the Kra damn. I believe this to be true. If we can somehow reach that place where they are camped, we will be safe."

"It is at least forty miles to the bridge and we are not all young," the Vice-Chancellor said, glancing inadvertently toward Alice.

Alice responded, "Even those of us who are not young would rather walk than die. Why not let those who wish to leave Mbordo on foot do so. Let those who do not wish to walk take the lorry."

A polite but definite knock at the door interrupted conversation. When Jeff opened the door he was greeted by a boy of about fourteen years of age. He recognized him as one of Chief Kanata's relatives.

"Sir," the boy said, "I have a most important message for you."

He removed a small folded paper from a pocket in his shorts and handed it to Jeff.

The words Jeff saw as he unfolded the paper were:

COME QUICKLY IF POSSIBLE.
PROBLEMS IN EVERY DIRECTION.
THE CHILD NEEDS YOUR HELP.
KANATA

Jeff refolded the note and stuffed it in his shirt pocket. He turned away from the boy and sat down in a chair near the door. His eyes focused on the cement floor of the bungalow as he struggled to absorb the content and meaning of the message.

Alice called to the boy, "Come in, come in and have something to drink and eat. You look as if you have come a long way."

A change in the boy's expression indicated his gratitude. He moved to the dining area and rapidly consumed the food and drink that Alice placed before him.

Jeff thoughts converged to a decision quickly.

"Very odd, how I could forget what should be most important," he chided himself. "Why did I not think of the danger to the child in Kwim? If men come from the north to Mbordo they would reach Kwim soon after."

"I must go to Kwim," he said in a soft but determined voice.

"How did you come to Mbordo?" he asked the boy.

"By the bush trail, sir," the boy replied as soon as he was able to swallow the food in his mouth. "If you wish to go to Kwim, I will show you the path."

Jeff packed his personal papers and a few small trinkets, reminders of the days with Enata, in a small carrying case. He told the boy to finish eating and moved around the room shaking hands, hugging and saying good-by. Karen found three bottles of Coke in the fridge and put them in his bag. Jeff followed the boy out into the heat of the early afternoon sun. They moved quickly and were soon out of sight on the forest trail that led toward the bungalow in which the Harrises lived.

"I hope he makes it," Jason said quietly as he blinked away tears.

The others nodded their agreement.

CHAPTER 18
Jeff Returns to Kwim

Jeff followed the boy from Kwim into the forest. He made no effort to analyze or understand the consequences of returning to Kwim with the messenger. The Chief's message that his son needed help was sufficient.

By forest trail, the distance from Mbordo to Kwim was less than thirty miles. The path was well kept and easy to walk. They moved rapidly along level portions. The boy led using his flashlight to watch for snakes.

"He is little more than a child," Jeff thought. "And he has already done more than twenty miles. No wonder in the village he is known as the 'one who walks.'"

Jeff thought back on the stories of his guide's endurance. In the Chief's compound, he had once heard a former student remark that if this boy's parents wanted a tin of milk or a newspaper not available in Kwim, they would send him to Mbordo on foot. Jeff now began to fully appreciate those stories as he struggled to maintain the pace set by the messenger. The boy noticed Jeff's labored breath and stopped.

When Jeff asked how far they had come, his guide smiled and replied, "It is still many miles to Kwim. But don't worry, you walk well. Better than many Africans."

Jeff half chuckled as he sipped one of the Cokes the boy carried for him and thought, "If you only knew how my body really felt."

After that first stop Jeff found it necessary to rest frequently. He had time to ask the 'one who walks' about what was happening in Kwim.

"Soldiers come from the north, Ave come from the west," the boy explained. "Maybe somebody come from the east, too. No good. None of them. All people who are able go to bush to hide. Only the sick people, old people stay in village. Chief Kanata stay with them. Very bad trouble there soon. Kwim is in wrong place. When I take you to the Chief's house, I will go to the bush, too. I will find my family."

Even with the extra time required for Jeff to rest, the messenger's rapid pace got them to the edge of the village by sunup. Jeff sensed immediately that his guide's description of what was happening was accurate. At this time of day men should have been on the way to farm, children should have been running about, playing and doing household chores, and palm wine sellers would have been returning from the forest with their wares. Instead, the village reminded Jeff of a ghost town. That sense of abandonment was broken only by the faces of a few old people observing from their doorways, part in fear and part in curiosity, the two intruders who walked alone toward the compound of Chief Kanata. A few recognized Jeff and the boy. He responded to their greetings and began to feel a little more comfortable.

At the entrance to the Chief's compound no one came forward to greet him. The boy did not go in with Jeff.

Instead, he said, "I must go now."

Jeff thanked him for his help. The boy moved away, his stride still firm, back in the direction of Mbordo.

The door to the courtyard stood open. At first he thought that no one was present. The courtyard seemed empty, no children running about, no women at work. Jeff sensed that he was not alone. He turned and saw Chief Kanata sitting in a shaded corner. The Chief's head was bowed, held in his hands. He took no notice of his visitor.

Jeff thought of the old medicine man who lived on the edge of the village and of the spirit world of African religions. "Whatever spirit it is that brings happiness and joy, that spirit has surely abandoned this place."

For a time Jeff waited quietly, but he grew impatient and walked over to the table where the Chief sat. The old man became aware of his presence and looked up.

"Sit down, please," he said. "It is good that you have come. We feared that you might already have left for Nkra."

"Are you well?" Jeff asked, puzzled by the Chief's failure to rise in greeting him.

"I am sorry," the Chief replied, "my own health is quite well, thank you, but that of my people and my country is not. The burden of that sickness is much too heavy for this old man. As you have seen, there is no village left here. Buildings, yes, but without people they will soon crumble into dust. This war was not our doing. We wish nothing more than to be left alone. But with the Bordo it is always so. We are a small tribe. In times of peace everyone is our friend. They partake of our hospitality. We turn away no one, be he Ave, Kroban, Hausa, Atan. They all come to this land; they live in our houses, eat our food, teach our children, grow rich on our cocoa. But now we are enemy to all only because we wish to be left in peace. To the Ave we are traitors because we do not wish to join them in committing suicide. To the Kroban and Atan we are just another type of Ave to be exterminated.

"Aiee, but perhaps I should not speak so harshly of the present. For us it has always been so. My father told me of his father's father, captured by the Atan in some long forgotten war with the Ave and sold into slavery, and the same man's brother taken in the same war by the Ave and also sold into slavery."

The Chief continued his monologue, seeming nearly to forget the presence of his guest.

"We are a most unfortunate people. We will die because we are Ave and because we are not Ave. It is beyond understanding. We did not make this war. We did not ask to be a part of it. Why cannot those who wish to fight do so elsewhere and leave us in peace? By whatever small power I have with the spirits of the earth, the sky and the water, I curse Kroban, Ave and Atan alike. May they destroy each other and leave the earth to those who know how to live in peace."

The Chief's head dropped. His eyes tried to focus on the ground in front of him but he saw nothing as he fought to control a surge of anger and frustration. The Chief stood up abruptly and walked away from the table. He motioned for Jeff to remain seated. Moments later he returned with a bottle of beer and two glasses. He opened the bottle and poured a glass for Jeff and himself.

"I am sorry," the Chief said, "that I was unable to greet you more kindly."

"Do not be concerned for my comfort," Jeff replied as he tried to keep his voice from cracking. "I understand a measure of the pain and sorrow that you feel even more than you would think possible."

The Chief nodded in reply.

"Why did you not go to the bush with the others?" Jeff asked.

"I could not do that," Chief Kanata said. "The sick and the old of this village are unable to leave. They would die quickly in the bush. I have a responsibility to them.

"Also," he continued, "to die in the bush later is not much better than to die in one's own home a little more quickly. But enough of my problems. I am certain that you wish to know why I asked you to come. The reason for my request is also a portion of my grief. Perhaps you remember my insistence only a few months ago that the boy remain here near the place where his mother was also a child. It grieves me deeply that it cannot be so. This war may destroy us all one way or another. If the child is taken into the bush he probably will not live to see his second year. The rains will soon come. A child so small, without proper food and shelter, does not often survive that cold time. For him to stay here in the village is an even greater danger. Kroban are to the north, Ave to the west, government troops to the east and roving bandits, evil men, all about. It is only a matter of time until this village becomes a battlefield. I have heard terrible stories. Many soldiers are not well disciplined. Sometimes they kill all, the old, women, children, all. Perhaps these stories are not completely true. But even if the child were allowed to live and the rest of us died, who would care for him? How could one so small survive and what would become of him without friends or family?

"This decision causes me great pain. The child is my link to Enata. But it cannot be otherwise. Please, take the boy with you. Take him with you to your home in America. You will be a good father to him. With you he will grow into a man."

Jeff was silent. The Chief's words had been expected. But only now did he begin to understand the full weight of his responsibility.

"It will not be easy to replace what the child has here," Jeff said.

"Yes," the Chief replied, "but I do know that whatever can be done, you will do."

"Yes, I will do what I can." Jeff said. "You knew that I would be willing to take the boy with me even before you sent the messenger."

The old man smiled for the first time that day and said, "Thank you, my son. Now, to help you, we have made certain preparations. Several years ago a nurse sent by the government left bottles with nipples behind. We have boiled milk and filled them in the way that she explained. We also have some powdered milk. The gas tank of my car is full, thanks to the contributions of a number of lorry drivers before they hid their trucks in the bush. The fighting seems to be concentrated to the east and north at present. If you drive to the south and west, you may be able to move some distance before you encounter trouble. The car has been prepared for your use. You will find bottled water, well boiled, and a bag to carry it in on the back seat. Come with me."

The two men walked to where the car was parked.

"I believe it best that you leave immediately in order to use all of the daylight hours. You should not drive at night. It would be much too dangerous."

Jeff interrupted to say, "I have heard that it is not safe to be on the road at any time for the Obroni. We are accused of being mercenaries."

"I know of this problem," the Chief replied, as he pointed to various signs and symbols newly drawn on the car. "We have done our best to mark the car so that those who see it will know that you are a peaceful traveler and my son. Those who know me will allow you to pass without hesitation, the others..." the Chief's voice trailed off as he struggled to find words to complete the sentence and then gave up.

"Here," the old man continued as he removed an old handmade map and compass from the glove compartment. "Go south toward Sanuway then west toward Malief. From the information I have that is the safest route. If you are forced to leave the car, this compass may be of some use."

Jeff nodded.

The Chief called out an instruction in Bordo. An old woman appeared at the courtyard door with a small bundle in her arms. She spoke to the Chief in Bordo. Jeff understood much of what she said, but the Chief translated for him anyway.

"If he cries, he is hungry or damp. In the car is extra cloth to provide for changes. There is a basket on the front seat large enough to carry the boy in."

No one spoke as the woman opened the front door of the old car and laid the baby in the basket. Then she turned slowly and walked back toward the compound. The Chief rested his hands on Jeff's shoulders.

"Jeff," he said, "I know that I cannot rightfully ask for more than that you take this child safely to America. But if it is at all possible, please, in some small way teach him that he is also African. And perhaps tell him of his grandfather the Chief of Kwim and his mother Enata who loved him dearly and whose spirits await him always in this small village."

Chief Kanata paused to remove a small stone from a hidden pocket, then continued, "Perhaps this will seem too odd or strange, but would you take this small stone which I have removed from one of the ancient holy places and keep it near the boy as he grows to be a man?"

"You need never worry," Jeff replied. "This stone will never be far from the child. And he will know as much as I am able to tell him of his grandfather the Chief of Kwim and of his mother Enata and of the village of Kwim. I promise that he will know that he is African as well as you yourself know it to be true. And should we all survive this time of war, the boy and I will return to this place and you, yourself can teach him of those things of the Bordo which I cannot."

CHIEF KANATA'S HANDMADE MAP

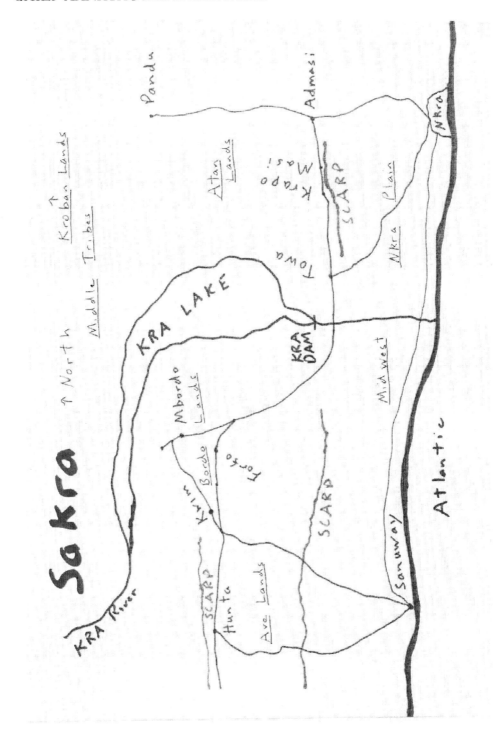

Chief Kanata did not reply. Instead, he opened the front door of the car for a last look at his grandson lying asleep in the small basket. He closed the door carefully and handed the keys for the car to Jeff. They clasped hands then fell into a full embrace.

The Chief released Jeff and said, "It is time. You must go."

The old man turned and moved rapidly away from the car. Jeff slid into the front seat and started the motor. In a momentary sideward glance, he saw Chief Kanata near one of the side entrances of the compound; no longer stiffly erect, but with shoulders slumped, head bowed, his entire body wracked with the pain of deep sorrow and the sounds of unbearable grief that Jeff had seen and heard before only from women in mourning. He drove away quickly through the empty streets of Kwim, but the image of the old man's grief remained with him as the car passed the last houses of the village. He looked at the small child in the basket next to him and tried to explain.

"I am sorry, my little one, to take you from your grandfather. You will miss his love more than you will ever know."

The Chief's old car was often the only vehicle in sight, but large numbers of people were walking on the road. All were moving south in the direction of Sanuway. The route planned by Chief Kanata would take them about halfway to Sanuway and then due west toward the Malief border. Twice that morning Jeff offered a ride to people who were having difficulty walking, once to an old man and later to a woman carrying a young child with two small ones following. Both times the Africans studied him and the automobile carefully then slipped away into the bush. About eleven, he spotted a student of the University-College walking along the road, one of those from the Ave brigade that had left Mbordo with Mr. West and several other teachers. Jeff stopped the car and motioned for him to approach. The student was at first hesitant but upon recognizing Jeff he moved quickly to the open window on the driver's side.

"Can I give you a lift?" Jeff asked.

The student responded in a polite but firm tone, "No thank you, sir. It is better that I walk."

"Why do you not wish to ride?" Jeff asked. "It will take you many days to reach Sanuway on foot."

"That is true," the student replied, "but it is better to reach there alive than not at all. We were nearly all killed because of the Europeans that traveled with us. There is much fear of mercenaries. Our own people fired on us. Several were wounded before we could make them understand that we were also soldiers of the Ave nation. If Mr. West had not been able to convince the captain who led those troops that none of us were mercenaries, I fear we all would be dead."

Were any of the teachers injured?" Jeff asked.

"Two were wounded," the student replied, "how badly, I do not know."

Jeff mused aloud as much to himself as to the student, "Now I understand why the old man and the woman would not ride with me. They too must be afraid of being seen with mercenaries."

"Perhaps, sir," the student smiled and commented, "that may be the case. But you should also know that your automobile carries on its body very powerful symbols of juju and the personal symbols of Kanata the Paramount Chief of the villages of Kwim. That might have frightened them away."

Jeff offered the student a ride again.

He replied, "No, it is better for me that I walk. Good-by and much good luck to you, sir."

The conversation left Jeff ill at ease. He would now have to decide whether to make an effort to avoid soldiers completely or simply stay on the road as long as possible and hope for the best. That decision was made for him when he rounded a sharp bend and saw a roadblock less than fifty yards ahead. His foot went lightly to the brake as he allowed the car to roll to a halt about ten feet from where the first soldiers stood. He recognized a mixture of Ave and Bordo words. One of the soldiers ordered him out of the car. Another frisked him as he stood near the door. They called for another young soldier. The others saluted and addressed him as Captain. He took several minutes to inspect the markings on the car. He also opened the front door on the passenger side and looked at the child.

Then he approached Jeff and said, "You may proceed, but take care. Before you reach Sanuway, others may question your right to drive on this road."

By one that afternoon, he had cleared two more checkpoints.

At the last, one of the soldiers had quietly whispered, "Do not go further south on this road. At the next place the soldiers will have no respect for your car or your life."

The decision to leave the car would have been difficult had not the gas tank been near empty. Thus far the trip had been almost pleasant. The car's motor was in good condition and finely tuned. But the few places they passed that had once sold gasoline looked as if they had been closed for years.

The motion of the car had kept the baby in a half awake, half asleep state. He had not done much more than whimper a few times during the stops at roadblocks.

"The Chief must have kept him up most of last night," Jeff thought.

A few miles beyond that last checkpoint the car's engine began to sputter. Jeff spotted a small downhill lane leading to an abandoned cottage. He coaxed the Chief's car into the lane. and braked to a halt a few yards from the mud and grass building.

The moment the car stopped the baby began to scream louder than Jeff would have believed possible for one so small. Jeff remembered the old woman's advice and looked for the bottles of milk. He found them packed carefully in the basket with the baby. There were eight. He took one out and leaned over the basket. The baby looked up. His eyes conveyed confusion and fear. For a moment the child refused to take the bottle, then hunger became his dominant instinct. The small boy took the nipple and rapidly drained the bottle of its precious fluid. The baby's vigorous sucking brought Jeff a moment of pleasure.

"This is easy. I do believe that I may yet qualify as a real father," he thought.

When the baby had finished the bottle, Jeff rinsed it out and refilled it with the boiled water from the old wine bottle that had also been furnished by the Chief. He noticed that the baby was still whimpering. Jeff remembered the rest of the old woman's advice and with a touch found that the child's diaper was quite wet, soaked, in fact. The one with which Jeff replaced it did not look much like the original, but it was dry. The small boy stopped crying and drifted back into sleep.

Jeff picked out items to carry. He filled a small bag with a full size cloth, clothes, and the powdered milk. In the space that remained in the bag, he placed the stone given to him by Chief Kanata, one full bottle of water, the map, a loaf of bread and a small bag of chocolates that someone must have given the Chief months or even years before. He slipped the compass into his shirt pocket and forced himself to drink what he could of the water in the other bottles.

By the time he had finished, the child was awake again, cooing softly. Jeff opened the door on the passenger side and picked the basket up by its handle. He slung the small bag over his other shoulder and walked away from the car. Jeff walked rapidly along the small lane. As he neared the highway, he stopped and looked back at the old automobile, intending to do so for only a brief moment. Thoughts of much that had happened involved the old Buick; the trip to Hunta, the small church on the scarp, the picnics, the accident, the birth of this child, Enata's death, the drive back to Kwim, images of the Chief's grief. Overcome by fatigue and sorrow, the shadows of the past seemed more than he could bear. For a moment he thought he could see Enata in the front seat of the car motioning for him to come. When the image faltered and disappeared he sat down suddenly by the side of the road. The Africans walking on the highway moved quickly to the other side and continued their journey. He was very much alone even in the midst of the other refugees, not really unhappy or even sad, but unable to cope with the beautiful but painful visions of the past.

The baby's near cry startled him.

He knew it could not be so, and yet he was sure that he heard a voice saying, "Let's go, let's go, daddy."

His mind cleared. The child was making noises. Not talking, of course, but he did seem to be asking in his own way why they had stopped so long. Jeff got up quickly, picked up the basket, and started walking.

He noticed with some small amusement that even though many others were moving in the same direction, they remained at least thirty yards ahead of or behind him.

"Ordinarily someone would be bothering me all the time," he mused. "children wanting a penny, students waiting to know what life is really like in America, young men asking for help in getting a scholarship to an American university. Maybe this fear of mercenaries does have its good aspects."

After a couple of miles, Jeff decided that his arms would not last even through the next checkpoint if he did not find a better way to carry the baby. The basket was an awkward and heavy burden. He already knew that the best way to carry a baby was on a woman's back. Unfortunately, no woman's back was available.

"I will look odd as hell," he thought. "Don't believe I have ever seen a man carry one that way. But if I don't do something, neither of us is going to make it."

He removed the large cloth that the old woman had packed. He spread it out full on the ground then folded it over once. He laid the baby down with its head near the top of the fold. He had always wondered why the child did not fall out of the blanket when it was wrapped around the mother's back. He had even been curious enough some months before to ask one of the women from the Chief's compound to demonstrate how it was done. She had been very pleased to show him. Unfortunately, he did not try to do it himself and now failed to remember some of the finer points involved in the technique. When he tried to secure the baby within the folds of the cloth behind him and at the same time tie the ends together in front, the small boy nearly fell to the ground. He tried again but gave up when he felt the child slipping down his back. Several of the Africans who had been walking well behind him noticed his difficulty. After some discussion, one of the women came forward to offer help. She demonstrated how the baby should be folded within the cloth and then tied high up on the back to balance the weight on the back and shoulders. Jeff tried doing it himself several times. He packed the bottles of milk in the empty spot left in the bag by the removal of the cloth and gave the basket to the woman.

Jeff became increasingly cautious in his efforts to avoid army checkpoints. Anywhere that a hill or curve obstructed his view of the road ahead, he moved off the pavement and through the bush until he could again see well forward. In the short distance that he walked that afternoon, they had passed three places where the road was cordoned off by the rebels. Each time he had seen the soldiers before they saw him and moved a good distance off the road.

By late afternoon he was travelling more off the road than on. The frequent checkpoints were bad enough, but he also had to dive off the road several times to avoid being seen by columns of soldiers marching up and down the highway in what seemed to be near aimless fashion. He decided that he must be in a training or staging area.

By dusk Jeff was exhausted, walking only from memory. He had nibbled on some of the chocolate but had eaten nothing else, preferring to save what he had until he stopped for the day. Had he been thinking clearly, perhaps he would already have looked for a safe place to spend the night. But his primary concern was the child. He knew it would be better if they reached a place of safety before the prepared milk supply was exhausted. He could use the bottle water to prepare more milk with the powder, but the chance of contamination would increase with each reuse of the bottles. Hence, he continued to move forward in the fading light. Few other people were still on the road. For the first time that day, Jeff could see no one either in front or behind. By watching the actions of others on the road, he had always been able to pick up some clues as to what lay ahead. But now he was alone. What he thought to be empty pavement straight ahead was a side road. The main road bent sharply to the left. Ahead, less than fifty feet, he saw a checkpoint manned by at least two dozen soldiers. His momentary indecision over whether to go forward or run like hell was resolved by the sound of gunfire. A bullet whistled above and to the right of his head. He plunged off a small bank near the side of the road and ran into a moderately thick growth of brush.

As he plowed ahead past small trees and vines, he heard a voice behind him yell, "Mercenary, get mercenary. Mercenary in the bush. Move that way. Don't let him back to road."

CHAPTER 19
The Walk Out

Jeff's abrupt departure had stunned those left in Alice's bungalow.

"It is a long way to Kwim on foot," Karen commented.

"Jeff is very strong and fit," the Vice Chancellor said. "He did a lot of physical labor in his school gardens. Certainly more than any of our students in the work programs."

"Yes," Jason added, "and after Enata died he quit drinking anything more than a beer or two a week."

"I hope it all works out for the best, but that doesn't have much to do with us right now," Alice said tersely. "Let's get back to business. I want to walk out of here. What do the rest of you want to do?"

The others in the room indicated their agreement.

"Then it is settled," the Vice-Chancellor said. "Those of us who wish to walk will walk. Those who don't like that idea can attempt the journey by lorry or I suppose just stay here."

"We should leave as soon as possible," the Sportsmaster said. "Every day that we wait the situation becomes more dangerous."

"Let's leave tomorrow morning," Gil suggested.

"Better that we leave tonight," the Sportsmaster replied. "During the day these men sometimes go into the forest. But at night they stay very near the roads. They are afraid of the juju and the snakes."

"Shouldn't we be afraid of the snakes too?" Karen asked.

"Which do you fear most?" the Sportsmaster asked. "The snakes that crawl on the ground or those that stand on two legs?"

"If I have to make a choice," Karen mused, "I believe that I would pick those that crawl on the ground."

"We have a small amount of serum," the Vice-Chancellor commented. "Before the Doctor left our small hospital he gave me the remains of the few drugs that he had left. He also gave me several needles to use for injections."

"Yes, then we agree I think," Jason concluded. "With the serum it is better we take our chances with the snakes of the forest and that we do so tonight."

The Sportsmaster expressed concern that those teachers who did not wish to walk toward Nkra might try to leave by lorry that afternoon. He was sure they would be stopped on the road and was afraid they would be forced to tell their captors about the people who still remained at the University-College.

The Vice-Chancellor smiled.

"Do not worry," he said. "I have already made certain that no one will leave in the school lorry until we give permission to do so. One does not travel far by truck without petrol."

After a quick lunch, Jason and the Vice-Chancellor visited all of the remaining staff members. Both Jason and the Vice-Chancellor feared that the meeting at four might break down into irrational bickering. They wished to give each individual or family the opportunity to think about the options they faced without also having to deal with an atmosphere of group hysteria.

The four o'clock meeting lived up to their expectations. The Vice-Chancellor opened the gathering with brief greetings and then proceeded to explain that he believed it to be too dangerous now for any of them to remain on the University-College compound. He left to Jason the explanation of the methods of evacuation.

Jason's intention had been to lay out the advantages and disadvantages of the two alternatives once more as clearly and carefully as possible. He had not gotten much past stating the two plans when Eric Thornton stood up. His body swayed as he tried to assert control over his balance.

"This is damnable foolishness," he bellowed. "We bloody well should get on that goddamn piece of junk they have the nerve to call a school truck and drive the hell out of here. No black bastard is going to stop any lorry that I am on. You fools won't get two miles on foot. They will find your bodies rotting in the jungle.

"Don't be misled by some of our so-called African friends," Thornton continued as he directed his eyes, now filled with a mixture of hate and contempt, toward the Vice-Chancellor. "Those buggers are just trying to save their own damned necks. They know they can't ride that lorry. We would not let them on anyway. They would get us all killed. It is their stupid war, not ours. They have to walk. They just want to take us along with them for extra protection."

Jason tried to shut Thornton up by pounding on the table in front of him with a cane, but Thornton, sensing that some of the others in the room might agree with him, became even bolder. His voice settled into that deep graveled bass that is the mark of an alcohol damaged larynx.

He shouted, "I am going to ride that lorry out of here and I am going to do it right now. Those of you who are not complete fools will follow me. The rest of you can stay here with your African friends."

Jason could not make himself heard above the spontaneous outburst of noise that enveloped the room. Several of the expatriates were already moving toward the door led by Thornton. Alice got up and moved to block the doorway.

Thornton's loud voice brought silence to the room, "Get out of the way, old woman, or you are dead! Do you understand? Dead!"

They stared at each other in silence. Then Thornton's concentration broke. He looked to those behind him for support, then dropped his head and stared at the floor.

Alice shook her head slowly and said, "You old drunken fool. You would lead these people?"

Then she looked at those who had planned to follow Thornton out of the room and continued, "Now just look at your leader. One or two more drinks and he won't even be on his feet. This is the man you think will lead you to safety? Stop and think for a minute. You may choose to use the lorry, but do so on your own, not led by this man. As for myself, I am older than any of you by quite a good margin. I intend to walk. You can do whatever you wish. But we are all in this together and I don't intend that Thornton or anyone else is going to do something that will take away my chances of getting to Nkra. Now, why don't you all sit down and listen before you make up your minds?"

"One more small item to consider," Jason added from the front of the room. "No one is leaving by lorry right now. We have hidden the gasoline. Those of us who plan to walk will not release it until we are ready to leave and that will be tonight under cover of darkness. I would suggest that the lorry not leave here before tomorrow morning. At night you may find yourself dead before anyone asks who you are."

"That is completely unfair," Mr. Springs, one of the River State people, said emphatically. "You seem to have already made all the decisions. I thought we came here to discuss what we were going to do and not just to be told what to do. Who gave you the right to do this?"

"This morning I thought it was very clear that you people asked the Vice-Chancellor, Mr. Pordoe and myself to go and make plans for evacuation," Jason replied. "That is exactly what we did. Walking is safest in our opinion. We cannot allow those who wish to use the lorry to jeopardize the safety of those who plan to walk."

"That is all well and good," the professor replied, "but what if the army from the North reaches Mbordo before we leave tomorrow morning?"

The Sportsmaster indicated that he wished to speak.

"Last night I went to the place on the river where the men from the North are now crossing. Not more than half have crossed and those on this side wait for the others. I used forest trails but an army of that size cannot move through forest they do not know. By road it is at least a two days' march from where they are to this place if they choose to move in this direction. They would not travel by night for fear of ambush. If you leave with the truck in the morning you will be far away before they could arrive."

The professor nodded. Jason suggested that if no one had anything further to say, each person should decide what they were going to do. Four of the British expatriates and three of the River State people, one couple and a single professor, decided to try the lorry. Almost everyone else, including the British couple, Ian and Beth Harris, had made up their minds to walk. Only Professor Whitland and his wife remained undecided.

After the meeting Whitland stopped Jason and asked, "What do you think our chances on the lorry are?"

Jason replied, "There are at least fifteen roadblocks between here and Towa. There are armed men at each one. Some may be honest soldiers. Most are not. First they will take your money. Then your clothes. What will they take when you have nothing left to give?"

"But can we really walk out of here?" Whitland responded. "That's a hell of a long way. I can probably make it, but what about Betty?"

"Only you can answer that question," Jason replied. "I intend to make it. Mr. Pordoe knows the trails and he knows which are safest. But only you and your wife can decide what is your best chance. If you choose to go with us, bring your things to the staff lounge by six-thirty. We will leave Mbordo before seven."

Alice, Jason and Karen were in the staff lounge by six. Each came with one small bag in which they carried vital papers, bottled water and a small amount of food. Ian and Beth carried a small briefcase containing their papers, food, and water. The Sakraian staff members who joined them carried nothing except a few folded papers for identification, small pouches of food and bottles filled with water.

At six-thirty Professor Whitland walked into the staff lounge carrying two large suitcases. His wife followed with two smaller ones. Another American couple, Ralph and Jean Block, followed the Whitlands into the room. They carried two medium sized bags.

Jason lifted one of Whitland's suitcases.

"My God, man," he exclaimed, "what in the hell do you have in here, books?"

"I only brought the most valuable of my collection," Whitland replied. "I left at least a thousand dollar's worth behind."

"What do you think this is?" Jason snapped, "A picnic? You have too much to carry. You won't make it half a mile. If you want to take those four bags, I suggest you wait and try the lorry in the morning.

Betty Whitland interrupted.

"They can help," she said, looking toward the Africans. "They don't seem to have much of anything to carry."

For one brief instant, Jason thought he would explode in a burst of indignation but instead he started to laugh. A sudden vision of the Vice-Chancellor, the Sportsmaster, and Gilbert dressed in loin cloths, hurrying through the jungle with huge suitcases carefully balanced on their heads and the Whitlands following serenely behind, brought Jason to a near hysterical state.

The others in the room looked on, somewhat puzzled, as Jason pointed at the Whitlands and said, "Me Tarzan, you Jane and another boyfriend. Africans here carry White Man's Burden."

Everyone in the room started laughing except the Whitlands.

When Jason stopped laughing, he looked at Whitland and said, "The Vice-Chancellor, Mr. Pordoe, and Mr. Adwin are not carrying much because they have brought with them exactly what they think they will be able to carry. I am sure that they have other possessions they would like to take with them if they wished to carry more. I don't believe there is any reason to discuss this matter further. Each person will carry his own belongings, no more, no less. If someone wishes to take more than they can carry, they should go on the lorry."

Then Jason added, "Cut down to one bag or less if you plan to come with us."

"Who the hell do you think you are?" Mrs. Whitland said.

"Why is this bastard giving orders?" she continued, looking around the room. "Who says we have to do what he tells us?"

"We are all in agreement, I think," the Vice-Chancellor said quietly but firmly. "Do as Mr. Wills says and do it now or get out."

Whitland glanced at his wife's suitcases.

Anticipating his intention she cried, "Oh no you don't, you SOB. I am not leaving anymore of my clothes behind just so that you can take those goddamn books. I don't want filthy niggers wearing my clothes."

Betty realized what she had said and started to cry. Through her tears she tried to explain.

"I never wanted to come to this shit-hole place anyway. Why did you do this to me? Weren't we happy in Indiana? Why?"

Alice's strong voice momentarily silenced Mrs. Whitland.

"I strongly suggest, Mr. Whitland, that you and your wife continue this discussion in private. We will wait fifteen minutes for your decision before we leave."

Whitland picked up his two suitcases and left. Mrs. Whitland followed in silence.

The Blocks had already started the process of sorting out what they would leave behind.

"I'm sorry about the way they acted," Ralph Block said to the Vice-Chancellor. "We know that nobody here is to blame for this mess."

"Thank-you," the Vice-Chancellor replied, "I don't know if I have ever formally expressed my gratitude for the quiet but good work you and your wife have done for our English program in your time here, but I did notice. The students at River State will be fortunate to have you both as teachers again. Thank-you for what you have done for the University College."

"You are very kind," Jean Block replied. "Now Jason, what exactly should we be taking?"

"Food, water, personal papers, and only those other things that are very important to you," Jason replied.

The Whitlands returned within the fifteen minute period. He carried one medium sized bag. She carried nothing except a bright red mark on one cheek. Mr. Whitland mumbled to Jason that they were ready.

Jason gave the keys of the school lorry to the Englishman who was to be the driver the next morning and explained where the supply of gas was hidden. Karen and Alice did a quick inventory of food and water carried by each person.

At seven they started westward toward Towa. They were quickly into the forest. Darkness became near complete with the end of the evening's meager twilight. The sky was clear, millions of stars were visible, but the moon was in its final quarter and provided only a weak flickering light through the canopy of branches over the trail.

"Use your torches carefully," Mr. Pordoe warned. "We don't need to let others who might still be in the forest know we are here and also we need to save the strength of the batteries for a time when there may be even less light."

"Torches?" Mr. Block asked.

"Flashlights," Mr. Pordoe answered. "I forgot that is the term you Americans use."

The path was dry and in places almost dusty since the heavy rains had not yet come. The trail chosen by Pordoe, the Sportsmaster, was wide and easy to walk on. It was more or less parallel to the main road and not far from it in many places. It passed through a number of small living areas with five or six houses each. The Bordo families who had once used these houses were no longer there. They had moved into Mbordo or deeper into the forest. The Sportsmaster avoided the little housing clusters by using smaller trails that bypassed the living areas. He feared that at least some of the men who manned the blockades on the road by day might be using these houses for shelter. During one of their rest stops, Mr. Pordoe explained to Jason that he had chosen this trail because it was wider and less rough than those deeper in the forest. They could move rapidly with little danger from snakes. Once daylight came they would have to move deeper into the forest since the strangers who stayed on or near the road by night tended to become bolder during the day.

After a few miles the little group settled into a single file pattern. The Sportsmaster moved along the trail with a quiet and graceful stride about a dozen yards ahead. Jason brought up the rear with Karen. The only torch lights they used were prearranged signals between the Sportsmaster and Jason to insure that they continued to walk as a group. They made good time, two to three miles per hour. However, by midnight, Betty Whitland was issuing a near continuous stream of complaints, all in rather foul language. Her choice of shoes, a pair of sandals with one inch heels, had been inappropriate and her feet were paying the price. Her most abusive comments were directed toward her husband.

"You goddamn son of a bitch," she seemed to repeat a hundred times in a quiet tone but with enough emphasis so that others could hear. "This is entirely your fault. My feet are ruined. I will never make it. You and those African bastards will have to carry me. This was a completely stupid idea."

Whitland bore most of her comments in silence. But, once when she sat down in the middle of the trail without warning, he couldn't stop and tripped over her.

"You clumsy idiot," she cried loudly. "What in the hell..."

Whitland interrupted, "Say what you please. But I am going to get up and start walking. You can get up and walk behind me if you want to or you can damn well stay where you are."

Whitland got up and moved along the trail. Betty, after a moment's hesitation, did likewise. Her comments continued but in a muted form that reflected concern with pain rather than anger. Jason noticed that the Blocks were also showing signs of fatigue and pain but were thus far bearing those burdens in silence. At midnight the Sportsmaster called a second halt for rest. Mr. Whitland indicated to Jason that he wished to talk with him.

"I know that I sounded pretty tough talking to Betty back there," he said, "but I really would not leave her out here alone. She is completely exhausted. Just plain done for. She says that she cannot go on."

"If she can't go any further, then we will have to leave both of you," Jason replied coldly.

"You are one real son of a bitch," Whitland said. "You and that Sportsmaster bastard are responsible for bringing us here. You better damn well get us out of this jungle or I will see to it that you spend the rest of your life in jail."

"You damn fool," Jason replied. "If you don't get out of here alive, how are you going to put anybody in jail? If we don't cover a lot of ground tonight, when are we going to be able to? Tomorrow the men on the road may know about us. We have to go deeper into the forest. The trails will be worse. We have to move fast and far tonight or we may never make it. Do you want to spend six weeks out here?"

Jason paused, then continued, "Now listen carefully. In a few minutes the Sportsmaster is going to start walking. Anybody that doesn't get up and start walking can stay right here. Your wife can still walk. She is not going to die of sore feet."

Whitland said nothing. He left Jason and returned to where his wife sat by the trail. In the darkness Jason heard her sharp voice. He saw Whitland's hand move and heard the crisp sound of his palm on her face. Jason's attention was diverted from the woman's sobs by a torch signal from the Sportsmaster that indicated his wish to start.

Jason said quietly but clearly, "All right, let's go."

At her husband's insistence Betty resumed her place in the column. She whimpered and moaned as she limped along. After about thirty minutes of walking she collapsed. Her husband moved quickly to her side. Karen paused as she reached the place on the trail where Betty had fallen. Jason caught up with them moments later.

He grasped Karen's arm and said, "Leave them. We will all die if we stay here. We must find a safe place to spend the daylight hours. Renegades will come by this spot tomorrow. Anyone who stays here will be in big trouble. If we make a few more miles tonight we will be in a safe place. We can rest there. I feel terrible about leaving them behind, but better for them to die alone than for all of us to die."

He pulled Karen past the place where the Whitlands sat on the trail and signaled the Sportsmaster to go on. Before they had covered another ten yards Jason heard Whitland's voice.

"Wait, please," he cried, "please God, wait, we are coming. Wait, please wait."

Jason sighed. Karen gave him an understanding nudge. He signaled Mr. Pordoe to stop the column. A few seconds latter two stooped figures limped and stumbled past where they stood and continued along the trail.

"Thank God they got up," Jason said to Karen. "I was afraid that we were going to have to carry them."

"You mean you weren't serious about leaving them behind?" Karen teased.

Jason tried to smack her bottom with a quick flip of the wrist but missed.

Karen noticed and commented, "My you certainly seem to have plenty of energy left. Maybe you should carry Mrs. Whitland."

The Whitlands moved slowly, but they did keep moving. Jason noticed that Whitland left the suitcase with books and his wife's extra clothing by the side of the trail.

During the next stop for rest, the Sportsmaster indicated to Jason that he wished to speak with him.

"We must now use a trail that is no longer popular. Since it is not cared for I fear that it will be too difficult for the Whitlands and the Blocks and maybe even Mrs. Manati."

"What must be done must be done," Jason replied. "If you believe that is the best and safest way then we will follow. Everyone's life should not be put in danger because some of us get tired. Perhaps if we rest more frequently, maybe every hour, it will help."

"Then you signal for the stops," Mr. Pordoe said. "We do not have to go that much farther. I know a very good place if only we can reach there before daylight. I think we can rest there the entire day and continue on at night."

As they moved on to the new path, Jason realized that the Sportsmaster had not exaggerated when he described the trail as difficult. For a time the Whitlands managed a constant stream of complaints. Jason didn't bother to answer as long as they kept walking. The Whitlands were not the only members of the contingent that found this little used trail exhausting. The rest stops on the hour soon became stops every half hour. By four o'clock the time needed for rest was almost as much as the time used in walking. They reached the spot the Sportsmaster had described just as the sun was coming up.

Mr. Pordoe had chosen well, a tiny glen in which a spring part-way up one side flowed from under large flat rocks down into a small pool.

"You will be safe here until evening," Pordoe explained. "No one comes to this place anymore. Rest well. Drink well. The water here is very sweet."

With the exceptions of Jason and the Sportsmaster, the little collection of humanity collapsed to the ground almost as a single entity.

"You are in excellent condition, my friend," the Sportsmaster said, "the only one still standing."

"I shall join them soon," Jason replied. "I am just admiring this place. It is beautiful."

"As a boy," Mr. Pordoe said, "I would be sent here for water when drought was at its worst. This place is fifteen miles from my house. Then I did not like it so well. But now I too see its beauty. But this spot is forgotten by most people. When it is dry, we now depend on the government or we go to the river near the University-College. That place is now more convenient to reach by road. But enough of the past. I will now return to the main road. I want to know what happens to those on the school lorry."

Jason's gasp was audible.

"Return to the main road!" he exclaimed. "That's a hell of a long way."

"Not as far as you might think," the Sportsmaster replied. "It is very important that we know what happens to that lorry. Our fate is tied to theirs. It they are stopped then our presence in the forest may become known and we will have to adjust our plans."

Jason nodded and shrugged.

"Have a nice walk," he said.

Once Pordoe had disappeared into the forest Jason looked around. No one else was awake. He knew that he probably should remain alert and serve as a watchman but he too was asleep almost as soon as he sat down.

Less than two hours later Jason was awakened by the light touch of Pordoe's hand on his shoulder.

"Jason," he said, "I am sorry that I cannot let you sleep longer, but we must talk now. By chance I reached the road a few minutes before the school lorry passed. I saw our people try to drive through a road block. But the men there had placed iron spikes on the road. The front tires exploded then the back ones also. The truck skidded sideways and turned over. One man fell out the side. He was caught beneath the truck. He must be dead or hurt very badly. The man who was driving and two others riding in front were thrown against the windshield. The other four in the back seemed shaken but still able to walk. It is possible that the men who set the roadblock are part of the regular army of the new Ave nation. But I don't know. It is difficult to tell from the distance that I watched. They made everyone who was still able to move lie face down in the road. The men chose Thornton to question first. He was riding in the front and was in great pain from the cuts and bruises on his face. They put a rope around his neck.

"Quite clearly I heard him say, 'Please, please, you must understand. We are not the mercenaries. We are only humble teachers. But we did see a group of mercenaries in the forest. They are over there in the jungle, trying to walk to Towa to join up with the government forces. They want to help them kill you. Don't you understand anything? If we were mercenaries, we would not be on the road traveling in the open like this. We would be sneaking through the forest like those other people.'

"I stayed long enough to watch the soldiers take all of those who could walk away into the forest. Perhaps there is an Ave encampment somewhere near. I am very much afraid that those men might have believed Thornton, especially if others in the group told the same lie about mercenaries in the forest. I heard some of the them talk of sending a patrol into the forest."

"So what does that mean for us?" Jason asked.

"We are no longer safe in this place," Mr. Pordoe replied. "Bandits or renegades would not move this deep into the forest, but a unit of even a poorly trained army might. I had not wished to move by day. I know that most of your people are exhausted and need more rest. But we have little choice. We cannot fight. And if we are found by those soldiers, you and your friends will have serious trouble. Mr. Thornton has already branded you as mercenaries."

CHAPTER 20
Jeff Becomes 'The Mercenary'

The repeated cry of "Get the mercenary!" provided Jeff with a burst of energy that even he found surprising. He moved quickly in the low but heavy vegetation. The branches of small trees punished his face and arms. He felt the sting of a thorn in his side. Knee-high grass seemed determined to slow the forward movement of his legs. He thought momentarily of throwing the bag aside but did not. Without food, he knew the child would soon starve.

"My God," he muttered as he ran, "now I am 'The Mercenary.' Am I that well known? Maybe they were looking for someone else. But that's no damn help. It doesn't matter. If they find me, I am it."

He reached an area in which the trees were larger and the brush beneath less thick. Little light from the moon filtered through the layered canopy of the forest above. The darkness was near total. Jeff continued to run, spurred on by the sounds of the soldiers that he assumed were following him. At times, he could see only well enough to dodge the trunks of the larger trees. Saplings and vines he tried to ignore by running straight over or through them. He pulled the cloth that held the baby on his back tight against his chest. Since the child had not complained, Jeff hoped the branches that whipped his face and chest were missing the child.

Jeff ran until he could run no more. He collapsed in a small clear spot between several large trees. He could still hear the voices of soldiers. Jeff's mind told him to get up. He tried, but his knees buckled and he sank back to the ground.

The baby murmured. Jeff moved it around to his chest and took another bottle of milk from the bag, hoping to keep the child quiet by feeding it. The voices moved closer. The baby cried. Jeff jammed the bottle into the small boy's mouth.

"Perhaps," Jeff hoped, "if the soldiers do not know about the child, they will mistake the cry for a bush baby."

The voices moved away. Jeff had understood enough of what they said to know that the men had decided to return to the roadblock and begin their search for 'The Mercenary' again in the morning.

What Jeff had not understood was that the area he had tried to walk through was under military control and a sundown to sunup curfew had been imposed. The soldiers at the roadblock had opened fire on him as a curfew violator and not as a mercenary, even though they had given him that name because of the light color of his skin. Perhaps it made little difference, since the penalty for being a curfew violator was to be shot on sight as opposed to summary execution if found guilty of being a mercenary.

Once Jeff was sure that the soldiers were well away from the spot where he had stopped, he untied the cloth and placed the child on the ground to finish its bottle. Then he lit a match to study briefly the map that Chief Kanata had given him. He decided that they must be within a few miles of the place were the Chief had suggested they turn west toward the Malief border. Jeff decided to avoid roads and move through the forest in that direction. That would also take them away from the soldiers.

That decision made, he rested his head against one of the large trees that had created the small clearing with the shade of its branches. His intended short rest was quickly a deep sleep. Only the child's angry cry kept him from sleeping through the night. Jeff decided that the child's soaked diaper was the reason for its anger and replaced it. He wrapped the child in the cloth, placed him on his back, tied the cloth in front, and used the compass to move westward. The moon, when he could see it through the canopy of the forest, was pretty much overhead and Jeff decided that it was not yet midnight. His progress was slow. The welts from branches were swollen and painful to even the slightest touch. He moved cautiously through the pathless forest to protect himself and the child. He was aware of the snakes that are a part of every forest and made a little noise as he walked to warn them of his approach. Jeff, when he was a small boy, had been told by his father that noise would scare them away. He hoped that was true.

At first he found only trails that seemed to run north to south. After several hours he did find a narrow but well-kept path that did lead in a westward direction. His concern for safety caused him to hesitate before staying on this trail until it occurred to him that little chance existed of anyone using this path while it was still dark. Few Sakraians would venture into the forest at night for fear of snakes and perhaps juju and none would do so without a flashlight. Jeff was not happy about moving along that narrow path without a light either, but he had left his flashlight behind in Mbordo and the Chief had not provided one. Walking on the trail was considerably easier than moving through the forest. However, much to Jeff's surprise, they did, twice that night, encounter others moving in the opposite direction. Both times he saw the light of a torch and moved off the trail. The first encounter was with a man moving along the trail in a near trot. A few minutes later a group of soldiers appeared, also moving at a pace faster than a normal walk. Jeff wondered briefly as he watched from the forest if the soldiers were following the man. Gunfire and a scream minutes later answered the question. He decided not to return to the path immediately and moved deeper into the forest.

Jeff fed the child and rested. He wished to be sure that the soldiers were no longer near before he tried the trail again.

The rest of that night's walk was uneventful. By early morning, he was exhausted and knew that he must stop again soon. He left the main trail and moved southward on a smaller trail looking for a safe spot. He had gone less than a hundred yards when he saw what he hoped was an abandoned farmer's hut.

He fed the child and fell asleep on the dirt floor of the hut. The baby's cry awakened Jeff from a deep sleep sometime around noon. He was shocked out of his half awake state by the return of the farmer who had built the hut. At first, the man saw only Jeff. He raised his machete as if to strike, but when he heard and then saw the baby, he dropped the machete to his side. He appeared frightened and nervous, not sure of what to do next. He tried to explain in a combination of broken English and Ave that if the men with guns found Jeff in his hut, they would kill them both and leave the baby to die. Jeff replied in almost a begging tone that he feared to travel by day and wished only a safe place to hide and rest until dark. The farmer motioned for him to pick up the baby and follow. He led them to a secluded spot about three hundred yards from the cabin. As the man started to move away, Jeff opened the small bag and showed the man the baby's bottles which were now empty except for one. The farmer shrugged. Jeff removed one of the packages of powdered milk from the bag and said the Ave word for water as he pointed to it. The man understood immediately. What Jeff found more difficult to explain was that the water should be boiled. But with the help of some sign language and pictures drawn on the ground, Jeff was able to make known the need for the water to be made very hot. The farmer protested that a fire might attract the attention of soldiers. After some further discussion and pleading, the farmer did agree to try to provide Jeff with the hot water that he wished. In about an hour, the man returned with three whiskey bottles filled with water. The bottles were still warm. Jeff hoped that the water had actually been boiled. He mixed some of the water with the powdered milk and had enough liquid to fill four of the empty bottles.

The farmer also brought sliced yam and a few small pieces of meat for Jeff. The morsels of meat were very tough, and the yam very dry, but Jeff found both delicious. He used all of his Ave vocabulary to thank the farmer in the humblest manner that he knew. The farmer replied graciously that the thank-you was unnecessary and that if his own family were ever in such trouble, he hoped that they would be fortunate enough to find someone that would help them as he had helped Jeff. The man returned again that evening with more food and water. Jeff filled all the baby's bottles and kept one of the full whiskey bottles for himself. At dusk Jeff said good-by to the farmer and moved back toward the trail that led to the west.

A light but persistent rain began to fall about midnight. Jeff found walking increasingly difficult. The moisture that dripped from the branches above combined with the moss-like growth on the rocks of the trail to create a filmy substance much like a mixture of oil and water on a highway after a brief shower. He found a plastic rain shirt in the bag and wrapped the child tightly, leaving only an opening for him to breathe. Then he placed the child in the cloth and tied it to his back again. The baby remained relatively dry, even in the worst of the rains. He checked often to see that the plastic did not shift and restrict the child's breathing. Jeff decided to move the baby around to his chest so that he would never be out of sight.

The rain seemed to bring out the mosquitoes. The night before, Jeff had noticed a few when he stopped to rest. Now they swarmed around his head and any other bare skin on his arms and legs, forcing him into a near trot to escape their torment. The pace of the rain increased to a heavy downpour. He slipped and fell into a low spot on the trail.

Jeff felt water rise around him and thought, "Eaten or drowned, wonder which is worse."

Then he heard a small murmur from the cloth and moved quickly sideways and back to his knees to keep the baby out of the water.

"Neither one right now," he said out loud. "Just keep moving somehow. Can't stop now. Can't stop."

CHAPTER 21
Sportsmaster Leads Deep into the Forest

Based on what Pordoe had seen and heard when the University-College lorry was stopped on the road, Jason agreed they needed to move deeper into the forest immediately.

They reluctantly woke the others from deep sleep. Most looked confused and disoriented. Betty Whitland reacted angrily.

"What the hell is going on?" she asked. "Can't you let us rest? We won't last an hour without more sleep."

"Just listen to what Mr. Pordoe has to say," Jason replied.

The Sportsmaster related again, in graphic terms, the way in which the soldiers on the road had treated Thornton and the other University-College teachers.

"What will happen to those people?" Betty asked.

"Damn if I know," Jason replied calmly, "but I am certain of one thing. Nothing that we can do will help them. Thornton has made it all too clear to those men on the road that we are mercenaries. If they find us, we would probably be dead before we could explain who we are. But if we keep our heads together we might be able to save ourselves by moving deeper into the forest."

No one argued with Jason's suggestion that they resume walking immediately.

Pordoe continued to choose narrow little-used trails remembered from his boyhood. Most were not in good condition. In some places they were passable only with the help of the machete carried by Pordoe. Jason suspected that some of the ground they covered had never been used as a trail. By noon even Pordoe was exhausted. But he insisted it was important to push deeper into the forest. No one disagreed, not even the Whitlands. Pordoe's vivid description of the methods used in the interrogation of Eric Thornton was still fresh in everyone's mind.

With the Whitlands quiet, Jason, from his position at the rear of the group, could turn his attention to how the others were holding up. From the way they moved Jason could tell that Ralph and Jean Block were having a lot of trouble with their feet. But otherwise they seemed to be all right. The Vice-Chancellor, Gil, Karen, Beth and Ian weren't having any trouble walking but they were obviously not enjoying the trip. The movement of Alice's legs was still strong, but her expression was grim, almost wooden. Jason noticed that she was having trouble walking straight ahead. She often stumbled back and forth across the path. When she almost fell before steadying herself by hanging on to the branch of a tree, Jason sent Karen ahead to help.

Karen quickly caught up with Alice and asked if she was all right. Alice mumbled something about having to prepare lessons for the next day. Minutes later Alice's legs buckled. She sat down in the middle of the trail. Karen tried to coax her back on her feet but failed. Jason signaled the Sportsmaster to stop. Jason and Pordoe moved quickly to where Alice had collapsed.

"Alice, Alice," Pordoe said insistently but quietly, "we have only a little farther to walk to find a very safe place where we can rest for a very long time."

Tears were streaming down Alice's cheeks as she tried to explain, "I am really so very sorry to let you all down like this. I just can't go any farther. I heard what you said to the Whitlands back there and you were right. Anybody who can't walk should be left behind. This is the end for me. I don't blame any of you. Leave me now while the rest of you still have a chance."

"You've seen too many war movies, Alice," Jason said. "Maybe I have too. The only reason I said all that stuff was because I knew damn well Betty could walk. We would not have left them behind."

Jason looked around at the others. Gil nodded when Jason looked in his direction, understanding what Jason was asking even before he put his thoughts into words. Between them they used their hands and arms to form a seat in a manner that Jason remembered from his days as a Boy Scout. Alice's protests were ignored as they lifted her between them and moved along the trail. When Jason and Gil grew tired, the Vice-Chancellor and Pordoe took a turn in carrying Alice. No one questioned the effort expended in carrying Alice, but it did add to the fatigue of even the strongest members of the little group. Pordoe had planned to travel until they once again reached a spot with water. However, by three not even he felt like going farther. The Whitlands and the Blocks had not really been walking for the last three hours. They had continued to move along the trail in some surrealistic combination of limping and stumbling. After a quick search, Pordoe found a spot about a dozen yards off the trail that he believed would be safe for at least the rest of the day.

Once settled in the little clearing, Jason understood why the Whitlands and Blocks were having trouble walking. When they removed their shoes Jason noticed that the socks of Whitland and the Blocks were a light pink in color. Betty's were a bright red, very nearly dripping with blood. The bottoms of both of her feet were a mass of blood blisters. He silently cursed himself for not having checked footwear before they started the trip.

"Damn, who else would think of that? It would certainly seem ridiculous to the Africans that anyone would wear something that would hurt their feet when they walked. Maybe she didn't have any good walking shoes."

Karen did what she could with the small medical kit carried by the Vice-Chancellor. The Band-Aids were useless because of the size and number of blisters. She applied disinfectant and told the Blocks and Mr. Whitland to keep their feet propped up and bare to allow the blisters to begin drying. She decided against leaving Betty's feet uncovered. The bottoms of both were little more than open wounds. Karen wrapped each foot lightly in gauze in an effort to prevent infection.

They all rested, even Pordoe. He had mentioned to Jason his plan to return along the trail they had walked that day to find out if the Ave soldiers were still a threat.

221

However, he was asleep only moments after he sat down. Jason's sleep was also sound. He did not awake until midnight. He looked around and saw that only Pordoe was awake.

When the Sportsmaster noticed Jason sitting up he said, "I think it best that we go now. I don't know how long those soldiers will look for us, but the farther we travel the safer we are."

They woke the others. There was some grumbling by the Whitlands and Blocks, but they were not yet awake enough to do more than mumble their complaints. When Jason touched Alice lightly, she awoke with an involuntary jerk of her head.

"Are you OK?" Jason asked.

"I am not sure just yet," Alice said slowly. "Give me a moment."

"Here," she said, reaching out with her hand, "help me up and let me test my legs."

"I think they will do for awhile," she said as she managed to walk a few steps. "I am so sorry about what happened yesterday."

"Nothing to be sorry about," Jason replied, "we are all just doing the best we can."

Karen rebandaged Betty's feet and helped her pull a clean pair of socks on over the gauze.

The Sportsmaster decided it was probably now safe to use the torches. With light, they would be able to move more rapidly and better avoid accidents. Mr. Pordoe continued to lead them along old, little known trails. He feared the possibility that the Ave soldiers might have in their company a Bordo guide. By sunrise Pordoe was confident that they were at least twelve miles north of the road. Jason asked him how far they were from Mbordo.

The Sportsmaster smiled slightly and with a nod toward the others, said, "That is the part that I would not tell them. From Mbordo we are no more than fifteen miles if we now walked straight in that direction. Yesterday and last night we moved away from the road but not away from Mbordo."

"That means," Jason said, "that we are at least thirty miles from the Kra river."

The Sportsmaster nodded.

"If we do ten miles a day," Jason continued, "it is possible that we could be there in three days."

"That would be true," Pordoe said, "but the trail we use for the next day or two is not at all good. After that I think the danger may be less and we can travel on a better trail."

"Should we plan on four days then?" Jason asked.

"Perhaps, if all goes well," the Sportsmaster replied. "Jason, you plan as you wish. I will look for the trail. You know some of your friends are not well. Their feet are not good for walking."

"I know. I wish some had not come. But little can be done about that now," Jason replied. "I guess I better tell them what to expect."

Jason motioned for the exhausted teachers and their wives to gather around him.

"I have some difficult news," he said. "Because we were forced to move away from the main road, it will take us a few days longer to reach Towa than we had at first thought."

"What the hell is going on here?" Whitland said brusquely. "Just who is leading this thing anyway? My wife's feet are destroyed. Look at them for Christ's sake. More blood than skin. How long do you intend to have us wandering around out here? How much of this shit do you think we can stand before we all collapse?"

"I am not sure I have answers to all of your questions," Jason replied. "But I can answer the last one. I hope that you, me and all of us can stand whatever we have to in order to reach Towa. The alternative is not reaching Towa, and I find that thought a little grim. You do remember what happened to our friends who thought they stood a better chance on the road?"

"And I am not at all sure we need to believe everything we have been told," Whitland said, pointing in the direction of Mr. Pordoe. "All we really have is his word for what happened on the road. Maybe he made it up."

"You are a grade-A stupid asshole," Jason snapped. "Mr. Pordoe could be in Towa right now if he had decided to travel alone. We don't do a damn thing except slow him down. You want to know something, Mr. Whitland? It does not matter what you think or how you feel about Mr. Pordoe. We are twelve miles from the main road. If you think you know how to get back, then just take your wife and get the hell out. We don't need you. We need Mr. Pordoe. The next time we get close to the road we will be happy to sit you down right in the middle of it. Any other questions?"

"Yes, Jason," Alice said quietly, "just how long do you mean by a few days?"

"Oh," Jason said with a slight laugh to cover his own nervousness, "I forgot to tell you how long. Plan on four days. We hope it takes less, but it could take that long. Ration your water and food to last at least that long."

"Four days," Betty Whitland cried, "you are out of your goddamn mind. We can't last four days. Our food is already gone."

The Sportsmaster turned toward where the Whitland's sat, picked up the small bag that contained what remained of his food, and threw it toward them.

"Here," he said quietly, "have my food."

Then he spoke to everyone. "The next six miles is very difficult. After that the trail is good. We will in time come to a place near the road. Perhaps by tomorrow, perhaps the next day. When we reach that spot, I will take those who wish to walk no further to the road and leave them there."

"You damn well better get us back to the road," Whitland muttered.

Pordoe hunched his shoulders ever so slightly but said nothing. Instead he moved toward the trail. The others followed. They walked until noon with only short stops for rest. The trail was difficult. They covered no more than three miles that morning. Mr. Pordoe found a small, abandoned hut a few yards off their path. He suggested that they rest there during the hottest part of the day and continue their journey that evening. They were all quickly asleep.

At five the Sportsmaster woke everyone and they began their struggle with the abandoned trail again. By seven the Whitlands and the Blocks were out of water. Jean Block said little, keeping the agony of thirst to herself, but Betty maintained a constant stream of complaints, making her thirst even worse. Alice finally grew tired of listening to Betty and shared her water with the two couples. They left her less than half a cup of what had been more than a pint. The Vice-Chancellor noticed Alice's look of dismay.

"Don't worry," he whispered, "I have enough for both of us to drink for a week. It was kind of you to share but I am not so kind."

Alice laughed as best she could manage and thanked the Vice-Chancellor.

"Not so kind perhaps," she commented, "but much, much wiser."

By two the next morning,. they did at last reach the better trail. A sense of relief swept the group as they realized that the path was relatively free of obstruction. In many places they could walk two and even three abreast.

That is not to say that they were now enjoying their journey. The look of anguish on Betty's face was not the result of imaginary sufferings. Her expression screamed with every step, but she had only the strength for an occasional moan. A little after three she collapsed. Her entire body shivered, driven by the pain from her feet. Neither Jason's threats nor Alice's supplications had any effect. She refused to take another step. Her husband observed what was happening quietly, too filled with his own exhaustion to take much interest in his wife's problems.

When Karen removed Betty's shoes she found even the bandages dripped with blood. She tried to remove a small portion of the gauze, but Betty's sharp scream stayed her hand. She decided to leave the bandages on when she realized that what was left of the skin on Betty's feet would probably come off if they were removed.

"I don't think we can help her," Karen said to Jason. "She can't walk at all with her feet in that condition."

"Then we will carry her as far as we can," Jason replied. "I wish we didn't have to do that."

The trail was wide enough so that two men could form a seat and carry Betty as they had Alice the day before. But Whitland, the Vice-Chancellor and Ralph Block were themselves close to exhaustion. That left only Jason, Gil, Pordoe, and Ian still capable of carrying anything other than their own weight. Beth and Karen would have tried but could not have lasted more than a few hundred yards. The Vice-Chancellor was persistent in his efforts to volunteer. Jason repeatedly explained that he would be used later when he was needed more. Jason prayed that 'later' would never come, since the Vice-Chancellor was already unsteady on his feet. The Vice-Chancellor and Alice began walking together, leaning on each other to provide mutual support.

Jason and Gil took the first turn in carrying Betty. Jason quickly became aware of his own fatigue. Pain seemed everywhere, with the worst of it shifting from spot to spot. Just as he would be on the verge of deciding that the agony signaled from his legs would allow him to go no farther, he would become aware of an even more intense pain in his arms, then in his back, and again back to his legs. He felt a deep, angry self-pity developing. But he needed only a quick glance at Alice and the Vice-Chancellor, struggling together to keep moving forward, to drain himself of those feelings. He felt instead a sudden wave of sorrow at the thought of the pain that Alice must be enduring as she stumbled along the trail. He had never thought of her as old before, but the years were now written clearly on her face.

His thoughts began to drift in time, to visits with Karen in Pandu, to his favorite classes at the University-College, even to his parents in Ohio. He became aware of his body going numb. Only a vague awareness persisted of the pain that he knew must still be there but his mind only dimly recognized. Then he felt nothing at all as he moved one foot in front of the other. Only a stumble and near fall told him that he could help carry Betty no farther. They stopped to rest. When they returned to the trail Pordoe and Ian replaced Gil and Jason. Jason at first moved to the front to lead but then decided to leave that job to Gil and his torch. Instead he moved back to Alice and took turns with Karen in helping the Vice-Chancellor steady her gait.

At the next rest stop they switched again and Pordoe moved back to the front. Ian and Beth walked just behind him. As night progressed toward day the turns in carrying Betty grew shorter and the periods of rest longer.

In the time of near light just before daybreak, Pordoe's foot disturbed the body of a sleeping snake that had been using the rocks of the trail to maintain a little of its body's warmth during the night. It reacted slowly and did not strike until Ian, a step behind Pordoe, passed where it lay. When Pordoe saw the outline of the snake he reached for its body. He caught it firmly in his hand near the end of its tail. The snake clung for a brief moment to Ian's heel before Pordoe was able to jerk it away. The Sportsmaster swung the snake rapidly in a circle to keep its head away from his own body. As he whipped the snake around he moved close to a large tree and bashed the snake's head against the trunk. He smashed the snake's body against the tree at least half a dozen times before he was satisfied that it was dead.

"What happened?" Jason asked.

"Green momba," Pordoe responded. "Very bad."

"Bad," Jason thought, "my God, nerve and blood poison."

Ian had not moved from where his body had dropped to the ground when the snake struck. The muscles of his face were taut. His eyes reflected fear and uncertainty.

He mumbled, "Am I going to die, am I going to die? Here? Die here? In this place? What am I going to do? Can you help me? Can you help?"

Beth's efforts to maintain composure were fractured by her husband's pleading.

She cried, "My God, can't you do something for him? Can't you see he is hurt? Please, Jason, somebody, please try to help."

Alice and the Vice-Chancellor were the last to reach the spot where Ian sat in the trail. The Vice-Chancellor understood what had happened immediately.

"What kind?" he asked as he removed the small medicine kit from the bag he was carrying.

"Green momba," Pordoe replied.

The Vice-Chancellor shook his head slightly as he prepared a syringe and hypodermic with antivenin serum. Alice gently pulled Beth away from where Ian sat to give the Vice-Chancellor room to administer the antidote. He used both vials of the serum, the kit's entire supply, to inject Ian in six different places on his heel. Each time the needle punctured his foot Ian's body tensed in pain but no sound came from his lips. He cried out only when the Vice-Chancellor made X-shaped incisions across each of the fang marks. Then the Vice-Chancellor drew blood from the cuts with his mouth and spat it on the ground. He continued to seek the poison in Ian's heel until the red spot on the ground where he spat was more than six inches in diameter.

The others watched in silence. When the Vice-Chancellor had finished Karen applied an antiseptic solution to the wounds and bandaged them. Ian no longer looked quite as frightened, but even in the early morning light, it was apparent that blood had drained from his face and shock became a very real and immediate possibility.

"Get his feet up in the air," Karen said. "Find something to cover him. Beth, talk to Ian. Make him talk."

A jacket was quickly produced and Ian's legs were propped up on a log. Beth knelt to talk with him.

Jason touched the Vice-Chancellor's arm to indicate that he wished to talk away from the others.

"Why did you make the incisions?" Jason asked. "Won't the serum counteract the snake's poison?"

"The Doctor who left it said it was very old," the Vice-Chancellor replied sadly. "I don't know how well it will work. But don't tell Ian. At least the mental effect will be positive. He is quite a strong young man. One of your Doctors once told me that few people actually die from the snake's poison. Most die of fear. I do hope that is true."

"I think there is a much better chance of that being true if one is home in bed from the bite of a cobra," Jason said. "But the momba poisons both the blood and the nerves. And even if we carry him, the movement of just his leg swinging will speed the flow of the venom to the rest of his body."

The Vice-Chancellor's eyes moistened as he replied, "I'm sorry, I don't know any more to do."

"Forgive me, my friend," Jason said quickly, "I didn't mean it that way. You have done more than the rest of us even know how to do."

Ian seemed to revive. He and Beth talked quietly and Ian's skin tone returned to near normal. The Vice-Chancellor returned to where he sat to look at the bite.

Ian smiled and said, "Glad you brought that kit along. You did a super repair job. Where did you learn to do that sort of operation?"

The Vice-Chancellor laughed in a small way and replied, "The Boy Scouts, many years ago of course. The organization was quite popular here before Dr. Agyenkwa took power. Mr. Harris, do you think that you can walk?"

"My condition is just as good now as when I sat down," Ian answered almost jauntily.

"Yes, I think it will be all right," the Vice-Chancellor said as he continued his examination of Ian's foot and leg. "But just to make sure Beth and I will walk on either side of you for a while."

The Vice-Chancellor moved quickly to where Jason stood watching.

"I am very much afraid," the Vice-Chancellor said in a whispered tone, "his leg is already a light blue color to the knee and the swelling reaches above the ankle. But I think we should say nothing to them."

"He should not be moved," Jason replied. "It will only speed the flow of the poison. But we have no choice. To remain here will do none of us any good. Is it possible that the serum might still take effect?"

"That is in God's hands," the Vice-Chancellor murmured.

The Vice-Chancellor and Beth helped Ian to his feet. They moved with some difficulty along the trail. At times Ian could do no more than drag his snake-bitten foot along the ground, using the two as substitutes for crutches. Karen walked with Alice. Only Jason, Gil, and Pordoe were now left to take turns in carrying Betty. The others walked with obvious pain but no longer complained.

By the morning, it was apparent that Ian's condition was deteriorating rapidly. The mild exertion of walking, even with help, quickly made him delirious and unable to put one foot in front of the other. The time needed for him to recover increased with each stop. Jason began to feel like a yo-yo. They would get up, walk a short distance, sit down, then up again then down. Ian was seldom coherent.

Pordoe had hoped to reach a point on the trail by noon that day where he could guide the Whitlands to the road. He now realized that Ian's condition would change those plans by hours if not by days.

Each sensed in their own way that matters were not going well. They no longer waited for Ian to regain a sense of where he was but instead got him up as soon as they thought he could walk. In what seemed like the thousandth time, they helped him to his feet. He managed less than ten yards before his bad leg gave way. Beth cried out in frustration and fear as she tried to support his weight. The Vice-Chancellor called ahead and the bedraggled column stopped again.

227

"That leg must be immobilized," he told Jason. "The poison is spreading rapidly. If too much reaches his brain or heart he will die. We must either stop here or try to carry him."

Jason and the Vice-Chancellor discussed their diminishing options with the others. They decided to move on, carrying Ian at least as far as the place on the trail near the road. Jason and the Vice-Chancellor shared Ian's weight. Gil and Pordoe continued to carry Betty. They took frequent rest stops but still managed to cover no more than half a mile in distance before the Vice-Chancellor's legs gave way. He collapsed and Ian fell sideways on top of him. Jason pulled Ian away. His sigh of relief was audible when the Vice-Chancellor demonstrated that he was able to stand.

Jason looked toward Betty. She said nothing but nodded. Jason and Beth carefully lifted Ian onto the arms of Gil and Pordoe, and they again moved slowly eastward.

Each step brought a murmur of pain to Betty's lips, but with her husband's help she moved along the trail. Alice, the Vice-Chancellor and Karen limped along together. Karen walked in the middle, providing support for both Alice and the now exhausted Vice-Chancellor. The Blocks moved with obvious difficulty but maintained a steady pace. Beth walked near the two men carrying Ian. As they moved slowly along the trail Ian became even less aware of where he was and whom he was with. Instead he spoke more and more of home and family. At times he seemed almost happy, especially when he talked of Christmas and Easter and of his love for his parents. Beth had difficulty controlling her tears. Often she left his side to regain her composure. Jason asked which of the two Africans needed a rest from carrying Ian. Even before they answered he knew from their faces that neither man could go much further. The soreness in his own arms told him that he would be good for at most a few hundred yards.

"Better to find a place to stop now for a long rest and continue tonight when it is cooler," he suggested to Pordoe.

Pordoe readily agreed. Jason took the Sportsmaster's place in carrying Ian and he moved ahead to find a secure resting spot. He returned moments later.

"I found an excellent spot," he told Jason, "a well hidden clearing not far off the trail. But I found no water. I hope we have enough left."

They reached the place minutes later, a small field now abandoned but not yet reclaimed by the forest. Everyone was quickly asleep with no thought given to posting a watch. Jason and Pordoe had planned to be on the trail again by six that evening. They awoke about the same time. Pordoe judged by the position of the moon that it was well past midnight. The others still slept quietly except for Ian who, though asleep, was never still. Pain was written across his forehead and lips. His ankle was swollen to at least twice its normal size.

They woke the others. Jason made a quick survey of remaining supplies. Their food was finished. But that seemed to matter little since no one was particularly hungry. More serious was the depletion of their water. The Vice-Chancellor had used most of his remaining supply cleaning the snake bite on Ian's heel. The others had little more than a few swallows left. The total was less than half a pint.

"What the hell are we going to do without food and water?" Whitland asked.

Pordoe replied, "I will lead you to a place not more than 600 yards from the road. It is less than two miles from where we now are. There each one can decide what is best. Those who choose to try the road may do so. Those who do not choose the road I will lead back into the forest. I know a place where good water is available but the distance is another five miles."

Pordoe's offer ended the discussion of alternatives. Ian's condition seemed improved. He was again lucid. He apologized to Pordoe and Gil for being such a bloody burden, as they prepared to take the first turn in carrying him. They joked that after a few more days without food Ian would be so thin that they wouldn't notice his weight. The others, with the exception of Betty, seemed recovered enough to give the appearance of almost enjoying the evening's walk. Her feet were oozing blood after only a few hundred yards. They moved with good speed for the first mile. After that everyone's energy was pretty well dissipated. Ian's condition worsened to the point that he was no longer able to sit up. The men carrying him had to walk closer together so that his back could rest against their shoulders. When he began thrashing about they would call a halt and lay him down until his body exhausted itself and they could lift him again. It was the better part of four hours and near daylight before they reached the place on the trail near the road. Pordoe left them in a hidden spot and moved to investigate conditions on the highway. As they lay waiting, Ian was for the moment lucid.

He said to Beth, "I love you so much. Please remember. I love you. The serum didn't work, did it? I know it didn't work It's almost over. It hurts worse than anything I could ever imagine. I don't mind dying. It might be better than the way I feel now. But I don't want to leave you. I do love you."

Before Beth could answer he lapsed back into talk of his parents and childhood.

Pordoe returned in less than half an hour.

He reported what he had seen quickly, "There is a road block. It is manned by a small group of soldiers. No more than ten. They have uniforms. The uniforms of the regular government soldiers of the army of Sakra."

"Thank God," Whitland said as he slapped Jason on the back. "Let's get the hell out of here. I can hardly wait to shower and get into clean clothes."

"Unfortunately it is not as good as we might think," Pordoe said. "No one seems to be in charge of these soldiers. The highest rank is Sergeant. They have been drinking spirits. I could see the bottles. While I watched, an old man passed by. When they found he had no money, they took his shirt and beat him before they let him go."

"I don't give a good goddamn about some old man," Betty said. "They won't hurt us. We have our passports. I am not going to walk another fucking inch on this goddamn trail. I couldn't if I wanted to. Look at what's left of my feet. It will be a year before they are fit to see again."

"And look at this useless bastard," she said, pointing in the direction of Ian. "He's already dead. How many more of us have to die before we get out of this goddamn hell hole?"

Beth sobbed.

"You didn't need to say that," Jason muttered.

"I am going to take Ian to the road, Jason," Beth said. "We cannot go on."

"If you want to stay with us, we will carry Ian," Jason said. "I promise you that."

"No," Beth replied, "it wouldn't help. That witch is right. If he doesn't get help soon he will die."

Jason reached for Beth's hand and held it tightly for a moment then said, "Those who wish to go to the road should do so now. The rest of us will move back into the forest."

"Why don't we all go together to where the soldiers are?" Ralph Block asked. "I believe we might have a better chance as a group than split apart."

"That might be true if I were not with you," Pordoe answered. "But they are quite drunk. They would not know that I am Bordo and not Ave. It is possible that I would be dead even before any of you had a chance to speak."

"The same might well be true in my case," the Vice-Chancellor added. "Pordoe, Adwin and I have little choice but to continue in the forest. It is best that we separate now. Those who can walk no farther or wish to walk no farther should try the road."

"I wish that we could have done more for your husband," the Vice-Chancellor said to Beth. "He is a fine man. But now each of us must do what is best as each of us sees the situation."

"All right," Jason said, "who is going to try the road?"

Mr. Whitland and Mr. Block immediately indicated that they and their wives were ready to take their chances with the soldiers.

Beth said to Jason, "I don't think Ian has any chance unless we find a doctor quickly."

"I guess you're right," Jason replied, near tears, "we will help you carry him as far as we can."

Gil and Jason carried Ian to within two hundred yards of where the soldiers had set their roadblock. Pordoe moved ahead to scout. Then Whitland and Block half carried, half dragged Ian to the road. Betty, Jean Block and Beth limped along behind. Pordoe found a tree a little taller than those around it and climbed up in order to see how the soldiers would react to the sudden appearance of six Obronies.

At first the soldiers did not react at all. Instead, they gave the impression that drunken men often do of seeing but not completely believing. They made no move to help with Ian even though it was obvious that Block and Whitland were struggling with his weight as they moved toward the makeshift barricade that the soldiers had put together across the road using a jeep, an old army truck and tree branches. Instead, they just watched.

When he was within a few yards of the barricade, Whitland began to wave his passport, and shouted, "Americans, we are Americans. Do you understand, Americans?"

The soldier in charge, a sergeant, took the passport, looked at it carefully for a moment, then threw it down and stepped on it.

Then he looked at Whitland and screamed, "We look for mercenaries. Are you mercenary?"

"No, no, please," Whitland cried, "we are not. Just look at the passport. I work for AI..."

The soldier cut short his words.

"Goddamn, motherfuck paper mean shit, mean nothing," he shouted.

"You understand," he continued as he grabbed Whitland's shirt and drew it tight about his neck. "Anybody get paper. That nothing. You prove you no mercenary or you die."

"On belly, all of you," he said as he flung Whitland to the ground on top of his passport.

Ian collapsed face down. The others quickly followed his unintended example. Betty was slowest. One of the other soldiers grabbed her hair and pushed her down.

"We will search them one at a time," the Sergeant ordered.

"You first," he said pointing at Whitland.

Two of the soldiers pulled him toward the jeep and forced him face down over its hood. They began stripping away his clothes.

"Oh my God," Pordoe muttered, still watching from the tree, when he saw the handle of a pistol revealed.

One of the soldiers gave a loud whoop as he pulled the gun from the holster that Whitland had attempted to hide in the small of his back. The Sergeant smiled cynically as he took the gun.

"So," he said, "you not mercenary. Just innocent American walking for pleasure in our forest. If you not mercenary, why you carry gun? This gun not legal in Sakra unless you in army. You not in army. Did not embassy tell you?"

Whitland tried to reply with bravado, "Listen you son of a bitch, I am an American citizen. If anything happens to me, you will be in a hell of a lot of trouble."

As Whitland talked, another soldier standing behind him drew his pistol and positioned the barrel just behind his left ear. The soldier gently squeezed the trigger. In the fraction of a second after the bullet entered his head, Whitland's expression registered, surprise, dismay, pain and finally emptiness as his body collapsed to the ground.

The Sergeant and the man who shot Whitland moved toward Ian.

"Get up," the Sergeant said. "You next to be searched."

Ian probably heard nothing of what the man was saying, and understood little of what was happening. Even had he understood, he could not have supported himself on his swollen and near useless leg.

Beth half cried, half shouted as she tried to get up, "He is very ill. Can't you understand that? Can't you see?"

"Look," she continued, pointing at his leg, "he was bitten by a snake. He can't stand up. He can't even move."

As she spoke the words, "He will die,..." another soldier smashed the butt of his riffle against the back of her head. She fell, half conscious but unable to move. Two soldiers of lower rank moved between the Sergeant and Ian.

"This man be very sick," one of them said. "Not good to beat wife when she try help."

The Sergeant pointed his handgun at the man who spoke and said, "Get out of the way fool. I in charge here. Do you wish die with them? I shoot you for treason. I know mercenaries when I see with my eye. We have orders. Find mercenary. Kill mercenary. Move back now or you die."

The two soldiers moved away.

The Sergeant turned his attention to Ian again.

He kicked Ian in the groin and shouted, "Get up, goddamn mercenary, get up before you meet same fate as other criminal."

No part of Ian's body moved.

The Sergeant grabbed a rifle with bayonet from one of the other men and shouted, "Get up now or you learn what it mean to disobey a Sergeant in the army of Sakra."

Ian remained motionless.

The Sergeant screamed every oath he knew as he plunged the bayonet into Ian's back again and again.

One of the other soldiers said, "He is dead. Can you not see?"

The Sergeant pointed the rifle at the man who spoke. Suddenly, his expression changed to a half smile.

"You are right," he said. "This man is very dead. He deserve to die and now he has as he deserve."

"Get up," he ordered Block.

The American advisor got up quickly. The Sergeant saw the passport in his shirt pocket and smiled.

"You see," he said to the other soldiers, "very clear. In pocket he carries same paper as man with gun. This man also mercenary. You two, take him there. Tie him to tree."

Block had only moments to contemplate his fate before three bullets from the Sergeant's pistol ended his life.

The Sergeant carefully reloaded his gun and returned to where Beth lay on the ground.

"I don't know if women can be mercenaries?" he said, posing the question to the other soldiers.

Then resting on one knee he asked Beth, "Are you mercenary?"

Beth said nothing. The soldier who had protested the Sergeant's treatment of Ian tried to explain to the Sergeant that as far as he was able to understand, women could not be mercenaries.

"You are fool," the Sergeant shouted in reply. "Of course women can be mercenaries. You no study war like me. You village idiot. Now, we search all."

"You two men, pick this one up," he said pointing to Beth. "Let us find out what she carries close to skin."

Two of the soldiers forced Beth to her feet. The Sergeant stripped away her blouse and ripped off her bra. Pordoe decided that it was pointless to watch longer. He climbed down quickly and returned to the place where Jason waited for him. Before Jason could ask what he had seen, they heard the sounds of a woman screaming.

"No, please. I didn't do anything. I will do what you say. I am not a mercenary. The mercenaries are over there in the woods. That's where you will find them. There are men over there. They are mercenaries. They are spies. Oh please, please don't hurt me. I will do anything you want. I will show you where the mercenaries are. Just give me a chance. Please don't..."

"We must try to help them," Jason cried as he moved toward the sound of Betty's voice.

Pordoe grabbed Jason's arm.

"We cannot help them by going to the road," he said sternly. "We would only die. The men are already dead. You have already been marked as a mercenary. We have no weapons. We can only help those still alive by moving ahead quickly and finding other troops. These men are part of the regular army. I heard one of them say so. If we find their commander, he may be able to save the rest. He is the only one who can control the actions of these soldiers. Come, we must get back to the others. If the soldiers believe Mrs. Whitland, they will soon be searching for us.

"I do not think that it would be wise to tell the others all that we know," Pordoe added as they walked. "We must move quickly."

Jason nodded in reply. They reached the place where the others waited.

"What is happening?" the Vice-Chancellor asked. "We heard the sound of guns and what we thought were the screams of a woman."

"The situation is not good," the Sportsmaster replied. "The troops are of the government but they are not well disciplined. We must move rapidly and seek their commander."

"I understand," the Vice-Chancellor replied.

CHAPTER 22
Breaking Point

Led by Pordoe, the six moved rapidly. The Sportsmaster decided to use the better trails close to the road. He reasoned that the soldiers on the road would probably be too preoccupied with the women to begin looking for other 'mercenaries' anytime soon. By midmorning, Alice was having serious difficulty. Jason and Gil provided support as she swung one foot in front of the other. Three times they had been forced to plunge quickly into the brush to avoid others using the trail. By eleven, everything seemed finished, their energy, their water, even the shoes and sandals on which they walked now had such thin soles as to be near useless.

The Sportsmaster was closer to total exhaustion than at anytime that he could remember. He could not recall any feelings similar to the intense sense of despair and sadness in the signals that his body was sending in a constant stream to his brain. In the moments that his mind was able to reflect on something other than his own pain, he found himself wondering how the others kept going. Alice no longer even walked. The effort to put one foot in front of the other was more than she could manage. Gil and Jason seemed to be half carrying, half dragging her. They looked totally exhausted. The Vice-Chancellor staggered from side to side, unable to maintain a straight course, but still moved in a forward direction.

"Sad," Pordoe thought as he watched him struggle. "Brave old man."

Karen limped along by herself.

By noon, Pordoe decided that it was pointless to go further without rest. He called a halt and found what he thought to be a secluded spot not visible from the trail. The fatigued Sportsmaster didn't notice the small but distinct path that connected the other side of their hiding place to a point further down the main trail. None of the six took much notice of what was around them in the clearing and were all quickly asleep.

Jason awoke to the sound of a gruff voice. He had difficulty comprehending what the man standing over him was trying to say. He could not quite remember where he was. He realized he was outside, that the sun was no longer visible but it was not yet dark.

He heard the man's voice again, this time more clearly, "Roll on your stomach and put your hands behind your head."

Where he was and the meaning of the man's words became all too clear to Jason. For just one quick moment he thought of resisting but a sideways glance at the weapon carried by the soldier convinced Jason to do exactly as ordered.

"Old woman," the man with the gruff voice said, looking at Alice, "you cannot be a mercenary. That much I am sure of. I am Nata, a Captain in the army of the nation of Sakra. Who are you and who are these people with you?"

"We are teachers from the University-College of Mbordo," Alice replied quickly.

"Then please tell me if you can," the Captain said almost impolitely, "why are you here in this place and not in Mbordo?"

"We heard that troops were coming from the east and north and that bandits were everywhere," Alice answered. "We did not know where we could be safe except with the Army of Sakra. We do not know who to trust. Our only choice was to walk in this direction in order to find soldiers who would protect us."

The Captain seemed pleased with what Alice had said.

"If this is true," he replied, "you have done very well. It is more than a day's journey from Mbordo. I would not have thought that teachers could have walked so far. But your condition indicates that it must be so. You will be safe with my men as long as you are careful. There are many rumors of mercenaries. Be cautious and do not do anything that might arouse suspicion. All of you may get up now, but remember, take care in how you move and what you say. We will take you to the Major, who is my field commander. He will decide what should be done.

"Sergeant," the Captain continued, "get these people some water."

Tears of relief eased from Alice's eyes and rolled down her cheeks as she used a small tree to pull herself up into a sitting position. But when she tried to move forward she stumbled and fell to the ground.

When Jason and Gil tried to move to where she had fallen, the Captain stopped them and said, "Do not worry, my men will carry her."

Two of the soldiers gently picked Alice up. Within minutes they were on the road to Towa. In less than two hours they were on the edge of the headquarters encampment of the Third Battalion of the First Army of Sakra. Their entry was hardly triumphant, with Alice being carried by the soldiers, Jason and Karen providing each other with support they both needed to keep upright and moving, and Gil and Pordoe virtually carrying the Vice-Chancellor.

The Captain took them immediately to the Major in charge of the garrison. Jason was the first into his tent. He said nothing to the man in uniform sitting behind a small desk, but instead handed him his passport.

"Peace Corps," the Major mumbled, "what in hell's name are you doing out here in the bush?"

"Walking," Jason replied.

"Where from, man?" the Major asked in a harsher tone.

"Mbordo," Jason said, too tired to provide a full explanation.

The others had by this time also been ushered into the tent.

"My God, man, the road is impossible," the Major continued in a softer tone. "You must have come through the bush."

Jason only nodded in reply.

"The old lady," the Major continued speaking to Jason but looking towards the folding chair in which the soldiers had placed Alice, "she is Mrs. Manati from the University-College, is she not?"

Jason nodded again.

"I did hear that she was a strong woman," he mused, "but I am surprised that she could come this far. How many days since you left Mbordo?"

"Four, I believe," Jason responded, somewhat unsure of his answer.

"Were you also a professor at the University?" the Major asked.

"Yes, I was," Jason answered.

"And the others?" the Major continued.

"Yes, they are also with the University," Jason replied. "That man is the Vice-Chancellor."

"Forgive me, sir," the Major said to the Vice-Chancellor as he rose to his feet and moved to where the Vice-Chancellor stood, "I did not immediately recognize you. It has been a number of years since we last met."

The Vice-Chancellor smiled broadly as he spoke, "Nor did I recognize you until now, my dear Kwame. You have grown into a man. It is a great relief to know that we are among friends again."

The Major spoke to the soldier who had escorted them to the camp.

"Captain," he said, "you have done very well in this matter. These people will be honored guests. Will you see to it that quarters are prepared?"

"Are there any others beside you who came from Mbordo?" the Major asked.

"Oh, my God yes," Jason said remembering the sound of gunfire and Betty's scream. "There were six others taken captive by some soldiers on the road not more than three miles from here in the direction of Mbordo. There were three men and three women. The men are probably dead, mistaken for mercenaries. We do not know the fate of the women."

"Could you tell of what army these troops were?" the Major asked.

"As best we could tell," Jason replied, "the Army of Sakra."

The Major instructed his aide to find the same Captain who had brought the teachers in from the forest.

Then he said, "I will send a special detail of men to the place where you found this roadblock. It will not take them long if they use one of our trucks. Since there is more than one battalion in this area I am not even sure under whose command these men are. However, we will do our best to find the rest of your people, or their bodies, and bring them back here. I do wish there was more that could be done, but I cannot promise anything. I am sorry."

"Thank you for all of your help," Jason said quietly.

A sergeant directed them to one of the few small houses still standing, near the edge of the camp. Inside they found food, soft drinks, beer and cots.

Alice awoke sometime in the night. At first she had no sense of where she was or why she was awake. The sounds of a very loud argument near the window where she lay answered the second question although the cause of the argument remained a mystery. As the memory of the past few days returned, she sat up quickly on the narrow army cot, almost tipping it over. She noticed that Jason was also awake. The others in the room lay motionless, oblivious to the noise outside. Alice and Jason got up and met at the door. They moved cautiously in the direction of the noise from the argument. As they drew closer, the outline of an old army truck took solid form. The driver stood on the running board waving his arms half talking, half shouting. A woman sat huddled on the passenger side with a cloth wrapped tightly around her shoulders.

"Oh my God," Alice cried, "it's Beth."

Alice reached for the door of the truck.

One of the men near the lorry grasped her arm, but let go when he heard the Major say, "It is all right, soldier. Let her through."

Alice opened the door of the truck and tried to put her arms around Beth's taut shoulders.

"Beth, Beth," Alice repeated.

Beth did not respond. Her body was neither stiff nor relaxed, but seemed to try even harder to curl inward. Her eyes were fixed on a place on the floor of the truck as if looking for something lost that could not again be found.

"Beth, it's me. Me! Alice, you know Alice. We were together only a few hours ago," Alice continued, more and more concerned that she was unable to get any reaction.

Finally, after much pleading, Beth's eyes did move, but not in the direction of her friend. They moved so slightly that Alice would have missed their almost imperceptible roll upward and toward the rear of the truck had she not been watching carefully. She followed that movement of Beth's eyes with her own. The sight of the bodies of the people with whom she had walked and struggled only hours before sent a shudder through every part of her body. A muffled half cry came involuntarily from her lips. She would have fallen backward out of the truck had not Jason been at the door. Alice struggled to regain control of her whirling head. She dimly saw Beth's hand reach toward her in a tentative offer of help and knew the moment could not be lost. She grasped the extended arm and pulled herself back into the cab of the truck, then swung her own arms around Beth, holding her as tightly as her remaining strength would allow. Beth began a gentle sob that increased in intensity until her entire body seemed immersed in grief.

The others came out of the small house to see what was happening. The argument among the soldiers continued. But Beth and Alice, still in each other's arms, seemed no longer aware of what was happening around them. Finally, Jason did gently suggest to Alice that they try to move Beth. Alice got down from the lorry. Beth followed. She would have collapsed with her first step, had she not been supported by Karen and Alice. The Major followed several steps behind to the door of the house.

He called softly when they reached the door, "Mrs. Manati, could I see you for a moment when you have finished there?"

Alice walked over to the door where the Major stood and stepped outside with him.

"Mrs. Manati," he said apologetically, "I know that you have been through a very difficult experience. I am sorry to have to ask more of you, but we will need your help tomorrow. Could you come to my tent for a few minutes and I will explain?"

They walked in silence to the Major's tent.

Once inside he said, "Please sit down. What I am about to ask is very difficult. Perhaps you heard the argument near the lorry. Did you understand what was being said?"

"No," Alice replied, "I made no effort."

"Of course," the Major continued, "your thoughts were with your friend. But what they were speaking of was the fate of the soldiers who were at the roadblock. They were discussing whether or not they should be punished. I took no part in the argument but the decision will fall to me. I know very well that crimes have been committed and that those who are guilty should be brought to justice. However, to do so I must have definite evidence of the crime. If I punish these men without such evidence, the soldiers under my command will lose confidence in my fairness. Mr. Pordoe has given me a very good account of what he saw. But that in itself will not be sufficient. I will need an account from someone who was at the roadblock of exactly what happened. I know that it would be unwise for me to question your friend. I do not wish to cause her further pain. But I do trust you completely and I believe that my men will also trust your account of what she is willing to say to you. If she can give you an account of what happened and you are willing to testify in an open hearing, that I believe would be evidence acceptable to all."

Alice replied without hesitation, "I will do my best."

The next morning Alice asked the others to leave her alone with Beth. She explained to Beth what the Major had asked her to do. At first Beth was reluctant to pull to the surface of her mind the memories of the previous day. But as they continued talking, Beth's sense of outrage and disgust at what had happened to Ian and herself overwhelmed her sense of shame and fear. She talked freely. Alice took careful notes. Later that morning, she presented Beth's testimony in full at the hearing conducted by the Major.

Beth had described the deaths of Ian, Mr. Whitland, and Mr. Block to Alice in detail, but she had found it difficult to talk about what happened next. The soldiers had found American passports when they stripped Mrs. Block and Mrs. Whitland. They were executed as mercenaries, but not before being raped by five of the soldiers. Then the soldiers had turned their full attention to Beth. Two soldiers raped her before three of the soldiers who had not participated in any of the violence intervened. They convinced the others that she should not be harmed further since she carried different papers.

Pordoe also testified about what he had seen and heard from his perch in the tree.

The hearing was completed before two o'clock. The Major decided that he had sufficient evidence. He declared five of the men including the Sergeant, who had been in command, guilty of murder and rape. Four others were found guilty of negligence in making no effort to prevent what had happened. The three soldiers who had made some effort to prevent the murder of Ian Harris and the rape of the women were found innocent of wrongdoing. The five men guilty of murder and rape were sentenced to die by firing squad that same day at sunset. Twenty lashes were ordered for the four found guilty of negligence. That punishment was inflicted immediately. Alice watched until she could no longer stand the screams of the men being whipped. Nevertheless, as she walked away she found herself taking grim satisfaction in the outcome of the trial.

"But," she thought, "even if I live another hundred years, I still could have done without this. I don't remember anything, not even the pain of my body the last few days, that was worse than getting Beth to talk about what happened. A thousand years would be too soon to go through something like this again."

Late that afternoon Alice woke from a fitful sleep. The sun was still visible but low in the sky. She got up, straightened her hair a bit, and left the house. She was not at that moment willing to admit, even to herself, where she was going. She joined the flow of soldiers moving toward a small valley just to the north of the encampment. She reached the crest of a small hill that marked the edge of the valley in time to see the five condemned men escorted under heavy guard downward into the valley, across a small stream to a place where five thin posts had been driven into the ground. The firing squad stood ready, not far from where Alice watched.

The five men were assembled in a short row and blindfolded. One tried to run away but got only a few feet before he was restrained by half a dozen soldiers and returned to his position in the line. The prisoners were bound hand and foot to the posts to prevent further efforts to escape.

Alice could hear their pleas for mercy, unmistakable in any language.

Strange, she thought, "They don't sound like murderers and rapists. More like frightened children."

She felt her stomach go queasy and fought to maintain control.

The Major's orders came quickly, "Aim, fire."

With the sound of the guns, three of the condemned men slumped against the posts and were still. The other two had on cue from the Major's voice slid their hands down the posts and knelt in a successful effort to avoid the bullets of the firing squad. The posts were not driven deeply into the ground. With quick jerks the two men pulled them up. With their hands tied behind their backs and their feet still bound together, the men moved like monstrous inch worms desperately measuring the last moments of their lives.

"It would be humorous to watch those poor sons of bitches hump around on the ground," Alice thought, "if it were not for the final result of this thing. This is really bad. Just get it done."

The Major again spoke, this time with a single command, "Fire."

The movement of the two men momentarily became even more sporadic and non-directed as the second round of bullets drove their bodies against the far hillside. Moments later they too were still.

Alice watched the same Captain who had discovered the Vice-Chancellor and the teachers in the forest inspect the bodies. She shuddered when a hand reached out to grasp the Captain's wrist. He quickly drew his sidearm, placed it against the man's temple and completed the execution. Alice's stomach once again nearly betrayed her.

The Captain said, "They are all dead, sir."

The Major turned to the soldier in charge of the firing squad and said, "Dismiss your men, Sergeant. Please arrange for a burial detail."

Then the Major walked over to where Alice stood.

"I am sorry," he said, "that you were here to see all of that. But it is better for us to dispatch these men immediately rather than to let them die slowly. Unfortunately, many of our troops are not well trained with their weapons. Some have been in the army only a few weeks."

"I certainly would not question the Captain's judgement," Alice said, "it's just I didn't expect it to be this way or feel the way I do now."

"I know how you feel more than you would think possible," the Major replied. "I have seen more executions than I care to remember and each one is just as unpleasant. It isn't something that you get used to."

"Is there not another way, jail or something?" Alice asked.

"In normal times in this country," the Major replied, "whatever those are, we don't have capital punishment. But now with the war, putting men in prison in a situation like this is not possible. We don't even have a stockade in this camp. That is why I ordered the others flogged. All punishment must be immediate."

But Mrs. Manati," he continued, "I have the feeling that you did not come here to discuss the philosophy of crime and punishment or to plead mercy for those men."

"You are right, of course," Alice replied, "that was not my reason."

"You came to be certain they are dead," the Major asserted.

"You know my feelings as well as I do myself," Alice replied. "But after seeing it done, I am not as sure about what I wanted. It was what should have been done. Of that much I am certain. But to see men die like that, reduced to nothing more than crawling..."

"I know, I know," the Major said. "If it helps any, I probably would have sentenced those men to death without the testimony that you presented. There is no doubt in my mind that the man who was bitten by the snake was murdered. Two of the other soldiers came to me in private and testified about this matter. I could not condemn any of them for killing the man with the gun. There is much talk of mercenaries and our orders are to execute any we capture. But to kill a helpless man, that is murder. War is an ugly matter. Some men become like animals. Not all, of course, but we never really know even about ourselves. We are all lowered in our humanity. No one can really escape that. A few months ago, I might have reprimanded the Captain for the way he executed that man. Now I find such behavior, if not pleasing, at least acceptable. Yet there must be some standard of conduct below which we will not let ourselves fall. But even with the help and guidance of God, I am not at all sure that I know what that level is. What happened to your friends on the road will happen in village after village in this country. I don't know how I will react the next time and the time after that and the time after that. My men, my soldiers, they come from small villages, many of them. Most would have been content to live out their lives with the food raised on a small plot of land, a wife, children, a little palm wine in the evenings. Instead, they find themselves asked to walk until they drop, go hungry, thirsty, to kill other men, to be prepared to die and all because of something they have little understanding of and would probably not want to be involved in if they really did know what it was all about. It is not some evil from within that turns them into animals, but the evil that surrounds them. They have little knowledge of why they fight, only that today they are alive and tomorrow they might well be dead."

"But I am sorry," the Major said, "I did not mean to excuse those men. They deserved their fate. If what we are doing turns us into barbarians, then the war itself has no meaning."

"Excuses are unnecessary," Alice said in a choked voice. "God help us all..."

She would have continued but tears held her intended words deep in her throat. The trees and men in front of her suddenly seemed to be at odd angles. She felt her shoulder touch the Major's chest. He put his arm around Alice and steadied her walk. They said nothing more as they made their way back to the small house. Jason helped the Major get Alice to a cot.

As he was leaving, Jason stopped the Major and said, "I wish to thank you for all that you have done for us. We owe our lives to you."

"I have only done my duty," the Major replied.

"Well, yes," Jason replied, "but not all men would see their duty as you have. Now I don't mean to sound ungrateful for your hospitality, but I think the sooner we get to Nkra the better for us."

The Major laughed and then said, "I well understand that this is not home for you or even the Hilton. You must be anxious to see your friends and families. With today's business complete, there is nothing more for any of you to do here. It is best that you wait until tomorrow to make your journey to the Capital. That will give you the full day and you will not have to worry about being on the roads after dark. I have a small truck that I will put at your disposal. The road in that direction is reasonably secure. I do not believe that you will encounter any problems. I have asked the Captain who found you in the forest to be your escort. I would accompany you myself, but I must remain here. There are rumors of a counterattack by the rebels."

The next morning the Major came to the little house with the Captain, the truck and driver, and safe conduct passes. They left after a brief farewell.

Alice sat in front with the Vice-Chancellor and the driver. Once they were underway she examined the papers that the Major had prepared. The signature at the bottom of her pass read, 'Major Joseph Kanata.' She nudged the Vice-Chancellor and pointed toward the signature.

"Yes," the Vice-Chancellor murmured, "I know him well. But he decided that we should act as if we were not acquainted. He did not wish his men to know that his father and I were friends. He was afraid they might think him biased in the judgement that he had to make on those evil men. But we were indeed fortunate. Another commander might have made no effort to save Mrs. Harris or been willing to take such forthright action against those who harmed her. I do pray that she recovers."

In the back of the mammy wagon style truck Karen sat on the first plank with her arms around Beth. The two women rode in silence. Jason sat beside Karen, ready to help if needed. Gil, Pordoe and the Captain sat together on the second plank using each other to soften the blows from the potholes in the rapidly deteriorating road that led toward Nkra. They talked a little at first, but after a few miles they were as silent as Beth. The prospect of being home with friends and family within a few days brought with it a sense of warmth and comfort that did not require words to share.

Jason wondered if his parents had any idea what he had been through in the last week and if they were worried.

"They are probably frantic, but I will never know unless my mother sees fit to tell me."

His thoughts tumbled back to when he had destroyed the family car at the age of sixteen. He remembered what he had said to his father on the phone.

"Dad, I've been involved in an accident. No one seems badly hurt. No other car was involved. I hit a hole in the road and turned over. I think my wrist is sprained or broken. Could you meet me at the hospital?"

Jason's mom had later told him that his father had been unable to change clothes without her help. However, by the time they met in the emergency room all traces of anxiety had been erased from his father's demeanor. After the wrist was set, they had hitched a ride back home to save taxi fare.

"Maybe in a few years," Jason mused, "they will tell me how they felt. Must send a telegram as soon as possible."

In less than an hour they were within sight of the Kra River. Jason marveled at what he saw. Signs of war were few, except for the ever present roadblocks. The small villages along the road bustled with people, looking no different than the last time he had made this trip: Men, women going to farm, children carrying water on their heads, schools in session with masters caning wayward children.

"Strange," Jason thought," that life continues so calmly just a few miles from hell. The war is just over there, but not here. I guess war means the destruction of someone else's land, the murder of someone else's father, the rape of someone else's wife, the starvation of someone else's child."

They crossed the Kra River. In less than an hour and a half they were at the outskirts of Nkra. The city seemed not much different. The only visible indications of the war were wall posters that exhorted the people of Sakra to defend their nation and an increase in the number of uniformed military personnel on the streets.

Jason asked the driver to take them to the American Embassy. A message from Major Kanata, relayed through army headquarters, had reached the Embassy ahead of them. They were met by the Peace Corps Director, a personnel officer of the Embassy, and a representative from the British Embassy down the street. Little was said as they got down from the lorry. Beth sat down on the running board of the driver's side of the lorry and looked away from the others.

The Vice-Chancellor hugged Alice and said, "May God grant that we meet again."

Alice started to cry and finally managed to say, "I hope that this awful thing is over soon. Write me when you are back at Mbordo and the school is open again. I will not be happy until that time."

The Vice-Chancellor smiled a little sadly as if to say, "It will be the same with me," then turned to say good-by to the others.

Gil also found himself saying good-by all around. When he reached Jason the two men paused then held each other tightly.

"Good-by old friend," Gil said, "I am deeply sorry that your stay here with us ended so badly. I hope you will return when times are better. When you think of Sakra and Mbordo, think of how it was before. That is what we really are. Not this madness."

Jason responded, "I will never think badly of Sakra. I remember even now as it was and as it will be."

Then Jason turned to Pordoe and said, "To you, good friend the Sportsmaster, we owe our lives. What you have done for us goes beyond friendship. We shall always remember."

Pordoe grasped Jason's hand and said, "We did what we could do. We did well, I think, all of us."

After another round of good-bys and thank-yous to the Captain, the three Africans left to see friends and family and begin the process of rebuilding their lives.

Throughout the farewells Beth had remained silent and unresponsive. When Alice and Karen tried to hug her she pushed them away. The aide from the British Embassy guided her toward a waiting car. She moved neither willingly or unwillingly. Beth's sadness left Alice, Karen and Jason at least for the moment depressed.

"It's over," Jason said as he sat down on the Embassy steps. "It's all goddamn over."

"How soon can we get out of here?" he asked the Peace Corps Director.

"There is a flight at two," the Director replied.

"Can we find some money to buy these people tickets?" he asked the Embassy Personnel Officer.

"Yes," the man replied, "I believe that will be possible. We have an emergency fund. Do you want me to make reservations?"

"Yes, thank you," the Director answered.

"Let's go inside," he said to the three volunteers. "While we are waiting for the tickets, perhaps you can provide me with some information that I need to wrap things up here."

They accompanied the Director into a small office and accepted his offer of food and drink.

When they had been served he said, "Now that you people are here, all of the Peace Corps volunteers from the Western region are accounted for except one that was assigned to Mbordo. Major Kanata's message indicated that five bodies of expatriates had been recovered, one British and four Americans. Was one of those Americans Jeff Johnson?"

"My God," Jason exclaimed, "we forgot Jeff. But to answer your question, no, he was definitely not killed at the roadblock. The Americans who died there were two AID advisors and their wives, Mr. and Mrs. Whitland and Mrs. and Mrs. Block.

Well, that is in agreement with the communication from Major Kanata, but we thought there might have been a mistake in identifying the bodies," the Director said. "Do any of you know anything about what might have happened to Jeff Johnson?"

"Well, yes, I do," Jason responded, "but I don't quite know how to explain."

Alice interrupted, "It's very simple, really. He received word that his son was in danger in Kwim and he left us to help."

"His son?" the Director asked.

"Yes," Alice replied emphatically, "his son, the child of Jeff and another teacher at the University-College, a boy only a few months old. The message asking for help came from Kwim on the night we were preparing to leave Mbordo."

"How long ago was this and what did Jeff intend to do?" the Director asked.

"I think it has been about five days," Alice replied, looking toward Jason for confirmation.

Jason nodded.

Alice continued, "I don't know what his plans were, other than to go to Kwim."

"He is right in the middle of this damn war," the Director mumbled. "There's not much we can do to help. We will try to tell both sides who he is and why he is out there. Our government does have some contact with the rebels."

"Tell me," the Director asked Alice, "were they actually married?"

"Not by the government," Alice replied, attempting to fudge her answer. "The baby's mother died in childbirth."

The Director shook his head slowly and said, "None of this sounds very good. The government and the rebels are going crazy with the mercenary issue. If Johnson is captured by either side in the war zone, it's a problem. That's for sure."

Alice started to cry.

"I'm sorry," she apologized, "it's just been too damn much."

"That's OK," the Director said. "I feel like crying myself. We will do what we can to help him. He'll probably be all right."

The Director drove them to the airport and saw them safely aboard a plane whose last stop would be New York. On the way back into the city, his thoughts turned to Jeff Johnson.

"Damn fool kid," he mused. "A baby. Hard to believe. Imagine him running around with his little bastard out there in the middle of nowhere. I was hoping to have this thing wrapped up by now and be on that plane myself. Oh well, wait around another week, I guess, and see if he makes it."

CHAPTER 23
The Priest's House

Jeff awoke to the baby's cry. The sun was near the peak of its daily journey. The sound was familiar. It echoed through thoughts of past pain and pleasure. His mind struggled to deal with who and where he was but the effort only led to more confusion.

"Start with small things," he thought.

He was in a bed, that much he was sure of. But it was a large soft bed with a canopy. He couldn't remember having been in a bed like this or even seeing one except perhaps in a movie. And the baby? He remembered a baby, but not very clearly.

"I have held babies," he thought. "But why is this one here and what is he mad about?"

The baby's cry had changed from a whimper to a furious yell.

Jeff remembered the sound now. That same sound close to his ear and the feel of the warmth of the baby on his back.

He remembered his instructions and wondered if there was any milk left.

"My son," the thought suddenly struck him as a disconnected but important revelation, "yes, it is my son."

"The baby's cry woke you, I see," a voice said.

The words came from a man standing near the bed. Jeff noticed that he wore a clerical collar.

"We are very glad to see that you are awake," he continued. "Your fever was quite severe. But it is now normal. Medicine is not very available in this area because of the war to the east. Fortunately, some local medicines are always obtainable. They work more slowly. The child as you can well hear is in better health than you. When you came, he suffered only from diarrhea which we were quickly able to stop with good milk and a little medicine. His African blood protected him from the worst of the malaria that you seemed to have contracted. You must have forgotten your chloroquine pills when you decided to make this trip.

"What is this place?" Jeff asked.

"My home," the Cleric replied. "You are now in Polama, the second largest city of the nation of Malief. Don't be worried. You and the child are quite safe here. You must rest now and regain your strength. I have to make a call now, but when I return we will talk again."

Jeff closed his eyes but struggled to keep his mind from drifting back into sleep. He heard the Cleric instruct someone to feed the baby and let the man rest. She was a large Black woman who must have had a nursing child of her own since she picked the baby up and offered him her breast.

As she fed the baby, Jeff tried to start a conversation.

"Could you tell me what day of the week this is?" he asked.

"Wednesday," she replied without elaboration.

"One day from Kwim to Malief," Jeff thought, "that would be possible only by plane."

"Do you know what day of the month it is?" he asked.

"The 19th of April," she replied without hesitation then continued, "but please do not worry yourself with such things. The Father says that you are to rest, and if that is what he says, it is best that you do so."

Jeff's mind was whirling.

"A week," he thought, "a lost week."

He struggled to reconstruct what had happened. Now the painful image of Chief Kanata leaning on the wall of his compound in Kwim was all too clear in his mind. He also remembered without difficulty the drive southward, walking with the baby on his back down the highway, fleeing into the forest to avoid capture, the kindness of the man at the hut, the mosquitoes and the rain.

As Jeff lay resting in the Cleric's huge bed, he could almost to see himself half walking, half stumbling with the child along the trail. He remembered reaching the first great scarp and facing the choice of finding some way down or walking an extra seventy-five miles to reach the Malief border.

He had rested that day near the edge of the scarp and then used the entire night to make his way down. The clear picture in his mind of the steep trail and of near disastrous slips in the darkness caused him to sit up quickly in the old bed as if to grasp the small trees and vines that had, on more than one occasion, prevented their falling to the rocks below. The woman in whose care he and the child had been left moved to the bedside.

"You must rest now," she said as her firm hands gently guided his trembling shoulders back against the warm softness of the bed. "Here," she continued as she handed him two small white tablets, "the doctor left these to help you rest."

Jeff slipped the tablets into his mouth and washed them down with the water from the glass she handed him.

"Water," he thought, "damn, at first not enough and then far too much."

His thoughts returned to the journey.

At the bottom of the scarp he had stopped long enough to trap rain water with the plastic shirt. He had only enough milk powder left to refill three bottles.

"Milk, precious milk," he thought.

As the tablets dissolved in his stomach, Jeff's thoughts became less connected. Walking, walking, he remembered walking, always walking. The compass guiding him west. Then running in fear, in pain. How far, how long. The days blended together. But always moving, moving to the west. Then for just a moment he saw himself clearly in the middle of a stream holding the baby up high. The water was so deep and so fast. It didn't look that deep from the edge. Near the middle, a deep hole. Water on his shoulders, his neck. He raised the baby over his head but his legs seemed to move away from him as if they belonged to the water. Again, he heard a voice yell from the far bank and saw the rope. He felt his hand grasp the rope and wrap it around his wrist. The man pulled them up out of the water. Jeff reached the shore exhausted and soaked. He collapsed a few feet from the edge of the river. When he opened his eyes to look at the man, he realized that he was a soldier. He clutched the baby to his chest and tried to run. He moved only two steps before he stumbled and fell.

The soldier said, "Look, my friend, I intend you no harm. If I wished you to die, I would have better left you in the water. Your time was very near its end. Please, take this dry cloth for the child."

Jeff gratefully nodded his appreciation.

"In normal times," the soldier continued, "I would invite you to my house to rest and eat before you continue your journey. Unfortunately, my house is at least five days' walk from this place."

He touched Jeff's forehead.

"You have much fever," he told Jeff. "My company is near here, but I am only a Corporal. My Captain talks of how much he wishes to capture a mercenary. I would fear for your safety with him. Even though you are ill, the distance to Malief is not far. You have only to follow this trail another ten miles. If you can still walk, it is best you go there. I will guide you part of the way."

Jeff's memory blurred as it tried to picture how he had stumbled along behind the soldier. When the man had offered to carry the baby, Jeff refused. He remembered thinking that when he could go no further, both he and his son would remain where he fell. The soldier accompanied him until they were within site of the border.

"Down there," the soldier said pointing to a path that was wide enough to be a small road. "This place is used mainly by smugglers. Sometimes the police or army comes here to catch them, but I see no one. I think it is safe. Go quickly."

He said good-by to the soldier. It wasn't much of a border. Just three strands of barbed wire that seemed to have spent more time pushed to the ground than in the air.

It became increasingly difficult for Jeff to hold together the bits and pieces of what he remembered after crossing the border. He knew that he had tried to walk for a while but had no idea of where he wanted to go. Then the heat and pain in his head overwhelmed all thoughts of fear. He vaguely remembered sitting down with the child in his arms, resting his head against a tree.

His next memory was of being carried.

He heard again a voice saying in Ave, "The Priest's home is the only place to take him. The police will only send them back across the border."

The pills took complete effect and Jeff's mind slipped into a deep unconscious state. He slept for hours. When he awoke, the blackness told him that it was night. A kerosene lantern near the bed provided light.

He heard voices and realized that two men were looking at him.

"The fever's gone now," one of them said, "but he did have a rough spell of it. He must have at least a full week of rest before he is moved."

"I do believe that he is awake," Jeff heard the familiar voice of the Priest say.

"How are you feeling tonight, young man?" he asked.

When Jeff tried to answer, he found his mouth almost too dry to form words.

He did manage to mumble, "All right, I guess."

Jeff tried to sit up, but dizziness forced him to lie back down.

"Just relax," the Doctor said, "don't try to move about too much yet. Do you think you could eat something?"

Jeff nodded.

"Good, good," the Doctor said.

He turned to the Priest and whispered, "If he can eat, we won't have to bother with intravenous feeding. Bloody mess that is, you know, with the sterilization and all that."

"Who are you?" the Priest asked Jeff. "The men who brought you said that you had nothing with you except the child. All that I found in your pockets was this small stone."

Jeff took the stone from the Priest's hand and held it in his own for a moment.

"It belongs to the child," he explained. "Would you place it on that table near his bed?"

The Priest took the stone and did as Jeff had requested. A woman appeared with food.

"Do you feel like talking while you eat?" the Priest asked, "or should we return after you have completed you meal?"

"I can do both," Jeff replied, his spirits improving with each spoonful of chicken broth. "My two favorite things, talking and eating. My name is Jeffrey Johnson. I am a citizen of the United States and in the Peace Corps. I was assigned to teach at Mbordo University-College."

"Mbordo," the doctor muttered, "that is at least one-hundred and fifty miles from here. No wonder this boy's feet look the way they do."

Jeff continued to eat as he gave the two men a brief description of his journey.

"In the morning I will send a messenger to the American Embassy in the Capital," the Priest said. "I am quite certain they will be delighted to know that you are safe and well. I would call or wire tonight, but it is not possible. The heavy rains that I am sure by now you are all too familiar with have damaged the lines."

The doctor found two more sleeping pills in his bag and offered them to Jeff.

"How is the child?" Jeff asked before he accepted them.

"Doing very well," the Priest replied. "Would you like me to put him on the bed with you?"

"Yes, I would," Jeff answered.

The woman whom Jeff had seen nursing the baby earlier that day picked the child up from his small crib and laid him on the bed. The boy was sound asleep. Jeff held him for a few minutes until he felt the sheet beside him growing damp. He called the woman and handed the child back to her.

The Doctor chuckled and said, "I think I would really like babies if it were not for that. You know, he is in much better shape than you are. Rest now. We can all talk more at a later time."

Jeff took the two pills and was soon asleep.

When he awoke it was midmorning. The Priest was again standing by his bed. Jeff found that he was able to sit up without feeling dizzy.

The Priest remarked, "It is good to see you awake. How do you feel today?"

"Very much better," Jeff replied.

"The message about you went by lorry this morning to your embassy. I expect they will send someone. I know that you must be anxious to go home. But for now, I have ordered a breakfast that I think you will like. I will return when you have finished eating.

With the sight of the morning meal Jeff's appetite returned. The eggs, toast, jam and tea brought by a woman received his complete and favorable attention. When the Priest returned, Jeff felt well enough to move from the bed to a chair.

"Excellent," the Father commented, "I do believe that within a few days your body will have little memory of your journey. Your mind, or course, is a different matter."

"Yes, certainly," Jeff replied. "I have been trying to sort it all out. Some of it I don't remember that well. But I do wish to thank you a great deal for the hospitality that you have shown me and the child."

"Oh, don't mention it," the Priest said. "It is a pleasure to have company. Not many strangers come this way, especially not in the manner that you arrived."

"I don't doubt that," Jeff said with a smile.

The Priest nodded, then changed the subject.

"Now as to the future," he said, "your man from the embassy will be here soon, I am certain. They will be happy to know that you are still alive. However, even with that happiness it will probably take them several days to do the paper work necessary to get you out of Malief. You are welcome to stay here until it is completed. That will give you time to decide what should be done about the child. I will look carefully for a good family to adopt him."

"I am sorry, sir," Jeff said, "if what I say sounds inhospitable. I am very grateful for your help, more so than I can express in words. But I will not leave the child. He is my own son. I am his father. Whatever happens, he will stay with me and I with him."

The Priest's brow furrowed. For the first time Jeff realized that he was not a young man, certainly past fifty.

He spoke deliberately, "That will make matters more difficult. Perhaps you are being a bit too emotional about this entire matter. Are you certain that this is your son?"

Jeff stood up. He wanted to grab the Priest and shake him or hit him but instead stumbled and collapsed to the floor well before he was able to reach the place where the Clergyman sat. The Priest moved to cushion his fall and tried to lift him back into the chair. Jeff resisted his help.

"Forgive me," the Priest said, "I should have known that the matter was of great importance to you. Few could or would have done what you did to bring the child to safety. I am deeply sorry that I said what I did. Perhaps if you would tell me how all of this came about, I will be able to help you."

After a deep sigh, Jeff began to recount aloud, as he had so very many times in the darkness of the night alone and silently, that part of his life tied so closely to Enata and her father. He told of his work in Mbordo, of how he and Enata met, of their happiness in Kwim, of her pregnancy, of the picnics at the Church, of the automobile accident, of the birth of the child, of Enata's death, of their plans to be married, of the Chief's decision to keep the child and of his grief when forced to send the boy away. Jeff's effort to explain all that had happened to bring him to the Clergyman's house exhausted his meager energy. He sat in the chair barely able to hold his head up.

He heard the Priest say, "And you would have married Enata if she had lived?"

He had used all that remained of his strength to answer emphatically, "Yes, yes most certainly, we would have been married within a few months."

The old man mumbled, "In Africa, at least, what should have been can be."

Jeff awoke later, still sitting in the chair and shouting, "No, no, you can't do that. I will stop you!"

He looked quickly for the child and was relieved to find him still in the room but crying loudly.

"My God," he thought, "what a horrible dream. Soldiers trying to tear the child away. Or maybe customs officials."

He tried to laugh at his fears but only partially succeeded.

"The child's cry must have prompted the dream. I sure as hell hope that I don't have that dream every time he yells."

Jeff pushed his body up from the chair and walked over to the basket. The small boy's scream sounded like the music of a symphony orchestra to him.

"Beethoven's Ninth, maybe," he mused.

The Priest's voice startled him.

"You should not be up and about just yet," he said. "By what name do you call the child?"

"I don't know," Jeff answered, "I believe that he was known only by his day name, Kwame."

The Priest replied firmly, "He must have a name."

Jeff thought for a moment then replied, "His name is Robert Kanata Johnson, after his grandfather."

The Priest smiled broadly and said, "An excellent choice."

Then he left the room.

He returned an hour later.

"Here," he said, motioning for Jeff to look at papers that he held, "I have two pieces of paper. One is the marriage certificate of Jeffrey Johnson and Enata Kanata. It is dated April 3. The rites were performed in the town of Mbordo. The second is a birth certificate for one Robert Kanata Johnson, dated, January 8, from the city of Hunta. In case you are wondering, there is a gentleman in this city who does this type of work for citizens of Sakra who wish to escape the war and are able to pay for his services. Unfortunately, he is not good at what he does. Most of the people who deal with him are sent back to Sakra.

"For that reason," the Priest continued, "I bought the proper paper from him and did the 'art' work myself. You need not worry about the quality of these certificates. I have dealt with the governments of both Malief and Sakra more often than I care to think about. I know the manner of all of these official documents quite well. There is little danger that these papers will be checked for accuracy with the original source. From what you have said, records in the town of Mbordo have most probably already been destroyed. None can be obtained from Hunta at this time.

"There is no way that I will ever be able to repay your kindness," Jeff said as he examined the papers.

"There would be no reason to attempt any repayment," the Priest answered. "You and the child really are what the papers say, nothing more, nothing less. You were Enata's husband, and she your wife. The baby was and is your son. I have done nothing more than what should have been done. Believe me when I tell you this, Jeff, in this life the best that pieces of paper can do is to verify what is true. They do not create or destroy. We do that ourselves."

The End

Epilogue
The War

Jason looked through the handful of mail he had removed from his parents' mailbox in front of their rural home in Ohio. He noticed one addressed to him. The return address was:

Jeff Johnson
c/o Mr. and Mrs. Willard Johnson
Box 318
Memphis, Tennessee 38118

He ripped the letter open. It began:

Dear Jason and Karen,

I am sorry to be so long in writing this letter, but the last few months have been busy.

"Karen, Karen!" Jason called, as he trotted toward the house waving the letter, "look what came in the mail."

"You know I don't like guessing games, Jason," Karen shouted from where she sat on the porch, "and you know I can't see that far."

Jason laughed and said, "I'm sorry. It's a letter from Jeff."

"Where is he?" she asked as she stood up.

"He's here," Jason answered, "that is, I mean he's in Tennessee."

"He says it took him two months to get out of Malief with Robert," Jason continued.

"Who is Robert?" Karen asked.

"Robert Kanata Johnson, his son," Jason replied.

"I'm so glad they got out," Karen said as she began to cry.

"If you're so glad," Jason teased, "then what are you crying about?"

"You know damn well why I'm crying," Karen replied. "Let's call Alice!"

"We'll see her Monday," Jason said with a shrug. "She wants us to come over and look for an apartment in her building. Why not tell her then?"

Only the interruption of their conversation by Jason's mother stayed Karen's stinging retort.

"There is a telephone call for you, Jason," she said. "It's a long distance from Washington DC. A woman wants to talk to you right away."

"I wonder who..." Jason started to say.

"Probably the same person you didn't want to call," Karen suggested.

It was Alice. She seemed to be laughing and crying at the same time as she tried to tell Jason the good news about Jeff.

Jason managed to calm her down a little by explaining, "We know. We got a letter. It was great news to hear about his son Robert. We are really happy that all worked out."

"Yes," Alice said, "I'm looking forward to seeing the little guy again, and Jeff too.

"And," Alice continued, sounding almost disappointed, "since you already know all about Jeff and Robert, I have some other news for you that you may not find quite so pleasant. I heard a rumor that the people downtown over-hired. If you really want to work here, it would be wise if you come as soon as possible and be sure to bring your contracts."

"Ah, yes," Jason mumbled, "those strange contracts. Do you really think that man works for the DC School System?"

"Don't knock it," Alice replied. "They may have destroyed their own copies but as long as you have yours, you're in good shape. I checked with the union."

"Didn't that whole business seem a little strange?" Jason asked Alice. "I mean, to meet someone on a plane from Sakra to New York who had just been flying around Africa trying to recruit white teachers for the Washington DC City School System?"

"At the time, it didn't seem out of the ordinary," Alice replied. "But why did you sign the damn things? Didn't I give you fair warning about what it's like to teach in Washington?"

"Well, it seemed like a reasonable thing to do at the time," Jason replied. "The man did say they were one-way contracts, binding on them but not on us. We thought that when we found something better we would just throw them away, but they are the best offers we have."

"Then they must be the only ones," Alice remarked.

"How did you guess?" Jason replied.

"Just wait," Alice said, "you'll see. You know I will do what I can to help, but really..."

"Now don't you worry about Karen and me," Jason said. "It can't be any worse than those last few weeks in Sakra. We are pretty tough, I think."

"That and some other things, but you'll see," Alice replied. "See you two on Monday."

They flew into National on the first Monday in August. They found Alice waiting for them near the entrance to the luggage area. She insisted that they stay with her until they found an apartment. The next day they were assigned teaching positions in the DC School System.

After Jason and Karen found their own place they continued to dine with Alice at least once each week. Usually they would start early in order to finish in time for the 6:30 news.

The war in Sakra received little attention from the major television networks. Most of the emphasis was on what was happening to offshore oil production. Some of the worst outrages were deemed worthy of a few minutes of coverage. Usually the hand of a mercenary or two was evident, especially if it involved the wanton destruction of entire villages. They worked for both sides. Most were little better than hired killers. They were often the same men who, working for European governments or private companies, had massacred Africans in Zaire, in Angola, in Zimbabwe. How ironic they must have found being hired by Africans to do the same type of work.

In those rare moments when film from the actual war areas was shown, the three ex-volunteers carefully scanned the small screen of Alice's TV in an effort to match the faces of soldiers, refugees, and other victims of the war with those of old friends and former students. Occasionally they would think they recognized someone, but they were never really sure. Only later would they began to understand how the war had actually unfolded.

****

After an initial surge by government forces and a counterattack by rebel troops, the war had settled into small-scale fighting over a few miles of territory. Most of that action occurred to the west and south of the Kra river in an area that included the traditional lands of the Bordo people. The rest of the nation of Sakra and even the western parts of the new nation of Dadze seemed to be functioning in a state of near normalcy.

However, the Commander in Chief of the Dadze forces secretly combined his second and third armies in the south near the coast. In October the rebel forces moved rapidly into and across the lower Midwest region. The small contingent of government forces stationed there had been surprised, and were not prepared to fight. The civilian population was also surprised and few had the time or resources to flee. The rapidly moving rebels took what they needed as they drove eastward. Civilians who resisted expropriation of their goods or property were executed as an example to others who might think their possessions valuable enough to risk their lives. Within a fortnight the Dadze army had taken control of all bridges on the lower Kra and moved 40,000 men across that river into the flat, dry Nkra Plain no more than forty miles from Nkra. Once the threat to the capital was clearly perceived by the former military men in charge there, segments of every part of the armed services of Sakra were moved into positions between the rebel armies and the city. The troops under Major Kanata's command were among those ordered to the south. The Dadze field commander decided to attack before even more government troops moved south. His decision led to the first major engagement of the war, the Battle of the Nkra Plain.

The Ave soldiers fought with brilliance and valor, but as the battle stretched from hours into days the numerical advantage of the government troops became the dominant factor. Once the forward movement of their troops had been stymied, the generals of the Dadze armies decided to move their men quickly back to the east bank of the Kra river and make a stand there. They hoped to regroup, move more men across the Kra and march toward Nkra again.

The government of Sakra continued to mass troops on the Nkra Plain in what was to become the largest concentration of troops ever assembled in the history of all of West Africa.

The Ave soldiers, with their backs to the Kra river, fought desperately, holding the government troops at bay for ten days. The end of the battle for the east bank of the Kra, when it did come, occurred so quickly that the rebel troops had time only to destroy one of three bridges as they retreated. Troops of the Sakra army were able to move across the remaining bridges and establish positions on the west bank. Major Kanata's unit was the first across. Two days later, Ave saboteurs blew up the two bridges. This left about twenty thousand government troops isolated on the west bank. The rebels counterattacked. The Ave generals hoped to demoralize the rest of the Sakra army by driving this small force into the river and inflicting heavy casualties.

When the Ave counterattacked, Major Kanata was much surprised to find that he was the senior officer on the west bank. A certain Colonel Kardar had fallen ill with fever only the day before and had not accompanied the troops under his command across the Kra.

The battle for the west bank of the Kra was intense. Government forces with their backs to the river fought well. They had to or die. Sakra's small air force dropped supplies. A small number of reinforcements were moved directly across the Kra in small boats commandeered from their owners. After a week of heavy fighting Colonel Kardar came by helicopter to resume command. On the night of his arrival, Ave troops again attacked in force and the Colonel's fever returned. The next day the Colonel decided that his illness could only be treated in Nkra. He boarded his helicopter and was never again seen on the Ave side of the Kra river.

General Mensah, known as 'Iron Kwasi,' arrived two days later to take command.

He called Kanata aside and explained, "Colonel, I knew you could do very well without my help. You have already won this battle. Your tactics are excellent, your choice of defensive positions and construction of fortifications outstanding. I think these men would follow you to the gates of hell. They should have promoted you to the rank of General, but those bastards in Nkra are too damn slow at everything. You know what they want us to do here?"

The General continued without waiting for an answer, "They want us to sit on our butts and just hold on. They want to move troops north again and try to take advantage of Ave weakness there. I think we could go at them right here, but they won't give me enough troops. To tell you the truth, Kanata, I can't stand to be away from the action very long and I have asked to be moved north. When I do go, they will send some son of a bitch even dumber than I am to take command here. They got a lot of them waiting around Nkra for something that looks safe. You already have this position secure. Not even a complete fool could lose it. Why don't you come north with me? You know that area."

Kanata readily agreed to become the General's personal aide. Two weeks later the General's request for transfer was approved. He assumed command of the newly created sixth army encamped a few miles west of Towa. Kanata remained behind for two weeks in order to insure an orderly transfer of command, then joined 'Iron Kwasi.'

The failure to drive Sakraian troops from the west bank of the Kra was a major setback for the Ave forces. The problems involved in resupplying their troops across the Midwest region seemed to multiply with every passing day. The intense level of fighting of the previous weeks had left the rebels short of ammunition, petrol, replacement parts for vehicles and other supplies. Food was becoming a problem. The Midwest region had already been ravaged by the rebel troops as they moved toward the Kra. Now little was left for anyone.

The first and third armies also sensed the possibility that their link with Aveland might be threatened. The rebel generals were aware, through intelligence reports, that at least one government army to the north was moving into a position from which it would be able to drive southward to the west of the Ave armies. The Dadze high command in Hunta decided that they could not risk losing one-third of their fighting manpower. They ordered the first and third armies to retreat.

The Ave movement was a complete surprise to the Sakra high command in Nkra. The General who had replaced Mensah on the west bank of the Kra had specific orders to keep his men where they were and maintain a defensive posture. Those orders remained unchanged for five days. Instead of pursuing the retreating rebels, the government forces moved only a few miles to the west.

The rebels took full advantage of this break in the fighting. They slowed their retreat just enough to remove from the Midwest everything and anything that they had missed on their drive toward the Kra. They recruited laborers and reinforcements when they found young men and women whom they thought might make good soldiers or workers. The bodies of those who did not wish to 'volunteer' were left in ditches along the highways. Jason, Karen and Alice saw quite a bit of this part of the war. The government of Sakra made good use of these unarmed dead to demonstrate to the world the inhumanity of the Dadze soldiers.

Rebel intelligence reports had been at least partially accurate. Government forces in the Towa area were split into two army level commands. One of these, the Fourth Army, was ordered to move in a southwestward direction and trap the Ave armies in the Midwest. However, the General in command of the fourth army was a cautious man and chose to move very slowly. Given the pace of the fourth army, the government strategy would have been successful only if the Dadze troops had remained in the Midwest another year. The remaining forces in the Towa area were regrouped into a new, but under-manned, Sixth Army. They had fallen back to a spot near the Kra River and established themselves in a comfortable and highly fortified position.

This was the army that Iron Kwasi was asked to command. Five days after his arrival, he ordered the elaborate defensive fortifications of the camp dismantled. What could be loaded into trucks and moved he ordered saved, the rest was destroyed. In just ten days the Sixth Army was on the move, eastward, along the highway that led to Hunta. They met with little resistance. The Ave forces retreated in the face of superior manpower. As they neared the Mbordo junction, scouts brought word that no large concentrations of Dadze troops remained in Bordo lands. General Mensah decided to split his forces. He, along with the main body of troops, would continue toward Hunta. The others were dispersed in relatively small units through Bordo lands to the north to secure the area and eliminate any rebel forces that remained there.

When General Mensah reached the Kwim junction he ordered a halt. Intelligence reports from the detached units to the north indicated that no large units of rebel soldiers had been found. But small units were frequently encountered and fought with tenacity when engaged. Often the rebels would barricade themselves in the best buildings of a village with food and water enough to last several weeks. The officers in the field indicated that the cleanup operation would take longer than anticipated. General Mensah decided to remain encamped at the Kwim junction until the operations to the north were completed. Colonel Kanata requested permission to visit his home village of Kwim. Permission was granted.

The road to Kwim was badly damaged. The short trip required three hours. As they approached, it was obvious that Kwim had been one of the cities contested by Ave troops. Buildings that were once churches and schools were now little more than piles of rubble. Few houses were left standing. At the Colonel's direction, the driver of the jeep steered carefully through the debris toward the home of the Chief. Only a portion of the front wall was still standing. Behind the wall, he found his father sitting upright with his back against the wall, his face turned away from what had been his home. Kanata knew he was dead before he reached his side. He lay the old man's head on his chest and held him in his arms.

"Not dead more than a few days," Kanata thought. "If only I had come sooner."

The old man's expression in death reflected no fear, not even pain. He looked now as the Colonel had remembered him always. As he held his father, a sense of rage and anger swept away his sadness.

"Father, my dear father," he said quietly, "they shall pay a thousand times over for your death."

Then he screamed, "Who did this thing? What manner of men murder the old and children? Who are they to destroy what is decent and good?"

One of the soldiers came running when he heard the Colonel.

"Is everything in order, sir?" he asked. "Do you need help?"

"No, I don't need help. I know what I must do," Kanata replied.

The soldier carried a small flag.

"What is that?" the Colonel asked.

"Something I found stuck in what is left of the far wall of this compound," the soldier replied. "It bears the symbol of one of our divisions. I believe they are known as the avengers of Allah."

"No doubt that flag was captured by rebel troops and left here as they retreated," Kanata speculated.

"This is possible, but I think not," the soldier replied. "Rebel troops were driven from Kwim several weeks ago in a major battle. No more than a dozen men were left behind to secure this area and even they seemed to have moved on. It is easy to understand why they left. There is little left here to secure. Is the old man someone that you know?"

Kanata did not answer, but instead asked, "Then who did this?"

The soldier shrugged and said nothing. The Colonel already knew the answer. The Avengers of Allah was a unit composed of men from the North. They were fierce and brave fighters who had held the northern front almost alone when other divisions had been moved southward to defend Nkra. But the fate of the civilians unfortunate enough to be caught in their path had become one of the sickest jokes of the war among other government troops.

Kanata sank to his knees beside his father and half cried, half mumbled, "Now I am denied even revenge. My God, what a miserable thing this war is."

****

One evening in December, Alice had, as usual, finished eating and turned on the 6:30 news. About halfway through the broadcast the commentator turned his attention to the Dadze War, as it was now labeled by the international press. Reporters and cameramen had been airlifted by the government to a village near the front in order to demonstrate to the world the cruelty of the rebel forces. The place looked a little familiar to Alice as the camera presented a distant aerial view of what once was a village.

She heard only the first sentence of the reporter's flat voice, "This is Kwim, or rather this was Kwim, a small African village caught in the midst of war."

Alice tried to blink away her tears as she searched the screen for signs of life in the midst of crumbling houses and destroyed buildings. She saw nothing but gasped as the camera zoomed in on a pile of decaying bodies near the remains of a church. Most seemed to be old, but a few were small and obviously children. A ten-second shot of soldiers preparing to bury the dead in another village was the end of the NBC's report of rebel atrocities.

259

****

Kanata's thoughts of his life in Kwim as a boy and his father's death were interrupted by the return of his driver to the compound.

"Should we not begin the return journey now in order to reach the main road before dark?" the soldier asked. "There may still be a few enemy soldiers in this area."

"You go with the others," Kanata replied. "I must stay here for a time."

Two days later General Mensah himself visited Kwim to find out why Kanata had not returned. He had come with the intention of telling the Colonel that the sixth army was again reunited and ready to move eastward. His plan was to order Kanata to rejoin him in that march or face court-martial.

But 'Iron Kwasi' was also an African. When he found Kanata sitting alone in the remains of his father's courtyard, he thought of what his own reaction might be to finding his father dead and the village of his childhood destroyed. When his Landrover moved away from Kwim an hour later, he left Kanata behind with a small detachment of soldiers and orders to protect and rehabilitate civilians in the Bordo area. To provide a military rationale for his decision, he also ordered Kanata to see to it that fields were cleared and crops planted so that government troops would have a food supply available should the war last beyond the next harvest time. In a special plea, he asked Kanata to rejoin him at the front as soon as he felt the area secure enough to leave in the hands of the others.

General Mensah did not anticipate needing the food, nor did he expect to see Kanata at the front again. He expected the war to end in a matter of a few months. However, the rebels retreated to the Ave heartland and there, as in times past, resisted armies from the North and East with great bravery and courage. As the time of war stretched from months into years, the stories of death by starvation and disease that filtered out of Dadze grew worse. In the thirtieth month of the war government troops were able to cut the last Ave link with the sea to the south. In the thirty-seventh month of the war, Major General Mensah, now the supreme commander of all armies of Sakra, ordered the Sixth Army, under the command of General Kanata, to move from a position north of Hunta near Malief southward along the border and cut off Dadze's last remaining land link with the outside world. General Kanata's Sixth Army, after several months of heavy fighting, completed that mission. The rebels' only remaining supply link was the airport in Hunta.

The Aves fought on, their pride and courage intact. Their leaders swore that they would fight to the last man and even beyond, that fathers would teach their sons how to live alone in the forest, to hide and wait for the time of a new rebellion. That resistance to domination from the North and East would be never ending.

However, after four years and six million dead, the Ave dream of nationhood collapsed. Repeated hammer-like blows inflicted by government armies against the remaining rebel forces trapped in a small area around Hunta ended the war. The top echelon of Dadze leaders fled to other African nations and those left in charge surrendered.

The end of the war brought some immediate improvement. The murdering of civilians by troops was halted except in isolated instances. Some executions were conducted, but not as many as foreign 'experts' had predicted. Mercenaries were, for the most part, given airline tickets and asked to leave. Units with the worst reputations for civilian abuse were moved out of Aveland.

The process of disbanding unneeded army units began soon after the end of the war. Many of the soldiers had been sickened and disgusted by the carnage of the war and were happy to turn in their guns and return to their villages and cities. They found pleasure in going back to a quiet, measured life.

For others, who found the travel and excitement of army life stimulating, return to village life was boring and unsatisfactory. Such men either drifted toward the cities of Sakra or idled their time away in their villages, telling all who would listen of their bravery and courage. Some did more than talk. Laws were still on the books forbidding the use and ownership of a gun by anyone other than regular troops of the army. But those laws were now only enforced in areas where the Aves lived. The war had brought with it the entire range of modern weapons -- handguns, rifles, shotguns and even machine guns.

The deadly combination of available guns and restless ex-soldiers led to a period of lawlessness that Sakraians who lived to the east and north of the Kra river found more dangerous than the time of war. It was not safe to travel between the major cities. Lorries and other passenger vehicles were often stopped by highwaymen. Those who were fortunate lost only their possessions.

In time, the government took decisive action. Lorries filled with well dressed men and women, soldiers in disguise, lured bandits into planned ambushes. The most notorious of the bandits were publicly executed in Nkra to convince the populace that they were really dead. Others were simply dispatched where and when they were caught. These tactics cleared the major roads of Sakra of highwaymen. Those bandits who survived either found a new way of making a living or confined their illegal activities to back roads and small villages.

Jeff and Robert

Gil had promised to write to the four ex-volunteers and tell them when the war was over and conditions had returned to normal.

Seven years and some months after they had parted at Alice's house in Mbordo, Jeff received a letter from Gil in which he wrote, "Once again, praise God, it is safe to travel our roads and live in our villages. I traveled to Mbordo last month for the first time since we left so quickly that night. General Kanata, who is the military governor of that region, has the support of the Bordo people in dealing with bandits. Even the bandits have been driven from the forest. If a robbery happens, the thief is quickly reported and usually captured by soldiers within days."

Jeff had been waiting for this letter since the end of the war. With the child nothing had been easy since he left the house of the Priest. He now well understood Chief Kanata's desire to keep the boy with him in Kwim, until the war had made that impossible.

The attitude of officials in the American Embassy in Malief had varied from discourteous to hostile. They had been reluctant to accept the papers that the Priest had prepared. The memory of one particular embassy employee was still vivid enough to bring tears of rage to his eyes. She was a particularly bitter person from some sector or another involved in administering AID projects. She suggested to Jeff that Enata had been just another African whore, that he should stop being a sentimental fool and ditch the child in the nearest orphanage. Jeff had started throwing whatever he could get his hands on and would have included her had she not been quick enough to elude his grasp. Only the Priest's intervention prevented the embassy personnel from bundling Jeff up in a straitjacket and putting him on the next plane to New York.

Jeff was quite sure that no one at the embassy believed his story, but they could not disprove the authenticity of the papers. Eventually the Priest had been able to arrange a meeting with the American Ambassador. When the Ambassador realized that Jeff had been waiting for two months and planned to wait indefinitely, he ordered that Robert Kanata Johnson be registered as an American citizen and that Jeff be issued a family passport that included Robert as his son.

They were in Tennessee three days later. His parents welcomed both him and the baby. Jeff found a teaching job in one of the Black suburbs of Memphis. His mother kept the baby for a few months until he was able to locate a competent baby-sitter housekeeper.

After two years, he decided to look for a new job. In Memphis he had found himself to be a person without a community. Living in a modest Black suburb near the school in which he taught had made the problem of acceptance of Robert less difficult. But he was and perhaps always would be an outsider. People were always kind, often very kind, but he found that he had no close friends. At his parents' home, he and Robert were always welcome, but he could almost feel eyebrows raise as he drove through the well-to-do neighborhood in which they lived. He knew that Robert felt little of this. But soon, very soon, the child would be old enough to begin understanding the nature of discrimination in whatever form it was packaged. Another more positive reason for changing jobs involved one of Robert's uncles who was in his third year of medical school at the University of Arizona. Jeff was not sure that he would find less discrimination in Arizona (although he reasoned that it might be directed more toward Indians and Mexican-Americans than Blacks), but he had felt certain that getting to know his uncle would be an interesting and important experience for Robert.

He found a teaching job near Tucson. True to his expectations, Uncle Josh and his wide circle of acquaintances within the community of African students at the University had made both Jeff and Robert feel welcome and at home. In Tucson Jeff also met and married a teacher who worked at his school.

By the time he was six, Robert knew much of the history and customs of the Bordo people and Kwim. He even had a small Bordo vocabulary. Robert's uncle remained in the Tucson area after graduation to complete a hospital internship and residency. He returned to Sakra about a year before Jeff received Gil's letter.

When Gil's letter came, Jeff decided that it was time for him and Robert to return to Sakra also.

After he had tried at some length to explain to his wife of four years his reasons for returning to Africa with Robert, she had replied, "I love you for everything that you are. I understand better than you think just how much that includes the part of your life that you spent in Africa. I wouldn't want you to be some different person."

Then, in a lighter tone, she added, "But do try to return before school starts in the fall. I don't want you to lose your job. And we will miss you."

Jeff was not sure that his two small children understood, but he hoped they would when they were older.

"Alice, that lady you knew from Sakra, called while you were at work," Jeff's wife remembered. "She said something about getting your letter and wanting to ask a favor."

Jeff returned the call immediately. Alice asked that he pick up a few African artifacts for her to use in presentations to school children. He agreed and she gave him a list of things to look for. Jeff decided to buy tickets that would allow him and Robert to stop in DC on the way back and deliver whatever he found personally. Four weeks later they flew into the Nkra airport, took a taxi into the city, and arranged for transportation by Benz bus to Kwim the next day.

Jeff nudged Robert, who was squeezed into a half seat next to the window and said, "This is the Kra river. The great lake that I told you about is a few miles north of here."

"Will we see the lake, daddy?" Robert asked.

"Not today," Jeff replied, "but before we leave Sakra I will try and take you there."

263

The boy complained, "Daddy, why is it so crowded? I don't have any room to move. It smells real bad. I don't feel very good."

Jeff, who had been enjoying his nostalgic ride in the old bus, was upset by his son's reaction to the trip.

"Be quiet," he scolded, "you are lucky that you are not bouncing your bottom off the boards of a mammy wagon. Perhaps your Uncle Josh gave you the idea that you would always ride in a fine car when you got to Africa. It will be good for you to learn that some things in life are difficult here."

Robert started to cry.

"Ah, heck," Jeff said, "I'm sorry, Robert. It was stupid of me to forget that the trip cannot be the same for you that it is for me. I'm sorry I said what I did. It wasn't fair, was it? This trip would make anyone tired and it does smell. Would you like to sit in my lap for a while?"

The small boy nodded his head slowly and sadly as he climbed into Jeff's lap. He was quickly asleep. With Robert quiet, Jeff's eyes searched the landscape for signs of the war. Little evidence remained. Even when he did see partially destroyed buildings, it was difficult to tell whether their condition was a result of the war or of natural processes.

About twenty miles beyond the Kra River bridge, the driver stopped the bus and got down. He motioned for Jeff to follow. Jeff shifted Robert carefully from his lap and rested his head against the seat. Then he got down from the lorry and followed the driver to the side of the road.

The driver said, "Two months before you come, a European woman also come this way. She come with old man. Her father, I think."

"I helped her to fasten that small piece of wood to the large tree," he said with a hint of pride in his voice. "She said this place was the place her husband died during the great war."

Jeff found the small plaque nailed in one of the concave portions of a huge Boabob tree.

It read:

In memory of Ian
Never forgotten
Always loved

Beth

Jeff had by letter remained in contact with Beth Harris. Their loss of loved ones was a special bond. He had done his best to write often and carefully. Beth's parents had sought professional help soon after she returned to England, both for her and for themselves. Beth's recovery from anger and depression in the aftermath of Ian's murder and her own rape had been a long and painful process. But she had put her life back together and gone back to work as a teacher. In her last letter, she told Jeff of her plans to remarry in the fall and of her planned return to Sakra to seal forever in a special place her bond with Ian and the past.

Jeff looked away to hide his tears from the driver.

"The final act of bravery from a lady of great courage," he thought. "God bless you, Beth and Ian, wherever you are."

When he reboarded the bus, Robert was awake. He looked pale and frightened.

"What's wrong?" Jeff asked.

"I thought you had gone away," Robert replied as he wiped away a tear.

Jeff laughed slightly then said, "Robert, Robert, I would never leave you, never."

He repeated the pledge in his own thoughts, "No, it was not possible then and it is not possible now. I would never leave you, never."

Jeff continued, "Anyway, you are safe here."

"Are we on Bordo land?" Robert asked.

"No," Jeff replied, "I don't think so. Not yet."

"Then this is Aveland?" the boy continued.

"Yes, I think it might be," Jeff said.

"Then I am not so safe," Robert stated with some authority. "Ave people capture Bordo children and sell them into slavery."

Jeff's loud laugh at Robert's remark startled several of the other passengers. They turned to see what had happened, but just as quickly looked away when they saw it was the American who laughed.

"Your uncle and his friends have taught you too well," Jeff said. "Those things you are talking about happened more than one hundred years ago. No reason to be afraid that would happen now. The Aves and Bordos and all of the other people who live in Sakra are no longer enemies. People don't fear each other now."

A well dressed gentleman, perhaps in his middle fifties, who sat beside them on the bus had been listening attentively to their conversation.

With Jeff's last sentence, he turned his head in their direction and politely interrupted, "Pardon me, sir, but how long ago did you tell the young man beside you that it had been since fear and hatred among the tribes had stopped?"

The man's question startled Jeff.

He replied, "I do not really know the answer. What is your opinion?"

The man replied without hesitation but in a tone of sadness that bordered on despair, "Perhaps it did end a few years ago, perhaps only yesterday, maybe tomorrow, or perhaps we are destined never to be at peace with ourselves. That child may understand us better in his own way than you do."

Jeff decided to introduce himself, "My name is Jeff Johnson. This is my son, Robert Kanata Johnson."

The man's eyes opened a little wider as he looked more closely at Robert.

"The grandson of Chief Kanata," he murmured.

"Yes," Jeff confirmed the man's thoughts.

The man extended his hand. "I am also from Kwim," he said. "I am brother to the old Chief. Pardon me, you would say cousin. We have waited for your return. My brother said that you would return. But, if you will again pardon me for saying so, I am more than a little surprised that you have come. It is a long journey from America to our poor country. Few men make the journey twice unless the trip becomes part of their business. But I am indeed happy that you and the boy are here. The last wake in Enata's memory should have been many years ago. However, Chief Kanata asked that we wait until you and the grandson returned."

Jeff nodded to indicate that he understood. A wake for Enata was not something that he had anticipated. He had hoped to visit Kwim, show his son the village of his mother and grandfather, then return to Nkra with as little ceremony and formality as possible.

His outward thoughts involved some speculation that a wake for his mother might frighten or depress Robert since the child had little experience with the African manner of celebrating death. But his true fear, that he hid even from himself, was that of his own reaction to returning to a time of intense pain in the remembering of Enata's death.

Once they reached Kwim, word quickly spread of the return of the grandson of the old Chief. A message was sent to the Chief's oldest son, General Kanata. Preparations began immediately for Enata's wake. The time was set for the next evening. Jeff and Robert were led into a cement block bungalow and shown to a large room with two beds. They were told the house belonged to General Kanata. It was equipped with its own gas powered electricity generator and had indoor plumbing. Robert was tired from the long lorry ride and soon fell asleep. Jeff decided to go out for a while and see how Kwim had changed. He found the village different and yet the same. Little remained to remind one of the war. No trace remained of the old middle school in whose garden he had spent so many hours. (He smiled a bit at the thought of the work he had put into the farming manual and wondered if any copies still existed.) But a new building constructed of concrete block had been erected on the same site. Also, Kwim now had a post office and several other new stores. One of the few areas left just as it had been at the end of the war was Chief Kanata's compound. General Kanata had ordered that it be left as a war memorial.

The General arrived the next day about noon. Although they had never met, he greeted Jeff as his brother and Robert as his nephew, which of course he was. Jeff was confused when the villagers greeted Kanata not only as an army officer, but also as royalty, until he realized that the General was now also the paramount Chief of the villages of Kwim. Robert did not seem at all surprised to find that his uncle was a chief. In fact, he probably would have been surprised to find otherwise, given the logic of a seven year old boy and the tales that his other uncle had told him of their family.

Kanata explained to Jeff that he had decided at the time of his father's death to help in the rebuilding of Kwim. At the end of the war the people of Kwim had asked for his help as Chief during the process of reconstruction. He expressed regret that he now had little time to devote to his duties as Chief. His appointment as military governor of the newly created Upper Midwest region a few months after the end of the war had taken much time and energy. He wished, he told Jeff, to step down from the position as Chief as soon as a suitable replacement could be found.

Kanata looked at Robert and said sternly, "Are you ready to replace me?"

Only a slight movement of his eyes indicated less than total seriousness. Robert beamed as he hid behind his father.

"He might well think so," Jeff replied looking down at the boy, "but I don't."

"Of course, I understand that well," the General replied with a broad smile. "His future is now with you in America. But should trouble ever come to either of you, please understand this very well: you will always have many good friends in Kwim who will help you in any and every way that they are able to. This village is and always will be a home to you."

Jeff's eyes were moist and he choked a bit as he replied, "I don't know how to say thank-you well enough. No sum of money or store of earthly goods could be worth more than what you have just given, your friendship and that of the people of Kwim."

"That you and the boy have come is more than we could have thought possible," the General said. "But enough of this serious talk. I brought with me a small present for Robert."

Robert's interest in the conversation increased.

The General continued, "I tried very hard to think what a young boy in America might want most from Africa, and this is what I decided would do best."

He called a man's name, and a soldier entered the room with a small wooden drum about eighteen inches in height. Robert tried the drum. His expression mirrored surprise and delight at the sound. The General nodded to the soldier. He left and returned with another drum about eight inches taller. Then he left and returned again with yet a bigger drum. Robert was quickly surrounded by six drums. He had to stand and stretch to reach the head of the tallest.

"I hope that they will cause you no difficulty in transporting them back to America," General Kanata commented.

"We can take them with us, can't we, daddy?" Robert asked eagerly.

"We certainly can," Jeff replied, "one way or another, even if we have to buy them a seat on the plane."

Jeff knew that the drums might be a problem on their return flight. But it didn't matter at the moment. He was just as excited and delighted with the gift as his son. He had never seen a finer set of drums.

For a few minutes the two men watched Robert experiment with the drums.

Then the General said, "The wake tonight will be a very long affair, perhaps the entire night. I slept little last night and must rest this afternoon if I am to properly perform my duties. I hope that you will excuse my absence for a while."

"Most certainly," Jeff replied. "You have been more than kind."

"A nap sounds like a good idea," he continued, looking in Robert's direction.

Robert made a wry face and said, "I would rather play the drums than sleep, if that is OK."

The General laughed and without consulting Jeff said to the man who had brought the drums into the room, " Sergeant, will you teach this small boy something about how to play?"

The soldier replied with a quick, "Yes, sir," and then added less formally, "It would be a pleasure, sir."

General Kanata introduced the soldier to Robert.

"This is Sergeant Asari," he said. "He also is from this village and is one of the finest drummers in all of Sakra. His family made these drums."

The Sergeant smiled and took charge of Robert. Kanata and Jeff retired to sleep in another part of the house.

Robert placed a small stool behind the eighteen-inch drum, sat down, held the drum between his knees and began to play one of the rhythms taught to him by his uncle in Arizona. The Sergeant was surprised by what the child already knew. That afternoon he explained to Robert how drums of different sizes spoke together. They practiced combining what Robert already knew on a single drum with the sounds of other drums.

The sound of the drums did not really help Jeff get to sleep, but it was reassuring. The steady, rhythmic sounds told him that Robert was occupied and happy. He knew that Robert's feelings and emotions would be well protected by himself and the boy's uncles. If there was any problem, someone would see to it that Robert left the wake and that care would be provided for him until morning. But he knew that as Enata's husband, no such escape was possible.

The drumming that signaled the beginning of the wake started at six. Jeff was not expected until later in the evening. He was awake by eight and decided to go a little early.

The celebration of the wake was not at all as Jeff had thought. He had, true to his own cultural norms, anticipated great sorrow. To be sure, the traditional mourners wailed and wept in the finest manner. But when their duty shifts were completed and they were replaced by others, they seemed no less happy and cheerful than the others present at the wake.

"As much a party as a funeral," he mused. "The celebration of death. Perhaps as it should be. There is little reason to cry now."

General Kanata arrived a few minutes after Jeff. They stood near a table filled with food and beverage. Enata's other brother, Josh, arrived a short time later. He greeted Robert warmly then joined the two men at the table. They stood together to formally greet all who came to the wake and to offer them refreshment.

Jeff noted that Robert had been accorded the honor of participating in some of the drumming that night. The small boy seemed totally absorbed in trying to play his part of the complex rhythms on one of his smaller drums.

When the tasks of greeting had been completed, Jeff sat alone under one of the thatched roofs and watched the others eat, drink and dance. He was nearly asleep when he felt a small tug on the sleeve of his shirt. He looked around and saw Robert at his side. The small boy's face betrayed concern.

"Is something wrong?" Jeff asked.

"I am not sure," Robert replied, "I don't really understand what is going on. I wish I understood. It worries me."

Jeff pulled another chair closer and asked Robert to sit down.

Then he said, "Now tell me, what is it that is worrying you?"

"Is this my real mommy's funeral?" Robert asked.

"Yes," Jeff replied, "only it's more like a second funeral. The first one was many years ago. This is called a wake."

"I know that," Robert said impatiently, "but if this is like a funeral, why is everyone happy but those women who are crying? Aren't they sad that my mommy died and went away?"

Jeff paused to wipe away a tear as he tried to think how to answer his son's question.

"Robert," Jeff said, then stopped.

"Yes, dad," Robert replied.

"Robert, they don't think she has gone away. They believe that she has moved to another world that is right here in this village. That if we need her or they need her she will always be here in this place. That is why they are happy."

"But daddy," Robert protested, "you told me that mommy went to heaven. In Sunday school I learned that heaven is way up in the sky, not here on the ground."

Jeff said nothing for a while. The boy waited patiently, realizing that he had asked a difficult question.

Finally, Jeff answered, "Nobody knows where heaven is. Not even your Sunday school teacher. She only told you where she thought it was. The people who live here in Kwim believe that a part of heaven is also in this place. They believe that when people die, their spirits remain here in Kwim, always still with them and not somewhere far away. Your grandfather, the old Chief Kanata, believed that. He told me so himself."

"Father," Robert said, "when I was playing the drums I was very happy. Then I felt bad because I was happy. I don't want to be happy about my mother being dead."

"I don't think it's wrong for you to be happy tonight, Robert. It is what your mother would want," Jeff tried to explain. "In fact, I believe that your grandfather was right. I think they both are here with us and are probably very happy when they hear you playing your drums."

"Could I talk to them?" Robert asked.

"No, I am sorry that is not possible. I wish it were. It would be wonderful," Jeff replied with a sigh. "There are people who believe that they can talk to those who have gone to another world. But I don't think anyone from this world can talk to people in heaven, no matter where it is. You just have to wait until you make that journey yourself. One thing I am certain of, though, and that is that your grandfather and mother would want you to be very, very happy tonight."

"Do you really think that it makes my mother happy to hear the drums that I play?" Robert asked skeptically.

"There is nothing of which I am more certain," Jeff replied as he did his best to control his own growing sense of pain and loss from the memories that his son's questions revived. "Be happy, my beautiful child of two lands, and Enata your mother will also be happy."

Robert gave his daddy a quick hug and asked to return to the drummers. His father, no longer able to form words, nodded his assent.

As soon as the boy was a few yards away, Jeff fled to a place behind one of the walls of the old Chief's compound. There he collapsed to the ground, making no effort to control his sobs of grief. After minutes of total anguish, he began the struggle to regain control and was able to do so only when he thought of how Robert might react if he found his father given over to such total despair.

The wake was over by six the next morning. Robert had collapsed at a much earlier hour and been put to bed. Jeff slept until noon. He found his son in another room with his drums.

When he saw his father, Robert said, "I fell asleep last night. I did not want to. I wanted to stay awake and see if my mother would come. Did I miss her? Did you see her?"

"No, I didn't see her," Jeff replied. "Robert, we do not see those who have died. What is important is that she did not miss you. You were here for her to see you, not for you to see her. I think that she must be very happy with her son. Do you understand?"

"Yes, I think so, daddy," Robert replied.

Then he returned to experimenting with the drums.

They stayed in Kwim another eight days. For Jeff, Kwim without Enata was depressing, even dull. This was especially true after Enata's two brothers returned to their normal duties in other parts of Sakra. But Jeff was determined that they would stay long enough for Robert to gain some understanding of what life might have been like had he remained in Kwim with his grandfather. Robert quickly became a celebrity in the village. He went to school with other children, watched the drum makers and carvers at work, drank palm wine (fresh) until it made him sick, and in general made a lovable pest of himself all over the small town. When the time came to leave Kwim for Nkra, they did so in the General's car, driven by the General's driver. Jeff would have preferred another lorry ride for old times' sake, but Robert's one experience with a long trip by Benz bus had been sufficient to convince him that there were better ways to travel. His son had accepted the General's offer of transport before Jeff had the opportunity to decline.

Jeff asked the driver to stop in Mbordo. The village itself looked much the same as Jeff had remembered, but all the buildings of the University-College were new. When he asked a laborer about the new buildings, he was told that every structure on the old compound had been destroyed during the war.

"Finished. All finished," was the way in which the African expressed what had happened.

That was no exaggeration. Nothing remained of the University-College as Jeff had known it except a few sidewalks. Nor was there anyone on the present staff who had worked there before the war. Jeff found that even more painful than the physical changes. In less than an hour, he was ready to leave.

Gil, Pordoe and Kwame Onanga (the Vice-Chancellor) met Jeff and Robert in Nkra for a brief reunion. The three men were all teachers now, Gil and Pordoe in another teacher training college and the Vice-Chancellor at the National University. They sat together in a hotel bar and reminisced until it was time for Jeff and his son to leave for the airport.

He had found most of what Alice wanted in Nkra and Kwim. The collection of items for Alice and the drums packed into crates looked like a small mountain in front of the Pan American ticket counter. The lady in charge winked and looked the other way as he slid some items past the counter without weighing them.

At National Airport, they loaded a taxi with the things purchased for Alice and directed the driver to take them to her apartment building. Robert had carried his smallest drum on board the plane as hand luggage and now held it tightly under his arm in the taxi. Jeff was surprised, but certainly pleased, to find Jason and Karen in the lobby of the building in which Alice lived. He knew they all had lived in the same building for a couple of years, but Jason and Karen were now in Indiana where Jason was enrolled in a graduate study program at River State. They greeted each other and laughed at the remarkable coincidence of turning up in that particular lobby at the same time. However, the mood of the conversation changed abruptly when Jeff asked about Alice.

"Alice is ill," Jason said simply. "She has been hospitalized. We came after we got a letter from her Doctor. He is very concern about her heart. He stopped short of saying she wasn't going to make it, but he did say her condition is very serious."

"We were on our way out to see her," Karen said. "Why don't you put you stuff in her apartment and come with us?"

"All right," Jeff said. "Do you think she is well enough to look at any of the things we brought her?"

"We'll pick out a few," Karen suggested.

"Would she like my drum, daddy?" Robert asked quietly.

"I am sure that she would enjoy that drum," Jason said, smiling at Robert.

"She spent most of her time the last five or six years talking to kids of your age, Robert, about Africa and what it is like to live there," Karen added.

"When she first returned, she found herself with a lot of time on her hands," Jason continued. "In those first months of the war, people's stupid questions about what was going on in Africa made her so mad that she wouldn't talk to anybody about Sakra. But some old friends of hers, ones she really couldn't refuse, invited her to their classrooms to talk about her experiences in the Peace Corps. She was reluctant at first but decided to ignore the painful parts and concentrate on the rest. Now she is known to school children all over Washington, DC as the 'Africa lady.'"

"I went with her once to a fifth grade classroom," Karen said. "It was pretty unbelievable. The kids were jumping up and down, standing on chairs, throwing everything imaginable when we walked in. Alice didn't say a thing. She just started laying out some cloth and carvings on a table to one side of the room. When the students saw what she was doing, they began to quiet down. One kid said, 'That stuff is from Africa, ain't it?' Alice nodded to indicate that he was correct. She never raised her voice when she talked to children about Africa. If anybody got loud the other students took care of them. No question about Africa was too silly or trivial for her to answer. If it was important enough for a student to ask, then Alice would answer it. Only questions about the war made her uncomfortable and even angry. She had tried to explain about the war, you know, why it started and how it affected people, stuff like that. But she grew tired of that and started to answer all questions related to the war with the same explanation."

"'The war is an aberration,' she would say. 'When it is over, Sakra will be as it was before. The war is not like Africa. War does horrible things to those involved. Some people, who were once kind and decent, become evil. It is that way in Africa. It is that way anywhere else. War is stupid. There are no winners in Sakra, Vietnam, the Middle East or anywhere else when man is so foolish as to take up arms against his fellow man.'"

"Good for Alice," Jeff said. "You know most of us do keep trying in one way or another to tell people what it is really like in Africa."

At the hospital they were told that Robert would not be allowed to visit Alice because of his age.

"This is her only grandson," Jeff protested.

The lady at the desk relented and allowed them all to go up to her room.

In the elevator, Robert asked his father, "Was Alice Chief Kanata's wife?"

Jason and Karen made an effort to hide their smirks as Jeff tried to explain.

"I'm sorry, my son," Jeff said, "I lied a little. She was a good friend of your grandfather's but not his wife. If your mother had lived, Alice would most certainly have been like your Godmother but not your grandmother. She will be happy to see you."

Alice was delighted to see all of them, and especially Robert.

"I am so very happy you are all here," she said. "But I did not at all intend for it to happen this way. I only asked Dr. Morgan to see to it that you got that small suitcase in the corner. You know how things get lost in the city. It contains a few things from Sakra that the Vice-Chancellor sent to me from time to time. I use them when I talk to the children about Africa."

Alice looked at Jeff and exclaimed, "Oh dear! The things that you brought back for me. I almost forgot. Don't think I will have much use for them now. Never mind that. Keep what you want and give the rest to the little African Museum on R street. I am sure they will use them well.

"I am so happy to see all of you, but I had no idea that the Doctor would send for you. Did they let you into my apartment?"

"Yes, of course," Jason replied, "they still remember us. We have everything prepared for your return."

Alice smiled a little sadly and said, "As you already know, my Doctor is a very kind man. He has explained everything to me. It makes planning so much easier. We have already agreed that I will not be kept alive by one of those awful machines. I don't want a funeral. I have already arranged for cremation, so don't worry about anything."

"But enough of that," Alice said abruptly. "I do feel better today. They started me on something new a few days ago. But they have tried so many things. I think all of you being here is the best medicine. Tell me, what do you have in those interesting looking bags and boxes? I certainly hope it's not food or flowers."

"No," Jeff replied, "just some of the things that you wanted me to get in Sakra."

"Well, let me see them," she said impatiently and half seriously. "I don't have forever, you know."

The cloth and carvings delighted Alice. But Robert's drum she found the most intriguing.

"That is truly a beautiful instrument," she said. "Is it from Kwim?"

"Yes," Jeff replied, "part of the set of six given to Robert by his uncle. The others are at the airport."

"Do you know what to do with this, young man?" Alice asked Robert.

Robert nodded and began to softly play. Alice smiled as she listened. Her ears heard a thousand drums and her eyes again saw the dancers of Kwim.

When Robert had finished playing, they talked of Sakra in the old days, of the University-College, of friends now dead and those still living. The hours of visiting passed all too quickly. They said their good-bys to Alice and she to them. Jeff and Robert returned to Arizona later that evening. The next morning Jason and Karen received a message from the hospital requesting that they come as soon as possible. When they arrived, a nurse met them in the lobby.

"You should speak with Doctor Morgan," she said. "I will page him."

"That's all right, nurse," Jason said. "It won't be necessary for us to see the Doctor. Is Mrs. Manati not doing well today?"

"No," the nurse replied, "quite the opposite. Here is the Doctor."

"Good morning," Dr. Morgan said. "Are you the folks that are friends of Mrs. Manati?"

"Yes," Jason replied.

"I would be embarrassed if I weren't so happy," the Doctor continued. "The initial tests we did three weeks ago indicated her heart function was so weak that it seemed she had only a short time to live. Nothing we tried seemed to work. Then Alice gave us the name of a Doctor who was a second cousin. On Tuesday we started a course of drugs her cousin recommended. It seems that her heart condition is a family trait and they have figured out how to deal with it. Her latest tests indicate an unusual rhythm but strong and stable heart function. I think she's going to be all right."

"That is so great!" Karen exclaimed.

"Alice is such a practical person," the Doctor said. "She told me this morning that you had come to say your final good-bys. I never really told her she was dying, but I think she drew that conclusion from some of the things she heard. I guess I gave you that impression, too."

"That's quite all right," Jason replied. "We know all about what a practical person Alice is."

"She wants out of here right now and I agree," the Doctor said. "But the problem is how to get her discharged and home. Someone should stay with her a few days to be sure she is all right."

"We can do that," Jason said. "Yes, we can do that."

End of Epilogue

ISBN 141200048-3

Edwards Brothers Malloy
Thorofare, NJ USA
September 14, 2016